KIM & KIM

Vol 1

"This Glamorous, High-Flying Rock Star Life"

writer
Magdalene Visaggio

pencils & inks
Eva Cabrera

colorist
Claudia Aguirre

letterer
Zakk Saam

editor
Katy Rex

cover
Tess Fowler
& Kiki Jenkins

additional design
Ryan Ferrier

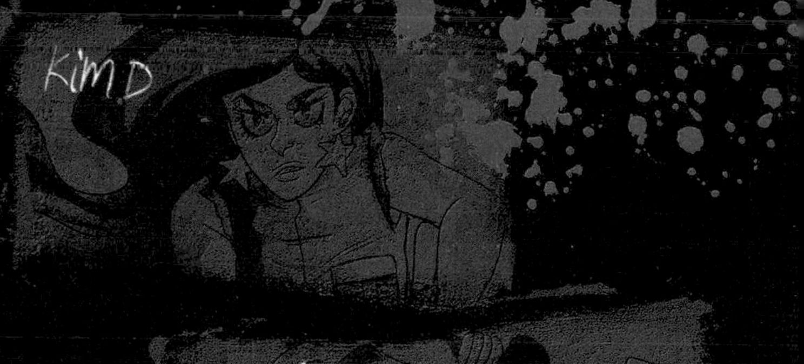
Kim D

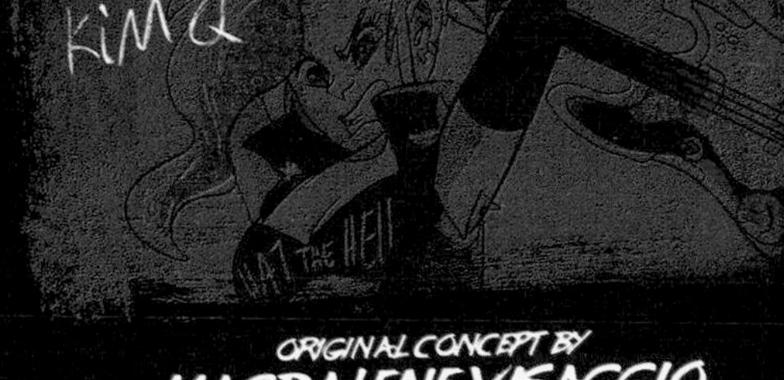
Kim Q

ORIGINAL CONCEPT BY
MAGDALENE VISAGGIO

SPECIAL THANKS TO: Moriah Hummer, Ryan Cady, Taylor Esposito, Christopher Sebela, Bryan Edward Hill, Kieron Gillen, Alex de Campi, Amancay Nahuelpan, Phil Smith III, Becca Farrow, Matt Wilson, Rachael Stott, Adam McGovern, Scott Smith, Kevin Roberts, and True Burns

BLACK MASK

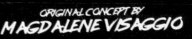

PUBLISHED BY BLACK MASK STUDIOS LLC
MATT PIZZOLO | BRETT GUREWITZ | STEVE NILES

Foreword

Look: the short version is that I talked a lot of shit about Neil Gaiman, and I'm sorry. I used to have this blog where I wrote about what I was reading and I got swept up in the Your Fav Is Problematic craze of the early mid 2010s. Maybe you remember this? It took place mostly on an internet hell made up primarily of pornography and self-righteousness called Tumblr, where people would write up little reports on how artists or singers or writers or whatever - your faves - had fucked up, so you could feel bad about liking their work and hate them forever.

It was fun, dude. You can't really argue with the sense of power you feel when you're taking down a famous or semi-famous or almost semi-famous person who has done something that makes you feel like you're better than them. Of course, when you're dividing people into two groups ("problematic" and "not yet problematic"), and those two groups roughly equate to "bad" and "good," you're not doing analysis as much as its opposite. But it's enticing, right? We all live in a culture that makes us feel shitty and hurt and powerless all the time. Of course we're all doing whatever we can to feel less powerless.

So okay. When I was a kid I loved Neil Gaiman's Sandman comics. And like a lot of teenage trans girls who haven't quite figured out that they're trans, I built myself an elaborate personal hall of mythopoetic mirrors in order to sort of understand that I was trans and sort of not know. And there were trans women in those Sandman comics! In the mid-nineties, in the rural part of New Jersey that they never seem to show on TV, I wasn't really seeing trans women anywhere else. I mean, they were there. We've always been there. I just didn't know yet, so the trans women in Sandman comics became really important to me. They were basically a lifeline.

On re-reading those comics a couple years ago, though, I noticed something kind of disappointing: the trans women in those comics kept dying. There were something like a dozen trans women who died offstage over the course of those comics, and I think one who died onstage? None live. So I did what any self-righteous grownup with a laptop would do: I talked a bunch of shit on the internet.

YOUR FAVORITE, NEIL GAIMAN, IS PROBLEMATIC, I hollered into the void.

Other jerks on the internet loved it. That post got passed around extensively. Neil himself seems still to have a career, which I am happy about, because at the time I don't think I had an endgame besides feeling powerful by attacking someone who was more powerful than me. And I regret it.

Neil, I'm sure you're reading this, and I apologize. I was being a jerk. We haven't met but I'm told that you are not, actually, a bad person who hates trans women. You yourself have said that if you had it to do over again you'd write those characters' stories differently. And honestly, while I still very strongly prefer stories in which trans women do not die, I've realized that I was never mad at you. I was mad that those comics were the best I could do at fourteen. You know? I was mad.

If there's a point to any of this, it's this: it rules that it's no longer the early mid 90s. Everything is awesome now. I mean... actually I guess there is a lot of stuff from now that is not awesome. A lot of stuff blows. But there is way more awesome stuff now than there used to be. The late mid 2010s are amazing: now it is the future and we have G.L.O.S.S. and Ryka Aoki and Janet Mock and Her Story and Tangerine and look. Check this out. If you want fun and monsters and spaceships and legit sexuality and gender stuff and hitting robot gorillas with bass guitars and cool girls giving a shit about each other and cute boys also giving a shit about those cool girls and interdimensional death magic, good news: we live in the future and we also get to have Kim & Kim.

I'm not sure how to tell you about this collection of Kim & Kim without spoiling the best parts. There's a bunch of stuff I could quote. I won't! You'll get to the part where the guy is making fun of the boys and the part with the word "fuckhead" and you'll see.

If Kim & Kim had existed when I was in high school, it would have fucked me up in such a good way. Even now it's a legitimately important contribution to the way we talk about and portray trans women. I mean, it is not a comic about being trans. It's a comic in which one of the protagonists is trans in a way that feels real - not "just happens irrelevantly to be trans" or "will not shut up about being gender." It's just a thing that comes up sometimes. You know? That's what being trans feels like to me and to a lot of my friends and one of the best tricks that writer Magdalene Visaggio pulls off here is to set a relatable version of being trans as the grounded heart of a story about sand worms and octopus monsters and what appears to be the van that the Teenage Mutant Ninja Turtles drove in the Saturday morning cartoons from the 80s, modified for space travel. It's a bright, fun, funny comic that works because at its center it's got this sweet, real relationship between two imperfect queer women who you fall in love with.

And also? I care about trans women, but you don't have to. There's plenty here for you even if you have a deep, profound indifference about that stuff: parent drama, the struggle to pay rent, organized space crime, cosmic bounty hunting, bright pink guns, you name it. You know: the stuff that makes comic books rule.

I've argued before that if readers can accept dragons and warp drives, they can probably also handle trans women with agency. In Kim & Kim, we get all three. And I'm happy to spoil this for you: over the course of these issues of Kim & Kim, no trans women die, as far as I can tell.

Your move, Gaiman.

Imogen Binnie
10/2016

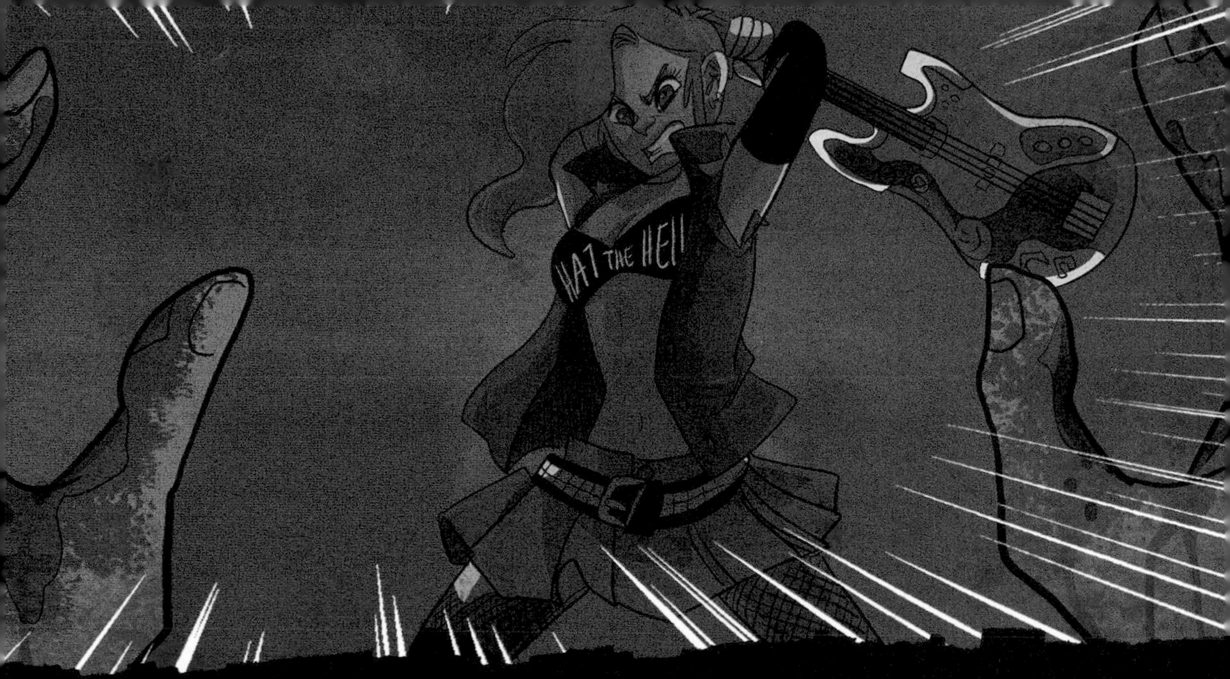

1

"THIS GLAMOROUS, HIGH-FLYING ROCK STAR LIFE"

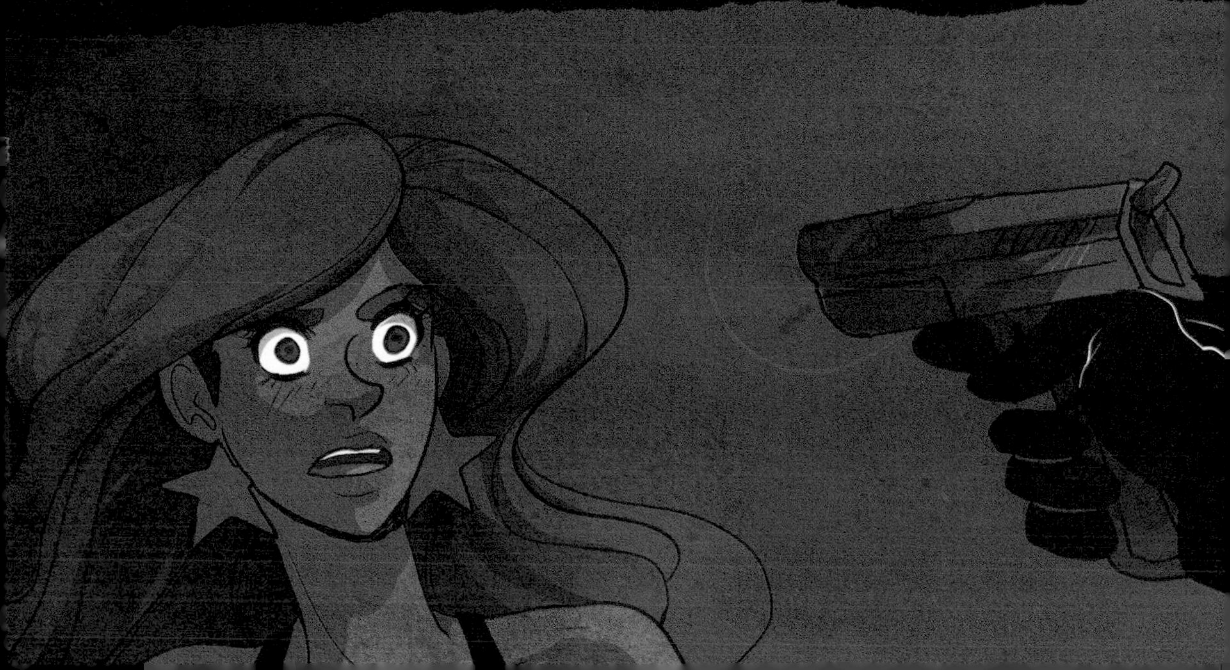

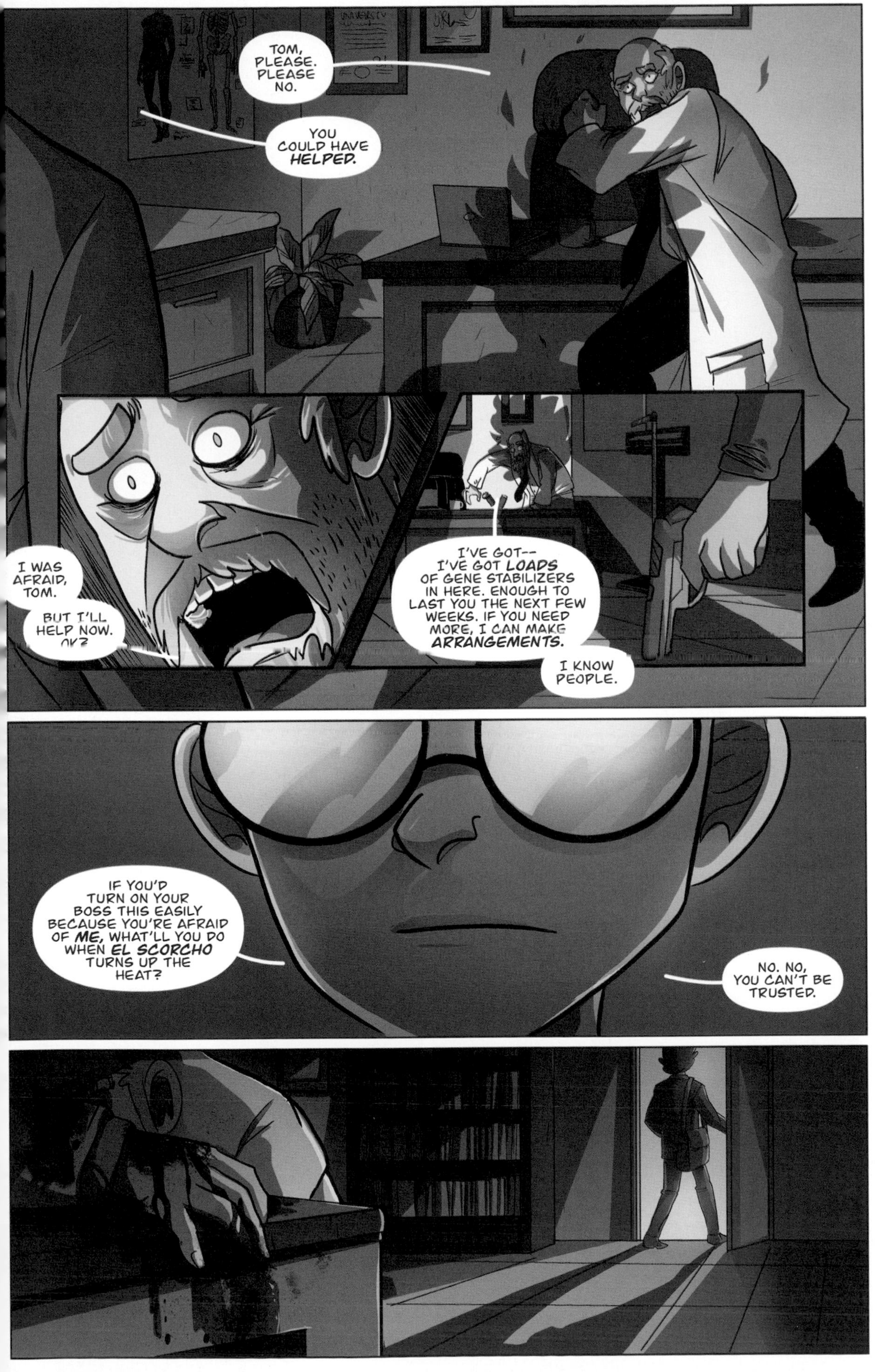
TOM, PLEASE. PLEASE NO.
YOU COULD HAVE HELPED.
I WAS AFRAID, TOM.
BUT I'LL HELP NOW. OK?
I'VE GOT-- I'VE GOT LOADS OF GENE STABILIZERS IN HERE. ENOUGH TO LAST YOU THE NEXT FEW WEEKS. IF YOU NEED MORE, I CAN MAKE ARRANGEMENTS.
I KNOW PEOPLE.
IF YOU'D TURN ON YOUR BOSS THIS EASILY BECAUSE YOU'RE AFRAID OF ME, WHAT'LL YOU DO WHEN EL SCORCHO TURNS UP THE HEAT?
NO. NO, YOU CAN'T BE TRUSTED.

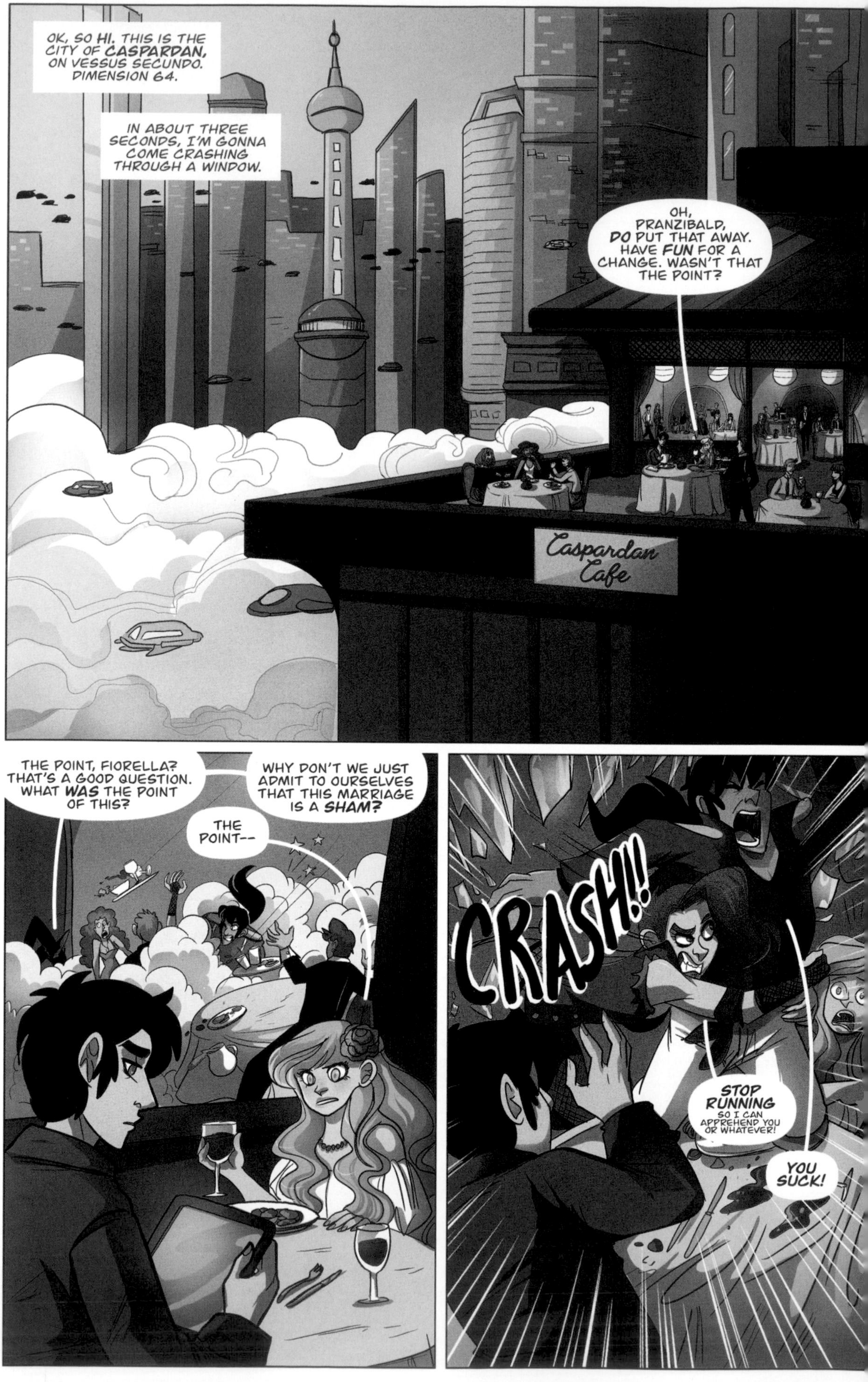
OK, SO HI. THIS IS THE CITY OF CASPARDAN, ON VESSUS SECUNDO. DIMENSION 64.
IN ABOUT THREE SECONDS, I'M GONNA COME CRASHING THROUGH A WINDOW.
OH, PRANZIBALD, DO PUT THAT AWAY. HAVE FUN FOR A CHANGE. WASN'T THAT THE POINT?
Caspardan Cafe
THE POINT, FIORELLA? THAT'S A GOOD QUESTION. WHAT WAS THE POINT OF THIS?
WHY DON'T WE JUST ADMIT TO OURSELVES THAT THIS MARRIAGE IS A SHAM?
THE POINT--
CRASH!!
STOP RUNNING SO I CAN APPREHEND YOU OR WHATEVER!
YOU SUCK!

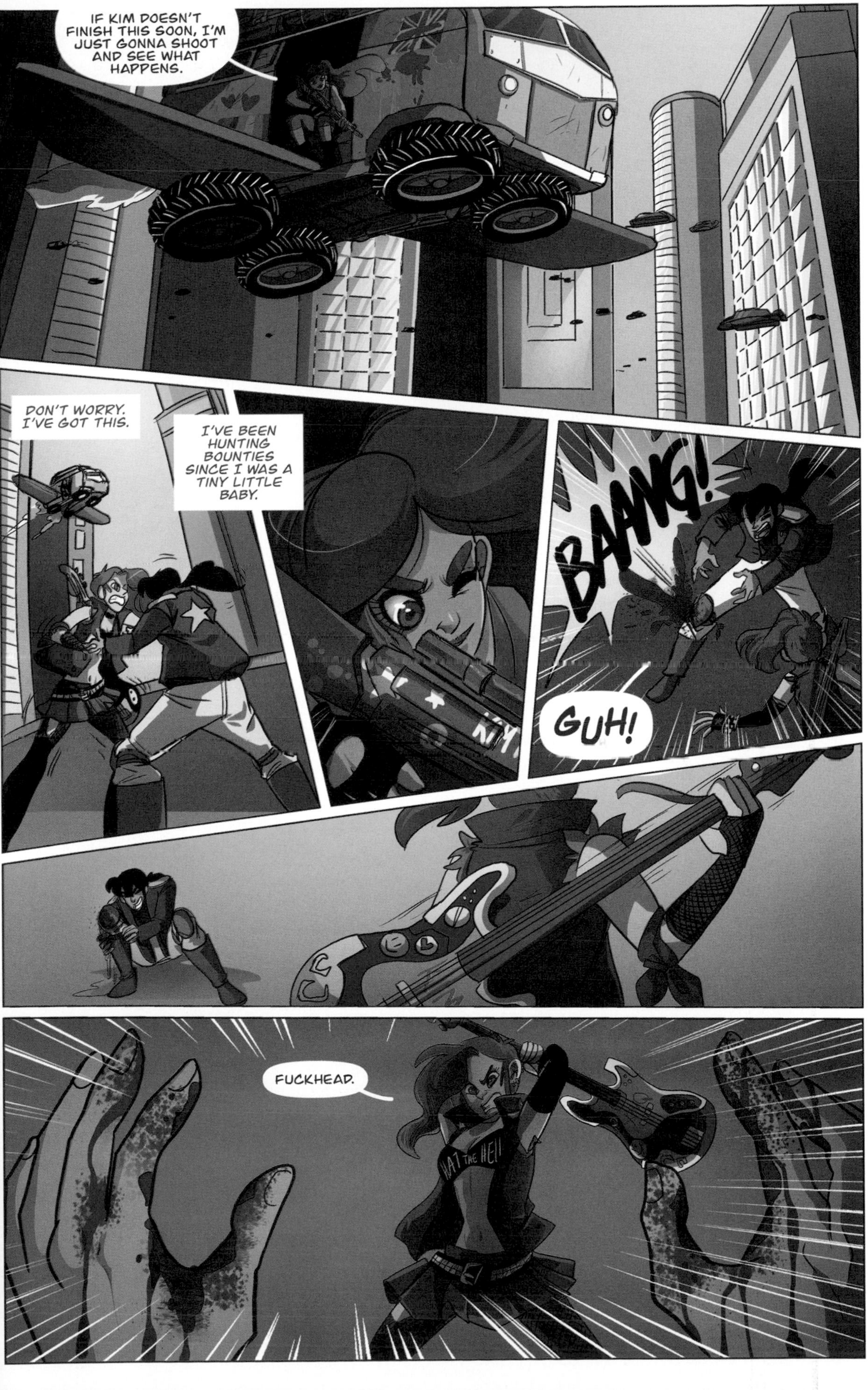
IF KIM DOESN'T FINISH THIS SOON, I'M JUST GONNA SHOOT AND SEE WHAT HAPPENS.
DON'T WORRY. I'VE GOT THIS.
I'VE BEEN HUNTING BOUNTIES SINCE I WAS A TINY LITTLE BABY.
BAANG!
GUH!
FUCKHEAD.

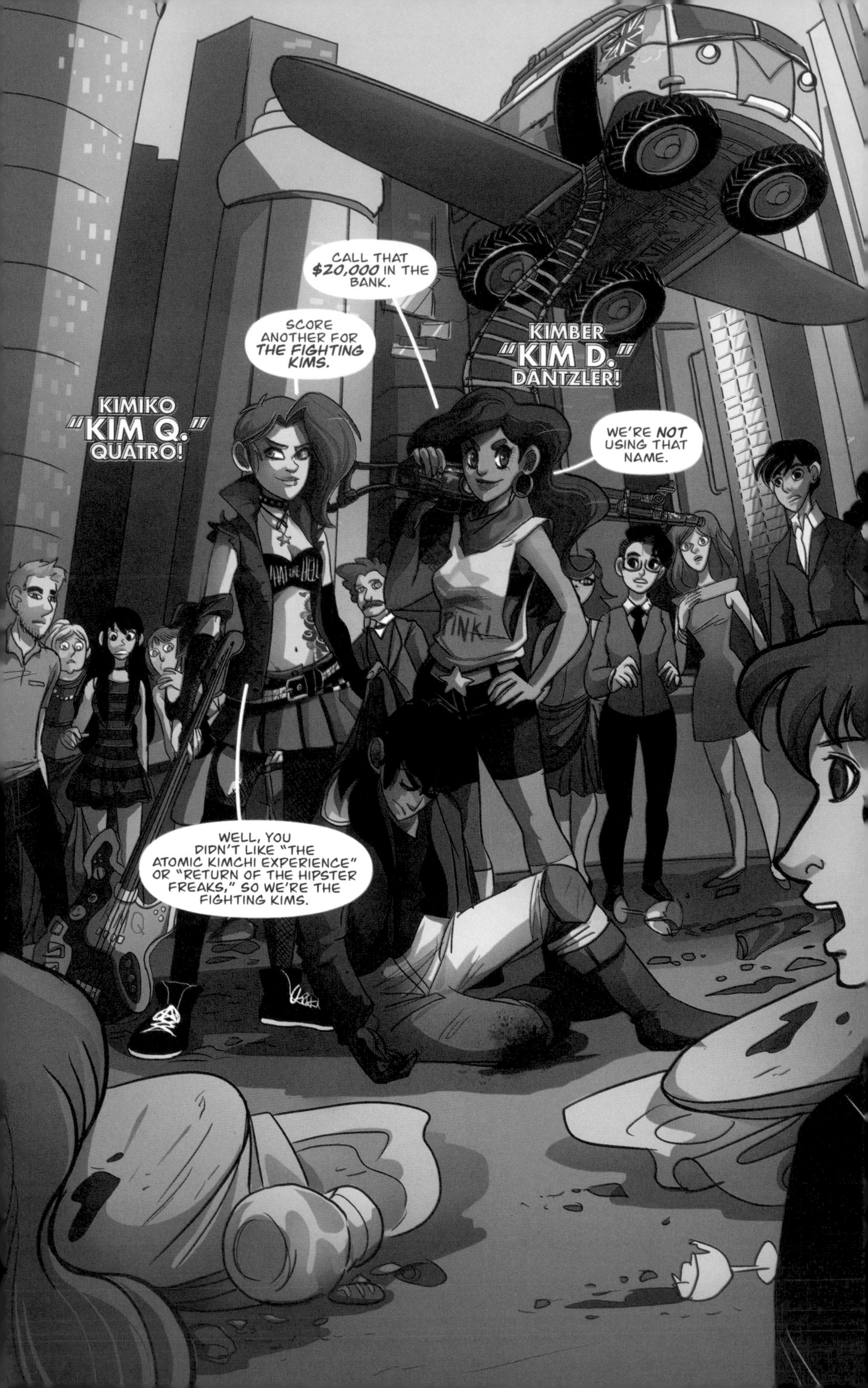

KIMIKO "KIM Q." QUATRO!
SCORE ANOTHER FOR THE FIGHTING KIMS.
CALL THAT $20,000 IN THE BANK.
KIMBER "KIM D." DANTZLER!
WE'RE NOT USING THAT NAME.
WELL, YOU DIDN'T LIKE "THE ATOMIC KIMCHI EXPERIENCE" OR "RETURN OF THE HIPSTER FREAKS," SO WE'RE THE FIGHTING KIMS.

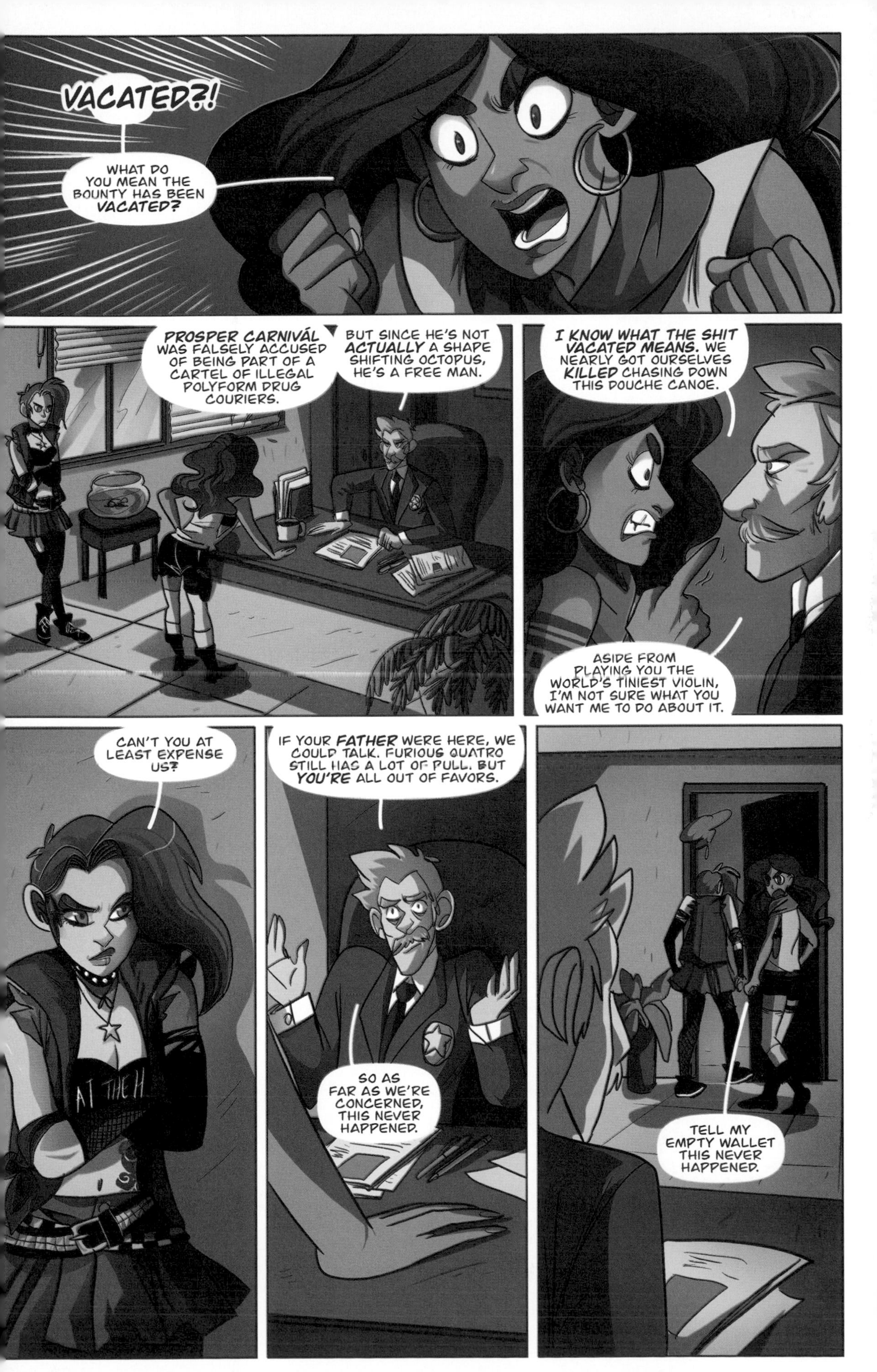
VACATED?!
WHAT DO YOU MEAN THE BOUNTY HAS BEEN VACATED?
PROSPER CARNIVÁL WAS FALSELY ACCUSED OF BEING PART OF A CARTEL OF ILLEGAL POLYFORM DRUG COURIERS.
BUT SINCE HE'S NOT ACTUALLY A SHAPE SHIFTING OCTOPUS, HE'S A FREE MAN.
I KNOW WHAT THE SHIT VACATED MEANS. WE NEARLY GOT OURSELVES KILLED CHASING DOWN THIS DOUCHE CANOE.
ASIDE FROM PLAYING YOU THE WORLD'S TINIEST VIOLIN, I'M NOT SURE WHAT YOU WANT ME TO DO ABOUT IT.
CAN'T YOU AT LEAST EXPENSE US?
IF YOUR FATHER WERE HERE, WE COULD TALK. FURIOUS QUATRO STILL HAS A LOT OF PULL. BUT YOU'RE ALL OUT OF FAVORS.
SO AS FAR AS WE'RE CONCERNED, THIS NEVER HAPPENED.
TELL MY EMPTY WALLET THIS NEVER HAPPENED.

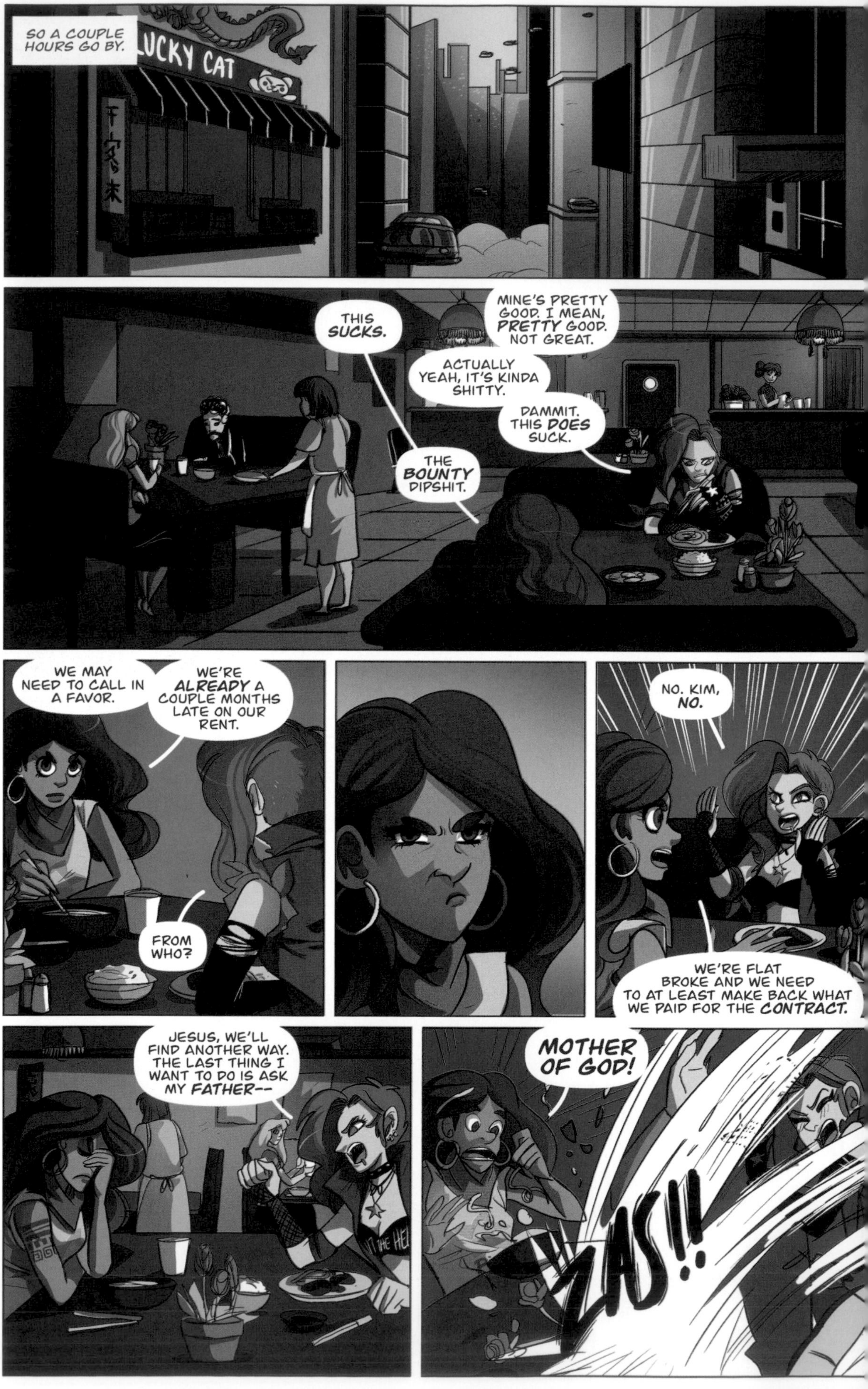
SO A COUPLE HOURS GO BY.
LUCKY CAT
THIS SUCKS.
MINE'S PRETTY GOOD. I MEAN, PRETTY GOOD. NOT GREAT.
ACTUALLY YEAH, IT'S KINDA SHITTY.
THE BOUNTY DIPSHIT.
DAMMIT. THIS DOES SUCK.
WE MAY NEED TO CALL IN A FAVOR.
WE'RE ALREADY A COUPLE MONTHS LATE ON OUR RENT.
FROM WHO?
NO. KIM, NO.
WE'RE FLAT BROKE AND WE NEED TO AT LEAST MAKE BACK WHAT WE PAID FOR THE CONTRACT.
JESUS, WE'LL FIND ANOTHER WAY. THE LAST THING I WANT TO DO IS ASK MY FATHER--
MOTHER OF GOD!
ZAS!!

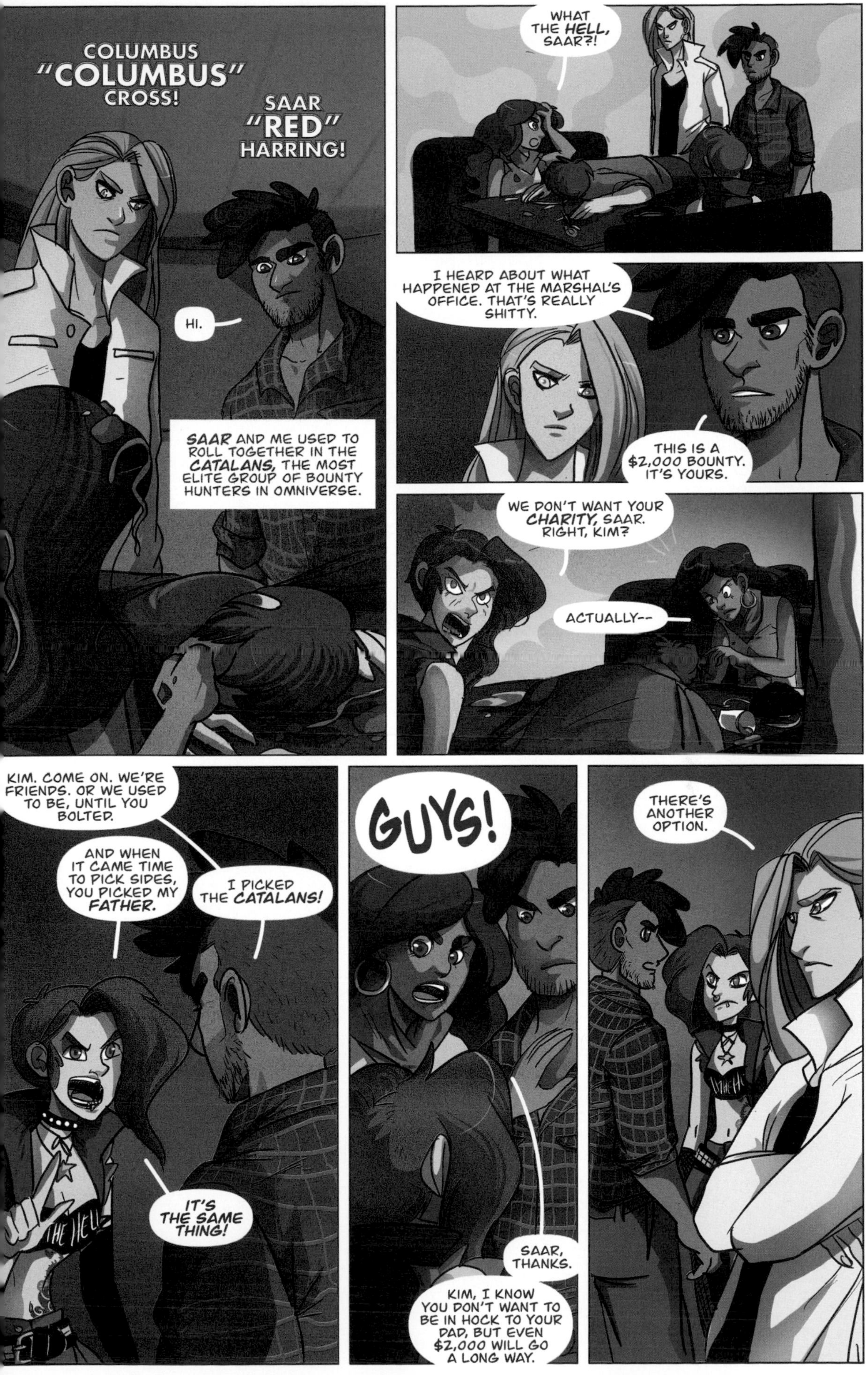
COLUMBUS "COLUMBUS" CROSS!
SAAR "RED" HARRING!
HI.
SAAR AND ME USED TO ROLL TOGETHER IN THE CATALANS, THE MOST ELITE GROUP OF BOUNTY HUNTERS IN OMNIVERSE.
WHAT THE HELL, SAAR?!
I HEARD ABOUT WHAT HAPPENED AT THE MARSHAL'S OFFICE. THAT'S REALLY SHITTY.
THIS IS A $2,000 BOUNTY. IT'S YOURS.
WE DON'T WANT YOUR CHARITY, SAAR. RIGHT, KIM?
ACTUALLY--
KIM. COME ON. WE'RE FRIENDS. OR WE USED TO BE, UNTIL YOU BOLTED.
AND WHEN IT CAME TIME TO PICK SIDES, YOU PICKED MY FATHER.
I PICKED THE CATALANS!
IT'S THE SAME THING!
GUYS!
SAAR, THANKS.
KIM, I KNOW YOU DON'T WANT TO BE IN HOCK TO YOUR DAD, BUT EVEN $2,000 WILL GO A LONG WAY.
THERE'S ANOTHER OPTION.

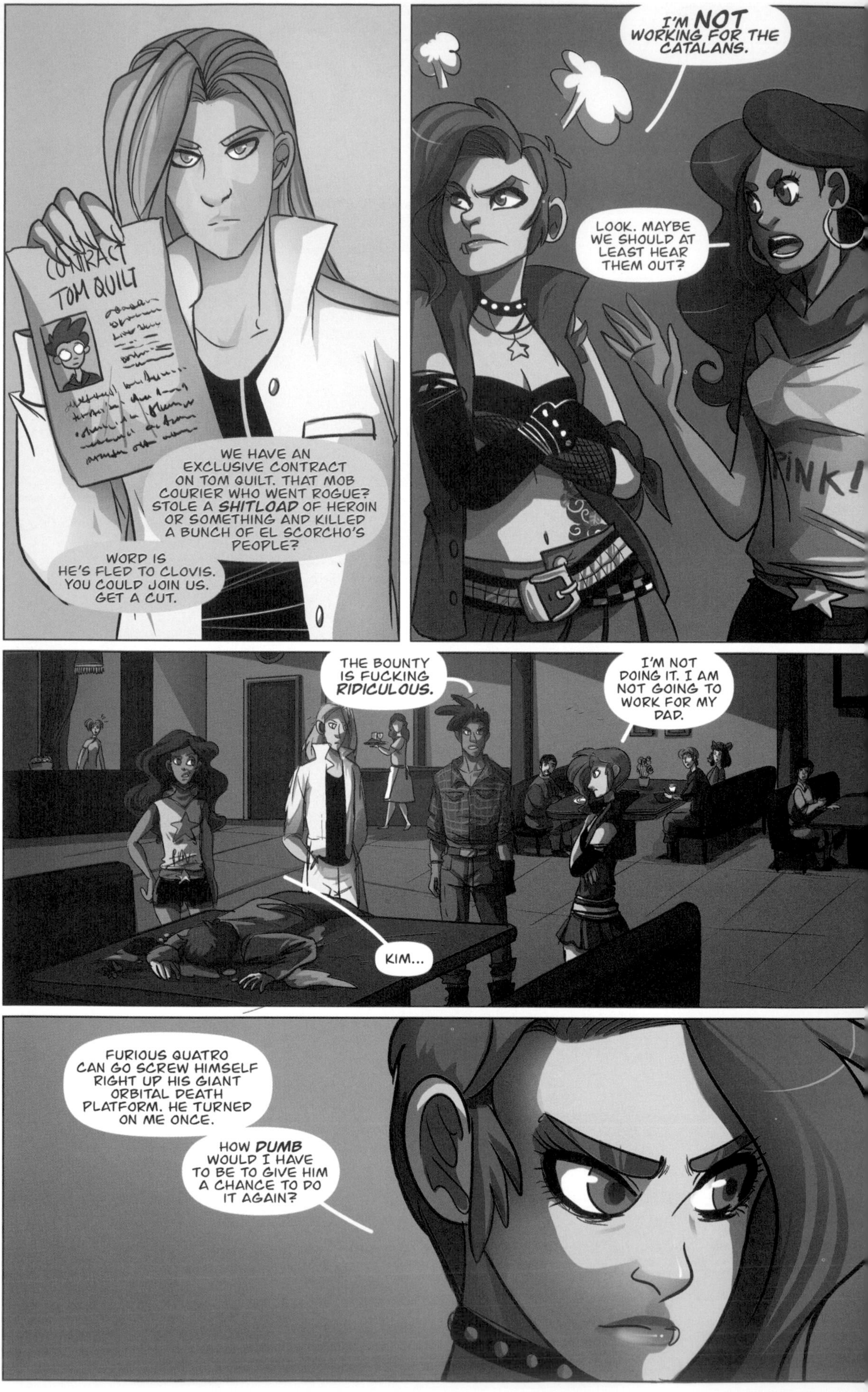
CONTRACT
TOM QUILT
WE HAVE AN EXCLUSIVE CONTRACT ON TOM QUILT. THAT MOB COURIER WHO WENT ROGUE? STOLE A SHITLOAD OF HEROIN OR SOMETHING AND KILLED A BUNCH OF EL SCORCHO'S PEOPLE?
WORD IS HE'S FLED TO CLOVIS. YOU COULD JOIN US. GET A CUT.
I'M NOT WORKING FOR THE CATALANS.
LOOK. MAYBE WE SHOULD AT LEAST HEAR THEM OUT?
PINK!
THE BOUNTY IS FUCKING RIDICULOUS.
I'M NOT DOING IT. I AM NOT GOING TO WORK FOR MY DAD.
KIM...
FURIOUS QUATRO CAN GO SCREW HIMSELF RIGHT UP HIS GIANT ORBITAL DEATH PLATFORM. HE TURNED ON ME ONCE.
HOW DUMB WOULD I HAVE TO BE TO GIVE HIM A CHANCE TO DO IT AGAIN?

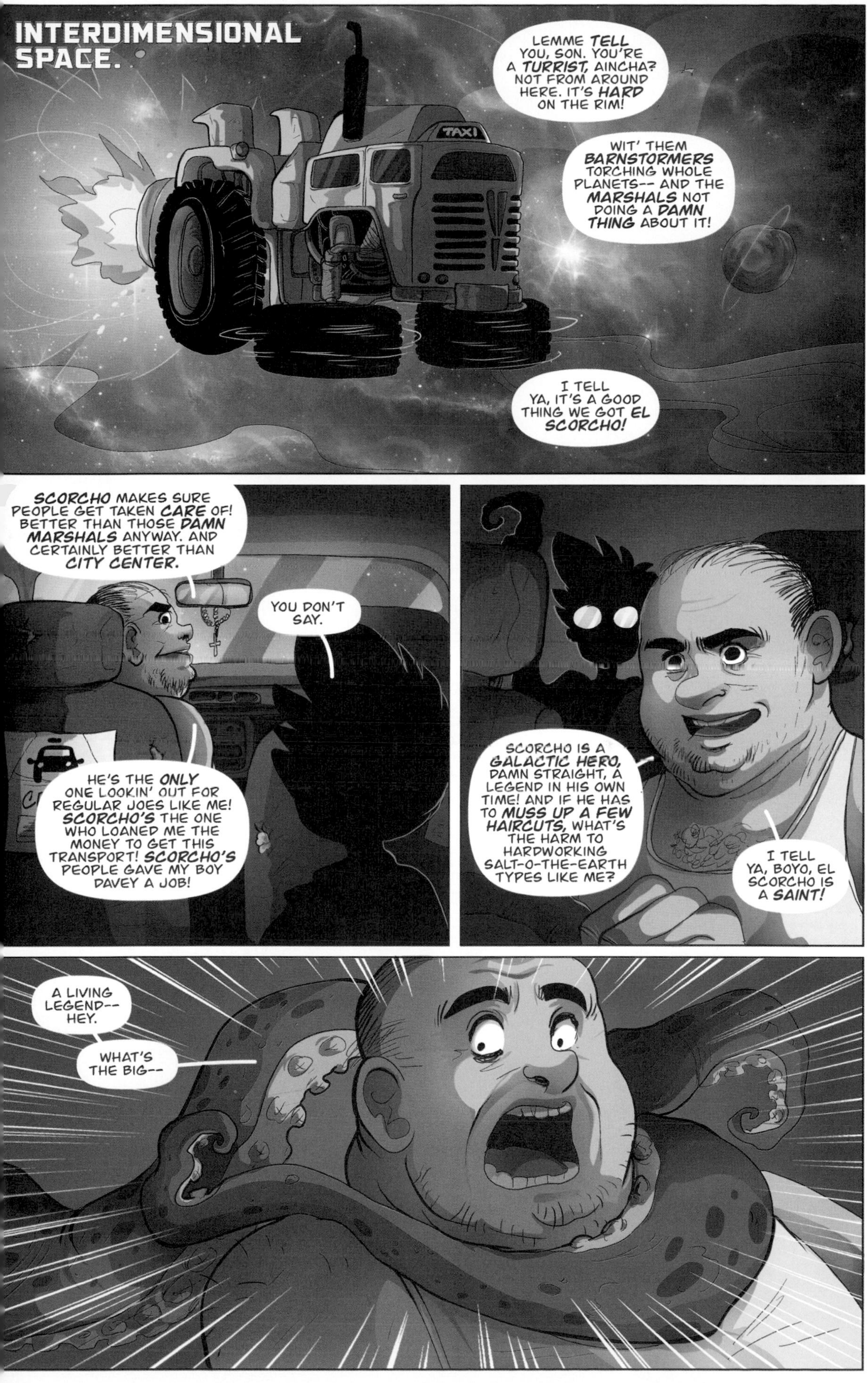
INTERDIMENSIONAL SPACE.
LEMME TELL YOU, SON. YOU'RE A TURRIST, AINCHA? NOT FROM AROUND HERE. IT'S HARD ON THE RIM!
WIT' THEM BARNSTORMERS TORCHING WHOLE PLANETS-- AND THE MARSHALS NOT DOING A DAMN THING ABOUT IT!
I TELL YA, IT'S A GOOD THING WE GOT EL SCORCHO!
TAXI
SCORCHO MAKES SURE PEOPLE GET TAKEN CARE OF! BETTER THAN THOSE DAMN MARSHALS ANYWAY. AND CERTAINLY BETTER THAN CITY CENTER.
YOU DON'T SAY.
HE'S THE ONLY ONE LOOKIN' OUT FOR REGULAR JOES LIKE ME! SCORCHO'S THE ONE WHO LOANED ME THE MONEY TO GET THIS TRANSPORT! SCORCHO'S PEOPLE GAVE MY BOY DAVEY A JOB!
SCORCHO IS A GALACTIC HERO, DAMN STRAIGHT, A LEGEND IN HIS OWN TIME! AND IF HE HAS TO MUSS UP A FEW HAIRCUTS, WHAT'S THE HARM TO HARDWORKING SALT-O-THE-EARTH TYPES LIKE ME?
I TELL YA, BOYO, EL SCORCHO IS A SAINT!
A LIVING LEGEND-- HEY.
WHAT'S THE BIG--

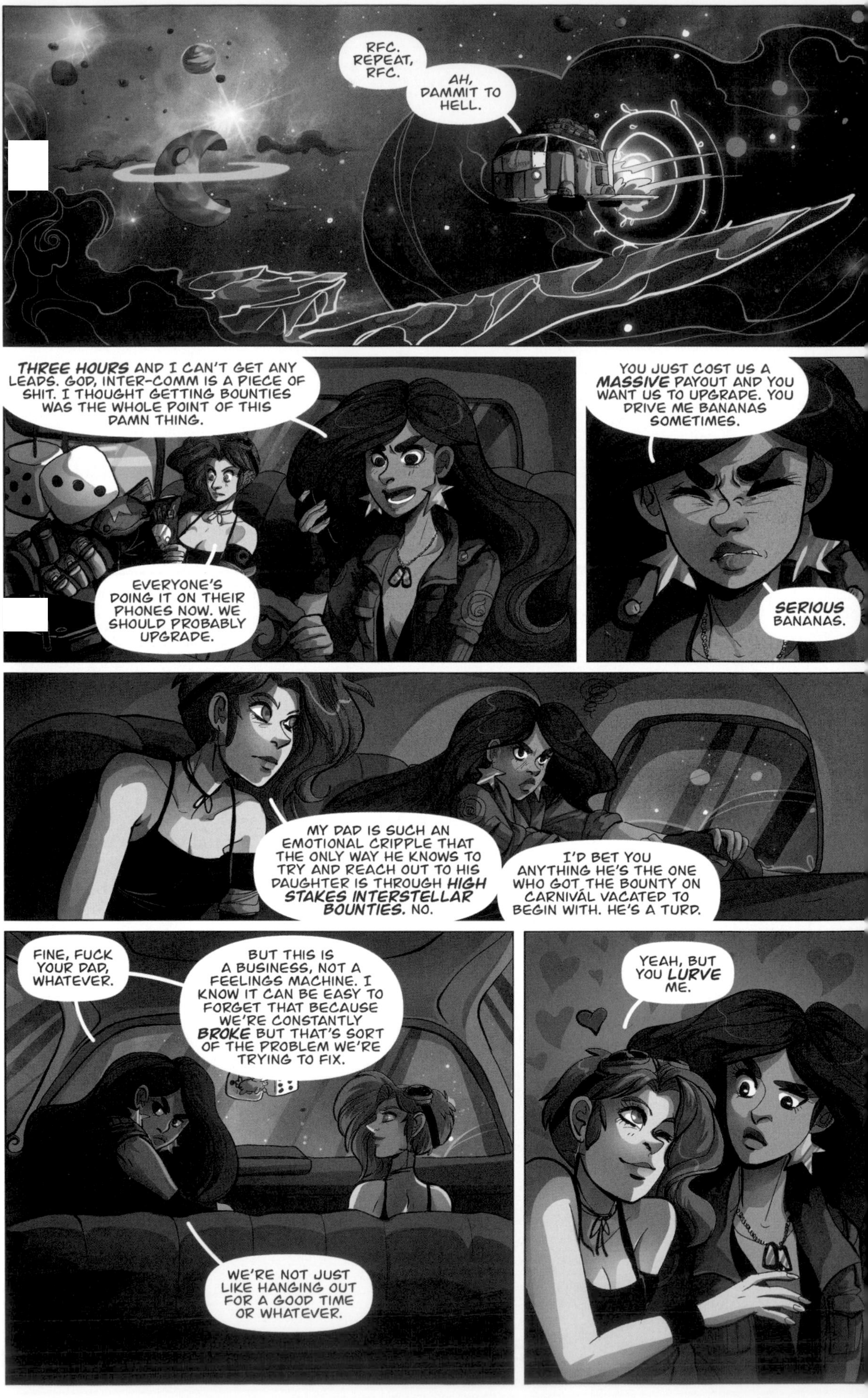
RFC. REPEAT, RFC.
AH, DAMMIT TO HELL.
THREE HOURS AND I CAN'T GET ANY LEADS. GOD, INTER-COMM IS A PIECE OF SHIT. I THOUGHT GETTING BOUNTIES WAS THE WHOLE POINT OF THIS DAMN THING.
EVERYONE'S DOING IT ON THEIR PHONES NOW. WE SHOULD PROBABLY UPGRADE.
YOU JUST COST US A MASSIVE PAYOUT AND YOU WANT US TO UPGRADE. YOU DRIVE ME BANANAS SOMETIMES.
SERIOUS BANANAS.
MY DAD IS SUCH AN EMOTIONAL CRIPPLE THAT THE ONLY WAY HE KNOWS TO TRY AND REACH OUT TO HIS DAUGHTER IS THROUGH HIGH STAKES INTERSTELLAR BOUNTIES. NO.
I'D BET YOU ANYTHING HE'S THE ONE WHO GOT THE BOUNTY ON CARNIVÁL VACATED TO BEGIN WITH. HE'S A TURD.
FINE, FUCK YOUR DAD, WHATEVER.
BUT THIS IS A BUSINESS, NOT A FEELINGS MACHINE. I KNOW IT CAN BE EASY TO FORGET THAT BECAUSE WE'RE CONSTANTLY BROKE BUT THAT'S SORT OF THE PROBLEM WE'RE TRYING TO FIX.
WE'RE NOT JUST LIKE HANGING OUT FOR A GOOD TIME OR WHATEVER.
YEAH, BUT YOU LURVE ME.

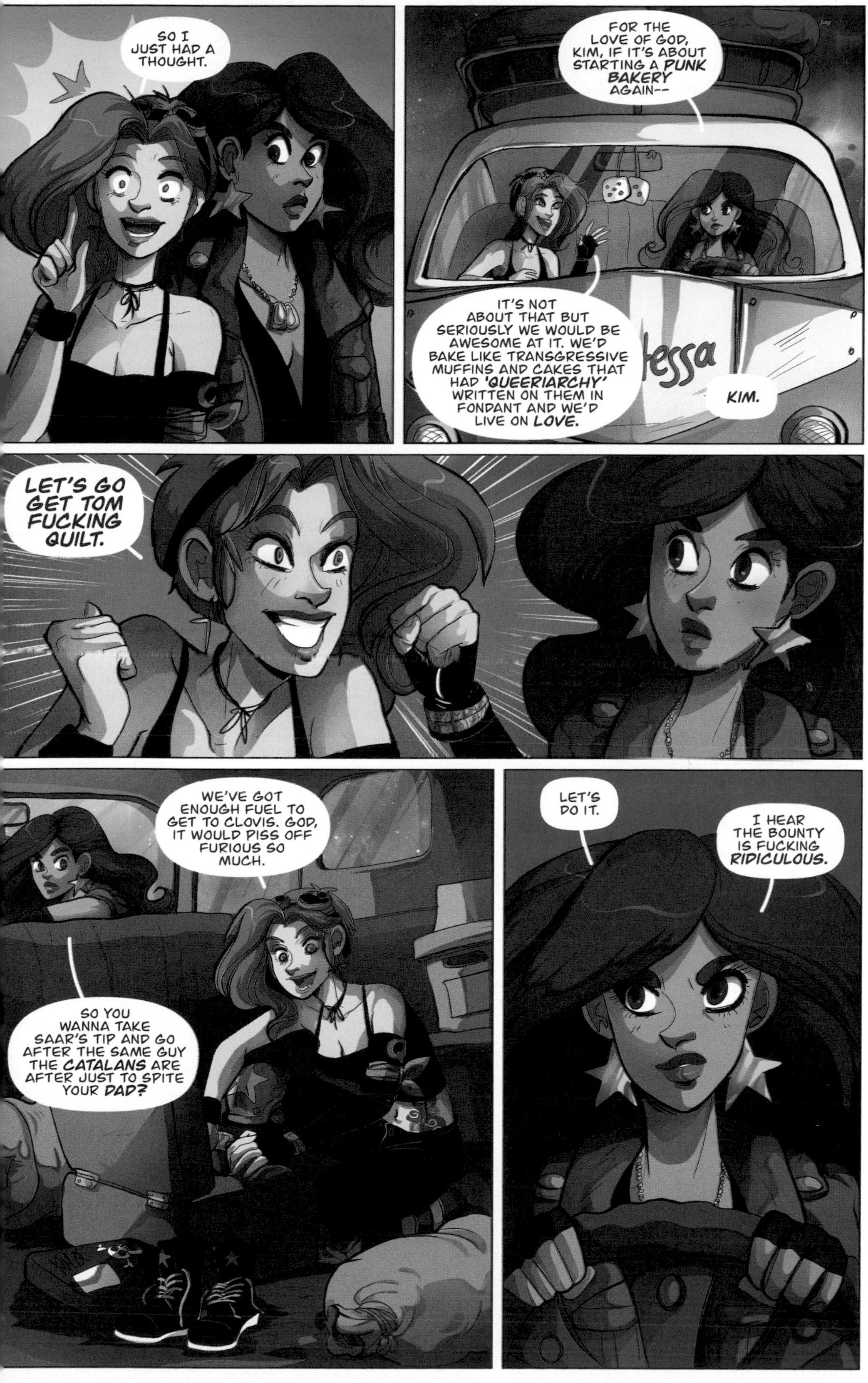
SO I JUST HAD A THOUGHT.
FOR THE LOVE OF GOD, KIM, IF IT'S ABOUT STARTING A PUNK BAKERY AGAIN--
IT'S NOT ABOUT THAT BUT SERIOUSLY WE WOULD BE AWESOME AT IT. WE'D BAKE LIKE TRANSGRESSIVE MUFFINS AND CAKES THAT HAD 'QUEERIARCHY' WRITTEN ON THEM IN FONDANT AND WE'D LIVE ON LOVE.
KIM.
LET'S GO GET TOM FUCKING QUILT.
SO YOU WANNA TAKE SAAR'S TIP AND GO AFTER THE SAME GUY THE CATALANS ARE AFTER JUST TO SPITE YOUR DAD?
WE'VE GOT ENOUGH FUEL TO GET TO CLOVIS. GOD, IT WOULD PISS OFF FURIOUS SO MUCH.
LET'S DO IT.
I HEAR THE BOUNTY IS FUCKING RIDICULOUS.

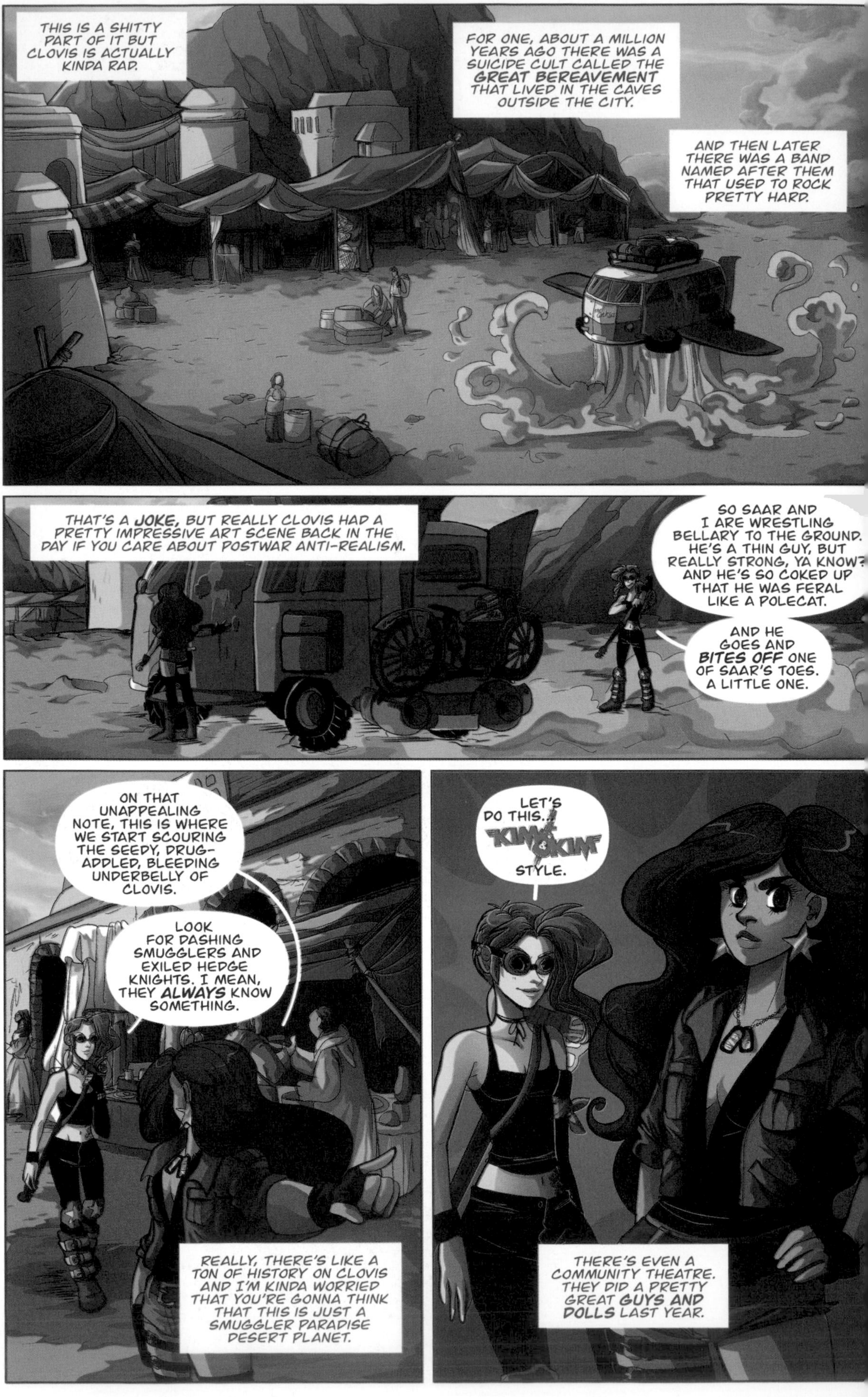
THIS IS A SHITTY PART OF IT BUT CLOVIS IS ACTUALLY KINDA RAD.
FOR ONE, ABOUT A MILLION YEARS AGO THERE WAS A SUICIDE CULT CALLED THE **GREAT BEREAVEMENT** THAT LIVED IN THE CAVES OUTSIDE THE CITY.
AND THEN LATER THERE WAS A BAND NAMED AFTER THEM THAT USED TO ROCK PRETTY HARD.
THAT'S A **JOKE**, BUT REALLY CLOVIS HAD A PRETTY IMPRESSIVE ART SCENE BACK IN THE DAY IF YOU CARE ABOUT POSTWAR ANTI-REALISM.
SO SAAR AND I ARE WRESTLING BELLARY TO THE GROUND. HE'S A THIN GUY, BUT REALLY STRONG, YA KNOW? AND HE'S SO COKED UP THAT HE WAS FERAL LIKE A POLECAT.
AND HE GOES AND **BITES OFF** ONE OF SAAR'S TOES. A LITTLE ONE.
ON THAT UNAPPEALING NOTE, THIS IS WHERE WE START SCOURING THE SEEDY, DRUG-ADDLED, BLEEDING UNDERBELLY OF CLOVIS.
LOOK FOR DASHING SMUGGLERS AND EXILED HEDGE KNIGHTS. I MEAN, THEY **ALWAYS** KNOW SOMETHING.
REALLY, THERE'S LIKE A TON OF HISTORY ON CLOVIS AND I'M KINDA WORRIED THAT YOU'RE GONNA THINK THAT THIS IS JUST A SMUGGLER PARADISE DESERT PLANET.
LET'S DO THIS... KIM & KIM STYLE.
THERE'S EVEN A COMMUNITY THEATRE. THEY DID A PRETTY GREAT **GUYS AND DOLLS** LAST YEAR.

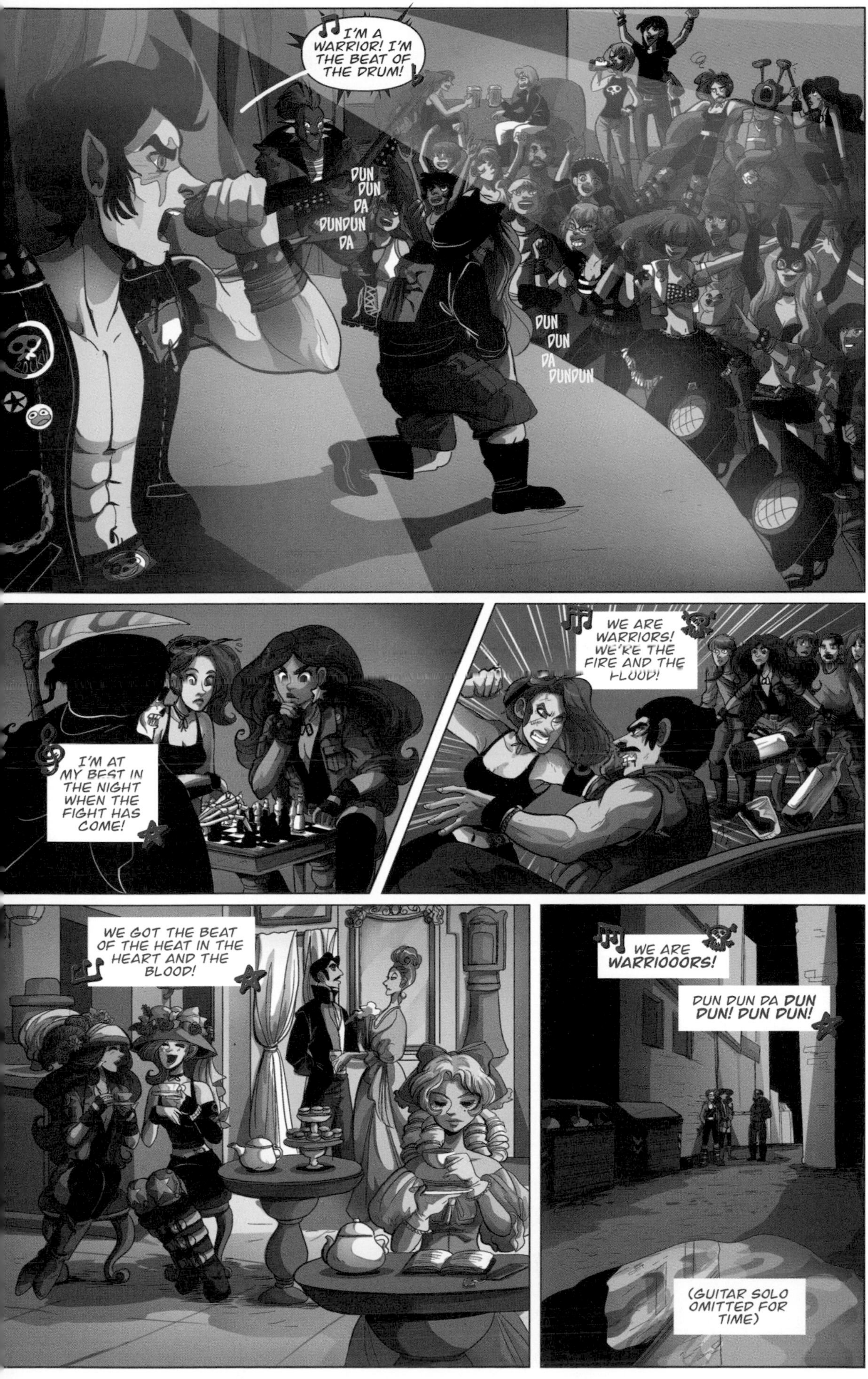

I'M A WARRIOR! I'M THE BEAT OF THE DRUM!
DUN DUN DA DUNDUN DA
DUN DUN DA DUNDUN
I'M AT MY BEST IN THE NIGHT WHEN THE FIGHT HAS COME!
WE ARE WARRIORS! WE'RE THE FIRE AND THE FLOOD!
WE GOT THE BEAT OF THE HEAT IN THE HEART AND THE BLOOD!
WE ARE WARRIOOORS!
DUN DUN DA DUN DUN! DUN DUN!
(GUITAR SOLO OMITTED FOR TIME)

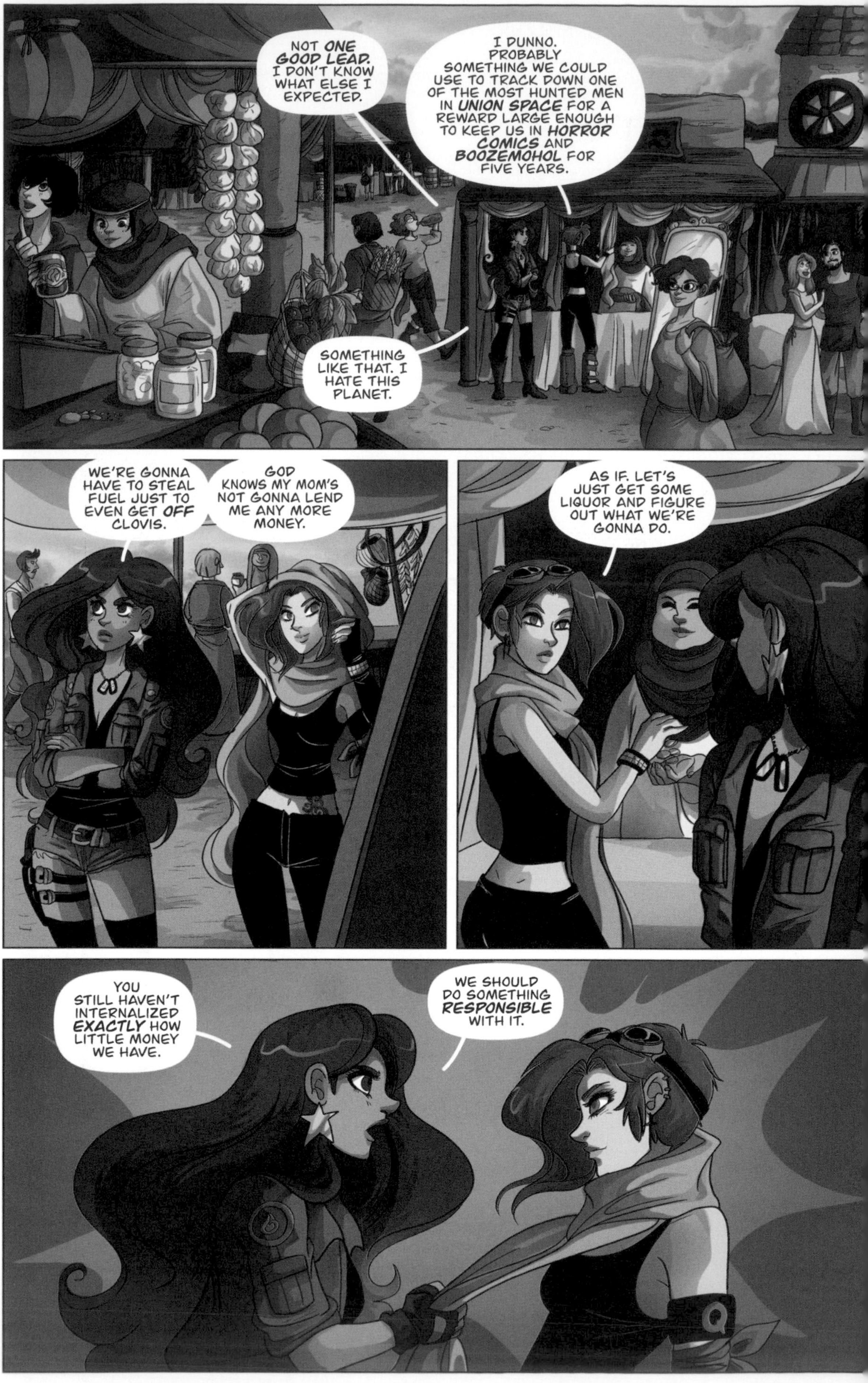
NOT ONE GOOD LEAD. I DON'T KNOW WHAT ELSE I EXPECTED.
I DUNNO. PROBABLY SOMETHING WE COULD USE TO TRACK DOWN ONE OF THE MOST HUNTED MEN IN UNION SPACE FOR A REWARD LARGE ENOUGH TO KEEP US IN HORROR COMICS AND BOOZEMOHOL FOR FIVE YEARS.
SOMETHING LIKE THAT. I HATE THIS PLANET.
WE'RE GONNA HAVE TO STEAL FUEL JUST TO EVEN GET OFF CLOVIS.
GOD KNOWS MY MOM'S NOT GONNA LEND ME ANY MORE MONEY.
AS IF. LET'S JUST GET SOME LIQUOR AND FIGURE OUT WHAT WE'RE GONNA DO.
YOU STILL HAVEN'T INTERNALIZED EXACTLY HOW LITTLE MONEY WE HAVE.
WE SHOULD DO SOMETHING RESPONSIBLE WITH IT.

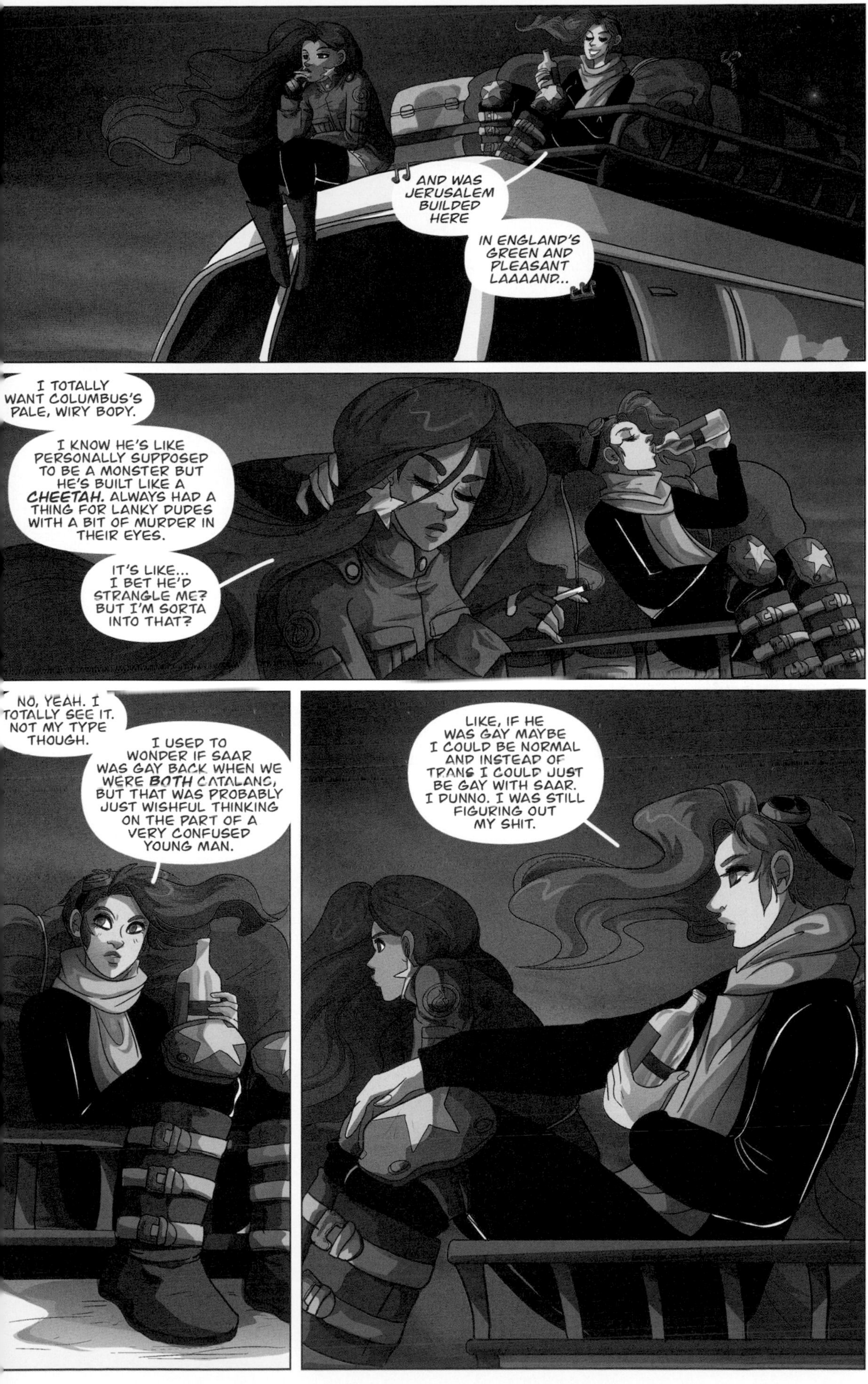
AND WAS JERUSALEM BUILDED HERE
IN ENGLAND'S GREEN AND PLEASANT LAAAAND...
I TOTALLY WANT COLUMBUS'S PALE, WIRY BODY.
I KNOW HE'S LIKE PERSONALLY SUPPOSED TO BE A MONSTER BUT HE'S BUILT LIKE A CHEETAH. ALWAYS HAD A THING FOR LANKY DUDES WITH A BIT OF MURDER IN THEIR EYES.
IT'S LIKE... I BET HE'D STRANGLE ME? BUT I'M SORTA INTO THAT?
NO, YEAH. I TOTALLY SEE IT. NOT MY TYPE THOUGH.
I USED TO WONDER IF SAAR WAS GAY BACK WHEN WE WERE BOTH CATALANS, BUT THAT WAS PROBABLY JUST WISHFUL THINKING ON THE PART OF A VERY CONFUSED YOUNG MAN.
LIKE, IF HE WAS GAY MAYBE I COULD BE NORMAL AND INSTEAD OF TRANS I COULD JUST BE GAY WITH SAAR. I DUNNO. I WAS STILL FIGURING OUT MY SHIT.

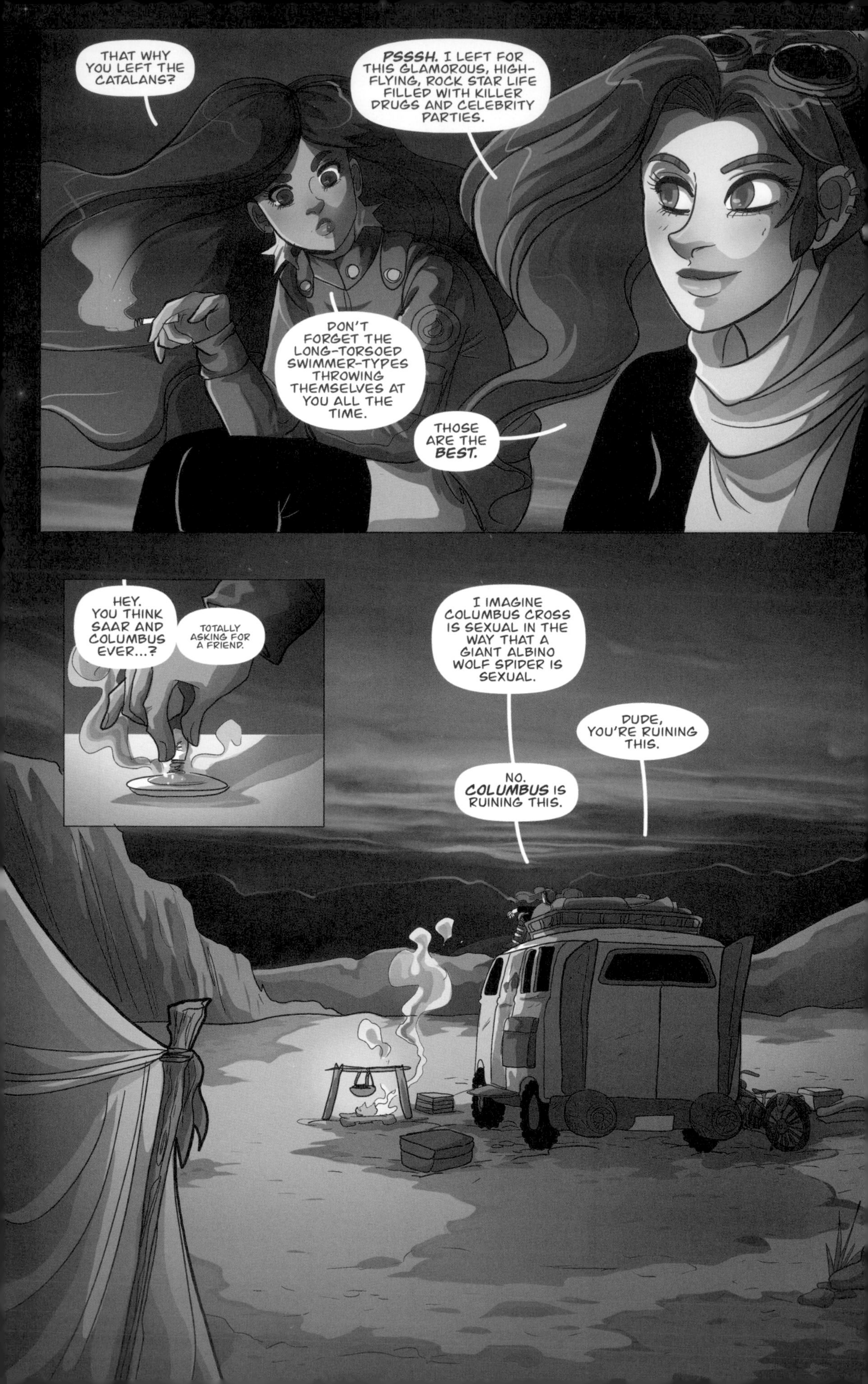
THAT WHY YOU LEFT THE CATALANS?
PSSSH. I LEFT FOR THIS GLAMOROUS, HIGH-FLYING, ROCK STAR LIFE FILLED WITH KILLER DRUGS AND CELEBRITY PARTIES.
DON'T FORGET THE LONG-TORSOED SWIMMER-TYPES THROWING THEMSELVES AT YOU ALL THE TIME.
THOSE ARE THE BEST.
HEY. YOU THINK SAAR AND COLUMBUS EVER...?
TOTALLY ASKING FOR A FRIEND.
I IMAGINE COLUMBUS CROSS IS SEXUAL IN THE WAY THAT A GIANT ALBINO WOLF SPIDER IS SEXUAL.
DUDE, YOU'RE RUINING THIS.
NO. COLUMBUS IS RUINING THIS.

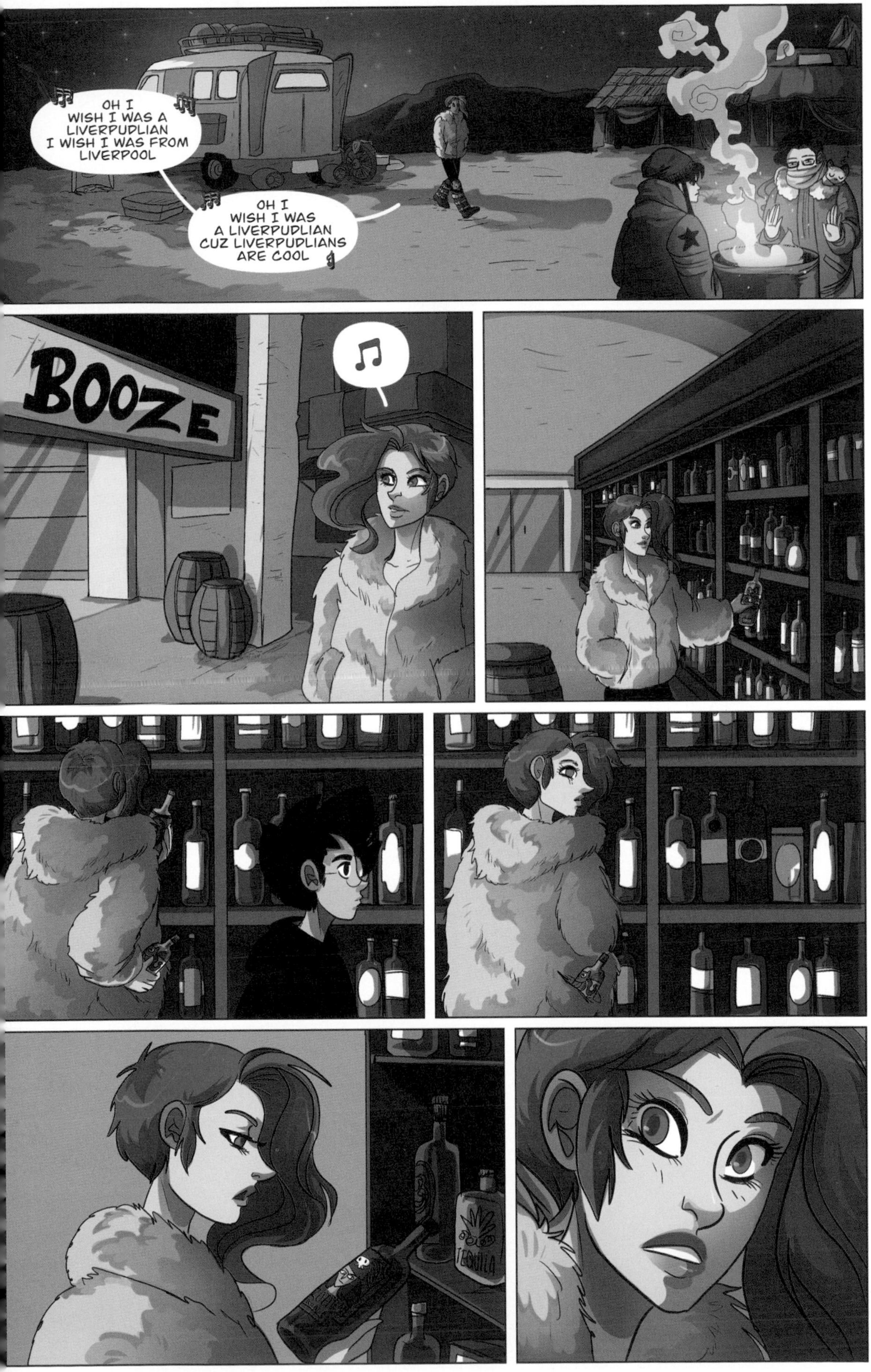
OH I WISH I WAS A LIVERPUDLIAN I WISH I WAS FROM LIVERPOOL
OH I WISH I WAS A LIVERPUDLIAN CUZ LIVERPUDLIANS ARE COOL
BOOZE
♫
TEQUILA

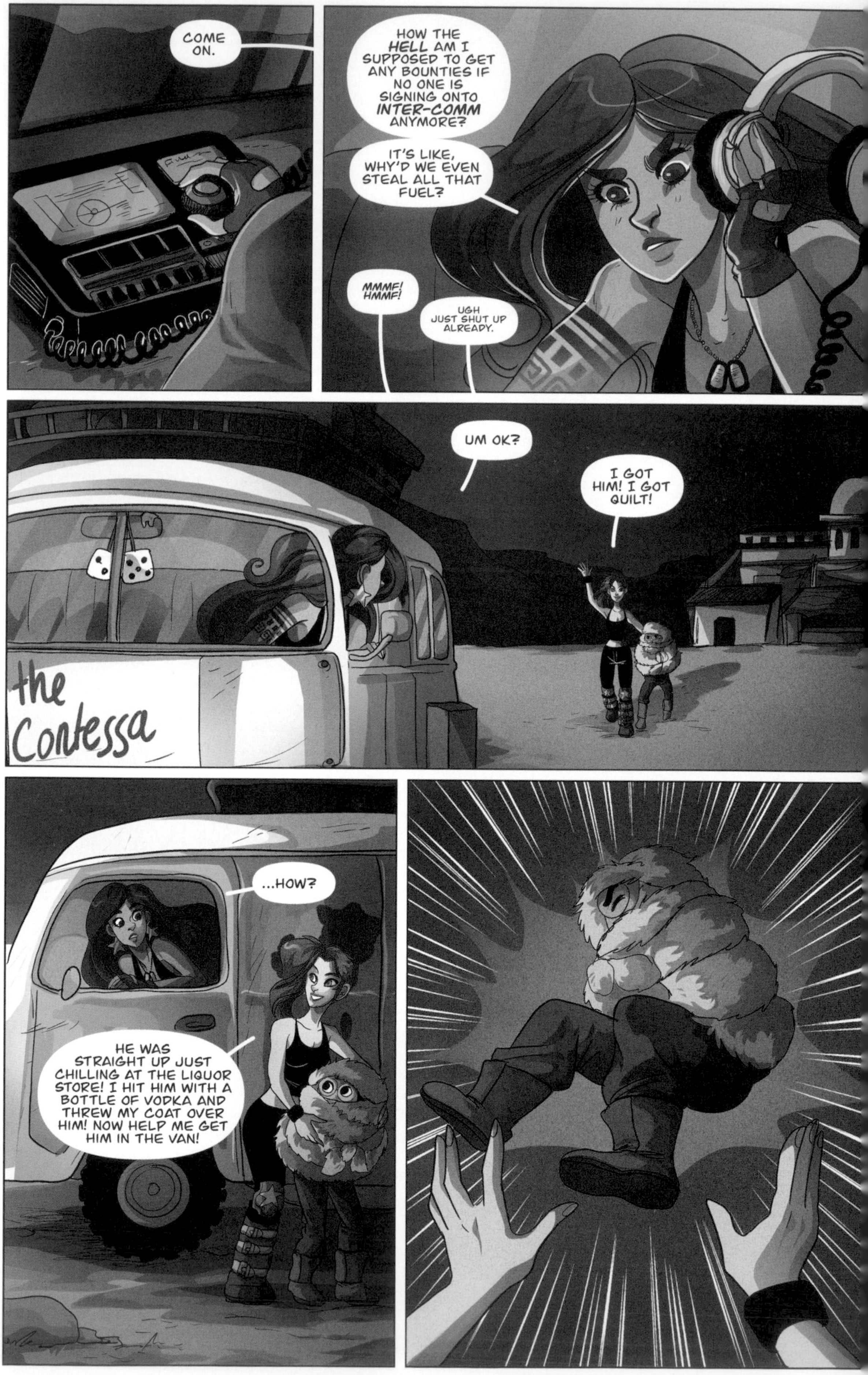
COME ON.
HOW THE HELL AM I SUPPOSED TO GET ANY BOUNTIES IF NO ONE IS SIGNING ONTO INTER-COMM ANYMORE?
IT'S LIKE, WHY'D WE EVEN STEAL ALL THAT FUEL?
MMMF! HMMF!
UGH JUST SHUT UP ALREADY.
UM OK?
I GOT HIM! I GOT QUILT!
the Contessa
...HOW?
HE WAS STRAIGHT UP JUST CHILLING AT THE LIQUOR STORE! I HIT HIM WITH A BOTTLE OF VODKA AND THREW MY COAT OVER HIM! NOW HELP ME GET HIM IN THE VAN!

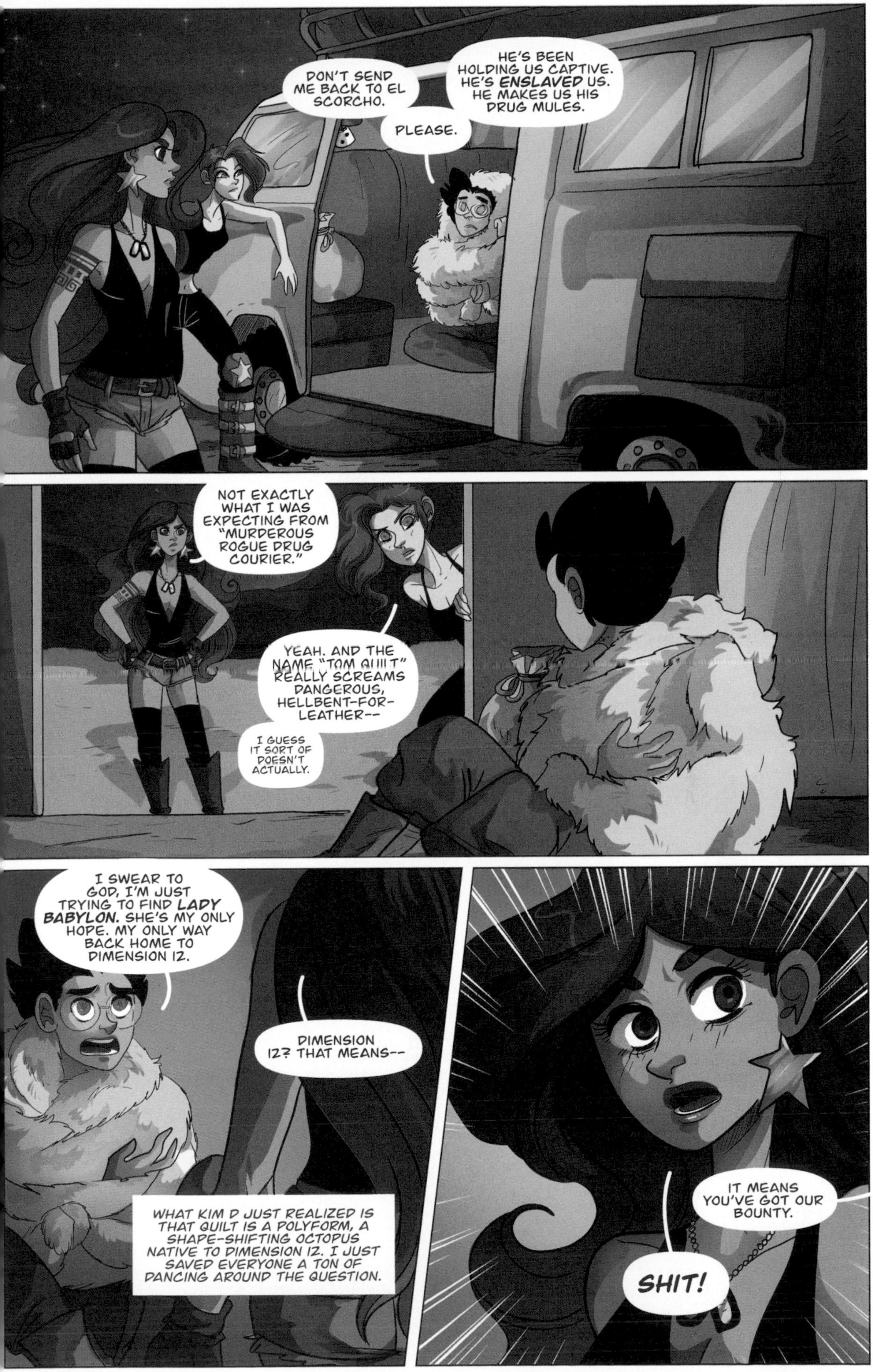
DON'T SEND ME BACK TO EL SCORCHO.
HE'S BEEN HOLDING US CAPTIVE. HE'S **ENSLAVED** US. HE MAKES US HIS DRUG MULES.
PLEASE.
NOT EXACTLY WHAT I WAS EXPECTING FROM "MURDEROUS ROGUE DRUG COURIER."
YEAH. AND THE NAME "TOM QUILT" REALLY SCREAMS DANGEROUS, HELLBENT-FOR-LEATHER--
I GUESS IT SORT OF DOESN'T ACTUALLY.
I SWEAR TO GOD, I'M JUST TRYING TO FIND **LADY BABYLON.** SHE'S MY ONLY HOPE. MY ONLY WAY BACK HOME TO DIMENSION 12.
DIMENSION 12? THAT MEANS--
WHAT KIM D JUST REALIZED IS THAT QUILT IS A POLYFORM, A SHAPE-SHIFTING OCTOPUS NATIVE TO DIMENSION 12. I JUST SAVED EVERYONE A TON OF DANCING AROUND THE QUESTION.
IT MEANS YOU'VE GOT OUR BOUNTY.
SHIT!

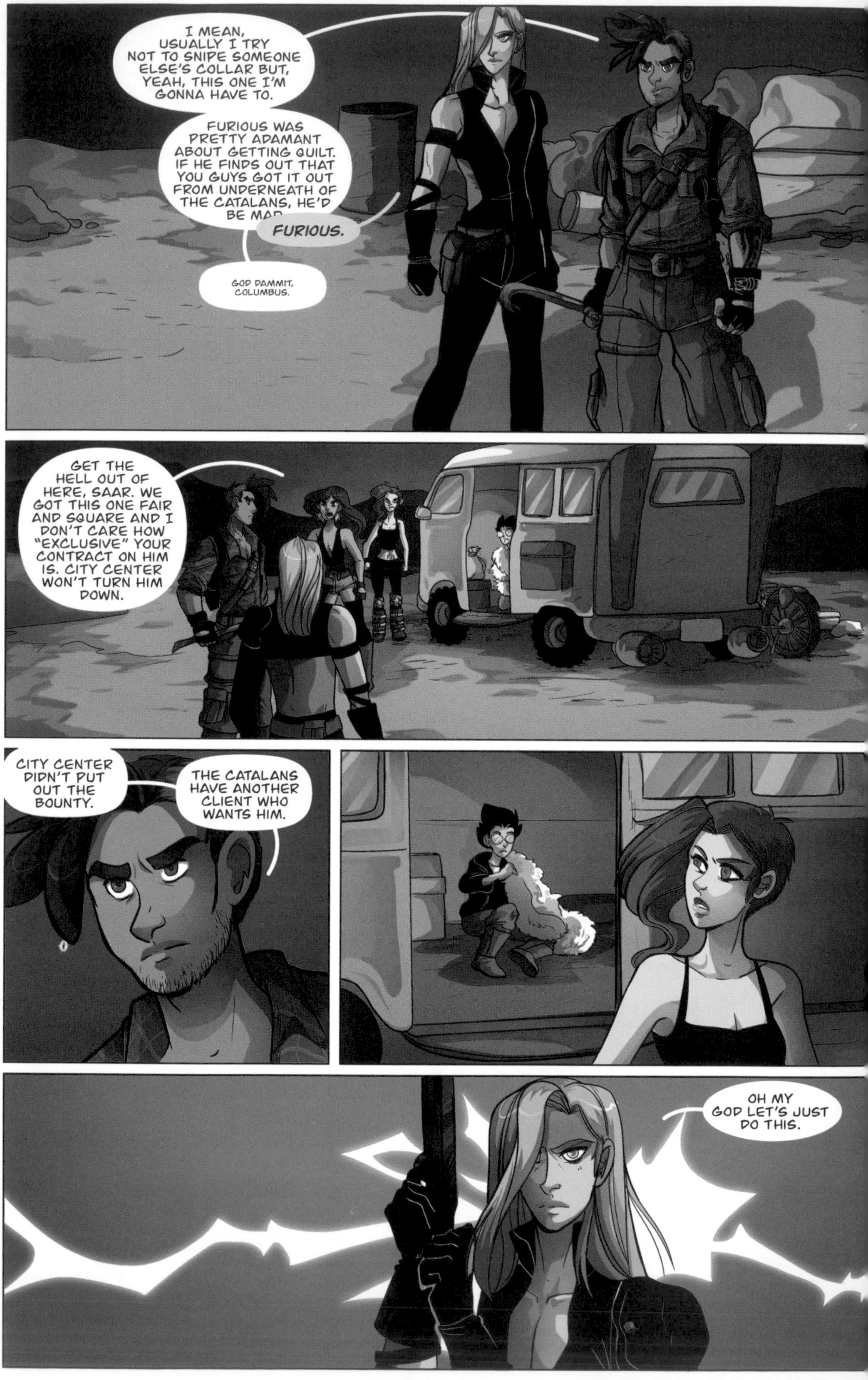
I MEAN, USUALLY I TRY NOT TO SNIPE SOMEONE ELSE'S COLLAR BUT, YEAH, THIS ONE I'M GONNA HAVE TO.
FURIOUS WAS PRETTY ADAMANT ABOUT GETTING QUILT. IF HE FINDS OUT THAT YOU GUYS GOT IT OUT FROM UNDERNEATH OF THE CATALANS, HE'D BE
FURIOUS.
GOD DAMMIT, COLUMBUS.
GET THE HELL OUT OF HERE, SAAR. WE GOT THIS ONE FAIR AND SQUARE AND I DON'T CARE HOW "EXCLUSIVE" YOUR CONTRACT ON HIM IS. CITY CENTER WON'T TURN HIM DOWN.
CITY CENTER DIDN'T PUT OUT THE BOUNTY.
THE CATALANS HAVE ANOTHER CLIENT WHO WANTS HIM.
OH MY GOD LET'S JUST DO THIS.

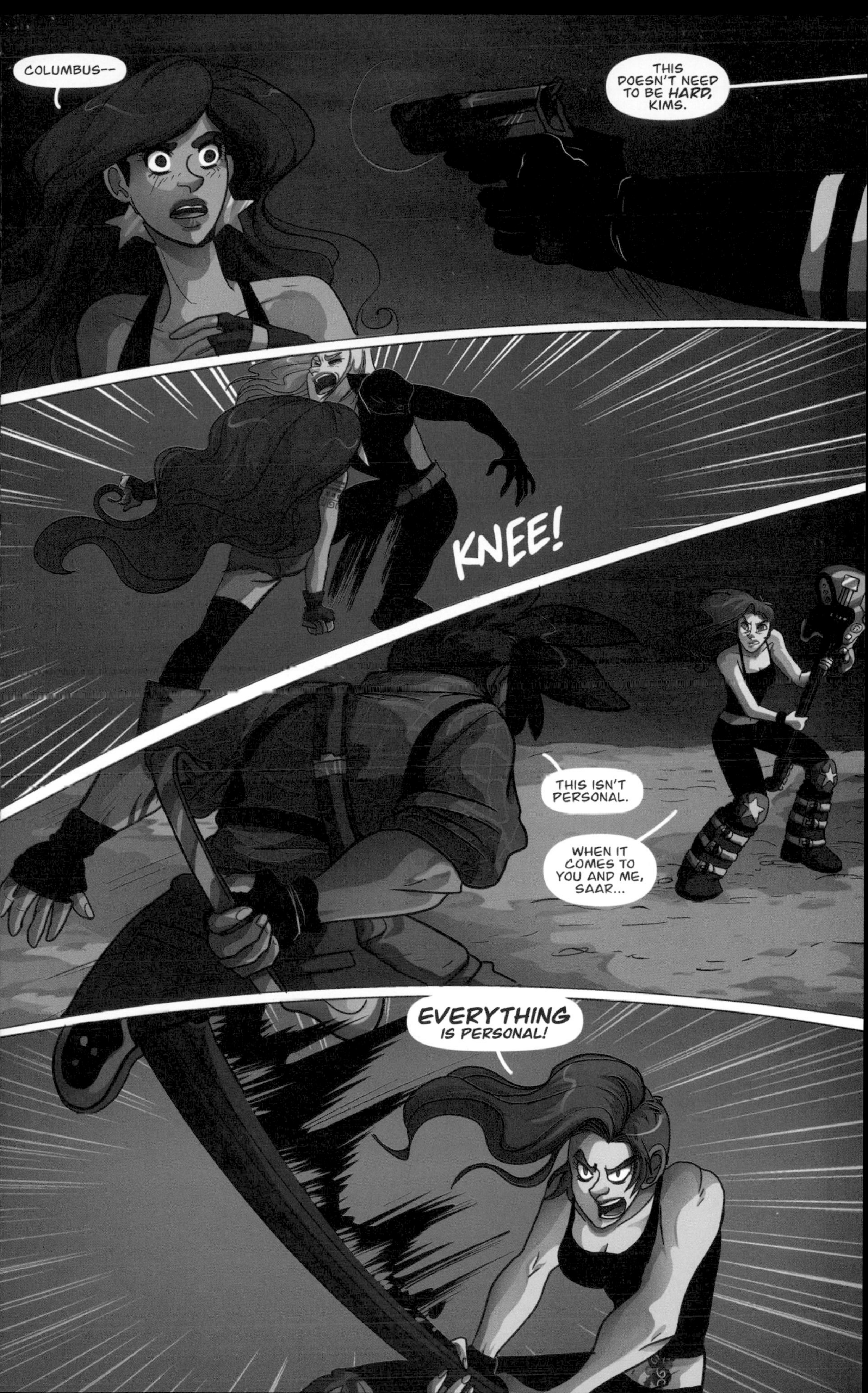
COLUMBUS--
THIS DOESN'T NEED TO BE HARD, KIMS.
KNEE!
THIS ISN'T PERSONAL.
WHEN IT COMES TO YOU AND ME, SAAR...
EVERYTHING IS PERSONAL!

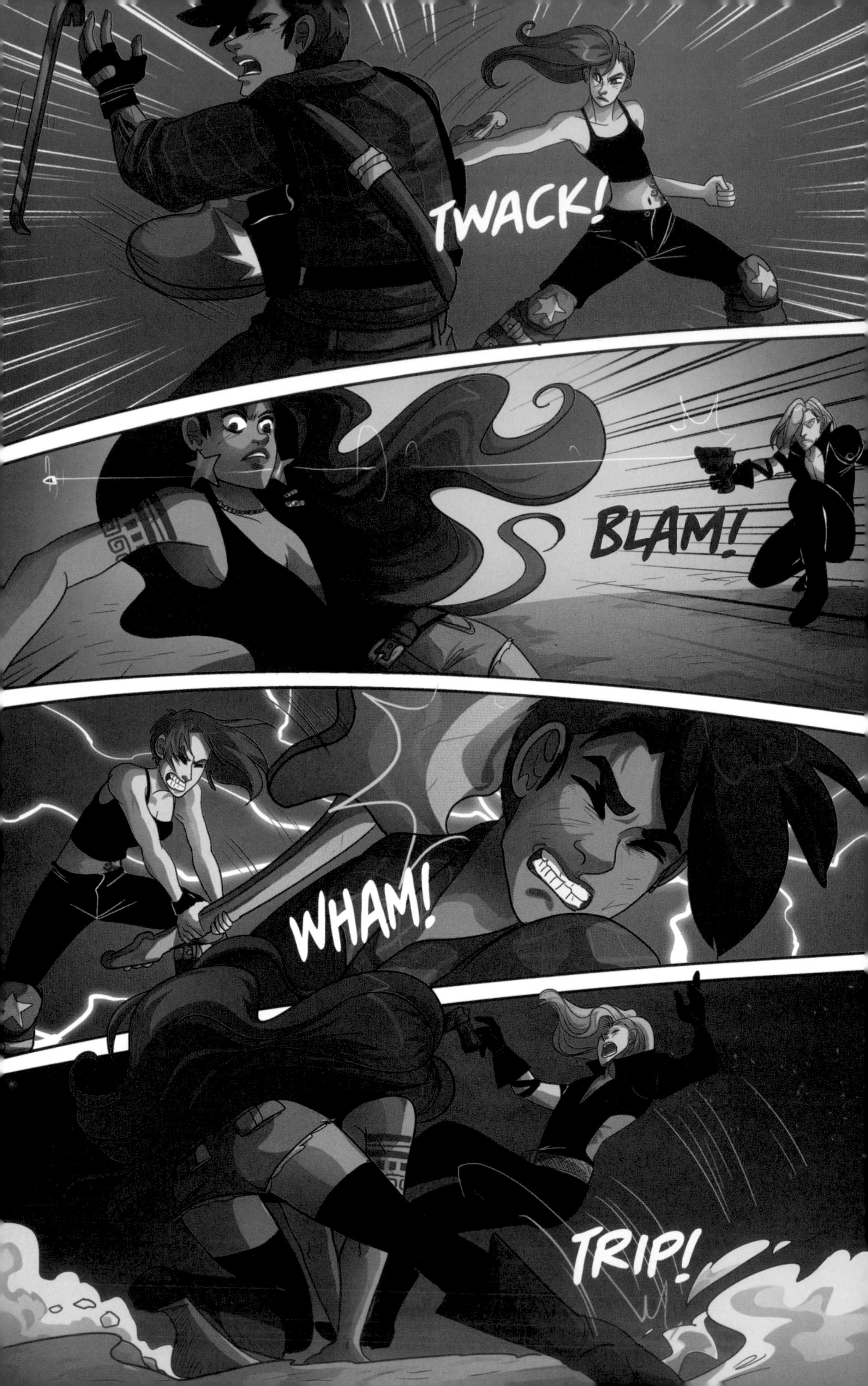
TWACK!
BLAM!
WHAM!
TRIP!

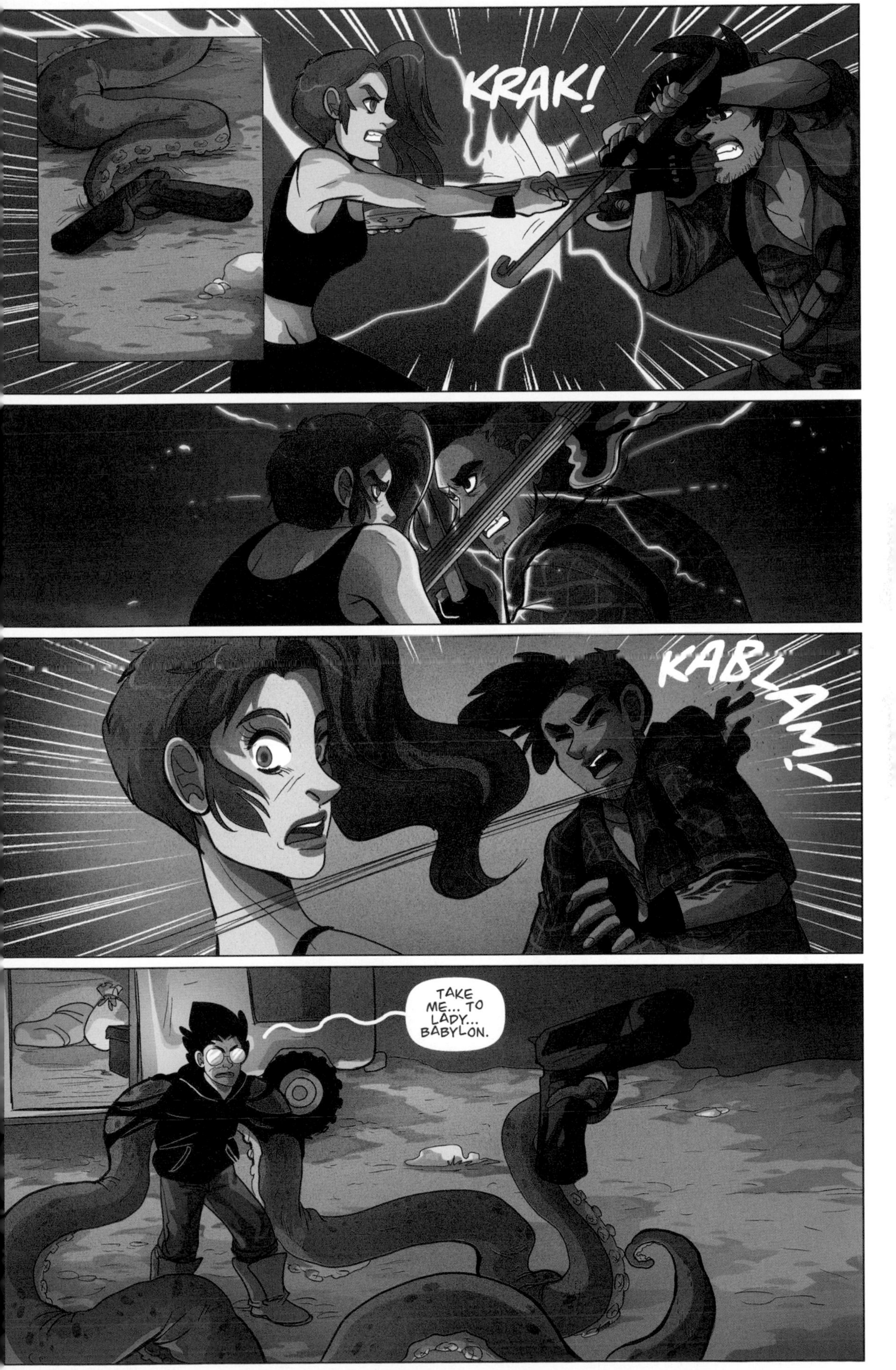

KRAK!
KABLAM!
TAKE ME... TO LADY... BABYLON.

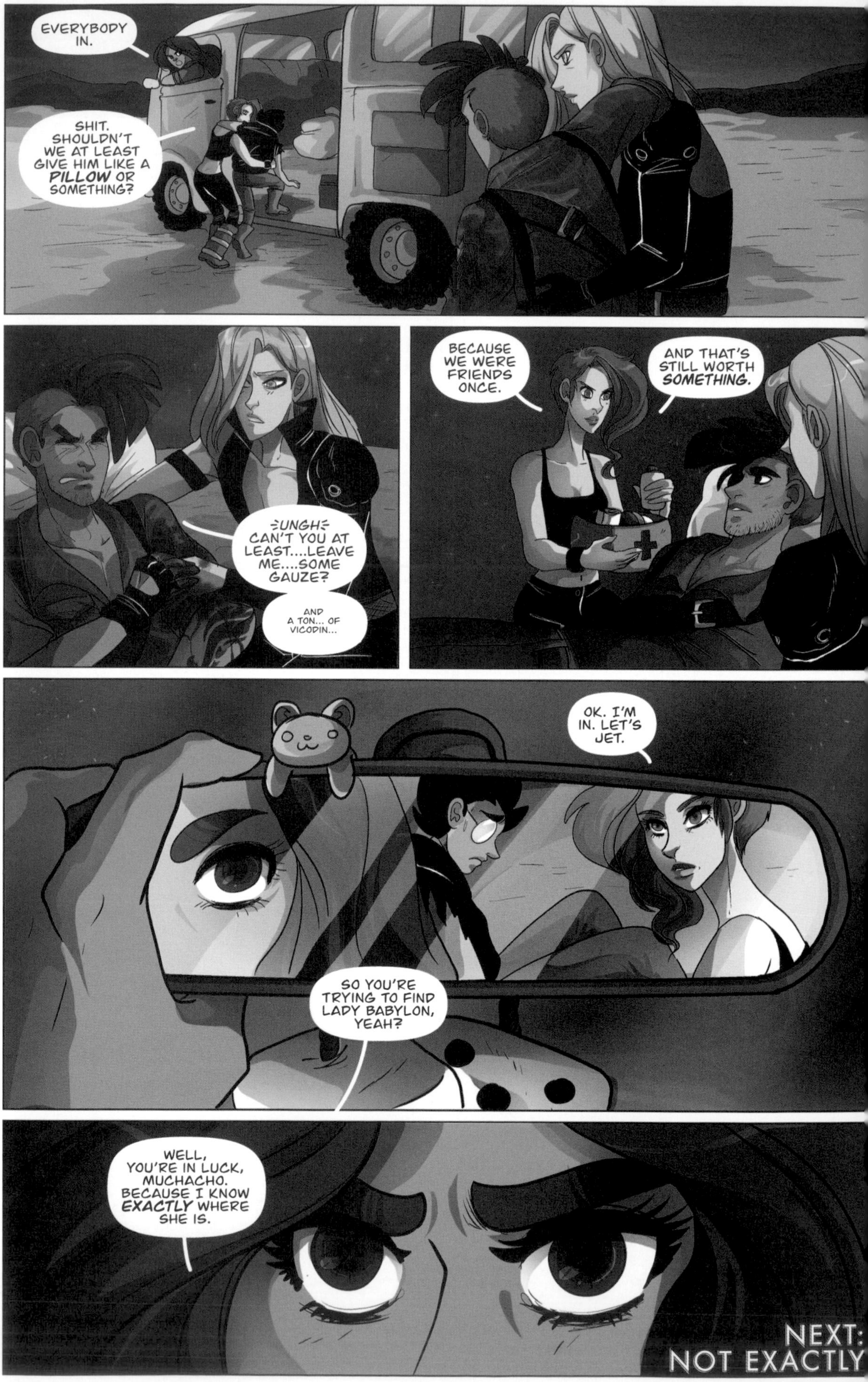
EVERYBODY IN.
SHIT. SHOULDN'T WE AT LEAST GIVE HIM LIKE A **PILLOW** OR SOMETHING?
=UNGH= CAN'T YOU AT LEAST....LEAVE ME....SOME GAUZE?
AND A TON... OF VICODIN...
BECAUSE WE WERE FRIENDS ONCE.
AND THAT'S STILL WORTH **SOMETHING.**
OK. I'M IN. LET'S JET.
SO YOU'RE TRYING TO FIND LADY BABYLON, YEAH?
WELL, YOU'RE IN LUCK, MUCHACHO. BECAUSE I KNOW **EXACTLY** WHERE SHE IS.
NEXT: NOT EXACTLY

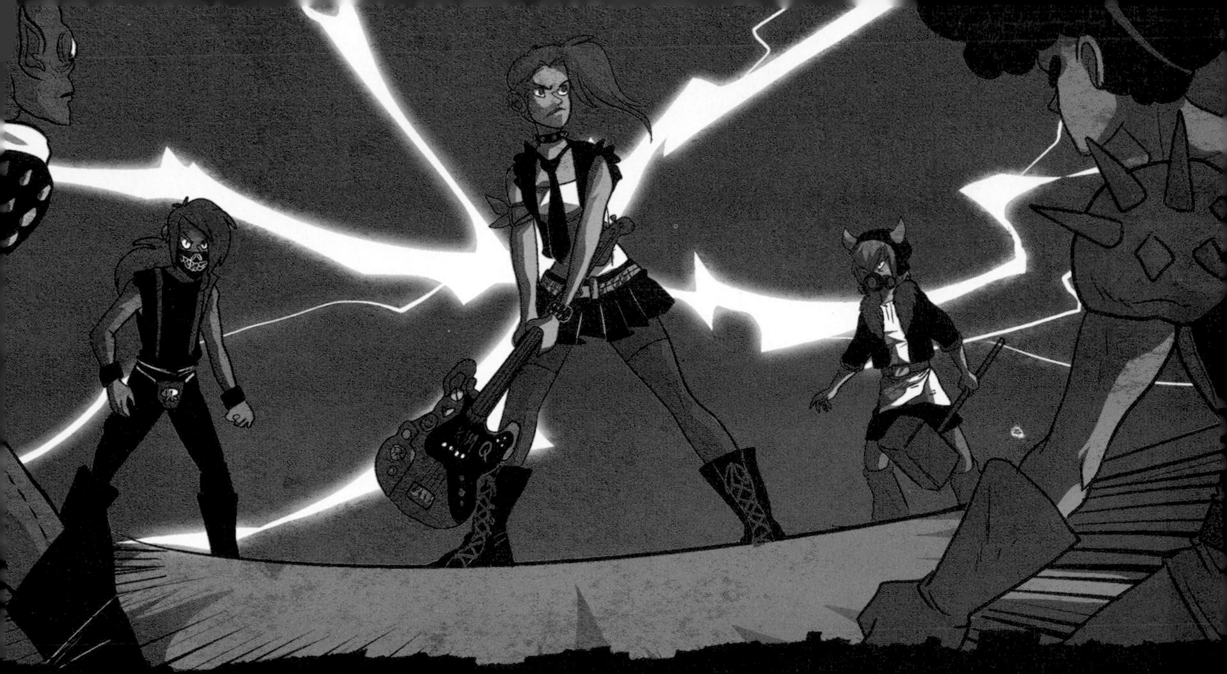

2

"NOT EXACTLY"

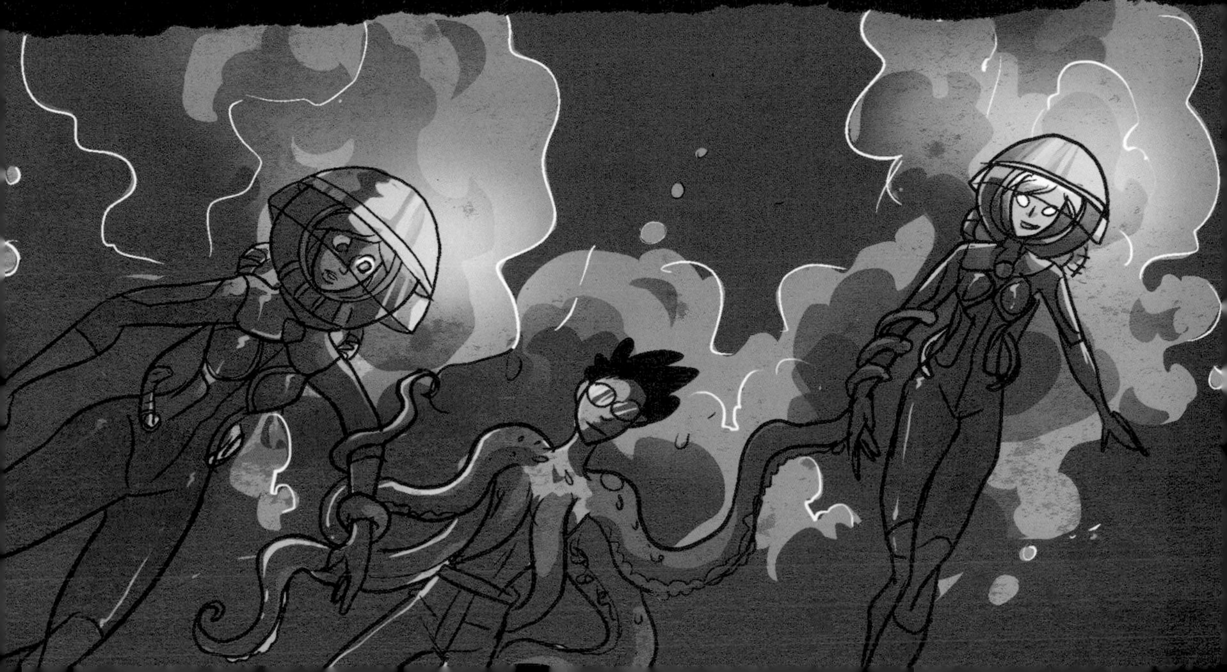

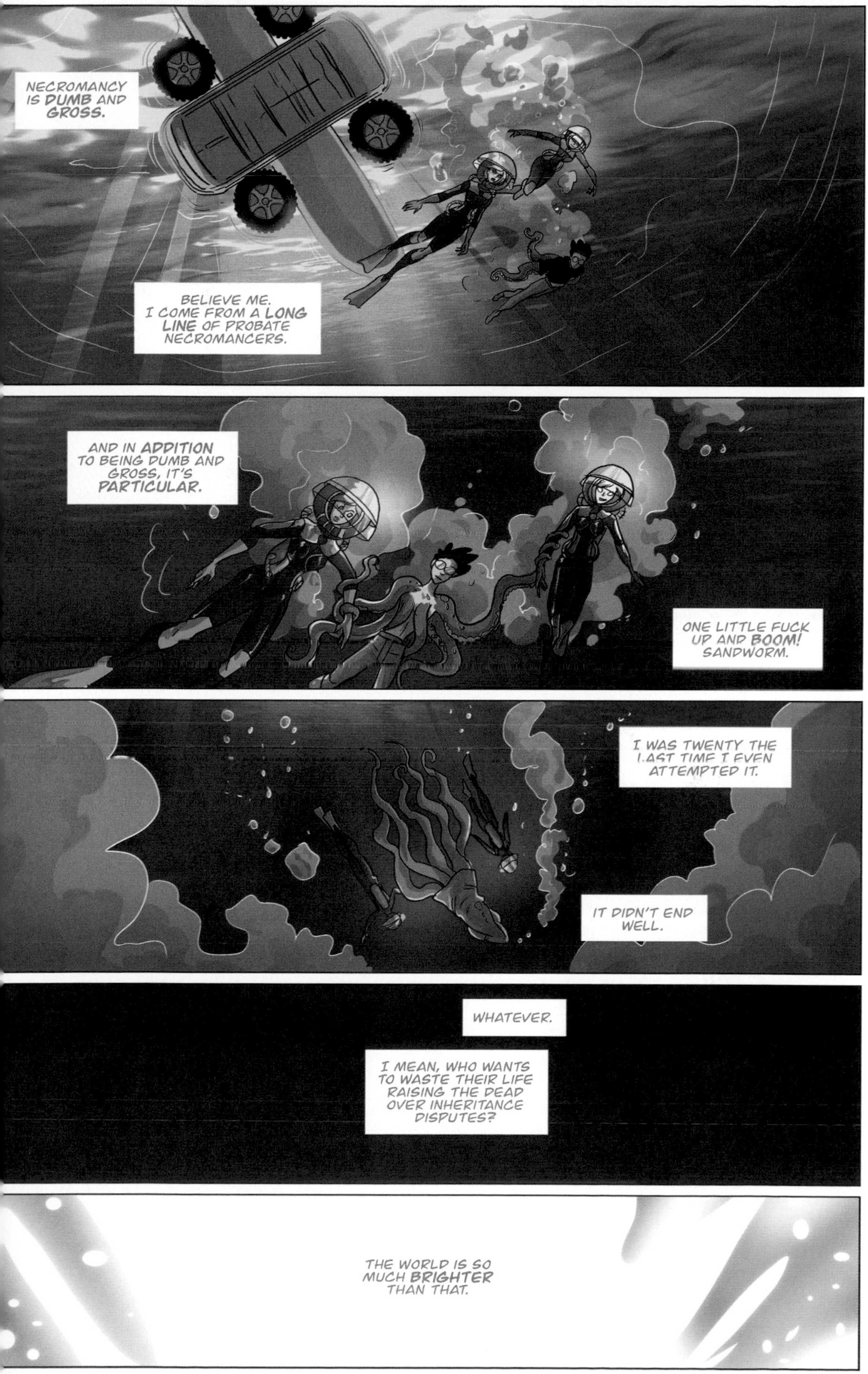
NECROMANCY IS DUMB AND GROSS.
BELIEVE ME. I COME FROM A LONG LINE OF PROBATE NECROMANCERS.
AND IN ADDITION TO BEING DUMB AND GROSS, IT'S PARTICULAR.
ONE LITTLE FUCK UP AND BOOM! SANDWORM.
I WAS TWENTY THE LAST TIME I EVEN ATTEMPTED IT.
IT DIDN'T END WELL.
WHATEVER.
I MEAN, WHO WANTS TO WASTE THEIR LIFE RAISING THE DEAD OVER INHERITANCE DISPUTES?
THE WORLD IS SO MUCH BRIGHTER THAN THAT.

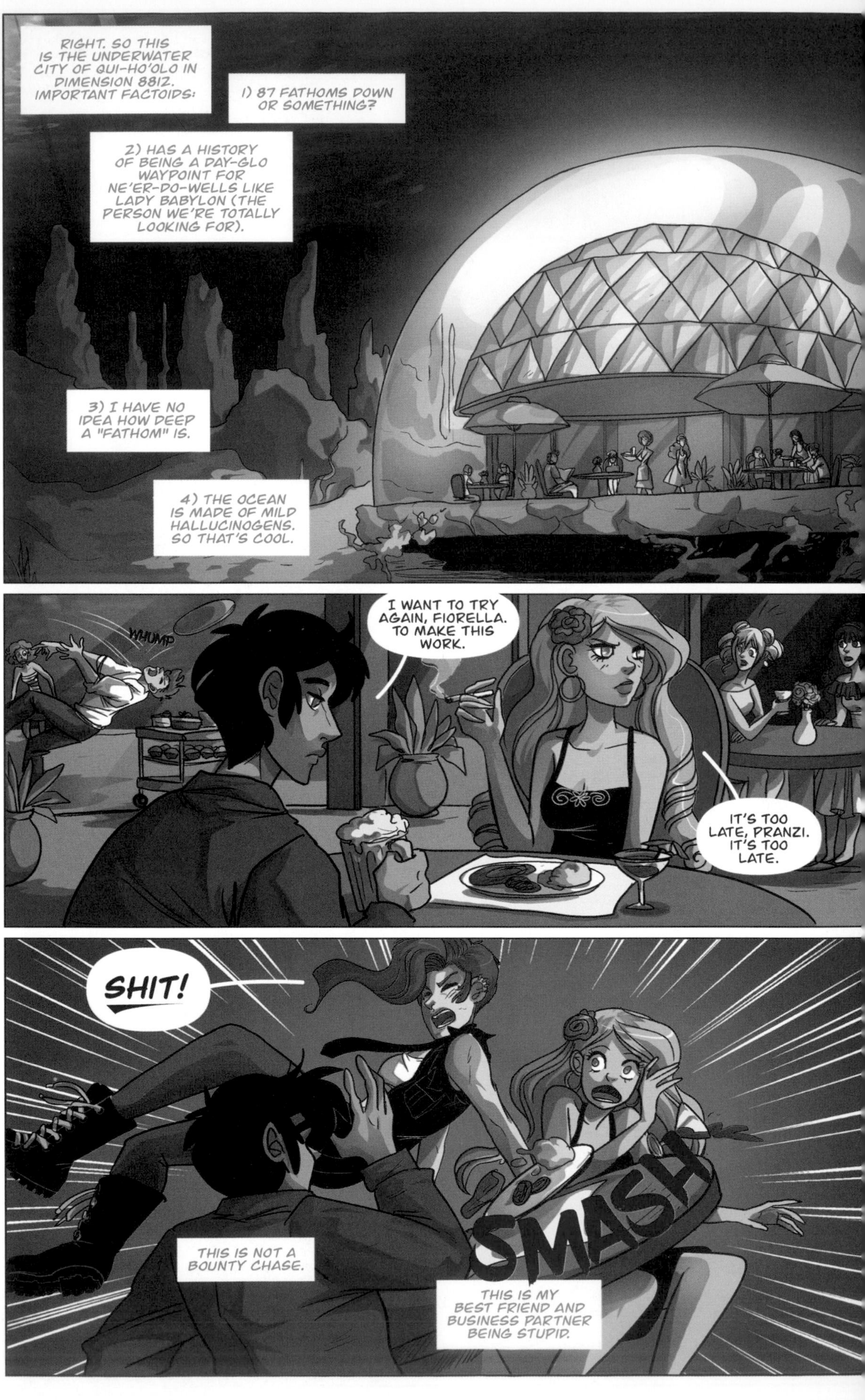
RIGHT. SO THIS IS THE UNDERWATER CITY OF QUI-HO'OLO IN DIMENSION 8812. IMPORTANT FACTOIDS:
1) 87 FATHOMS DOWN OR SOMETHING?
2) HAS A HISTORY OF BEING A DAY-GLO WAYPOINT FOR NE'ER-DO-WELLS LIKE LADY BABYLON (THE PERSON WE'RE TOTALLY LOOKING FOR).
3) I HAVE NO IDEA HOW DEEP A "FATHOM" IS.
4) THE OCEAN IS MADE OF MILD HALLUCINOGENS. SO THAT'S COOL.
WHUMP
I WANT TO TRY AGAIN, FIORELLA. TO MAKE THIS WORK.
IT'S TOO LATE, PRANZI. IT'S TOO LATE.
SHIT!
SMASH
THIS IS NOT A BOUNTY CHASE.
THIS IS MY BEST FRIEND AND BUSINESS PARTNER BEING STUPID.

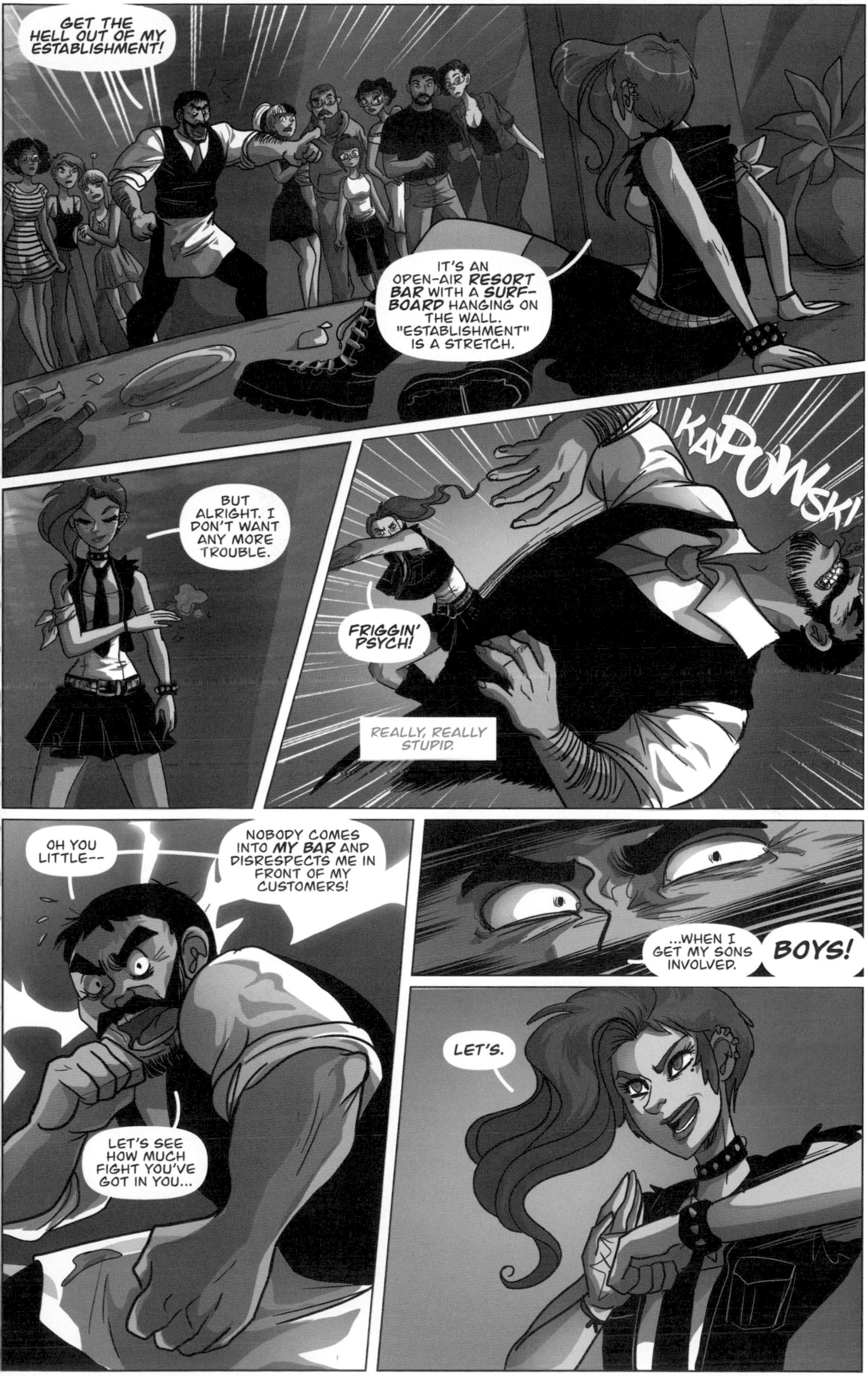
GET THE HELL OUT OF MY ESTABLISHMENT!
IT'S AN OPEN-AIR RESORT BAR WITH A SURF-BOARD HANGING ON THE WALL. "ESTABLISHMENT" IS A STRETCH.
BUT ALRIGHT. I DON'T WANT ANY MORE TROUBLE.
KAPOWSKI
FRIGGIN' PSYCH!
REALLY, REALLY STUPID.
OH YOU LITTLE--
NOBODY COMES INTO MY BAR AND DISRESPECTS ME IN FRONT OF MY CUSTOMERS!
LET'S SEE HOW MUCH FIGHT YOU'VE GOT IN YOU...
...WHEN I GET MY SONS INVOLVED.
BOYS!
LET'S.

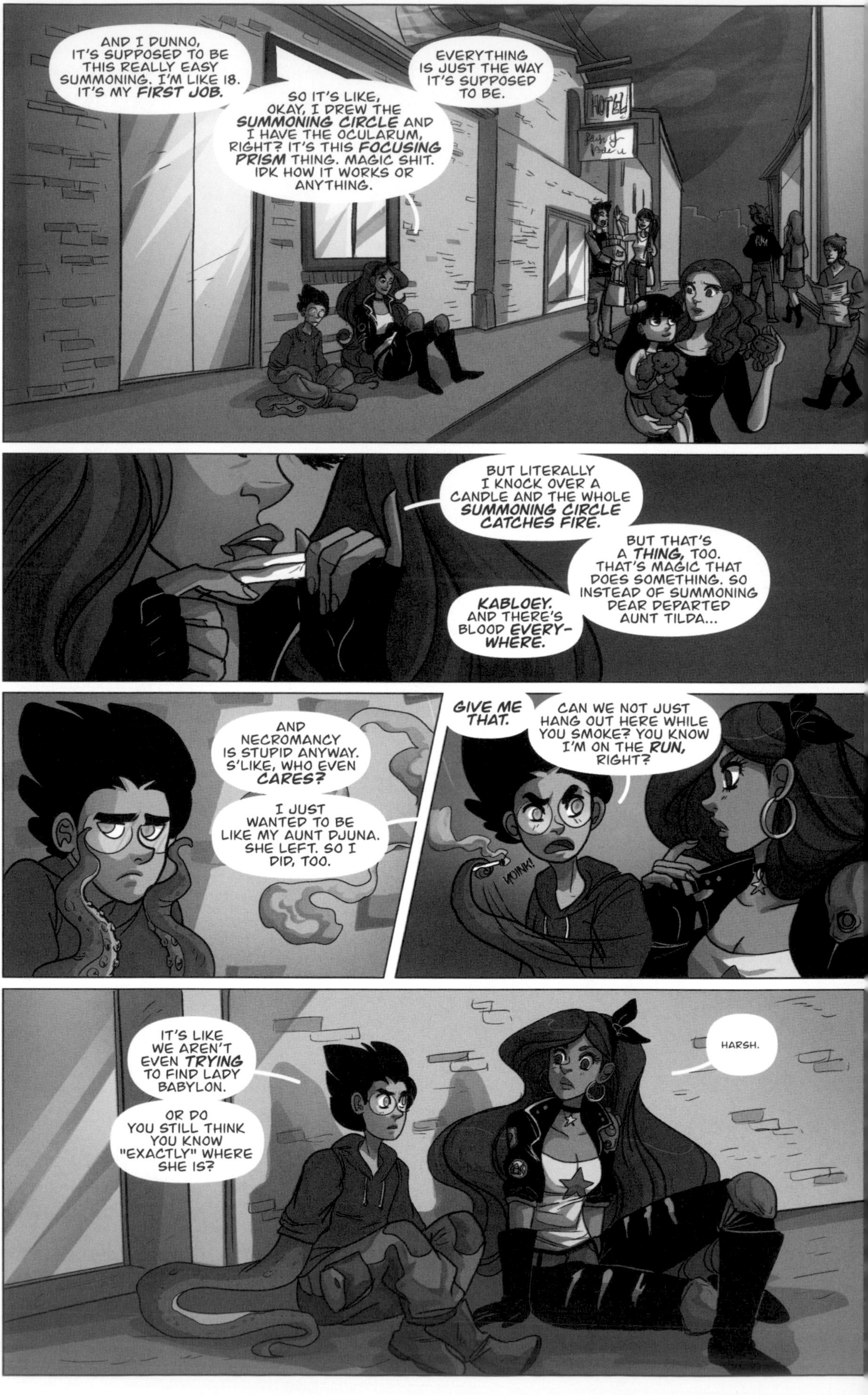

AND I DUNNO, IT'S SUPPOSED TO BE THIS REALLY EASY SUMMONING. I'M LIKE 18. IT'S MY FIRST JOB.
SO IT'S LIKE, OKAY, I DREW THE SUMMONING CIRCLE AND I HAVE THE OCULARUM, RIGHT? IT'S THIS FOCUSING PRISM THING. MAGIC SHIT. IDK HOW IT WORKS OR ANYTHING.
EVERYTHING IS JUST THE WAY IT'S SUPPOSED TO BE.
HOTEL
BUT LITERALLY I KNOCK OVER A CANDLE AND THE WHOLE SUMMONING CIRCLE CATCHES FIRE.
BUT THAT'S A THING, TOO. THAT'S MAGIC THAT DOES SOMETHING. SO INSTEAD OF SUMMONING DEAR DEPARTED AUNT TILDA...
KABLOEY. AND THERE'S BLOOD EVERY-WHERE.
AND NECROMANCY IS STUPID ANYWAY. S'LIKE, WHO EVEN CARES?
I JUST WANTED TO BE LIKE MY AUNT DJUNA. SHE LEFT. SO I DID, TOO.
GIVE ME THAT.
CAN WE NOT JUST HANG OUT HERE WHILE YOU SMOKE? YOU KNOW I'M ON THE RUN, RIGHT?
YOINK!
IT'S LIKE WE AREN'T EVEN TRYING TO FIND LADY BABYLON.
OR DO YOU STILL THINK YOU KNOW "EXACTLY" WHERE SHE IS?
HARSH.

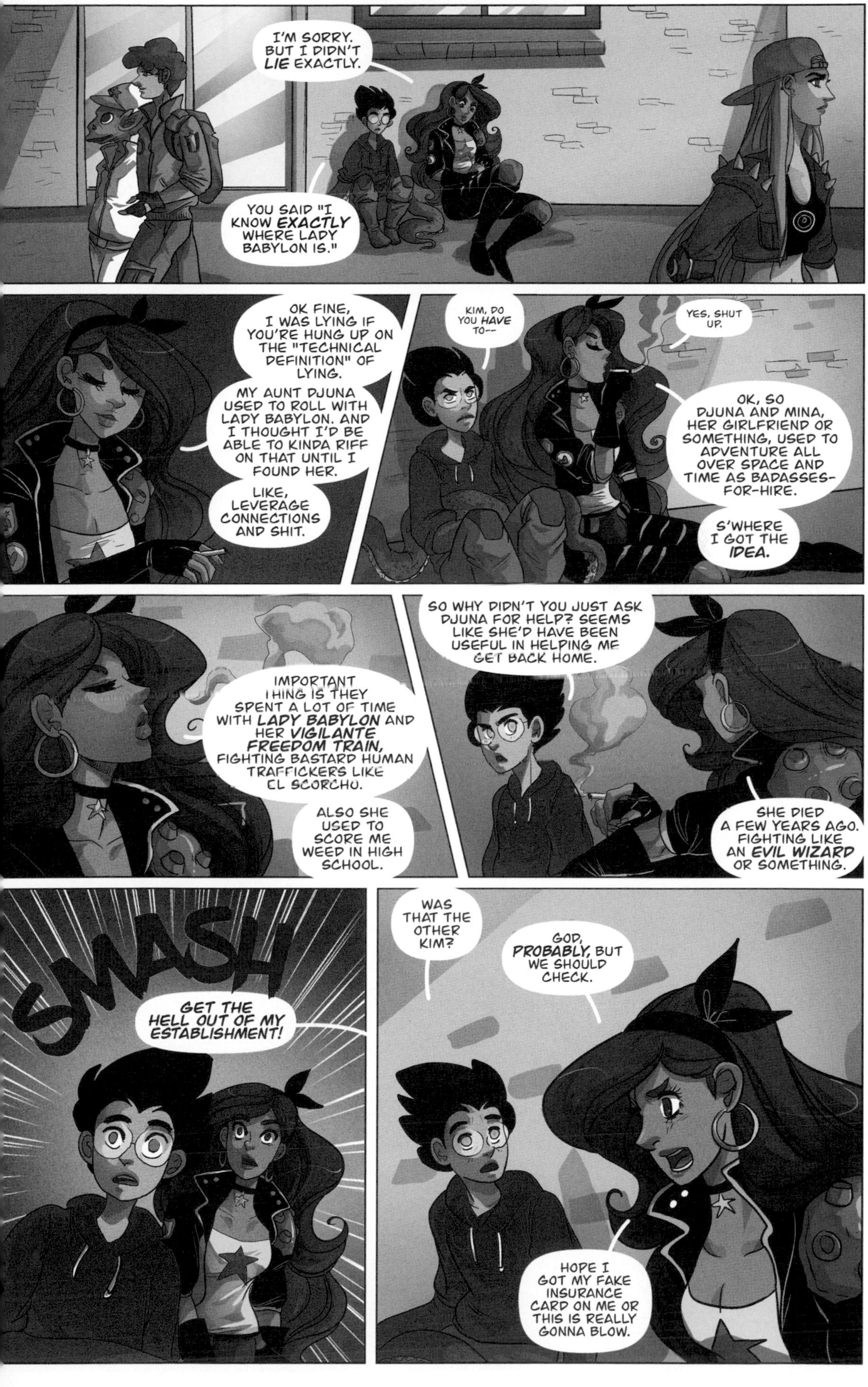
I'M SORRY. BUT I DIDN'T LIE EXACTLY.
YOU SAID "I KNOW EXACTLY WHERE LADY BABYLON IS."
OK FINE, I WAS LYING IF YOU'RE HUNG UP ON THE "TECHNICAL DEFINITION" OF LYING.
MY AUNT DJUNA USED TO ROLL WITH LADY BABYLON. AND I THOUGHT I'D BE ABLE TO KINDA RIFF ON THAT UNTIL I FOUND HER.
LIKE, LEVERAGE CONNECTIONS AND SHIT.
KIM, DO YOU HAVE TO--
YES, SHUT UP.
OK, SO DJUNA AND MINA, HER GIRLFRIEND OR SOMETHING, USED TO ADVENTURE ALL OVER SPACE AND TIME AS BADASSES-FOR-HIRE.
S'WHERE I GOT THE IDEA.
IMPORTANT THING IS THEY SPENT A LOT OF TIME WITH LADY BABYLON AND HER VIGILANTE FREEDOM TRAIN, FIGHTING BASTARD HUMAN TRAFFICKERS LIKE EL SCORCHO.
ALSO SHE USED TO SCORE ME WEED IN HIGH SCHOOL.
SO WHY DIDN'T YOU JUST ASK DJUNA FOR HELP? SEEMS LIKE SHE'D HAVE BEEN USEFUL IN HELPING ME GET BACK HOME.
SHE DIED A FEW YEARS AGO. FIGHTING LIKE AN EVIL WIZARD OR SOMETHING.
SMASH
GET THE HELL OUT OF MY ESTABLISHMENT!
WAS THAT THE OTHER KIM?
GOD, PROBABLY, BUT WE SHOULD CHECK.
HOPE I GOT MY FAKE INSURANCE CARD ON ME OR THIS IS REALLY GONNA BLOW.

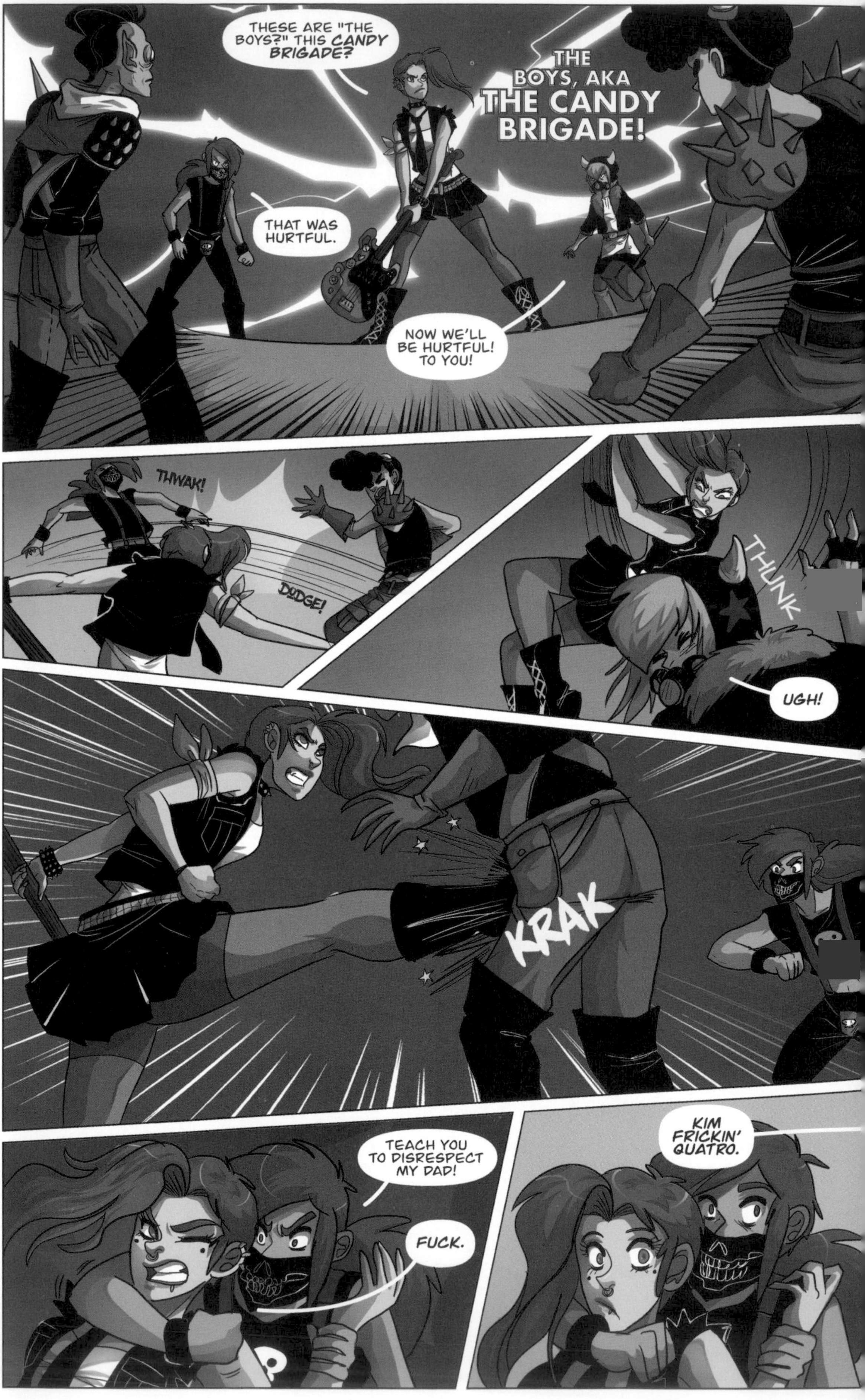
THESE ARE "THE BOYS?" THIS CANDY BRIGADE?
THE BOYS, AKA THE CANDY BRIGADE!
THAT WAS HURTFUL.
NOW WE'LL BE HURTFUL! TO YOU!
THWAK!
DODGE!
THUNK
UGH!
KRAK
TEACH YOU TO DISRESPECT MY DAD!
FUCK.
KIM FRICKIN' QUATRO.

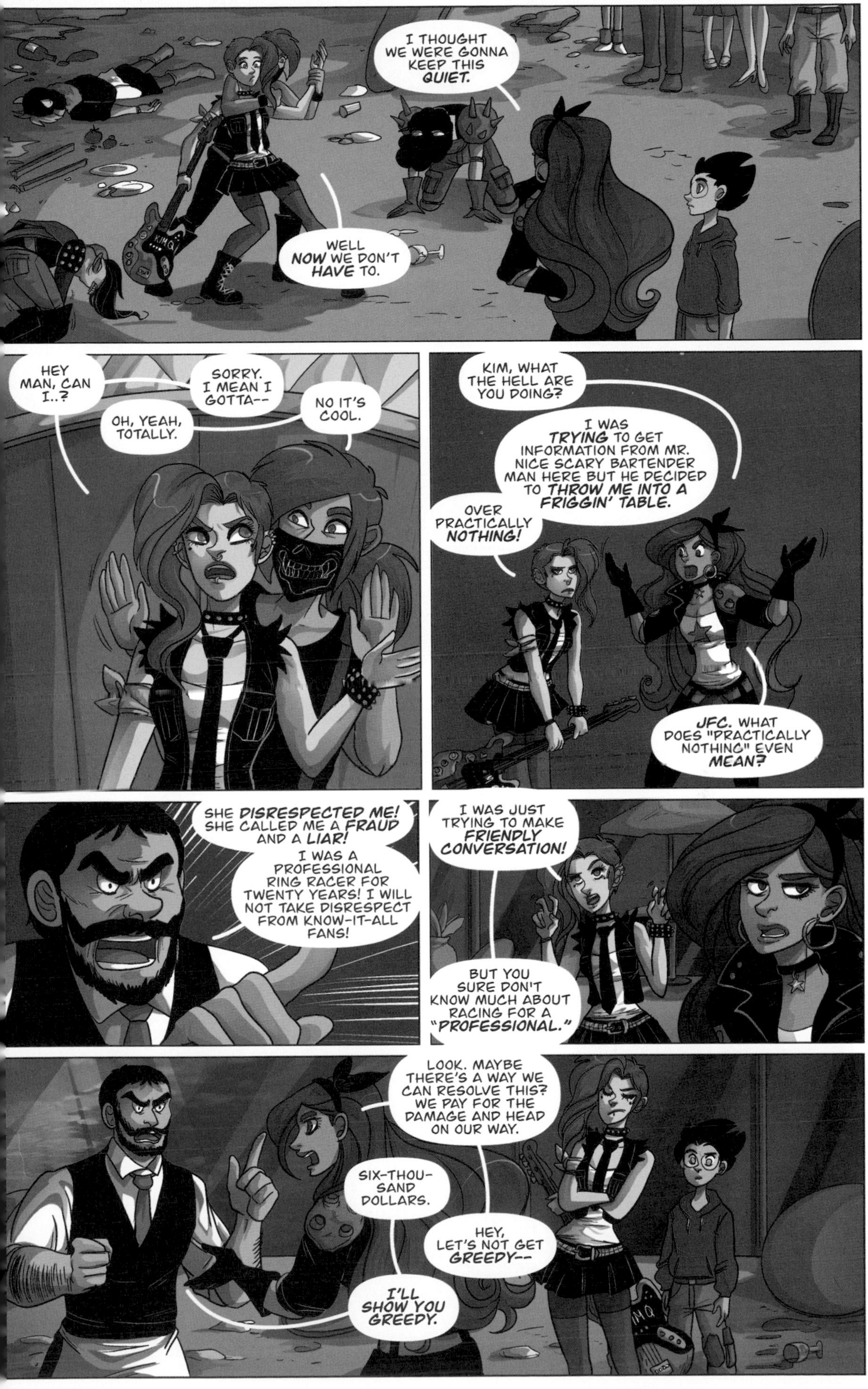

I THOUGHT WE WERE GONNA KEEP THIS QUIET.
WELL NOW WE DON'T HAVE TO.
KIMQ
HEY MAN, CAN I..?
SORRY. I MEAN I GOTTA--
OH, YEAH, TOTALLY.
NO IT'S COOL.
KIM, WHAT THE HELL ARE YOU DOING?
I WAS TRYING TO GET INFORMATION FROM MR. NICE SCARY BARTENDER MAN HERE BUT HE DECIDED TO THROW ME INTO A FRIGGIN' TABLE.
OVER PRACTICALLY NOTHING!
JFC. WHAT DOES "PRACTICALLY NOTHING" EVEN MEAN?
SHE DISRESPECTED ME! SHE CALLED ME A FRAUD AND A LIAR!
I WAS A PROFESSIONAL RING RACER FOR TWENTY YEARS! I WILL NOT TAKE DISRESPECT FROM KNOW-IT-ALL FANS!
I WAS JUST TRYING TO MAKE FRIENDLY CONVERSATION!
BUT YOU SURE DON'T KNOW MUCH ABOUT RACING FOR A "PROFESSIONAL."
LOOK. MAYBE THERE'S A WAY WE CAN RESOLVE THIS? WE PAY FOR THE DAMAGE AND HEAD ON OUR WAY.
SIX-THOUSAND DOLLARS.
HEY, LET'S NOT GET GREEDY--
I'LL SHOW YOU GREEDY.

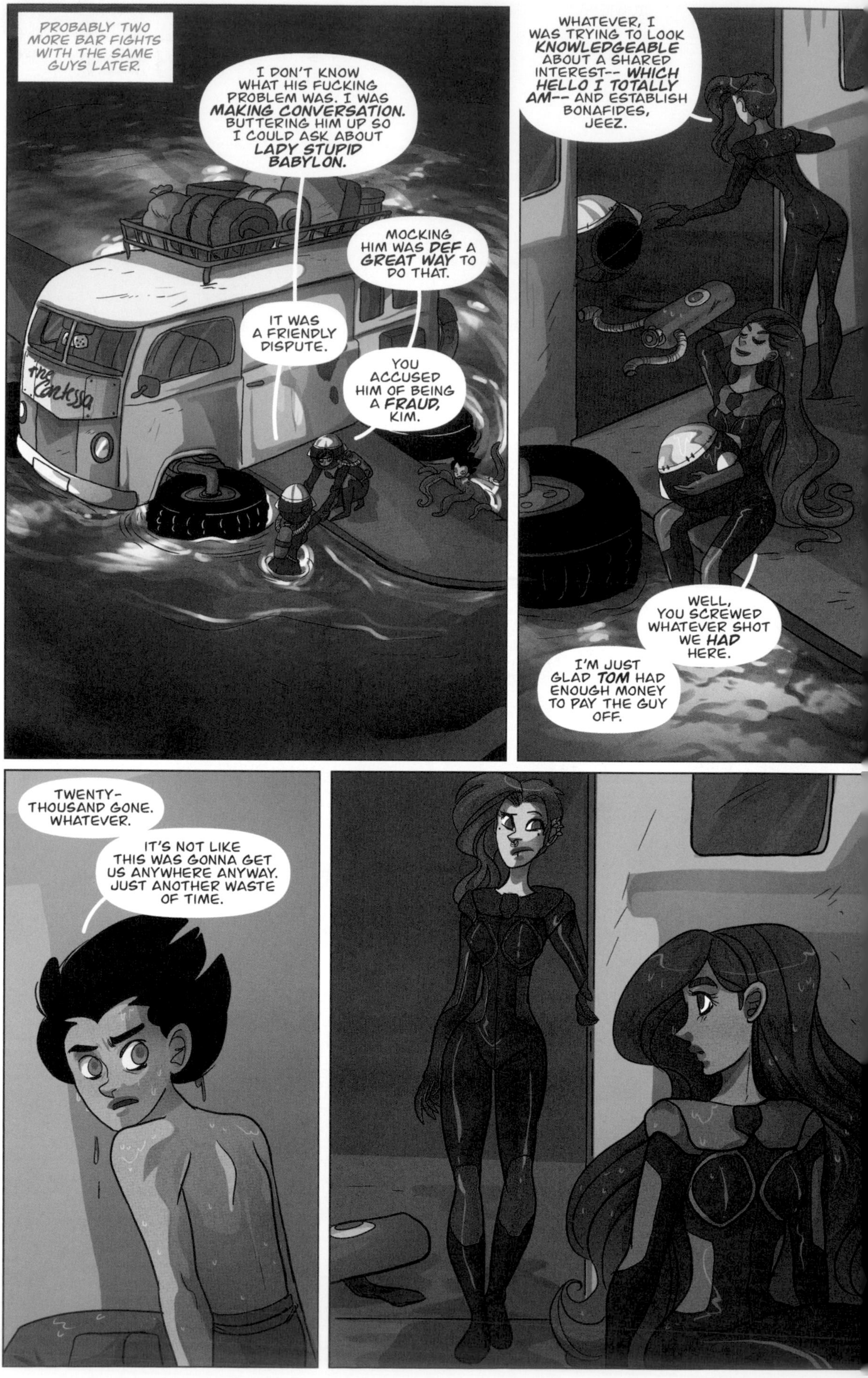
PROBABLY TWO MORE BAR FIGHTS WITH THE SAME GUYS LATER.
I DON'T KNOW WHAT HIS FUCKING PROBLEM WAS. I WAS MAKING CONVERSATION. BUTTERING HIM UP SO I COULD ASK ABOUT LADY STUPID BABYLON.
MOCKING HIM WAS DEF A GREAT WAY TO DO THAT.
IT WAS A FRIENDLY DISPUTE.
YOU ACCUSED HIM OF BEING A FRAUD, KIM.
WHATEVER, I WAS TRYING TO LOOK KNOWLEDGEABLE ABOUT A SHARED INTEREST-- WHICH HELLO I TOTALLY AM-- AND ESTABLISH BONAFIDES, JEEZ.
WELL, YOU SCREWED WHATEVER SHOT WE HAD HERE.
I'M JUST GLAD TOM HAD ENOUGH MONEY TO PAY THE GUY OFF.
TWENTY-THOUSAND GONE. WHATEVER.
IT'S NOT LIKE THIS WAS GONNA GET US ANYWHERE ANYWAY. JUST ANOTHER WASTE OF TIME.

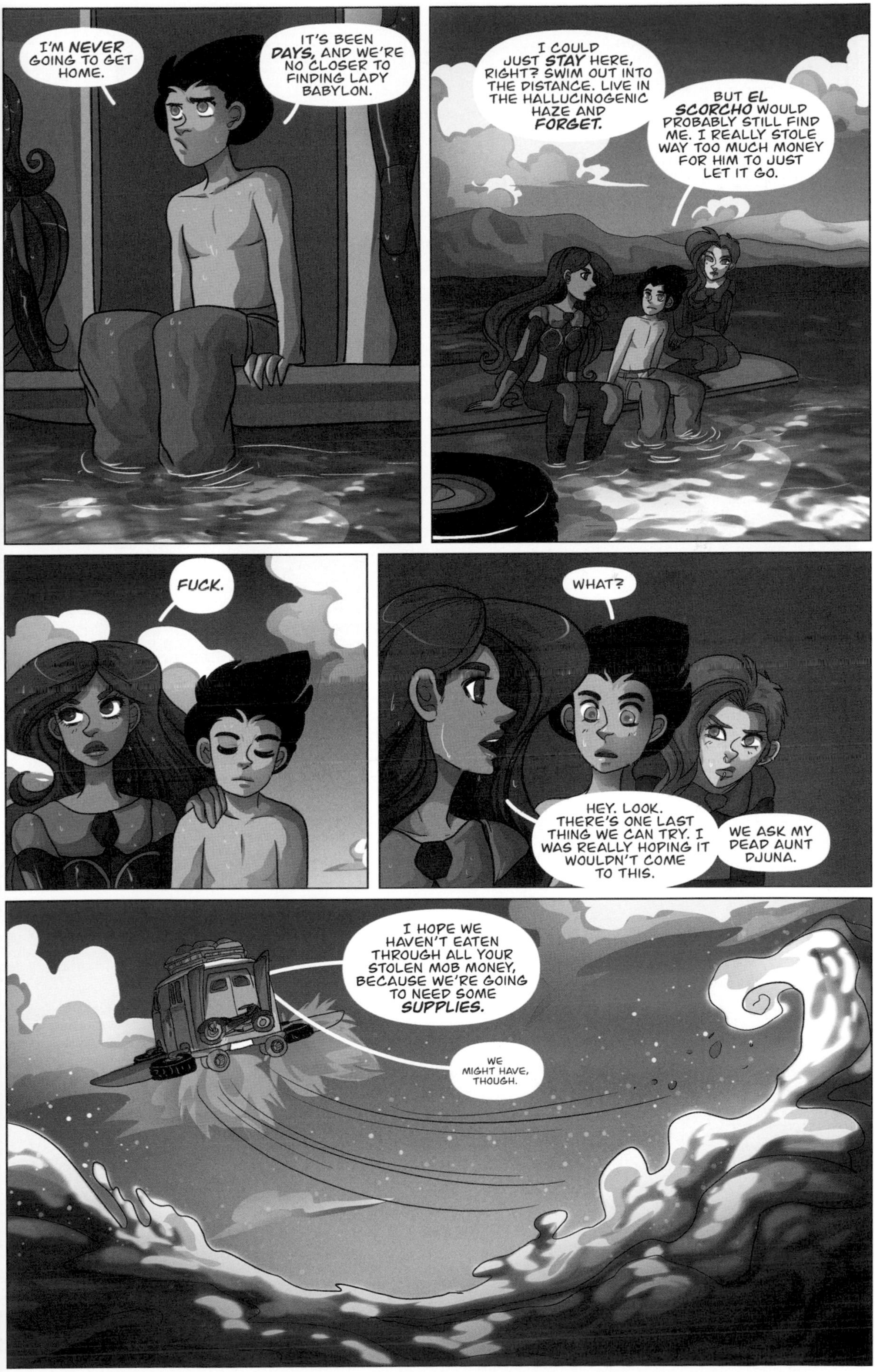

I'M NEVER GOING TO GET HOME.
IT'S BEEN DAYS, AND WE'RE NO CLOSER TO FINDING LADY BABYLON.
I COULD JUST STAY HERE, RIGHT? SWIM OUT INTO THE DISTANCE. LIVE IN THE HALLUCINOGENIC HAZE AND FORGET.
BUT EL SCORCHO WOULD PROBABLY STILL FIND ME. I REALLY STOLE WAY TOO MUCH MONEY FOR HIM TO JUST LET IT GO.
FUCK.
WHAT?
HEY. LOOK. THERE'S ONE LAST THING WE CAN TRY. I WAS REALLY HOPING IT WOULDN'T COME TO THIS.
WE ASK MY DEAD AUNT DJUNA.
I HOPE WE HAVEN'T EATEN THROUGH ALL YOUR STOLEN MOB MONEY, BECAUSE WE'RE GOING TO NEED SOME SUPPLIES.
WE MIGHT HAVE, THOUGH.

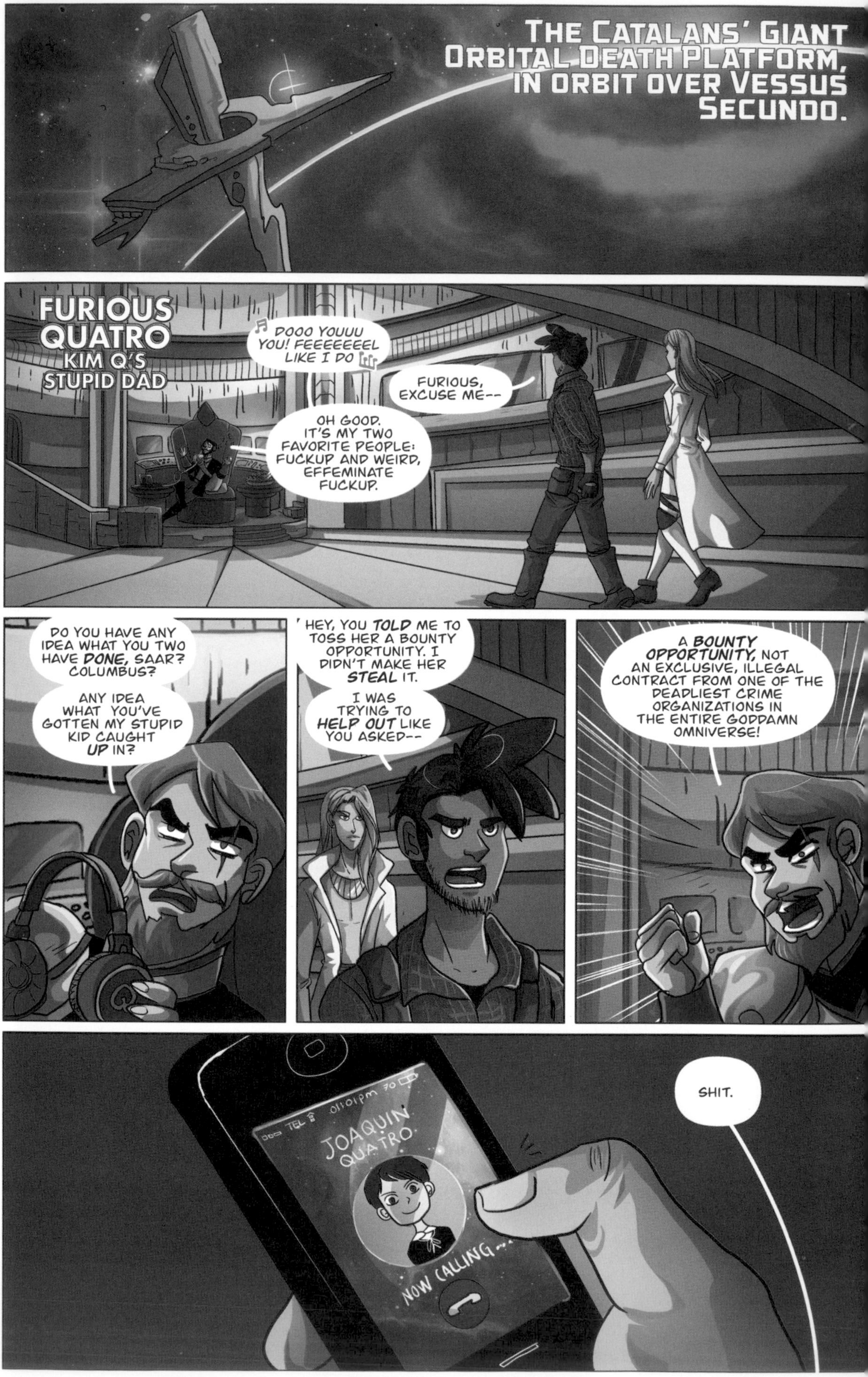
THE CATALANS' GIANT ORBITAL DEATH PLATFORM, IN ORBIT OVER VESSUS SECUNDO.
FURIOUS QUATRO
KIM Q'S STUPID DAD
DOOO YOUUU YOU! FEEEEEEEL LIKE I DO
FURIOUS, EXCUSE ME--
OH GOOD. IT'S MY TWO FAVORITE PEOPLE: FUCKUP AND WEIRD, EFFEMINATE FUCKUP.
DO YOU HAVE ANY IDEA WHAT YOU TWO HAVE DONE, SAAR? COLUMBUS?
ANY IDEA WHAT YOU'VE GOTTEN MY STUPID KID CAUGHT UP IN?
HEY, YOU TOLD ME TO TOSS HER A BOUNTY OPPORTUNITY. I DIDN'T MAKE HER STEAL IT.
I WAS TRYING TO HELP OUT LIKE YOU ASKED--
A BOUNTY OPPORTUNITY, NOT AN EXCLUSIVE, ILLEGAL CONTRACT FROM ONE OF THE DEADLIEST CRIME ORGANIZATIONS IN THE ENTIRE GODDAMN OMNIVERSE!
TEL
JOAQUIN QUATRO
NOW CALLING...
SHIT.

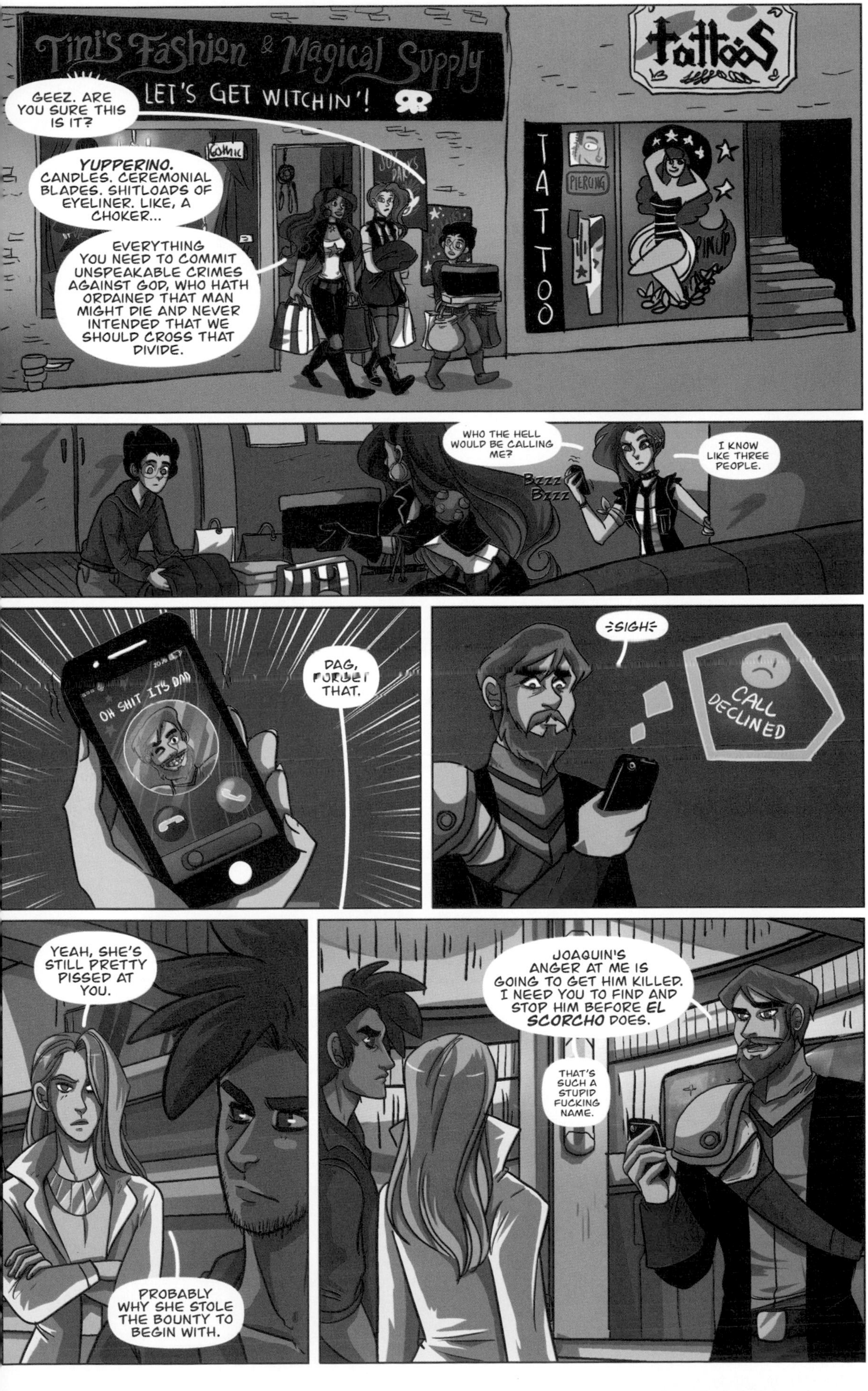
Tini's Fashion & Magical Supply
LET'S GET WITCHIN'!
tattoos
TATTOO
GEEZ. ARE YOU SURE THIS IS IT?
YUPPERINO. CANDLES. CEREMONIAL BLADES. SHITLOADS OF EYELINER. LIKE, A CHOKER...
EVERYTHING YOU NEED TO COMMIT UNSPEAKABLE CRIMES AGAINST GOD, WHO HATH ORDAINED THAT MAN MIGHT DIE AND NEVER INTENDED THAT WE SHOULD CROSS THAT DIVIDE.
WHO THE HELL WOULD BE CALLING ME?
Bzzz Bzzz
I KNOW LIKE THREE PEOPLE.
OH SHIT IT'S DAD
DAG, FORGET THAT.
SIGH
CALL DECLINED
YEAH, SHE'S STILL PRETTY PISSED AT YOU.
PROBABLY WHY SHE STOLE THE BOUNTY TO BEGIN WITH.
JOAQUIN'S ANGER AT ME IS GOING TO GET HIM KILLED. I NEED YOU TO FIND AND STOP HIM BEFORE EL SCORCHO DOES.
THAT'S SUCH A STUPID FUCKING NAME.

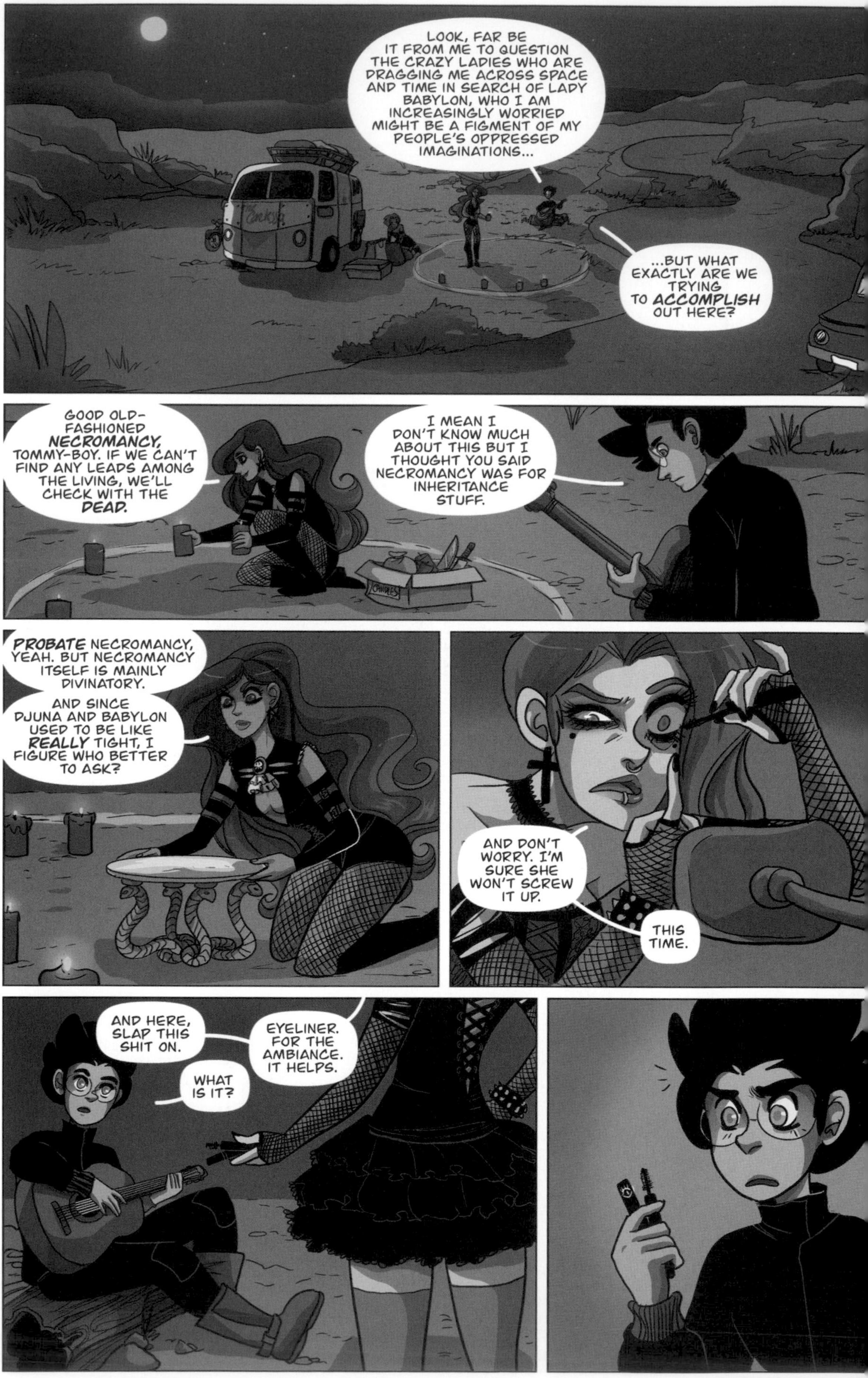
LOOK, FAR BE IT FROM ME TO QUESTION THE CRAZY LADIES WHO ARE DRAGGING ME ACROSS SPACE AND TIME IN SEARCH OF LADY BABYLON, WHO I AM INCREASINGLY WORRIED MIGHT BE A FIGMENT OF MY PEOPLE'S OPPRESSED IMAGINATIONS...
...BUT WHAT EXACTLY ARE WE TRYING TO ACCOMPLISH OUT HERE?
GOOD OLD-FASHIONED NECROMANCY, TOMMY-BOY. IF WE CAN'T FIND ANY LEADS AMONG THE LIVING, WE'LL CHECK WITH THE DEAD.
I MEAN I DON'T KNOW MUCH ABOUT THIS BUT I THOUGHT YOU SAID NECROMANCY WAS FOR INHERITANCE STUFF.
PROBATE NECROMANCY, YEAH. BUT NECROMANCY ITSELF IS MAINLY DIVINATORY.
AND SINCE DJUNA AND BABYLON USED TO BE LIKE REALLY TIGHT, I FIGURE WHO BETTER TO ASK?
AND DON'T WORRY. I'M SURE SHE WON'T SCREW IT UP.
THIS TIME.
AND HERE, SLAP THIS SHIT ON.
WHAT IS IT?
EYELINER. FOR THE AMBIANCE. IT HELPS.

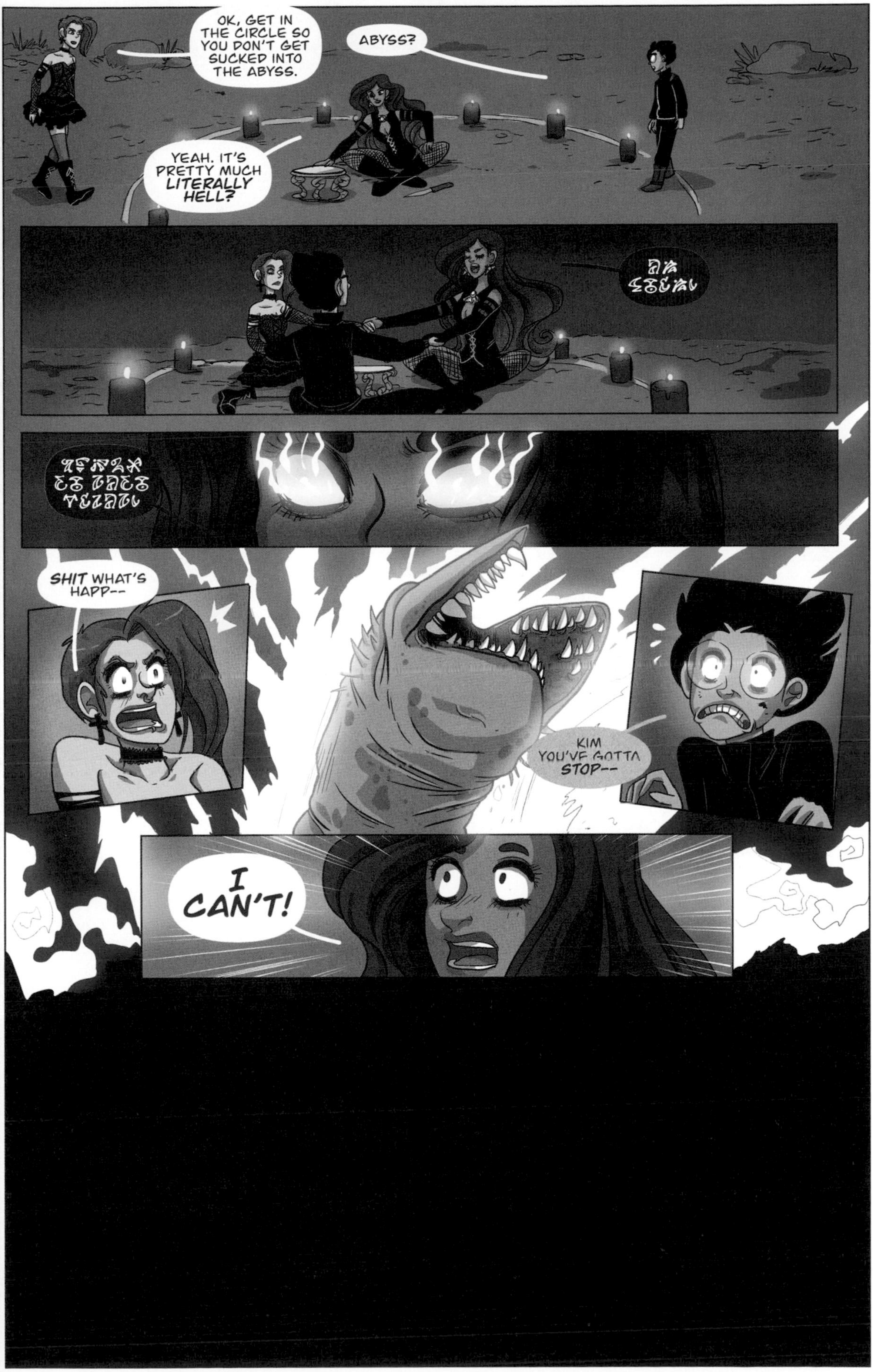
OK, GET IN THE CIRCLE SO YOU DON'T GET SUCKED INTO THE ABYSS.
ABYSS?
YEAH. IT'S PRETTY MUCH LITERALLY HELL?
SHIT WHAT'S HAPP--
KIM YOU'VE GOTTA STOP--
I CAN'T!

[redacted]

[redacted]

[redacted]

[redacted]

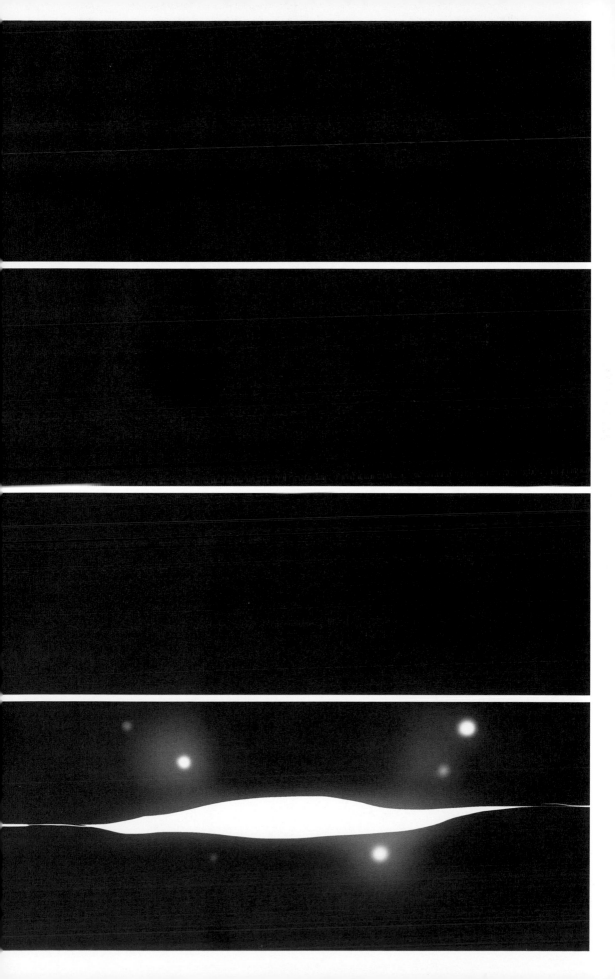

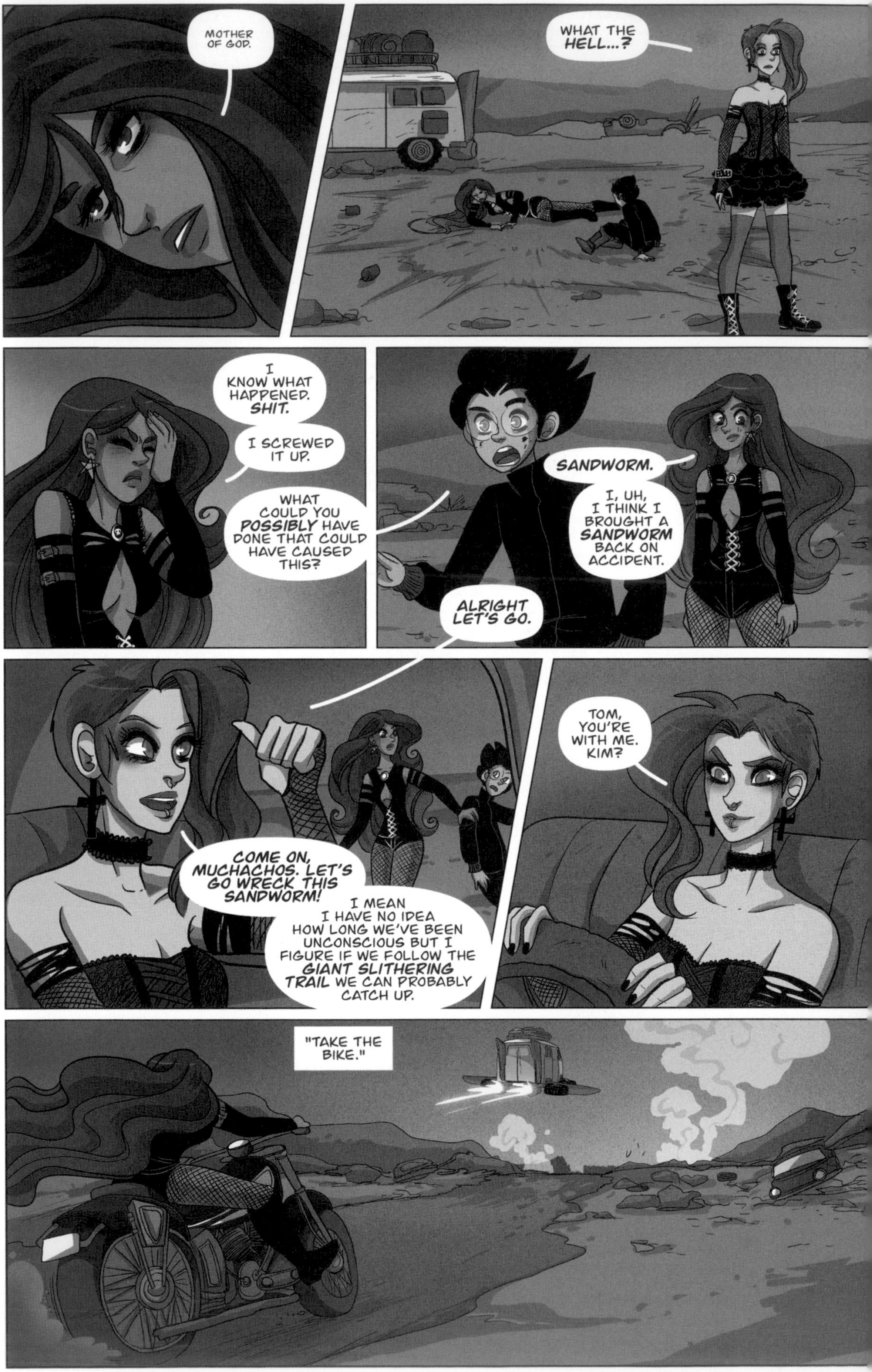
MOTHER OF GOD.
WHAT THE HELL...?
I KNOW WHAT HAPPENED. SHIT.
I SCREWED IT UP.
WHAT COULD YOU POSSIBLY HAVE DONE THAT COULD HAVE CAUSED THIS?
SANDWORM.
I, UH, I THINK I BROUGHT A SANDWORM BACK ON ACCIDENT.
ALRIGHT LET'S GO.
COME ON, MUCHACHOS. LET'S GO WRECK THIS SANDWORM!
I MEAN I HAVE NO IDEA HOW LONG WE'VE BEEN UNCONSCIOUS BUT I FIGURE IF WE FOLLOW THE GIANT SLITHERING TRAIL WE CAN PROBABLY CATCH UP.
TOM, YOU'RE WITH ME. KIM?
"TAKE THE BIKE."

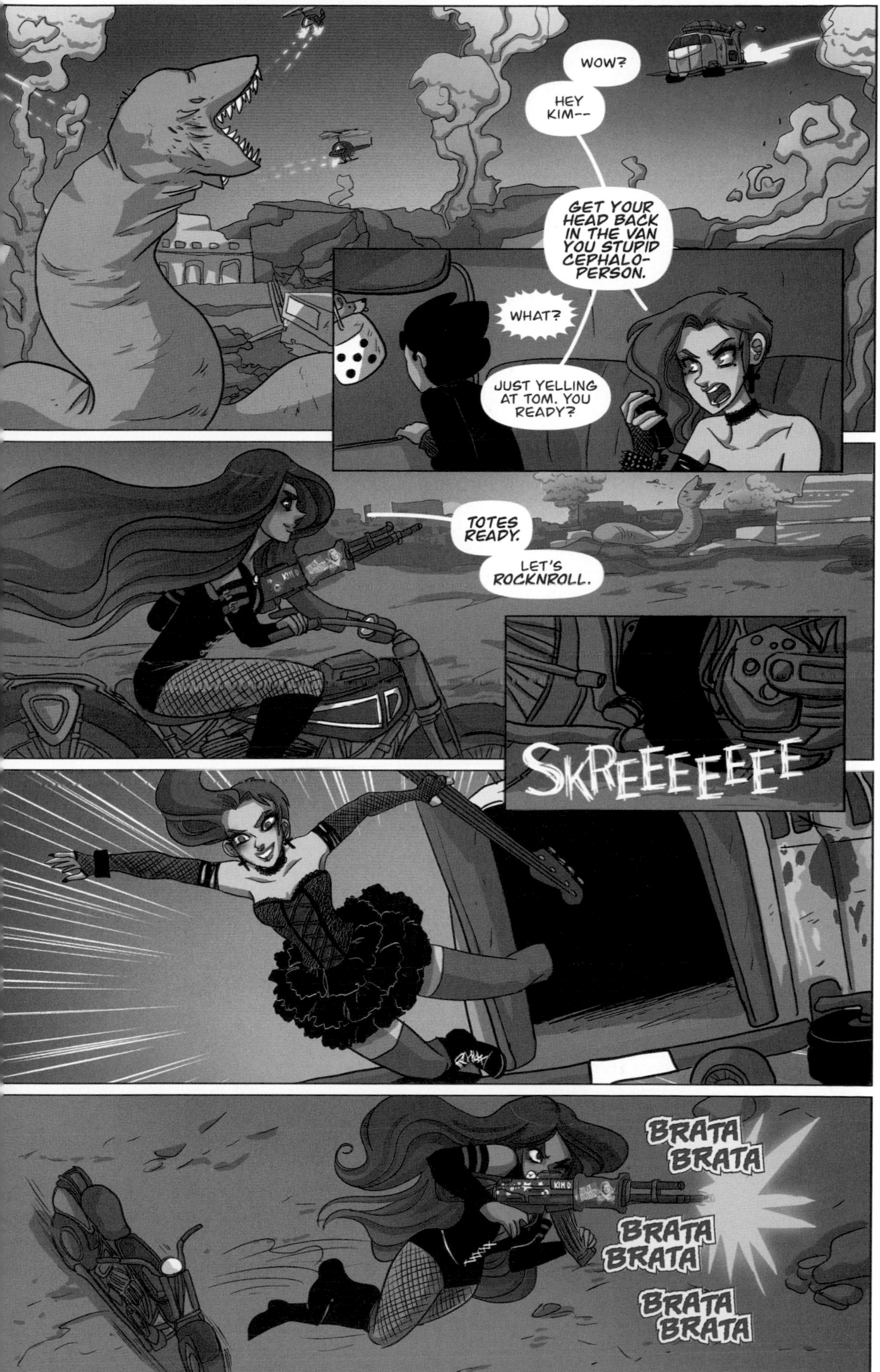
WOW?
HEY KIM--
GET YOUR HEAD BACK IN THE VAN YOU STUPID CEPHALO-PERSON.
WHAT?
JUST YELLING AT TOM. YOU READY?
TOTES READY.
LET'S ROCKNROLL.
SKREEEEEEE
BRATA BRATA
BRATA BRATA
BRATA BRATA

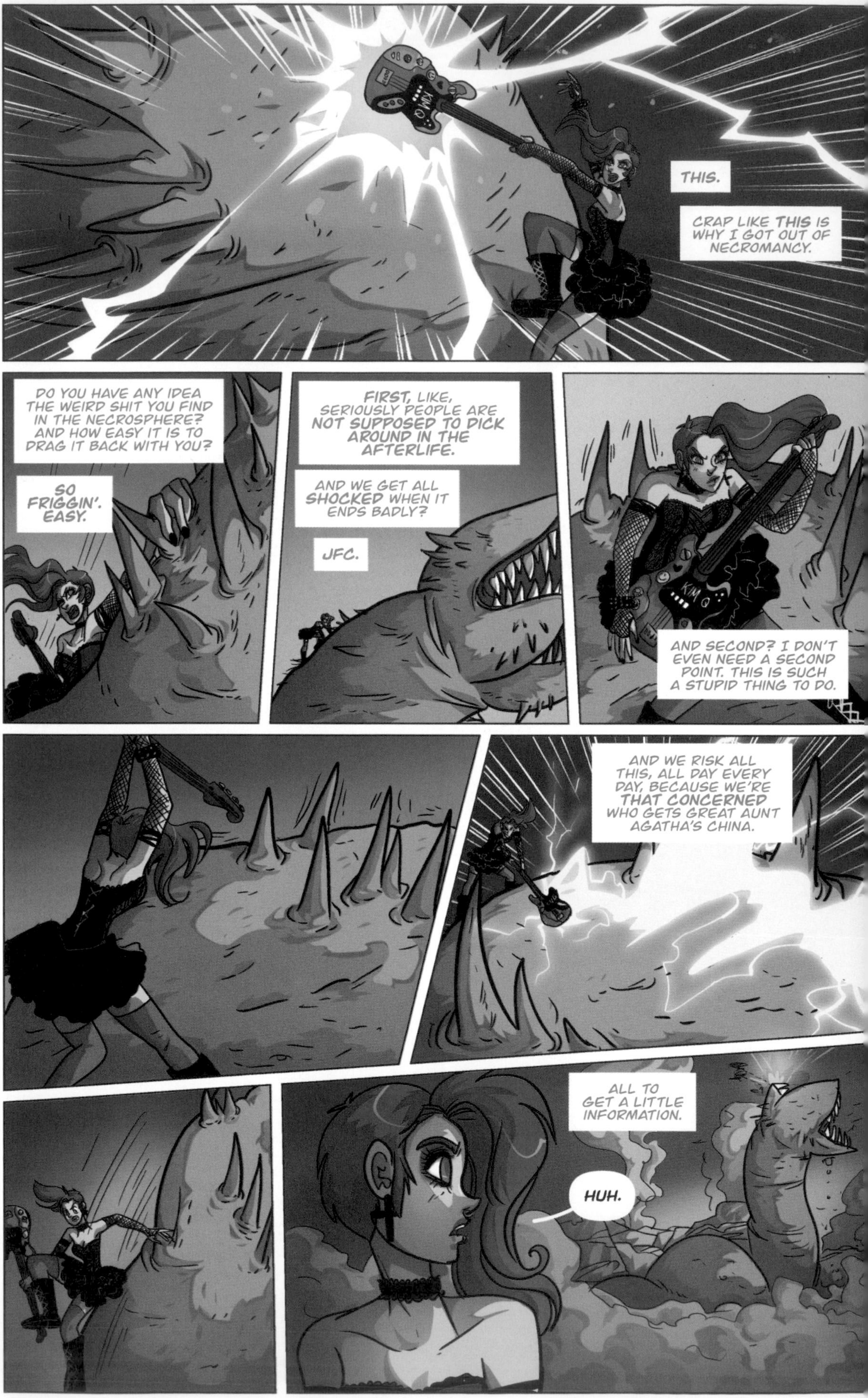
THIS.
CRAP LIKE THIS IS WHY I GOT OUT OF NECROMANCY.
DO YOU HAVE ANY IDEA THE WEIRD SHIT YOU FIND IN THE NECROSPHERE? AND HOW EASY IT IS TO DRAG IT BACK WITH YOU?
SO FRIGGIN'. EASY.
FIRST, LIKE, SERIOUSLY PEOPLE ARE NOT SUPPOSED TO DICK AROUND IN THE AFTERLIFE.
AND WE GET ALL SHOCKED WHEN IT ENDS BADLY?
JFC.
KIM Q
AND SECOND? I DON'T EVEN NEED A SECOND POINT. THIS IS SUCH A STUPID THING TO DO.
AND WE RISK ALL THIS, ALL DAY EVERY DAY, BECAUSE WE'RE THAT CONCERNED WHO GETS GREAT AUNT AGATHA'S CHINA.
ALL TO GET A LITTLE INFORMATION.
HUH.

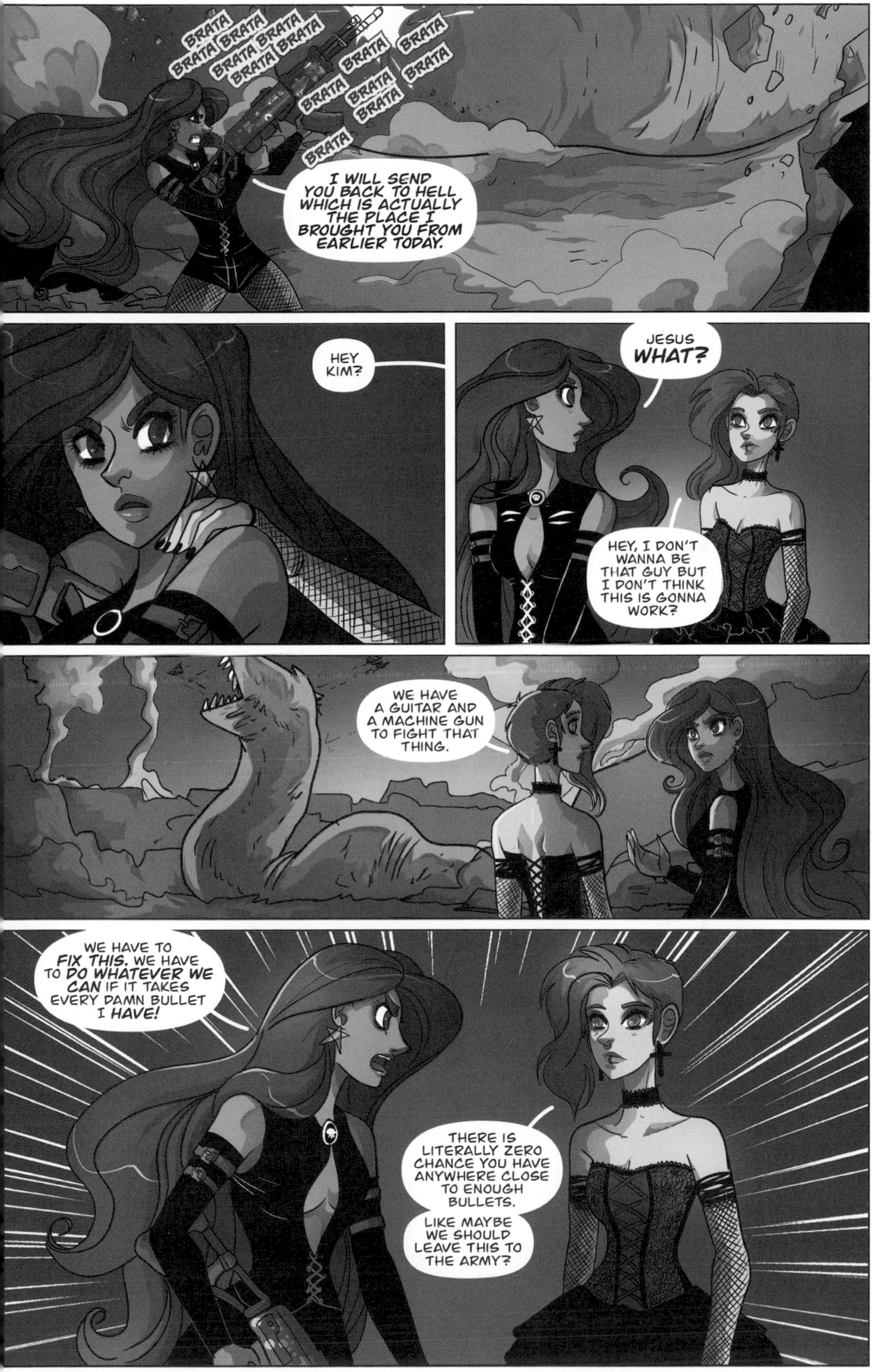
BRATA BRATA BRATA BRATA BRATA BRATA BRATA BRATA BRATA BRATA BRATA BRATA BRATA BRATA
I WILL SEND YOU BACK TO HELL WHICH IS ACTUALLY THE PLACE I BROUGHT YOU FROM EARLIER TODAY.
HEY KIM?
JESUS WHAT?
HEY, I DON'T WANNA BE THAT GUY BUT I DON'T THINK THIS IS GONNA WORK?
WE HAVE A GUITAR AND A MACHINE GUN TO FIGHT THAT THING.
WE HAVE TO FIX THIS. WE HAVE TO DO WHATEVER WE CAN IF IT TAKES EVERY DAMN BULLET I HAVE!
THERE IS LITERALLY ZERO CHANCE YOU HAVE ANYWHERE CLOSE TO ENOUGH BULLETS.
LIKE MAYBE WE SHOULD LEAVE THIS TO THE ARMY?

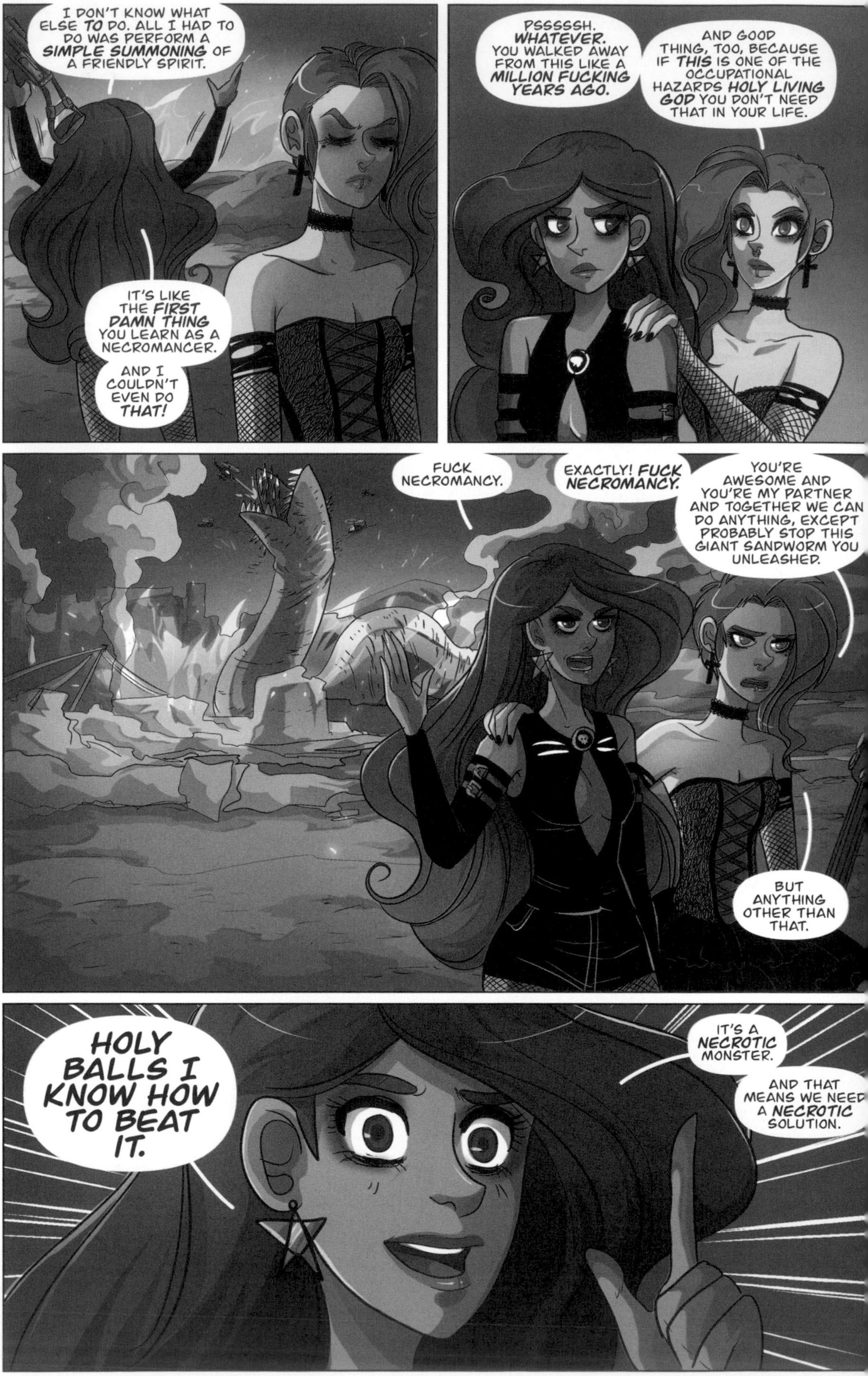
I DON'T KNOW WHAT ELSE TO DO. ALL I HAD TO DO WAS PERFORM A SIMPLE SUMMONING OF A FRIENDLY SPIRIT.
IT'S LIKE THE FIRST DAMN THING YOU LEARN AS A NECROMANCER.
AND I COULDN'T EVEN DO THAT!
PSSSSSH. WHATEVER. YOU WALKED AWAY FROM THIS LIKE A MILLION FUCKING YEARS AGO.
AND GOOD THING, TOO, BECAUSE IF THIS IS ONE OF THE OCCUPATIONAL HAZARDS HOLY LIVING GOD YOU DON'T NEED THAT IN YOUR LIFE.
FUCK NECROMANCY.
EXACTLY! FUCK NECROMANCY.
YOU'RE AWESOME AND YOU'RE MY PARTNER AND TOGETHER WE CAN DO ANYTHING, EXCEPT PROBABLY STOP THIS GIANT SANDWORM YOU UNLEASHED.
BUT ANYTHING OTHER THAN THAT.
HOLY BALLS I KNOW HOW TO BEAT IT.
IT'S A NECROTIC MONSTER.
AND THAT MEANS WE NEED A NECROTIC SOLUTION.

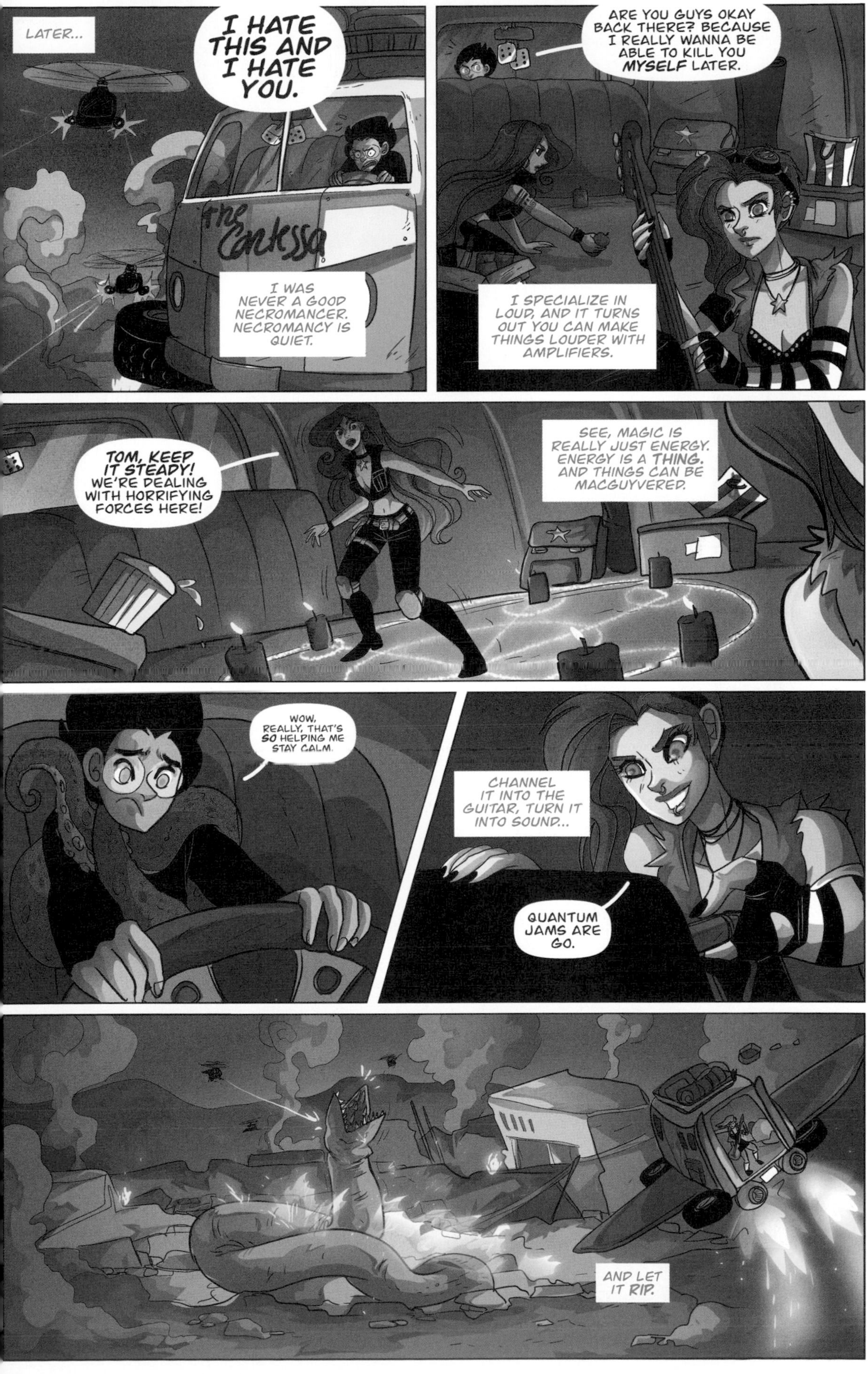
LATER...
I HATE THIS AND I HATE YOU.
The Cankssa
I WAS NEVER A GOOD NECROMANCER. NECROMANCY IS QUIET.
ARE YOU GUYS OKAY BACK THERE? BECAUSE I REALLY WANNA BE ABLE TO KILL YOU MYSELF LATER.
I SPECIALIZE IN LOUD, AND IT TURNS OUT YOU CAN MAKE THINGS LOUDER WITH AMPLIFIERS.
TOM, KEEP IT STEADY! WE'RE DEALING WITH HORRIFYING FORCES HERE!
SEE, MAGIC IS REALLY JUST ENERGY. ENERGY IS A THING. AND THINGS CAN BE MACGUYVERED.
WOW, REALLY, THAT'S SO HELPING ME STAY CALM.
CHANNEL IT INTO THE GUITAR, TURN IT INTO SOUND...
QUANTUM JAMS ARE GO.
AND LET IT RIP.

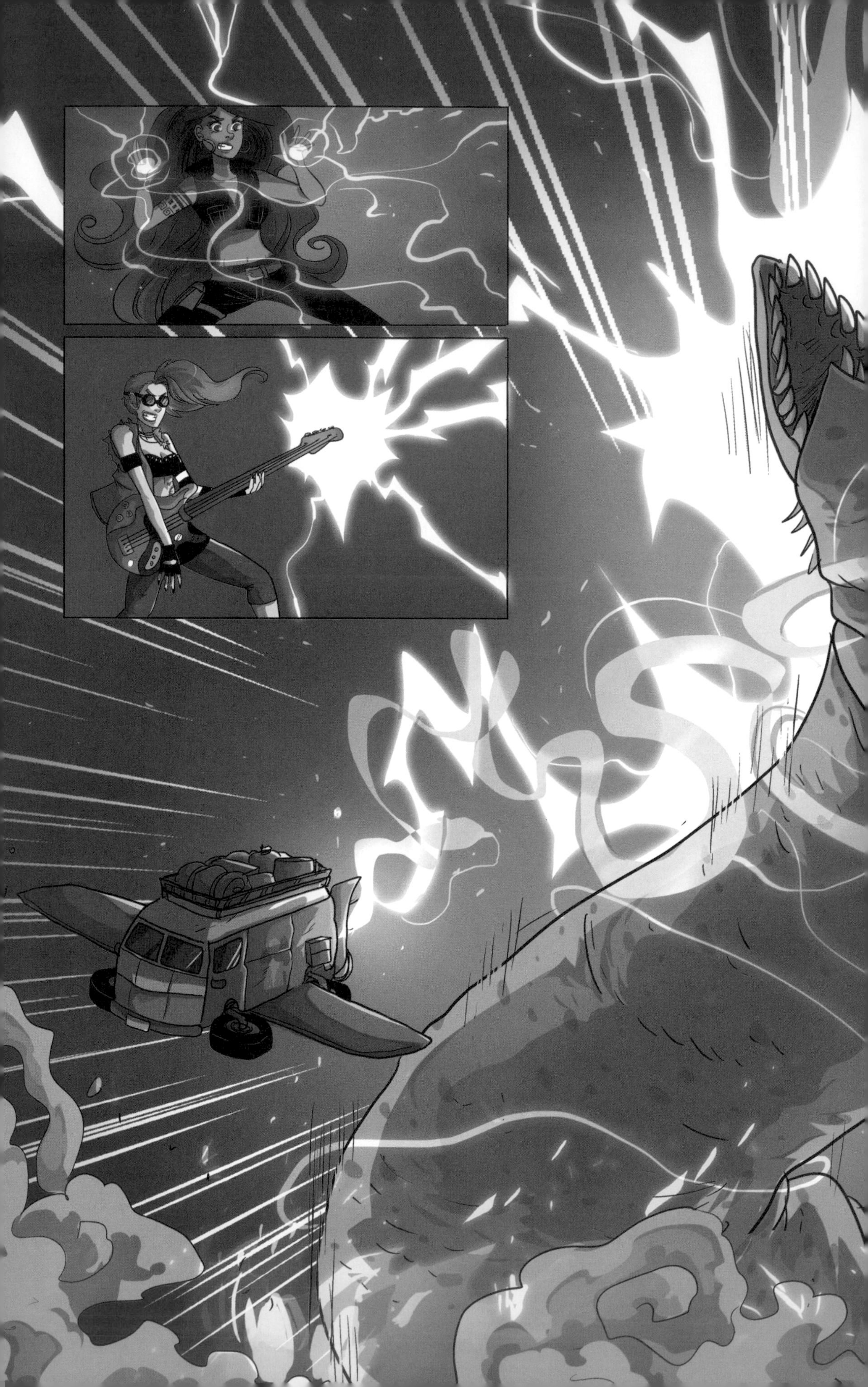

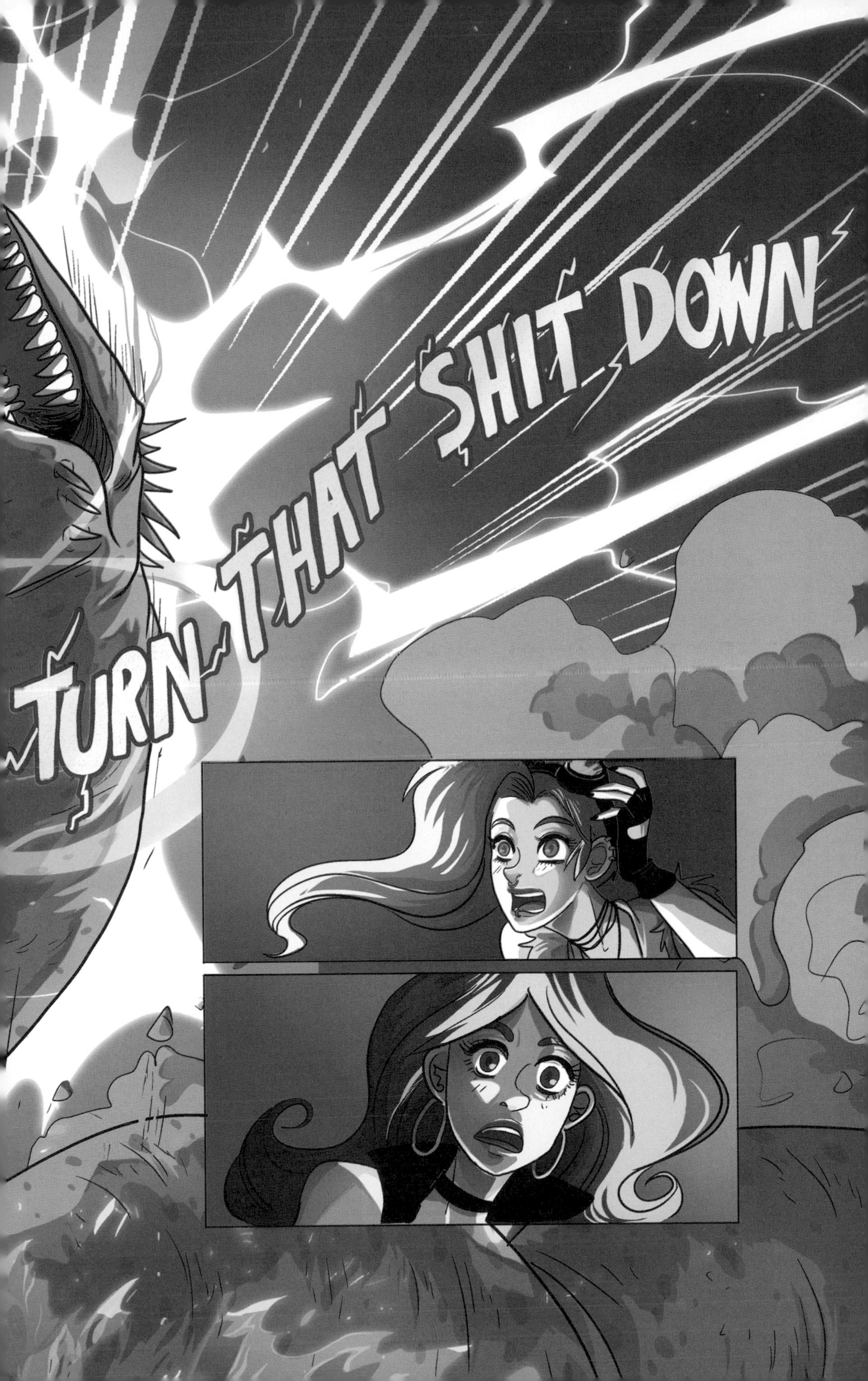
TURN THAT SHIT DOWN

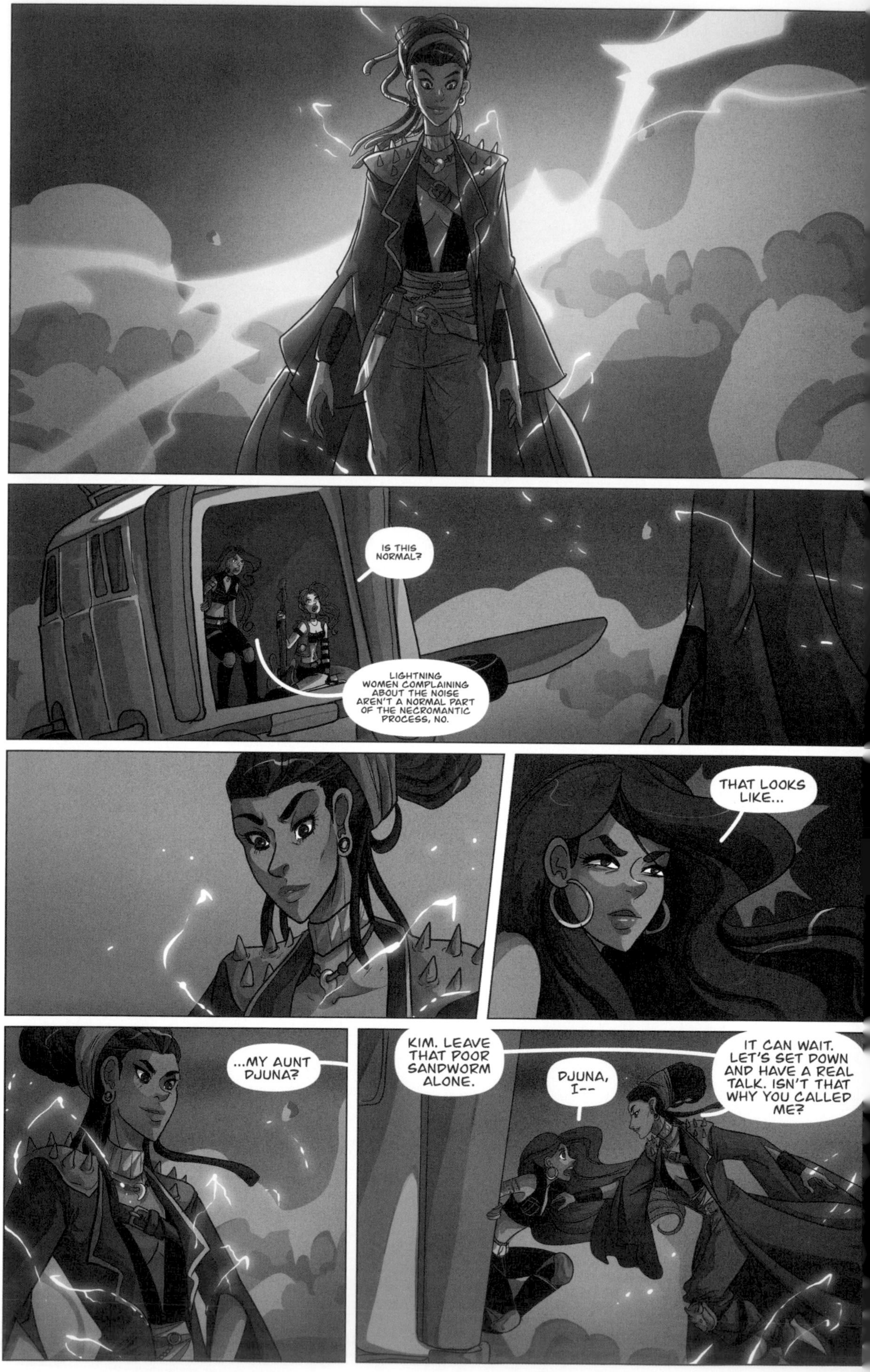
IS THIS NORMAL?
LIGHTNING WOMEN COMPLAINING ABOUT THE NOISE AREN'T A NORMAL PART OF THE NECROMANTIC PROCESS, NO.
THAT LOOKS LIKE...
...MY AUNT DJUNA?
KIM. LEAVE THAT POOR SANDWORM ALONE.
DJUNA, I--
IT CAN WAIT. LET'S SET DOWN AND HAVE A REAL TALK. ISN'T THAT WHY YOU CALLED ME?

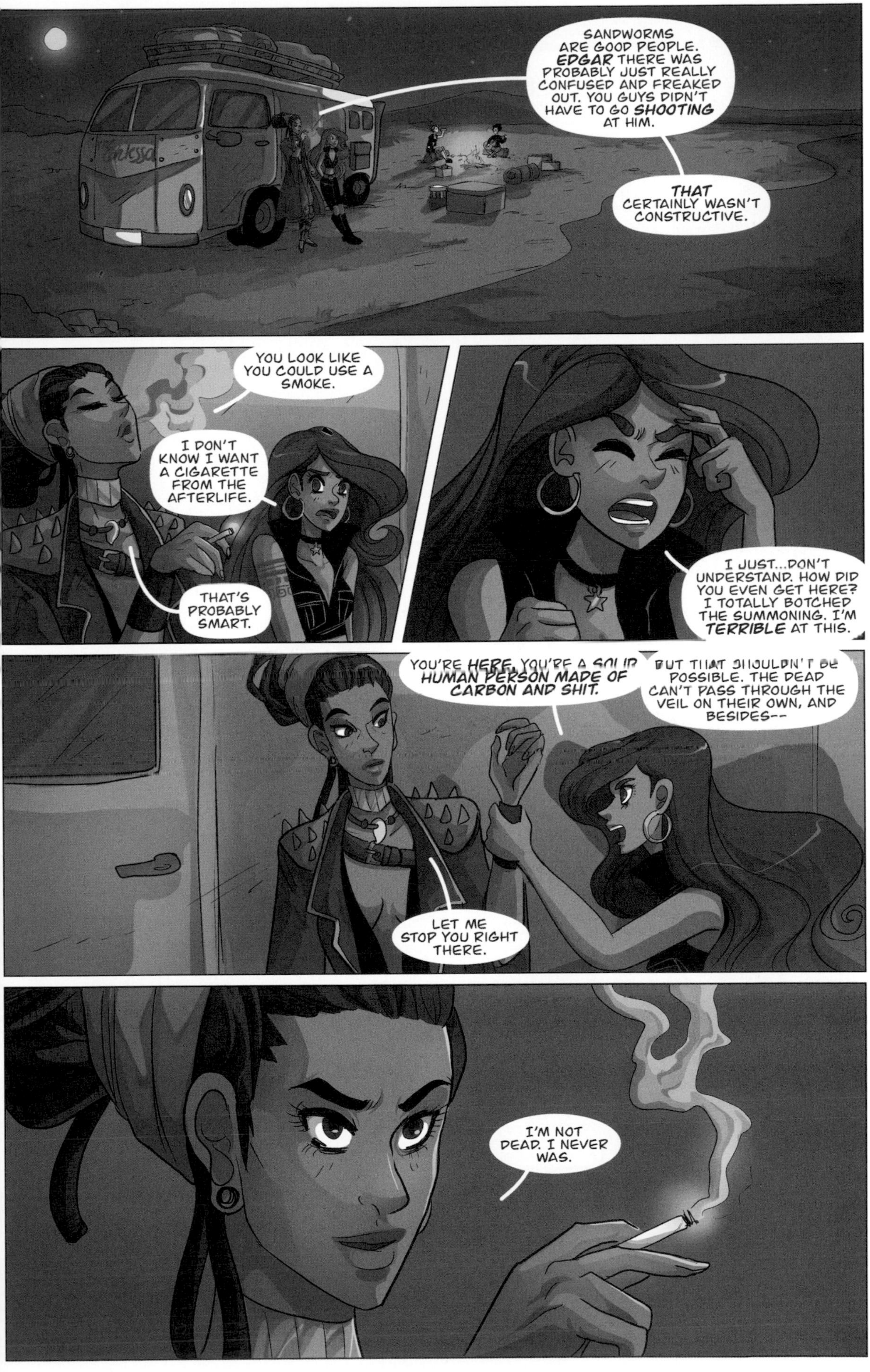
SANDWORMS ARE GOOD PEOPLE. EDGAR THERE WAS PROBABLY JUST REALLY CONFUSED AND FREAKED OUT. YOU GUYS DIDN'T HAVE TO GO SHOOTING AT HIM.
THAT CERTAINLY WASN'T CONSTRUCTIVE.
YOU LOOK LIKE YOU COULD USE A SMOKE.
I DON'T KNOW I WANT A CIGARETTE FROM THE AFTERLIFE.
THAT'S PROBABLY SMART.
I JUST...DON'T UNDERSTAND. HOW DID YOU EVEN GET HERE? I TOTALLY BOTCHED THE SUMMONING. I'M TERRIBLE AT THIS.
YOU'RE HERE. YOU'RE A SOLID HUMAN PERSON MADE OF CARBON AND SHIT.
BUT THAT SHOULDN'T BE POSSIBLE. THE DEAD CAN'T PASS THROUGH THE VEIL ON THEIR OWN, AND BESIDES--
LET ME STOP YOU RIGHT THERE.
I'M NOT DEAD. I NEVER WAS.

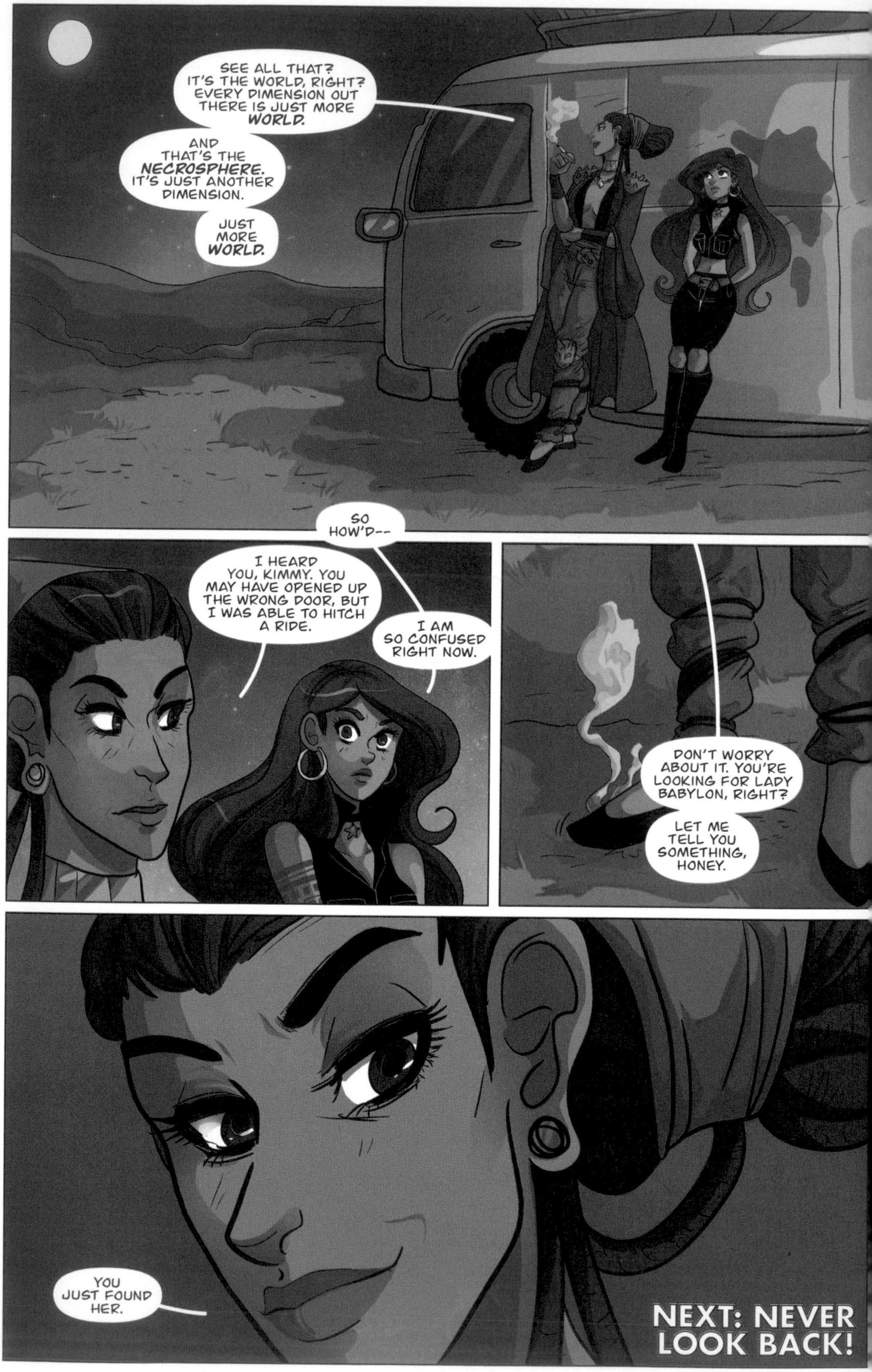
SEE ALL THAT? IT'S THE WORLD, RIGHT? EVERY DIMENSION OUT THERE IS JUST MORE WORLD.
AND THAT'S THE NECROSPHERE. IT'S JUST ANOTHER DIMENSION.
JUST MORE WORLD.
SO HOW'D--
I HEARD YOU, KIMMY. YOU MAY HAVE OPENED UP THE WRONG DOOR, BUT I WAS ABLE TO HITCH A RIDE.
I AM SO CONFUSED RIGHT NOW.
DON'T WORRY ABOUT IT. YOU'RE LOOKING FOR LADY BABYLON, RIGHT?
LET ME TELL YOU SOMETHING, HONEY.
YOU JUST FOUND HER.
NEXT: NEVER LOOK BACK!

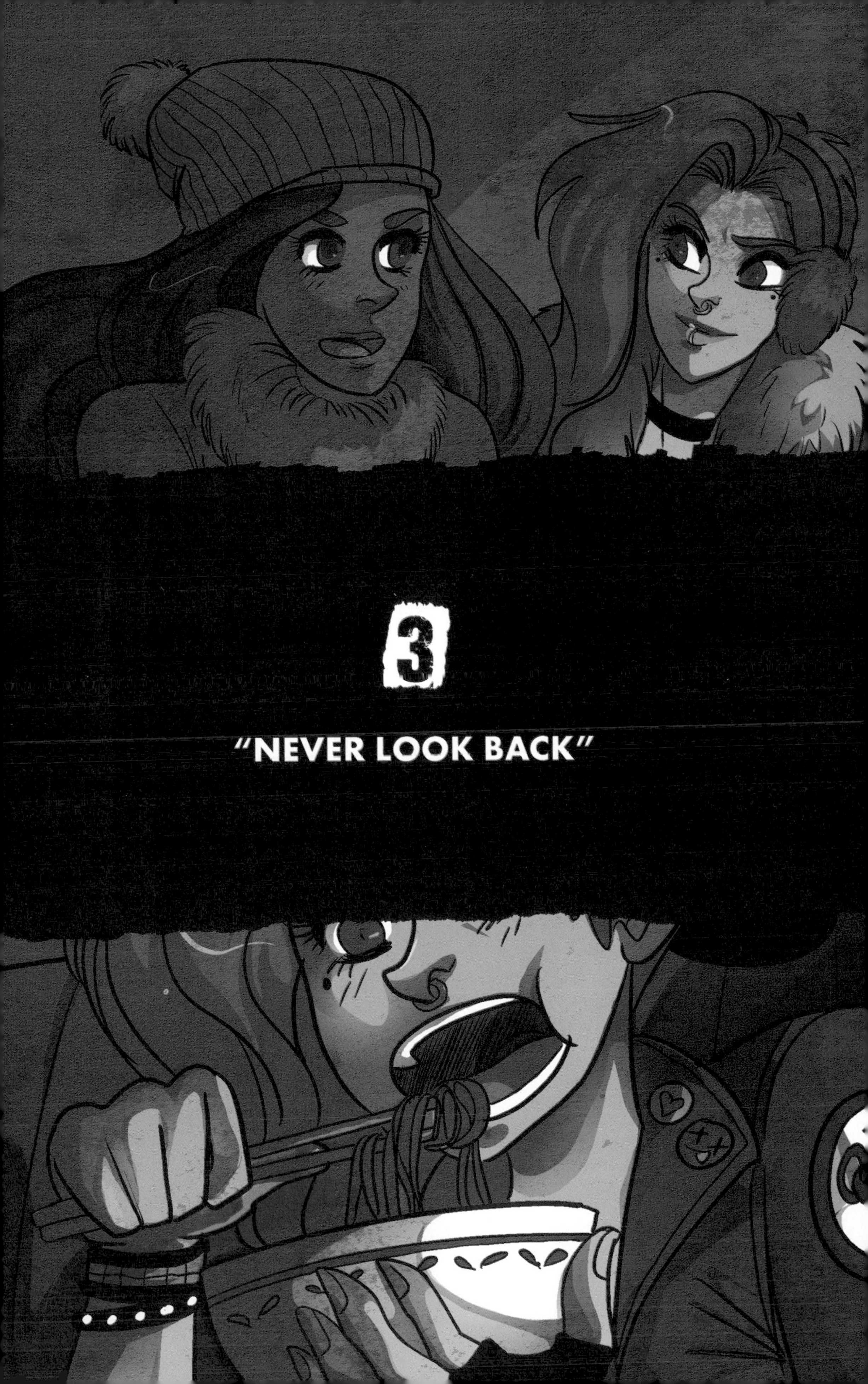

3

"NEVER LOOK BACK"

OK, SO MY FIRST SOLO BOUNTY GIG WASN'T SOLO. IT WAS WITH SAAR. MY DAD SENT US AFTER A DUDE NAMED STEFANO BELLARY. MINOR MOB ENFORCER.

THIS IS BEFORE I HOOKED UP WITH KIM D.

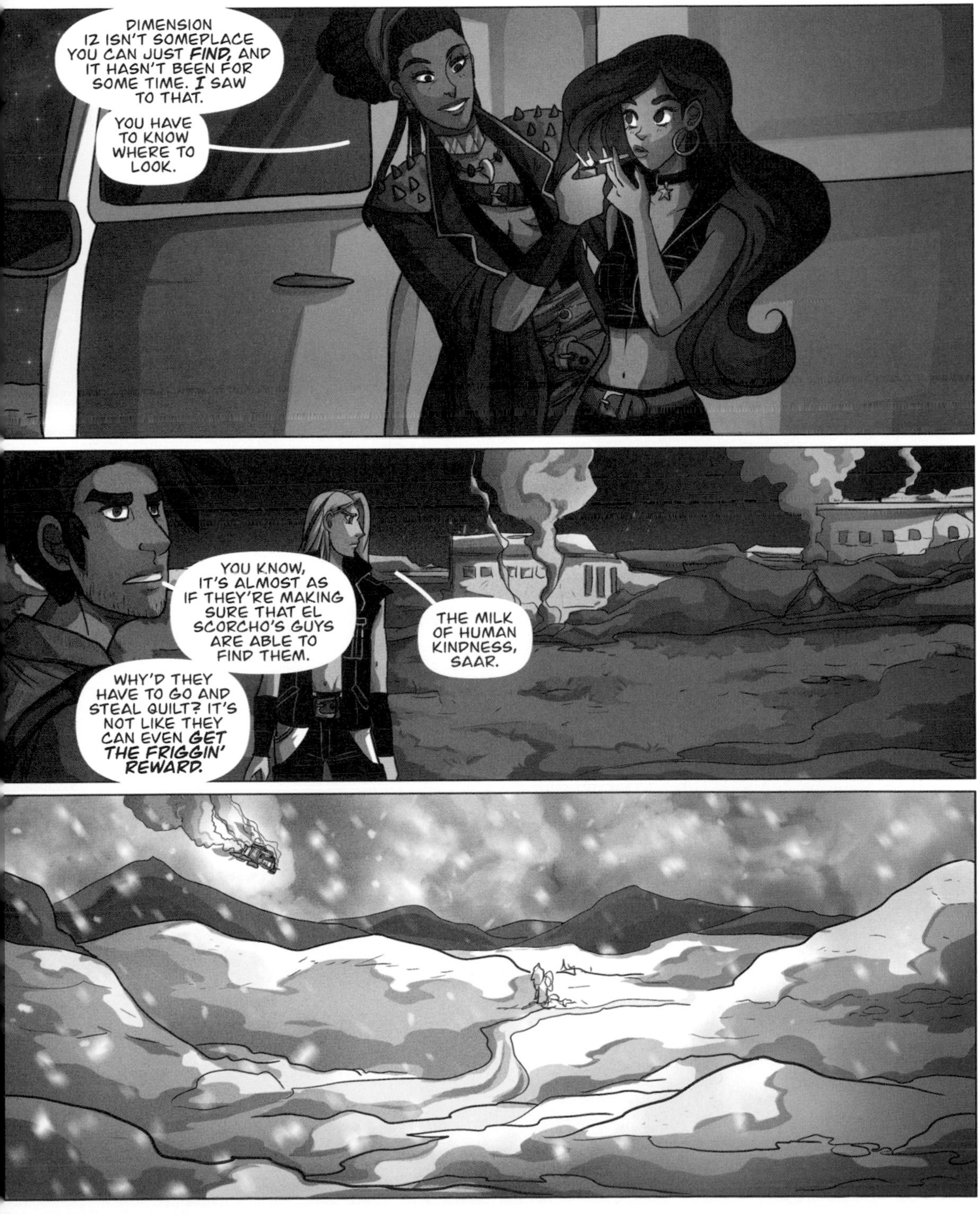

DIMENSION 12 ISN'T SOMEPLACE YOU CAN JUST **FIND,** AND IT HASN'T BEEN FOR SOME TIME. ***I*** SAW TO THAT.
YOU HAVE TO KNOW WHERE TO LOOK.
YOU KNOW, IT'S ALMOST AS IF THEY'RE MAKING SURE THAT EL SCORCHO'S GUYS ARE ABLE TO FIND THEM.
THE MILK OF HUMAN KINDNESS, SAAR.
WHY'D THEY HAVE TO GO AND STEAL QUILT? IT'S NOT LIKE THEY CAN EVEN **GET THE FRIGGIN' REWARD.**

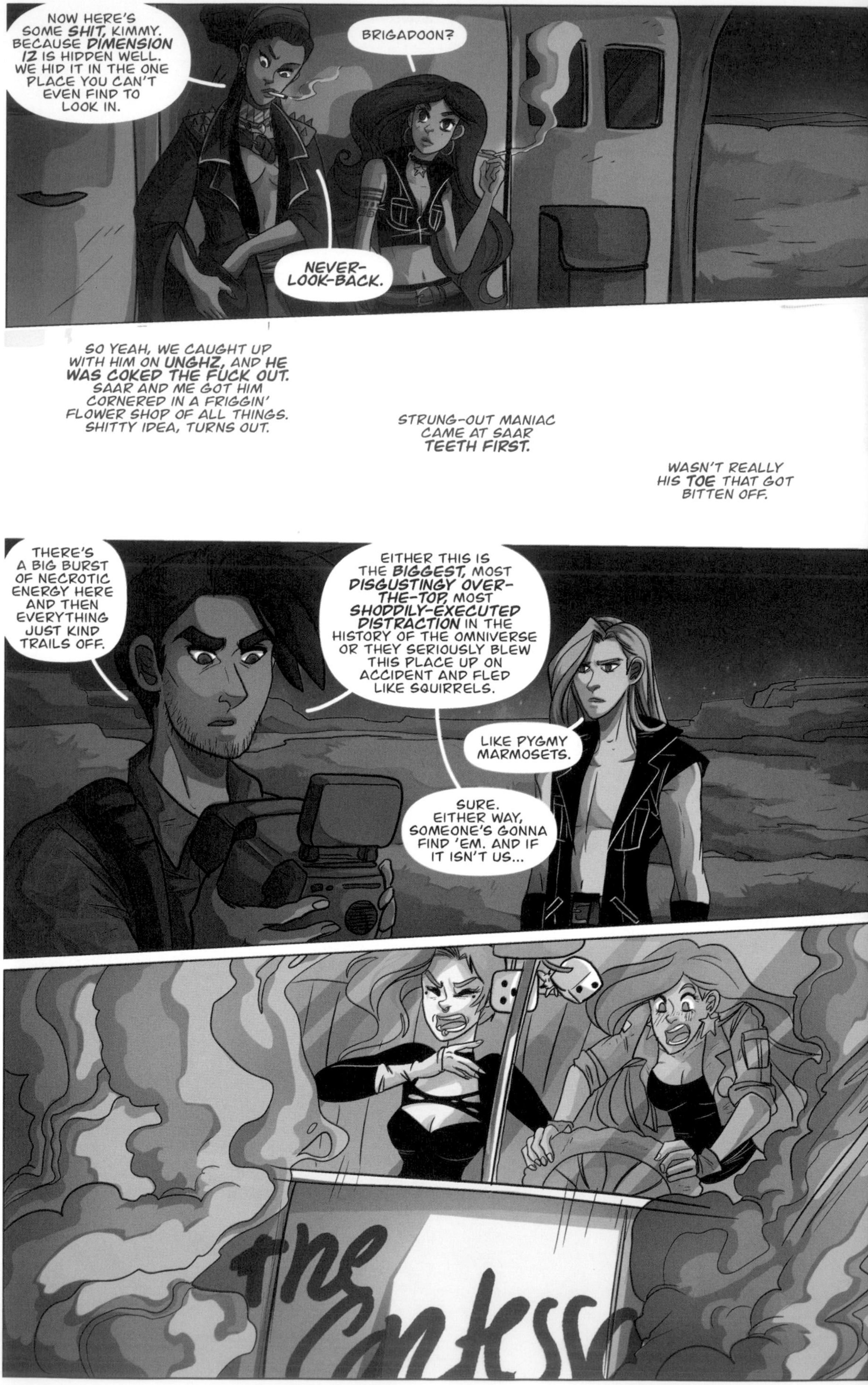
NOW HERE'S SOME **SHIT,** KIMMY. BECAUSE **DIMENSION IZ** IS HIDDEN WELL. WE HID IT IN THE ONE PLACE YOU CAN'T EVEN FIND TO LOOK IN.
BRIGADOON?
NEVER-LOOK-BACK.
*SO YEAH, WE CAUGHT UP WITH HIM ON **UNGHZ,** AND **HE WAS COKED THE FUCK OUT.** SAAR AND ME GOT HIM CORNERED IN A FRIGGIN' FLOWER SHOP OF ALL THINGS. SHITTY IDEA, TURNS OUT.*
*STRUNG-OUT MANIAC CAME AT SAAR **TEETH FIRST.***
*WASN'T REALLY HIS **TOE** THAT GOT BITTEN OFF.*
THERE'S A BIG BURST OF NECROTIC ENERGY HERE AND THEN EVERYTHING JUST KIND TRAILS OFF.
EITHER THIS IS THE ***BIGGEST,*** MOST ***DISGUSTINGY OVER-THE-TOP,*** MOST ***SHODDILY-EXECUTED DISTRACTION*** IN THE HISTORY OF THE OMNIVERSE OR THEY SERIOUSLY BLEW THIS PLACE UP ON ACCIDENT AND FLED LIKE SQUIRRELS.
LIKE PYGMY MARMOSETS.
SURE. EITHER WAY, SOMEONE'S GONNA FIND 'EM. AND IF IT ISN'T US...

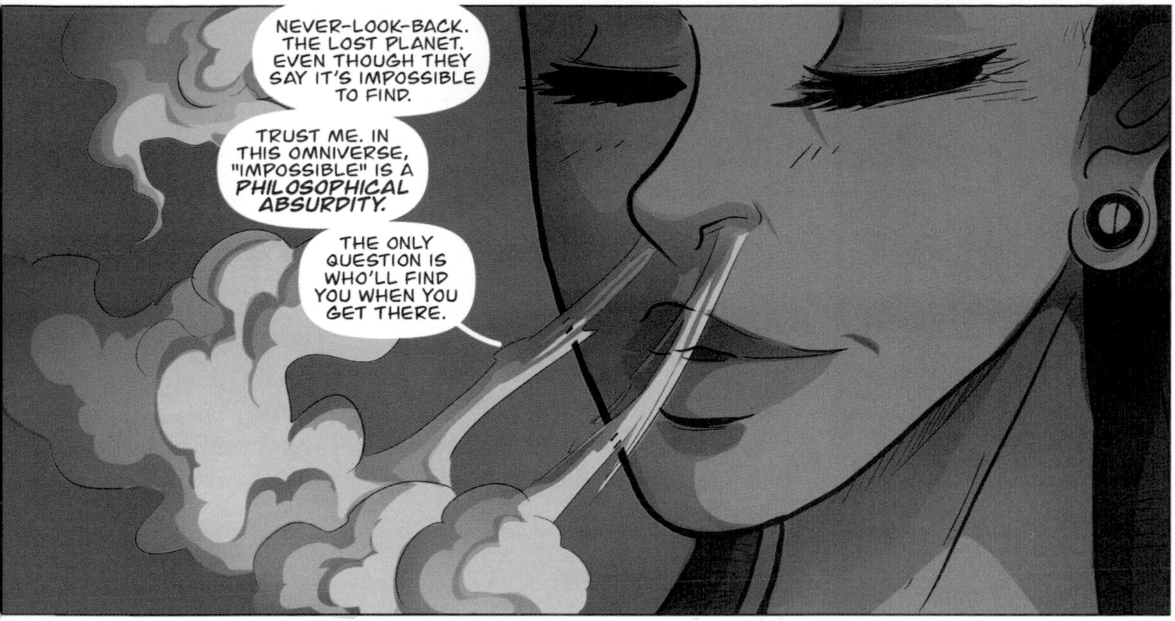
NEVER-LOOK-BACK. THE LOST PLANET. EVEN THOUGH THEY SAY IT'S IMPOSSIBLE TO FIND.
TRUST ME. IN THIS OMNIVERSE, "IMPOSSIBLE" IS A **PHILOSOPHICAL ABSURDITY.**
THE ONLY QUESTION IS WHO'LL FIND YOU WHEN YOU GET THERE.

*BUT THIS? **THIS** IS BULLSHIT.*

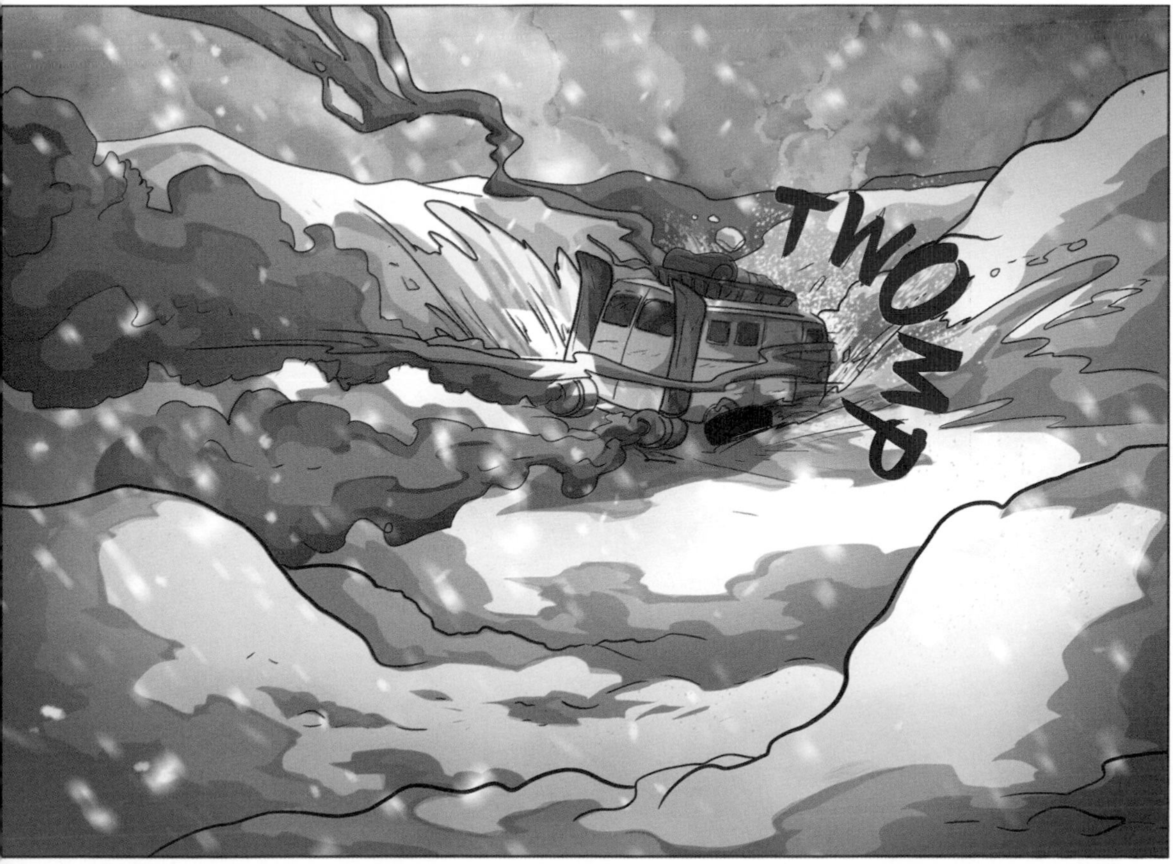
TWOMP

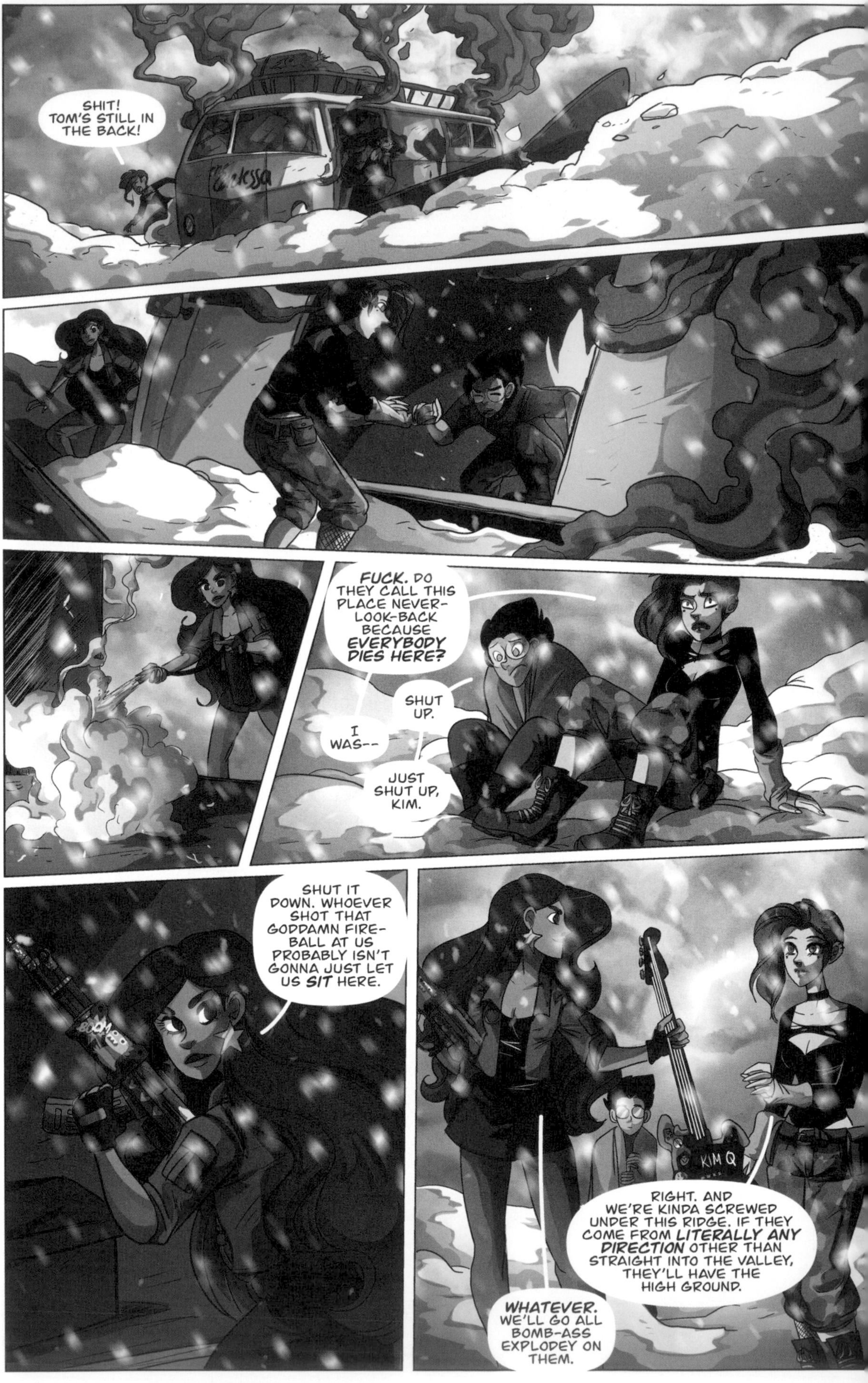
SHIT! TOM'S STILL IN THE BACK!
FUCK. DO THEY CALL THIS PLACE NEVER-LOOK-BACK BECAUSE EVERYBODY DIES HERE?
I WAS--
SHUT UP.
JUST SHUT UP, KIM.
SHUT IT DOWN. WHOEVER SHOT THAT GODDAMN FIRE-BALL AT US PROBABLY ISN'T GONNA JUST LET US SIT HERE.
RIGHT. AND WE'RE KINDA SCREWED UNDER THIS RIDGE. IF THEY COME FROM LITERALLY ANY DIRECTION OTHER THAN STRAIGHT INTO THE VALLEY, THEY'LL HAVE THE HIGH GROUND.
WHATEVER. WE'LL GO ALL BOMB-ASS EXPLODEY ON THEM.

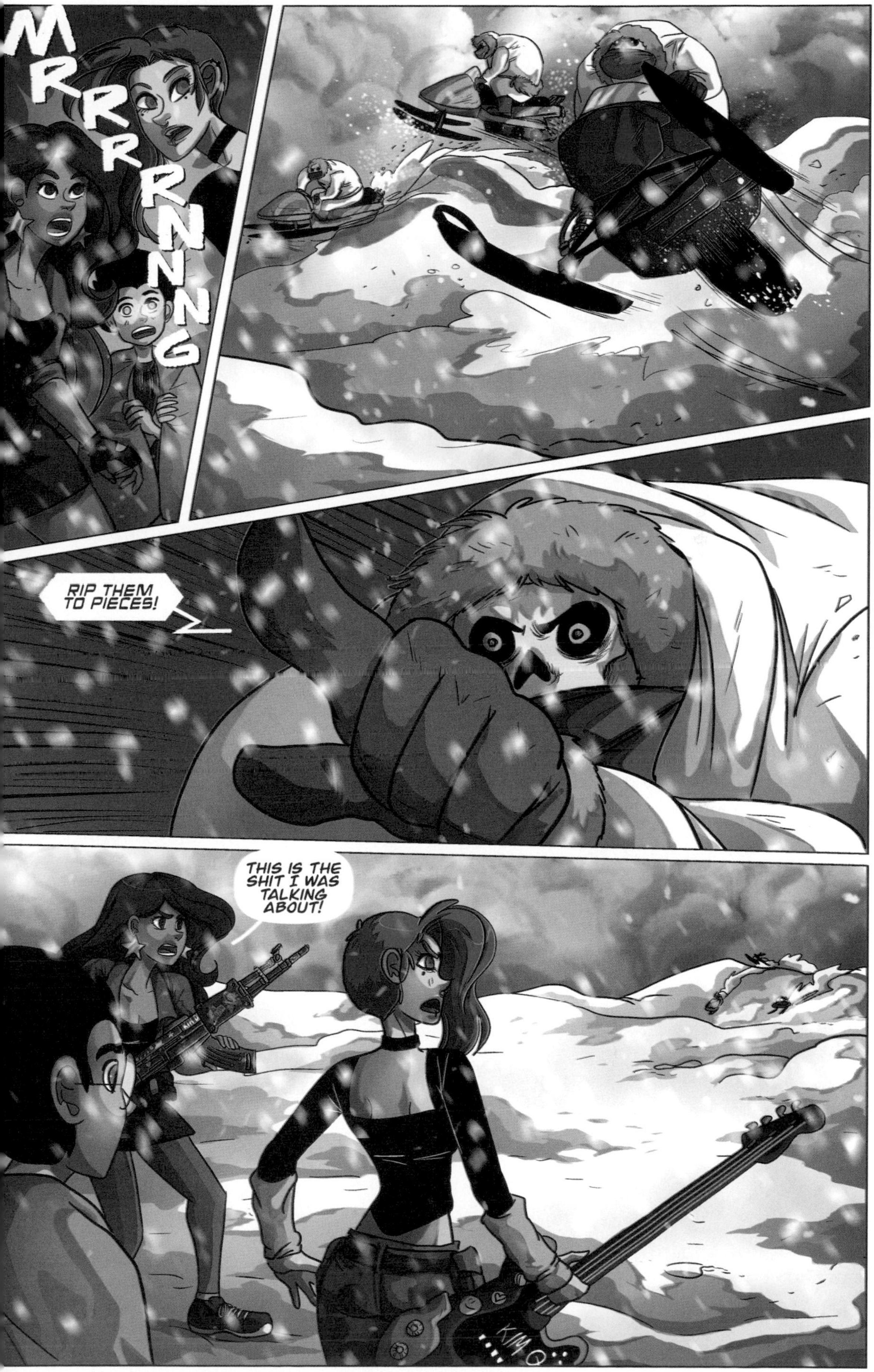
MRRRRRNNNG
RIP THEM TO PIECES!
THIS IS THE SHIT I WAS TALKING ABOUT!

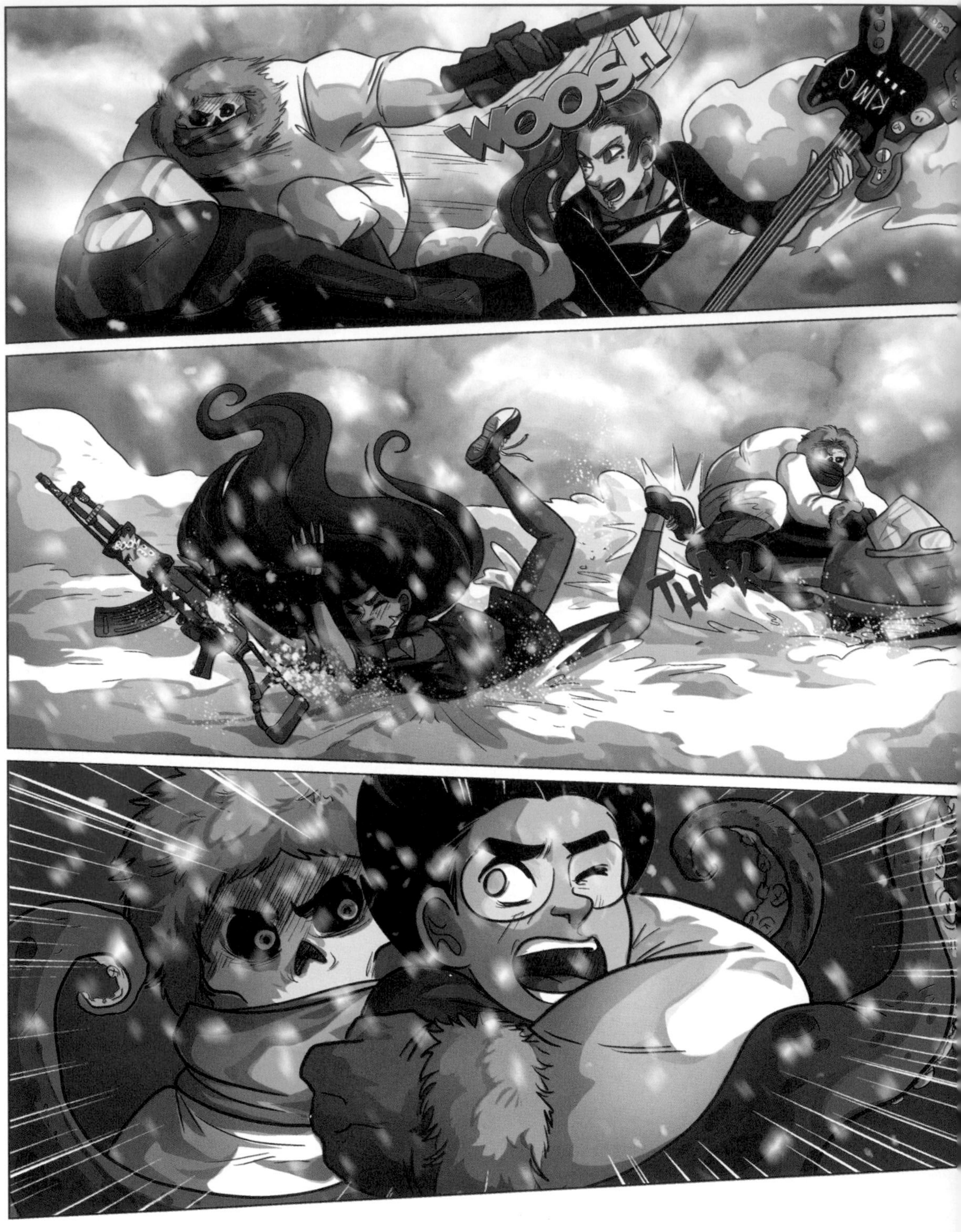
WOOSH

THIS IS THE SHIT KIM D.
WAS TALKING ABOUT.

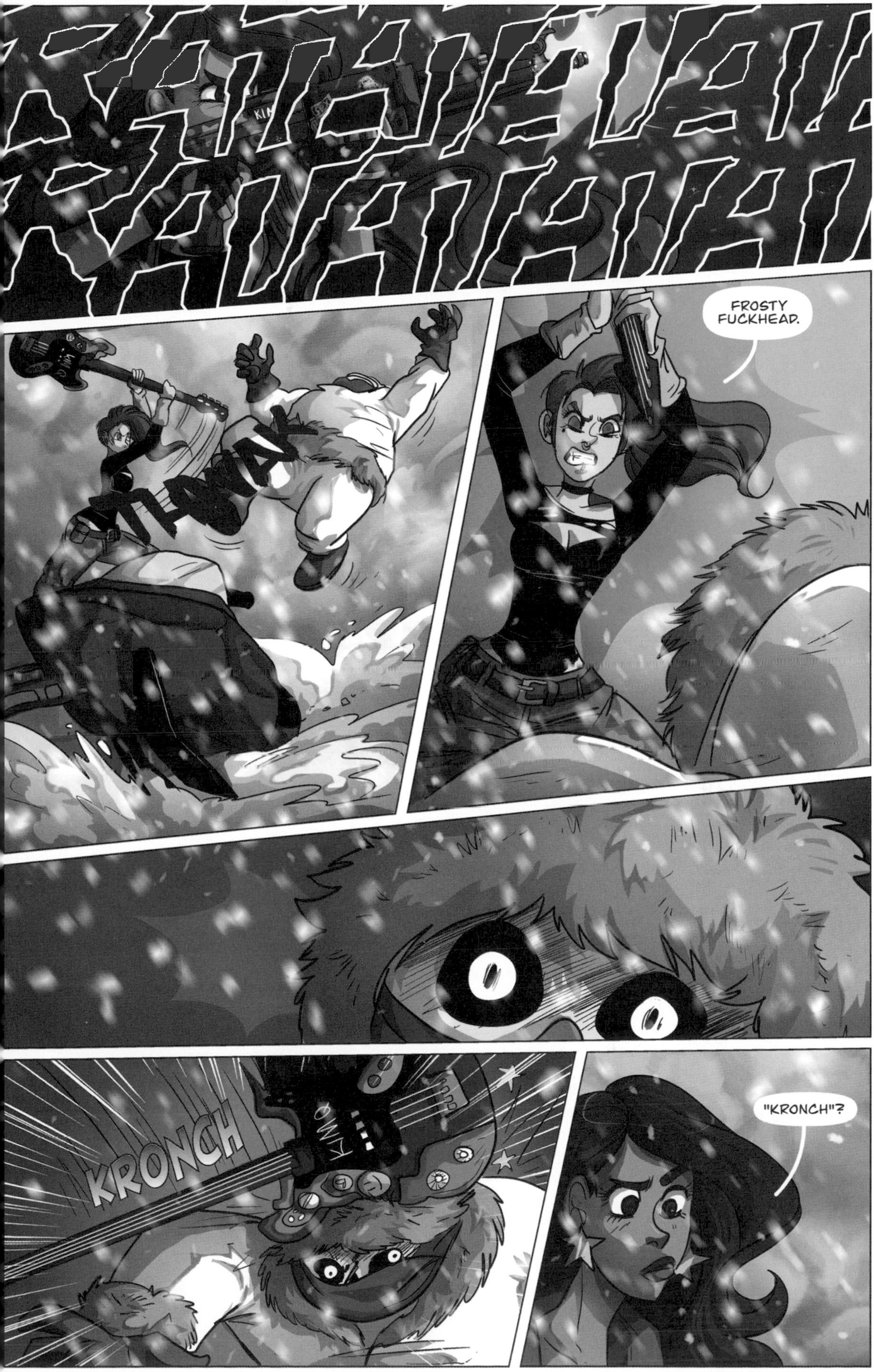
FROSTY FUCKHEAD.
KRONCH
"KRONCH"?

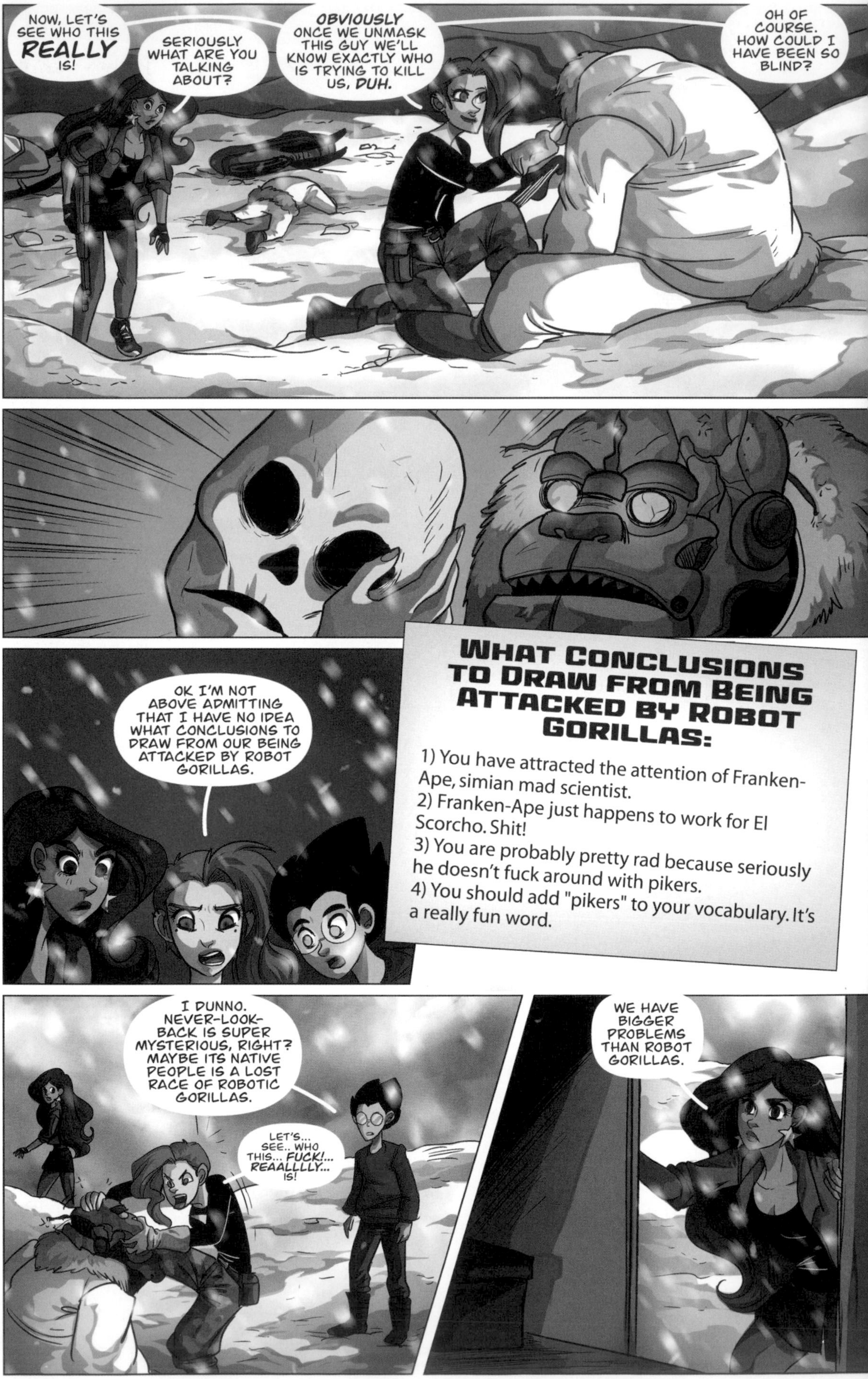
NOW, LET'S SEE WHO THIS REALLY IS!
SERIOUSLY WHAT ARE YOU TALKING ABOUT?
OBVIOUSLY ONCE WE UNMASK THIS GUY WE'LL KNOW EXACTLY WHO IS TRYING TO KILL US, DUH.
OH OF COURSE. HOW COULD I HAVE BEEN SO BLIND?
OK I'M NOT ABOVE ADMITTING THAT I HAVE NO IDEA WHAT CONCLUSIONS TO DRAW FROM OUR BEING ATTACKED BY ROBOT GORILLAS.
WHAT CONCLUSIONS TO DRAW FROM BEING ATTACKED BY ROBOT GORILLAS:
1) You have attracted the attention of Franken-Ape, simian mad scientist.
2) Franken-Ape just happens to work for El Scorcho. Shit!
3) You are probably pretty rad because seriously he doesn't fuck around with pikers.
4) You should add "pikers" to your vocabulary. It's a really fun word.
I DUNNO. NEVER-LOOK-BACK IS SUPER MYSTERIOUS, RIGHT? MAYBE ITS NATIVE PEOPLE IS A LOST RACE OF ROBOTIC GORILLAS.
LET'S... SEE.. WHO THIS... FUCK!... REAALLLLY... IS!
WE HAVE BIGGER PROBLEMS THAN ROBOT GORILLAS.

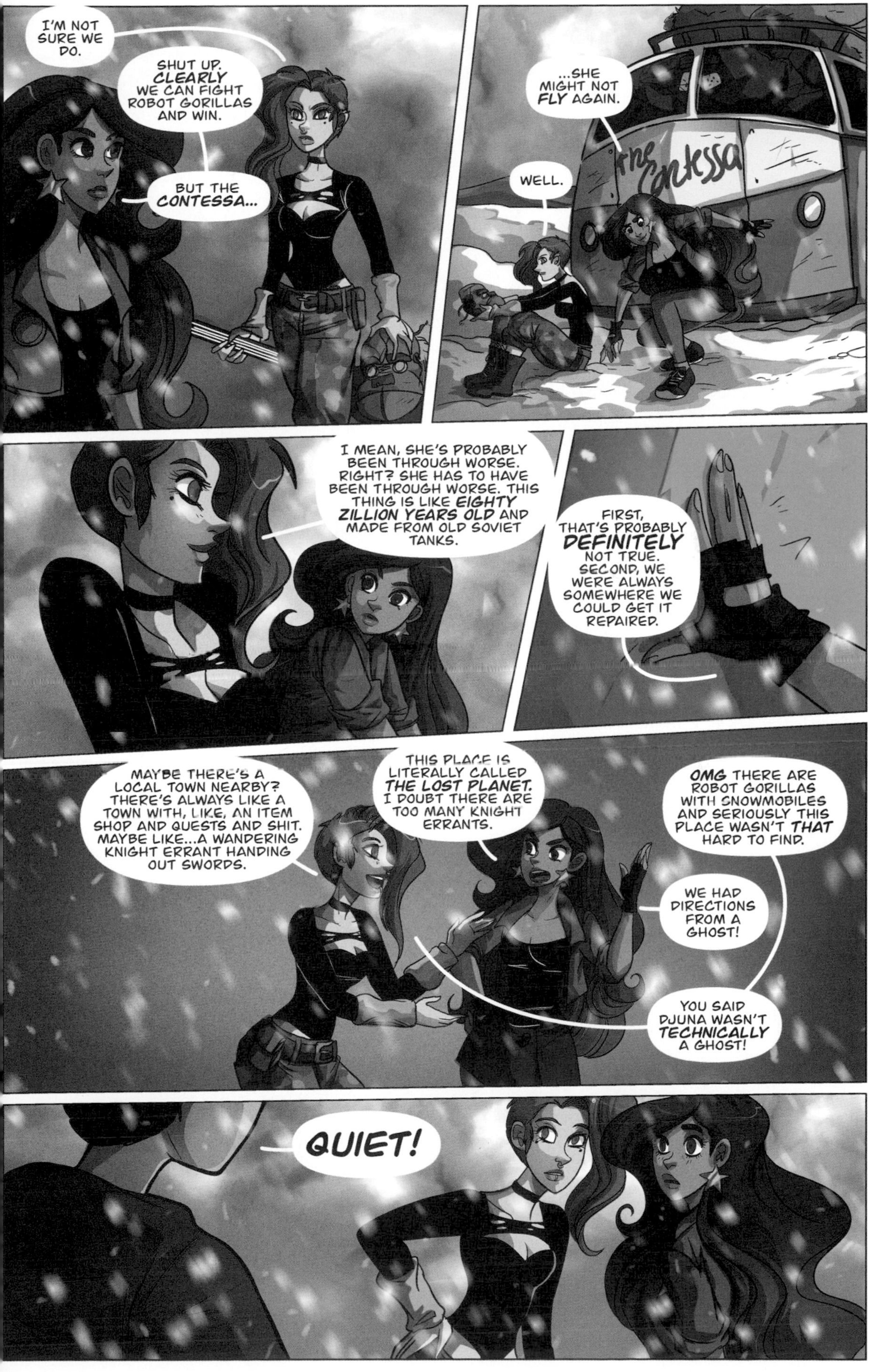
I'M NOT SURE WE DO.
SHUT UP. CLEARLY WE CAN FIGHT ROBOT GORILLAS AND WIN.
BUT THE CONTESSA...
...SHE MIGHT NOT FLY AGAIN.
THE CONTESSA
WELL.
I MEAN, SHE'S PROBABLY BEEN THROUGH WORSE. RIGHT? SHE HAS TO HAVE BEEN THROUGH WORSE. THIS THING IS LIKE EIGHTY ZILLION YEARS OLD AND MADE FROM OLD SOVIET TANKS.
FIRST, THAT'S PROBABLY DEFINITELY NOT TRUE. SECOND, WE WERE ALWAYS SOMEWHERE WE COULD GET IT REPAIRED.
MAYBE THERE'S A LOCAL TOWN NEARBY? THERE'S ALWAYS LIKE A TOWN WITH, LIKE, AN ITEM SHOP AND QUESTS AND SHIT. MAYBE LIKE...A WANDERING KNIGHT ERRANT HANDING OUT SWORDS.
THIS PLACE IS LITERALLY CALLED THE LOST PLANET. I DOUBT THERE ARE TOO MANY KNIGHT ERRANTS.
OMG THERE ARE ROBOT GORILLAS WITH SNOWMOBILES AND SERIOUSLY THIS PLACE WASN'T THAT HARD TO FIND.
WE HAD DIRECTIONS FROM A GHOST!
YOU SAID DJUNA WASN'T TECHNICALLY A GHOST!
QUIET!

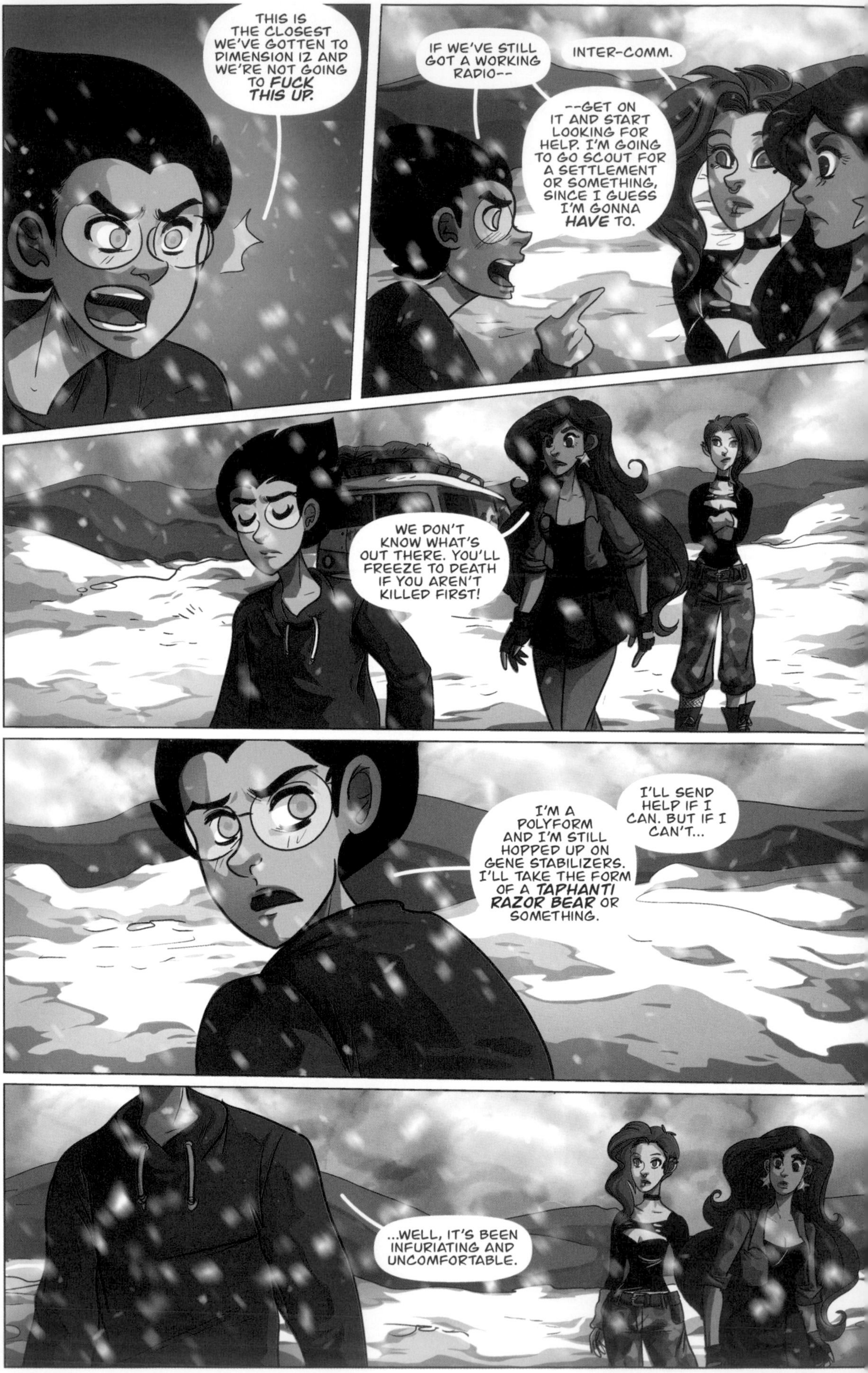
THIS IS THE CLOSEST WE'VE GOTTEN TO DIMENSION 12 AND WE'RE NOT GOING TO FUCK THIS UP.
IF WE'VE STILL GOT A WORKING RADIO--
INTER-COMM.
--GET ON IT AND START LOOKING FOR HELP. I'M GOING TO GO SCOUT FOR A SETTLEMENT OR SOMETHING, SINCE I GUESS I'M GONNA HAVE TO.
WE DON'T KNOW WHAT'S OUT THERE. YOU'LL FREEZE TO DEATH IF YOU AREN'T KILLED FIRST!
I'M A POLYFORM AND I'M STILL HOPPED UP ON GENE STABILIZERS. I'LL TAKE THE FORM OF A TAPHANTI RAZOR BEAR OR SOMETHING.
I'LL SEND HELP IF I CAN. BUT IF I CAN'T...
...WELL, IT'S BEEN INFURIATING AND UNCOMFORTABLE.

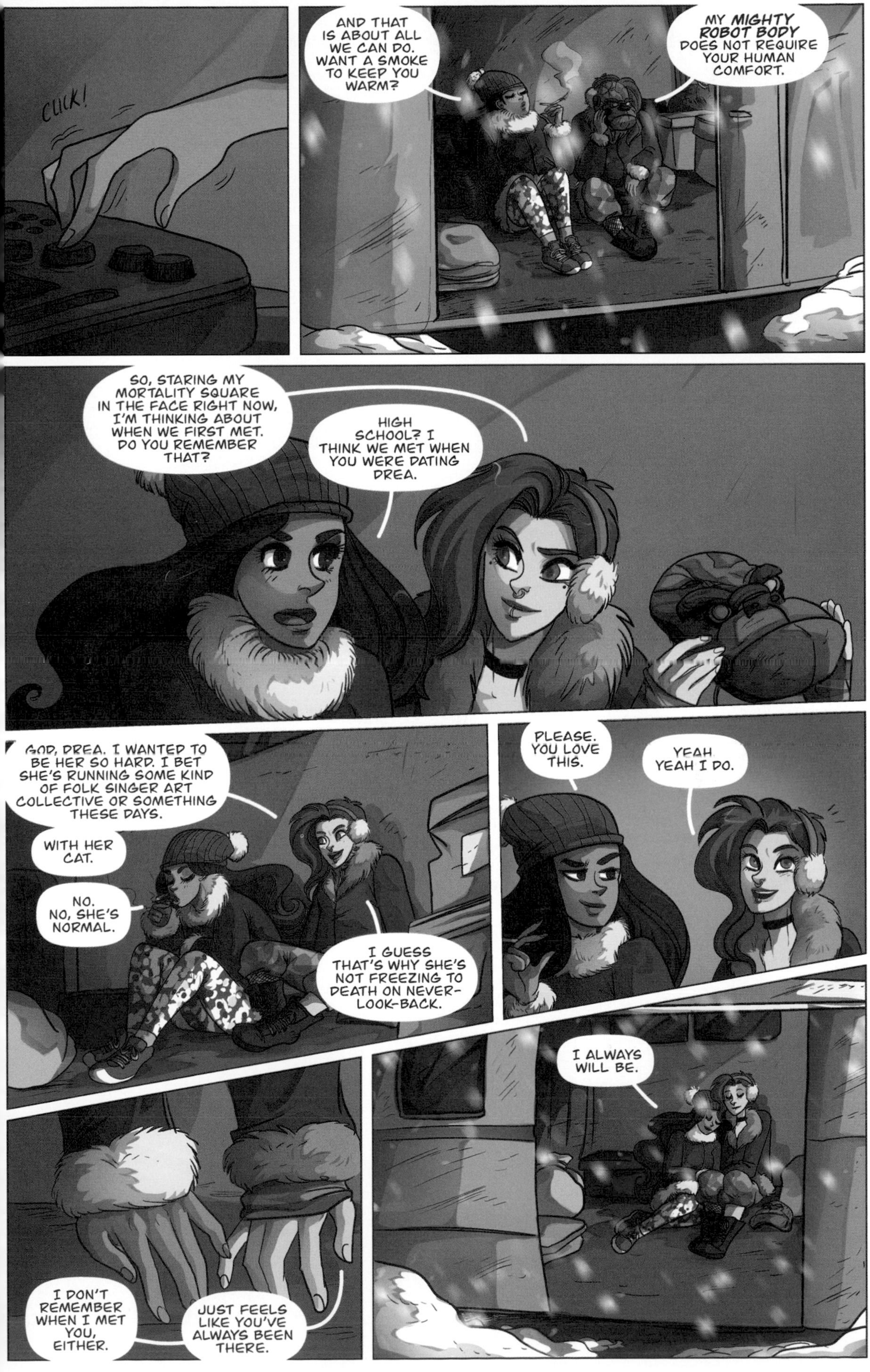
CLICK!
AND THAT IS ABOUT ALL WE CAN DO. WANT A SMOKE TO KEEP YOU WARM?
MY MIGHTY ROBOT BODY DOES NOT REQUIRE YOUR HUMAN COMFORT.
SO, STARING MY MORTALITY SQUARE IN THE FACE RIGHT NOW, I'M THINKING ABOUT WHEN WE FIRST MET. DO YOU REMEMBER THAT?
HIGH SCHOOL? I THINK WE MET WHEN YOU WERE DATING DREA.
GOD, DREA. I WANTED TO BE HER SO HARD. I BET SHE'S RUNNING SOME KIND OF FOLK SINGER ART COLLECTIVE OR SOMETHING THESE DAYS.
WITH HER CAT.
NO. NO, SHE'S NORMAL.
I GUESS THAT'S WHY SHE'S NOT FREEZING TO DEATH ON NEVER-LOOK-BACK.
PLEASE. YOU LOVE THIS.
YEAH. YEAH I DO.
I DON'T REMEMBER WHEN I MET YOU, EITHER.
JUST FEELS LIKE YOU'VE ALWAYS BEEN THERE.
I ALWAYS WILL BE.

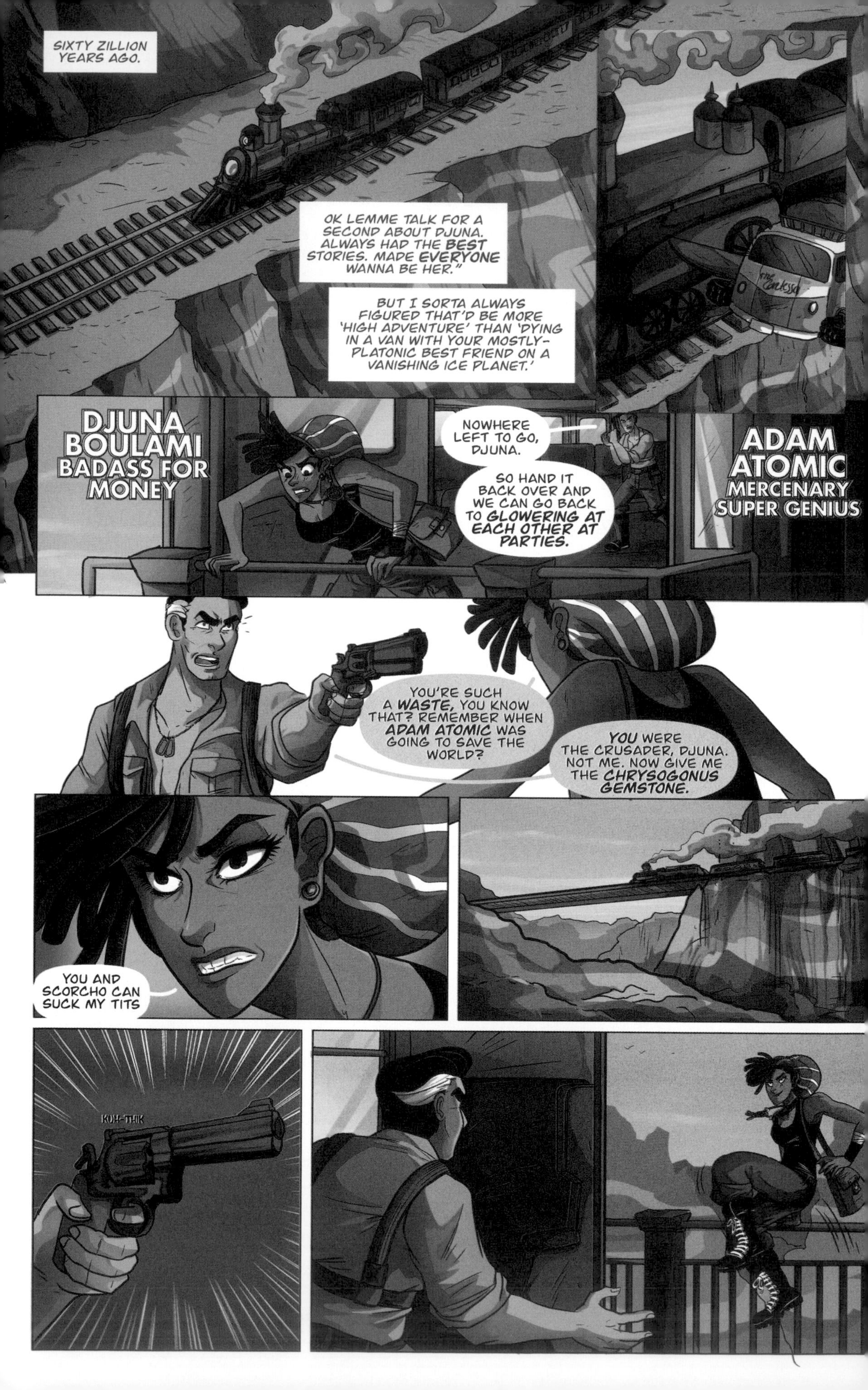
SIXTY ZILLION YEARS AGO.
OK LEMME TALK FOR A SECOND ABOUT DJUNA. ALWAYS HAD THE BEST STORIES. MADE EVERYONE WANNA BE HER."
BUT I SORTA ALWAYS FIGURED THAT'D BE MORE 'HIGH ADVENTURE' THAN 'DYING IN A VAN WITH YOUR MOSTLY-PLATONIC BEST FRIEND ON A VANISHING ICE PLANET.'
DJUNA BOULAMI BADASS FOR MONEY
NOWHERE LEFT TO GO, DJUNA.
SO HAND IT BACK OVER AND WE CAN GO BACK TO GLOWERING AT EACH OTHER AT PARTIES.
ADAM ATOMIC MERCENARY SUPER GENIUS
YOU'RE SUCH A WASTE, YOU KNOW THAT? REMEMBER WHEN ADAM ATOMIC WAS GOING TO SAVE THE WORLD?
YOU WERE THE CRUSADER, DJUNA. NOT ME. NOW GIVE ME THE CHRYSOGONUS GEMSTONE.
YOU AND SCORCHO CAN SUCK MY TITS
KUH-THIK

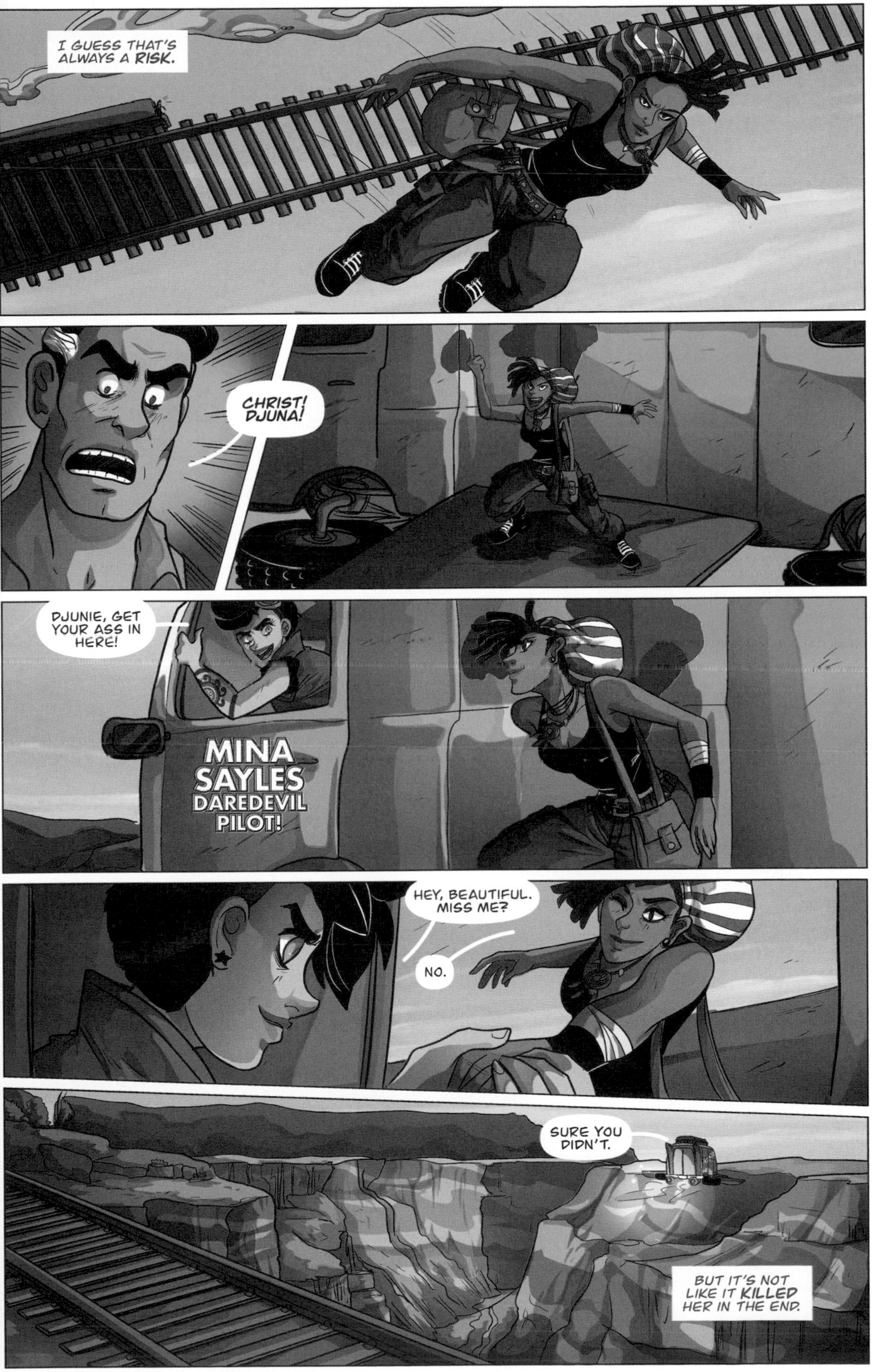
I GUESS THAT'S ALWAYS A **RISK**.
CHRIST! DJUNA!
DJUNIE, GET YOUR ASS IN HERE!
MINA SAYLES DAREDEVIL PILOT!
HEY, BEAUTIFUL. MISS ME?
NO.
SURE YOU DIDN'T.
BUT IT'S NOT LIKE IT **KILLED** HER IN THE END.

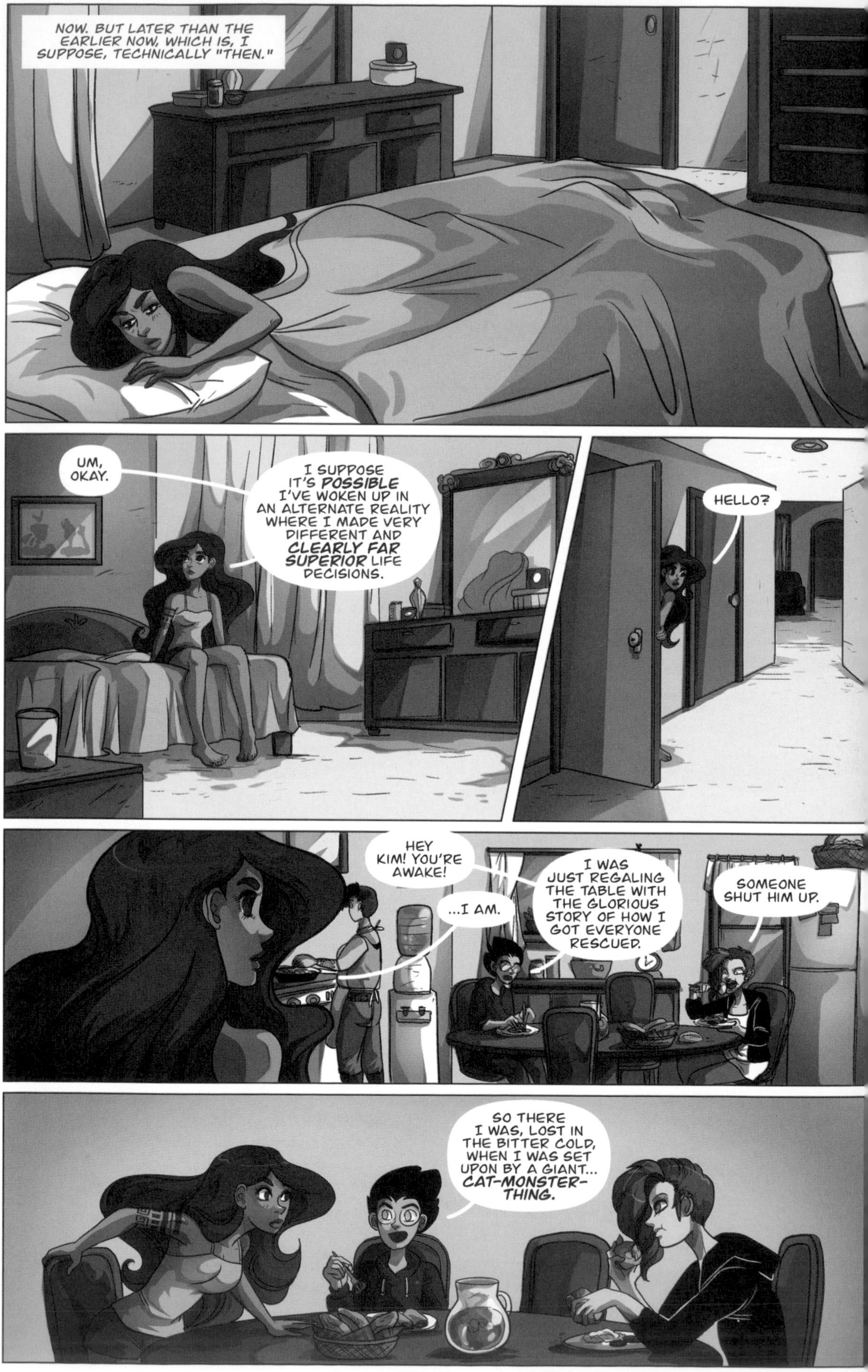
NOW. BUT LATER THAN THE EARLIER NOW, WHICH IS, I SUPPOSE, TECHNICALLY "THEN."
UM, OKAY.
I SUPPOSE IT'S **POSSIBLE** I'VE WOKEN UP IN AN ALTERNATE REALITY WHERE I MADE VERY DIFFERENT AND **CLEARLY FAR SUPERIOR** LIFE DECISIONS.
HELLO?
HEY KIM! YOU'RE AWAKE!
...I AM.
I WAS JUST REGALING THE TABLE WITH THE GLORIOUS STORY OF HOW I GOT EVERYONE RESCUED.
SOMEONE SHUT HIM UP.
SO THERE I WAS, LOST IN THE BITTER COLD, WHEN I WAS SET UPON BY A GIANT... **CAT-MONSTER-THING.**

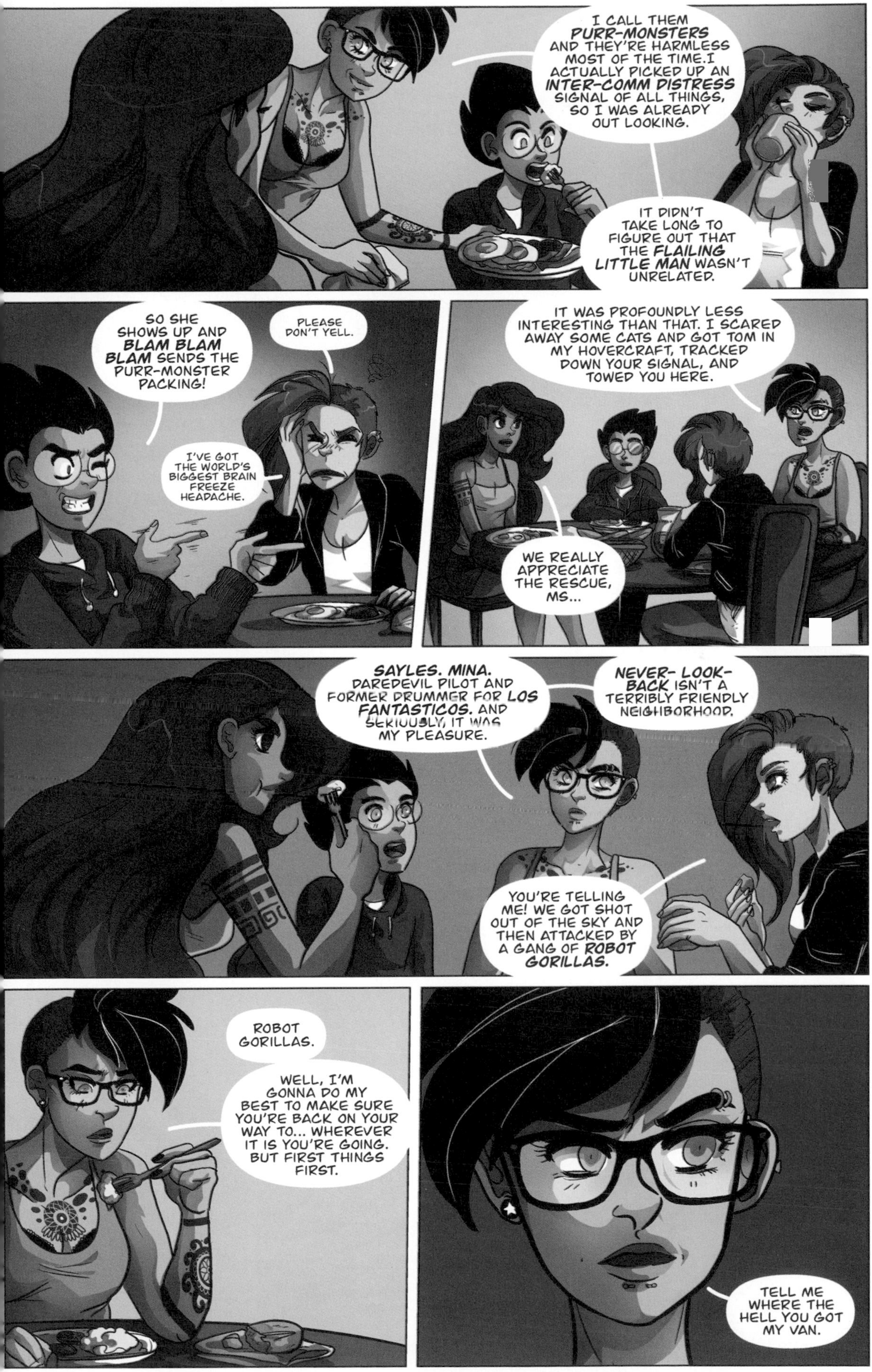
I CALL THEM PURR-MONSTERS AND THEY'RE HARMLESS MOST OF THE TIME. I ACTUALLY PICKED UP AN INTER-COMM DISTRESS SIGNAL OF ALL THINGS, SO I WAS ALREADY OUT LOOKING.
IT DIDN'T TAKE LONG TO FIGURE OUT THAT THE FLAILING LITTLE MAN WASN'T UNRELATED.
SO SHE SHOWS UP AND BLAM BLAM BLAM SENDS THE PURR-MONSTER PACKING!
PLEASE DON'T YELL.
I'VE GOT THE WORLD'S BIGGEST BRAIN FREEZE HEADACHE.
IT WAS PROFOUNDLY LESS INTERESTING THAN THAT. I SCARED AWAY SOME CATS AND GOT TOM IN MY HOVERCRAFT, TRACKED DOWN YOUR SIGNAL, AND TOWED YOU HERE.
WE REALLY APPRECIATE THE RESCUE, MS...
SAYLES. MINA. DAREDEVIL PILOT AND FORMER DRUMMER FOR LOS FANTASTICOS. AND SERIOUSLY, IT WAS MY PLEASURE.
NEVER- LOOK-BACK ISN'T A TERRIBLY FRIENDLY NEIGHBORHOOD.
YOU'RE TELLING ME! WE GOT SHOT OUT OF THE SKY AND THEN ATTACKED BY A GANG OF ROBOT GORILLAS.
ROBOT GORILLAS.
WELL, I'M GONNA DO MY BEST TO MAKE SURE YOU'RE BACK ON YOUR WAY TO... WHEREVER IT IS YOU'RE GOING. BUT FIRST THINGS FIRST.
TELL ME WHERE THE HELL YOU GOT MY VAN.

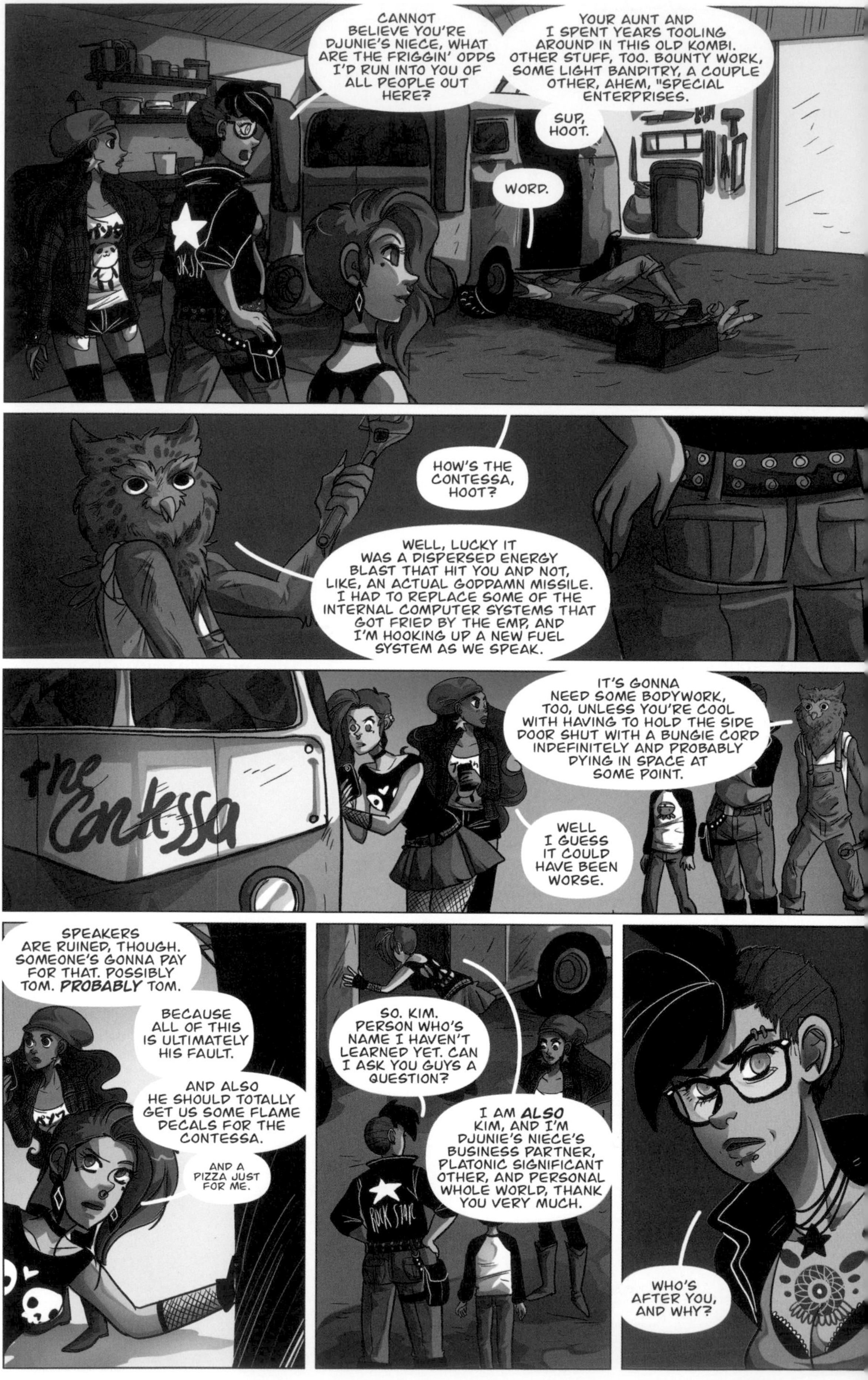

CANNOT BELIEVE YOU'RE DJUNIE'S NIECE, WHAT ARE THE FRIGGIN' ODDS I'D RUN INTO YOU OF ALL PEOPLE OUT HERE?
YOUR AUNT AND I SPENT YEARS TOOLING AROUND IN THIS OLD KOMBI. OTHER STUFF, TOO. BOUNTY WORK, SOME LIGHT BANDITRY, A COUPLE OTHER, AHEM, "SPECIAL ENTERPRISES.
SUP, HOOT.
WORD.
HOW'S THE CONTESSA, HOOT?
WELL, LUCKY IT WAS A DISPERSED ENERGY BLAST THAT HIT YOU AND NOT, LIKE, AN ACTUAL GODDAMN MISSILE. I HAD TO REPLACE SOME OF THE INTERNAL COMPUTER SYSTEMS THAT GOT FRIED BY THE EMP, AND I'M HOOKING UP A NEW FUEL SYSTEM AS WE SPEAK.
the Contessa
IT'S GONNA NEED SOME BODYWORK, TOO, UNLESS YOU'RE COOL WITH HAVING TO HOLD THE SIDE DOOR SHUT WITH A BUNGIE CORD INDEFINITELY AND PROBABLY DYING IN SPACE AT SOME POINT.
WELL I GUESS IT COULD HAVE BEEN WORSE.
SPEAKERS ARE RUINED, THOUGH. SOMEONE'S GONNA PAY FOR THAT. POSSIBLY TOM. **PROBABLY** TOM.
BECAUSE ALL OF THIS IS ULTIMATELY HIS FAULT.
AND ALSO HE SHOULD TOTALLY GET US SOME FLAME DECALS FOR THE CONTESSA.
AND A PIZZA JUST FOR ME.
SO. KIM. PERSON WHO'S NAME I HAVEN'T LEARNED YET. CAN I ASK YOU GUYS A QUESTION?
I AM **ALSO** KIM, AND I'M DJUNIE'S NIECE'S BUSINESS PARTNER, PLATONIC SIGNIFICANT OTHER, AND PERSONAL WHOLE WORLD, THANK YOU VERY MUCH.
ROCK STAR
WHO'S AFTER YOU, AND WHY?

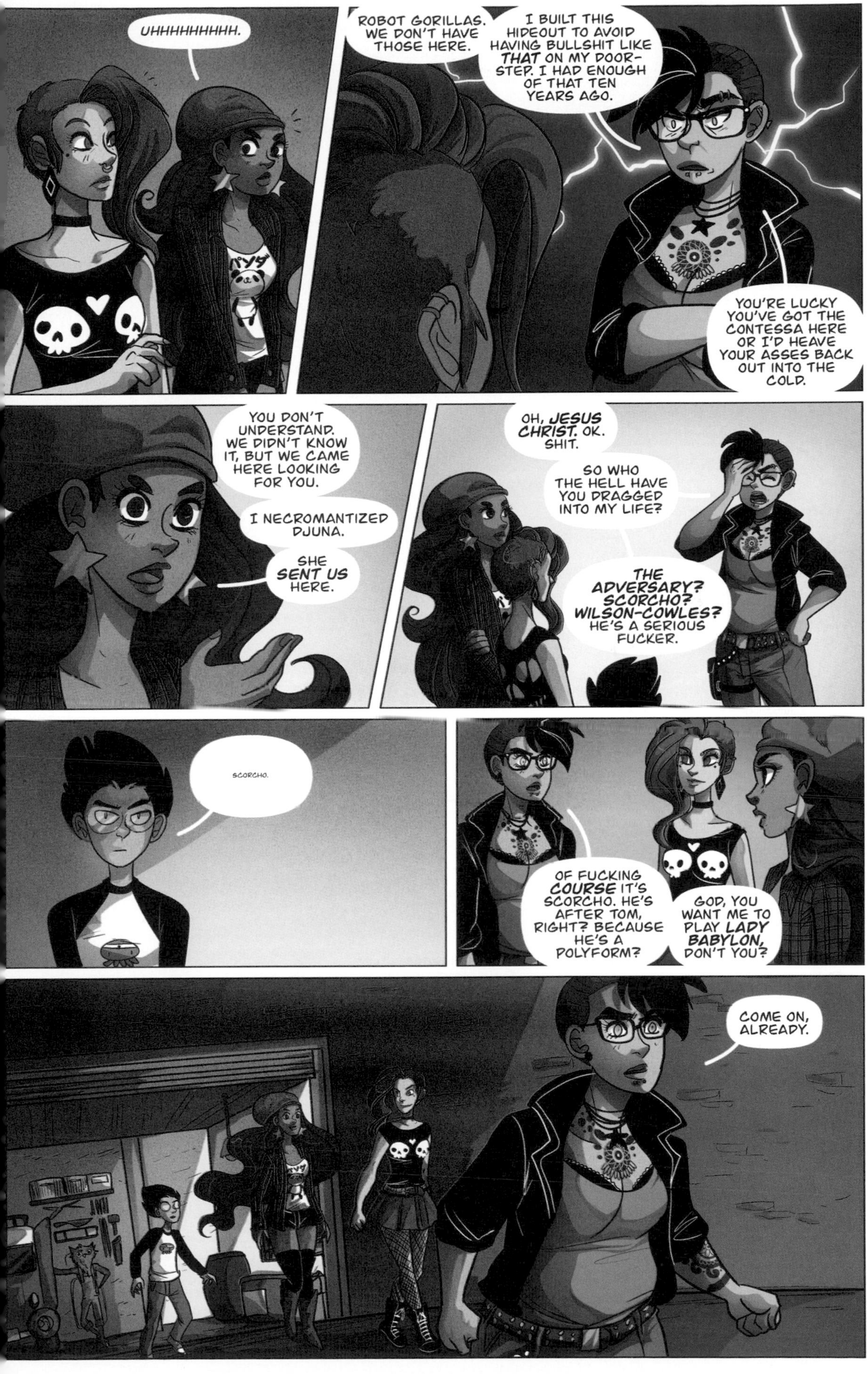

UHHHHHHHHH.
ROBOT GORILLAS. WE DON'T HAVE THOSE HERE.
I BUILT THIS HIDEOUT TO AVOID HAVING BULLSHIT LIKE THAT ON MY DOOR-STEP. I HAD ENOUGH OF THAT TEN YEARS AGO.
YOU'RE LUCKY YOU'VE GOT THE CONTESSA HERE OR I'D HEAVE YOUR ASSES BACK OUT INTO THE COLD.
YOU DON'T UNDERSTAND. WE DIDN'T KNOW IT, BUT WE CAME HERE LOOKING FOR YOU.
I NECROMANTIZED DJUNA.
SHE SENT US HERE.
OH, JESUS CHRIST. OK. SHIT.
SO WHO THE HELL HAVE YOU DRAGGED INTO MY LIFE?
THE ADVERSARY? SCORCHO? WILSON-COWLES? HE'S A SERIOUS FUCKER.
SCORCHO.
OF FUCKING COURSE IT'S SCORCHO. HE'S AFTER TOM, RIGHT? BECAUSE HE'S A POLYFORM?
GOD, YOU WANT ME TO PLAY LADY BABYLON, DON'T YOU?
COME ON, ALREADY.

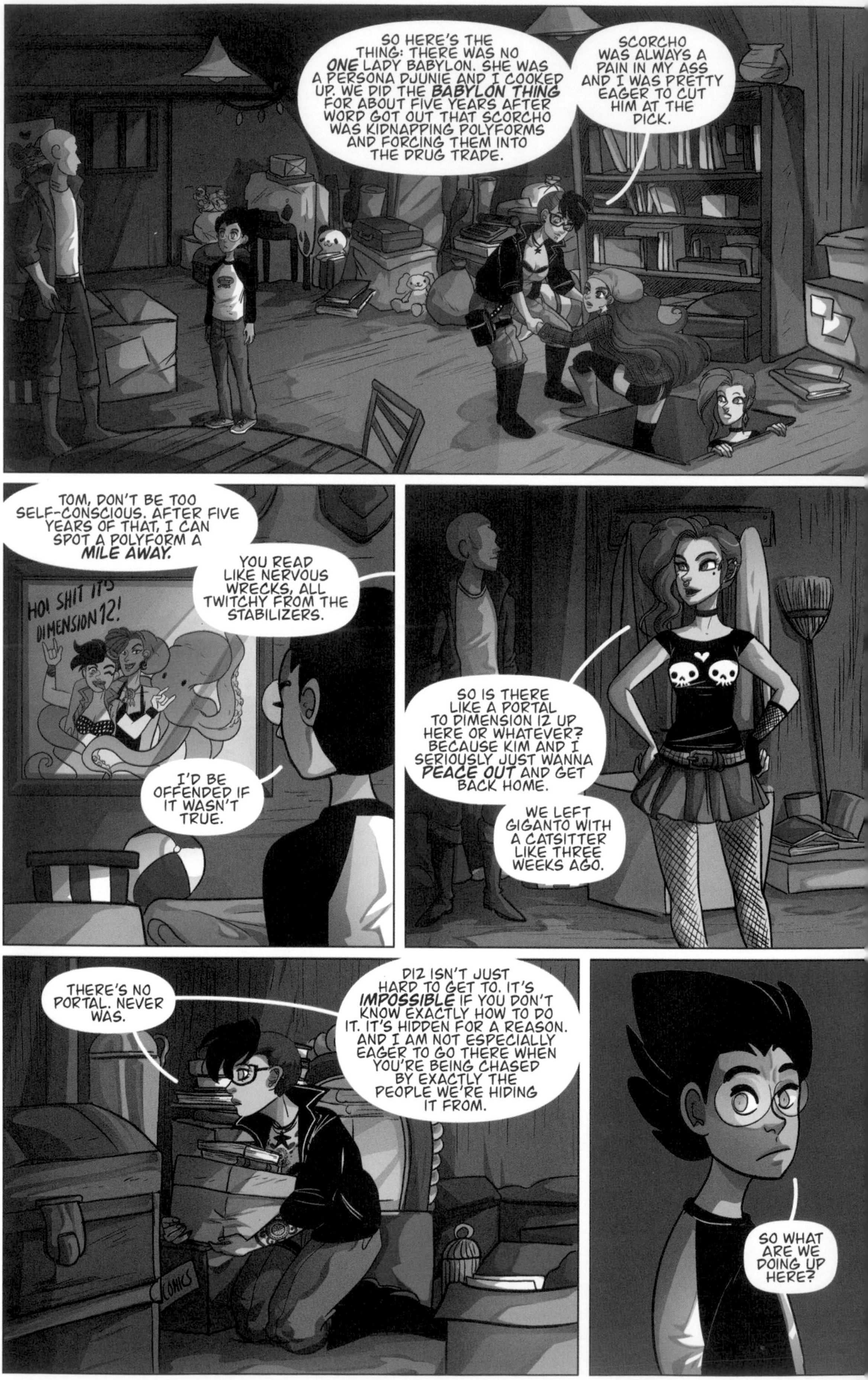
SO HERE'S THE THING: THERE WAS NO ONE LADY BABYLON. SHE WAS A PERSONA DJUNIE AND I COOKED UP. WE DID THE BABYLON THING FOR ABOUT FIVE YEARS AFTER WORD GOT OUT THAT SCORCHO WAS KIDNAPPING POLYFORMS AND FORCING THEM INTO THE DRUG TRADE.
SCORCHO WAS ALWAYS A PAIN IN MY ASS AND I WAS PRETTY EAGER TO CUT HIM AT THE DICK.
TOM, DON'T BE TOO SELF-CONSCIOUS. AFTER FIVE YEARS OF THAT, I CAN SPOT A POLYFORM A MILE AWAY.
YOU READ LIKE NERVOUS WRECKS, ALL TWITCHY FROM THE STABILIZERS.
HO! SHIT IT'S DIMENSION 12!
I'D BE OFFENDED IF IT WASN'T TRUE.
SO IS THERE LIKE A PORTAL TO DIMENSION 12 UP HERE OR WHATEVER? BECAUSE KIM AND I SERIOUSLY JUST WANNA PEACE OUT AND GET BACK HOME.
WE LEFT GIGANTO WITH A CATSITTER LIKE THREE WEEKS AGO.
THERE'S NO PORTAL. NEVER WAS.
D12 ISN'T JUST HARD TO GET TO. IT'S IMPOSSIBLE IF YOU DON'T KNOW EXACTLY HOW TO DO IT. IT'S HIDDEN FOR A REASON. AND I AM NOT ESPECIALLY EAGER TO GO THERE WHEN YOU'RE BEING CHASED BY EXACTLY THE PEOPLE WE'RE HIDING IT FROM.
COMICS
SO WHAT ARE WE DOING UP HERE?

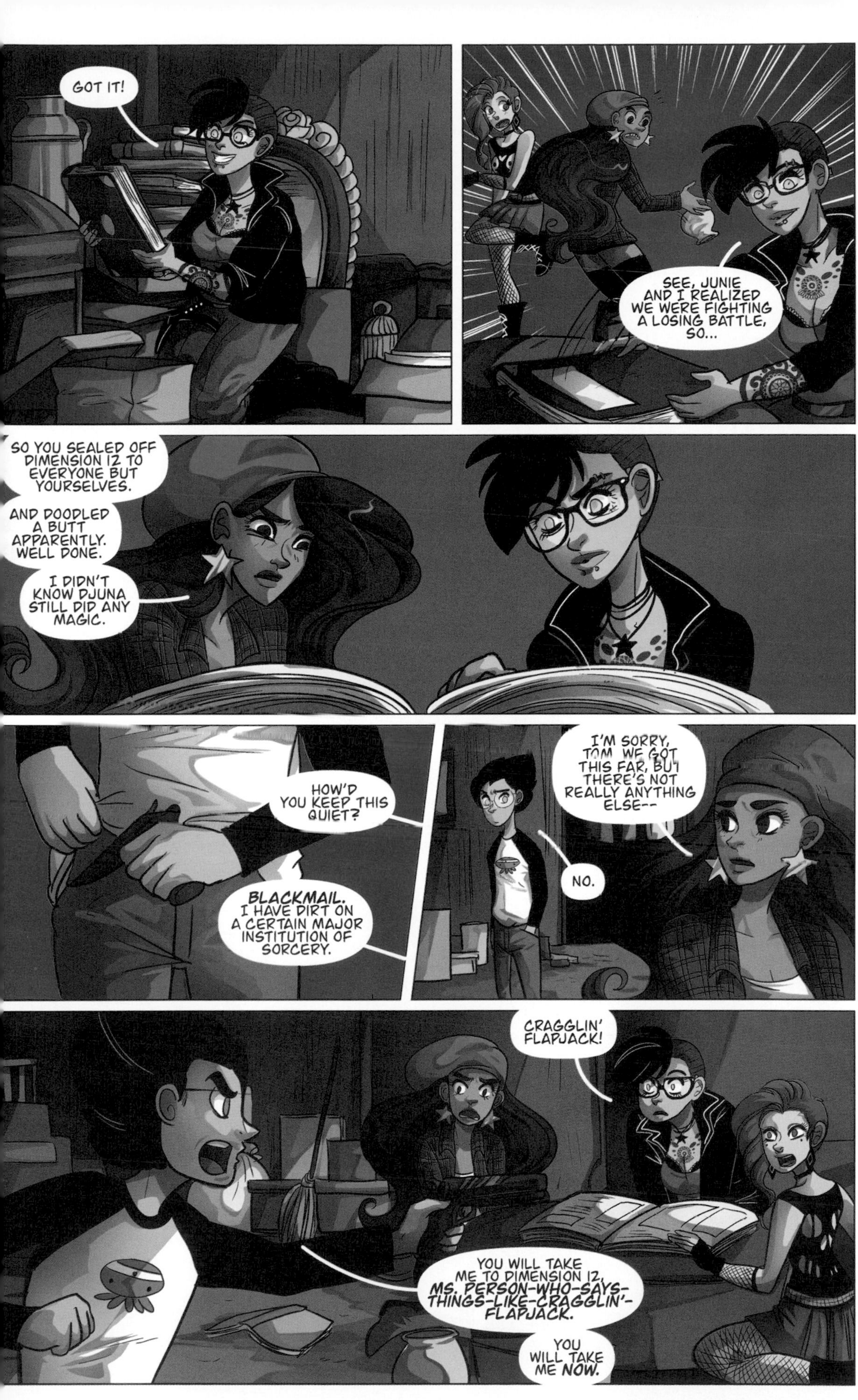
GOT IT!
SEE, JUNIE AND I REALIZED WE WERE FIGHTING A LOSING BATTLE, SO...
SO YOU SEALED OFF DIMENSION 12 TO EVERYONE BUT YOURSELVES.
AND DOODLED A BUTT APPARENTLY. WELL DONE.
I DIDN'T KNOW DJUNA STILL DID ANY MAGIC.
HOW'D YOU KEEP THIS QUIET?
BLACKMAIL. I HAVE DIRT ON A CERTAIN MAJOR INSTITUTION OF SORCERY.
I'M SORRY, TOM. WE GOT THIS FAR, BUT THERE'S NOT REALLY ANYTHING ELSE--
NO.
CRAGGLIN' FLAPJACK!
YOU WILL TAKE ME TO DIMENSION 12, MS. PERSON-WHO-SAYS-THINGS-LIKE-CRAGGLIN'-FLAPJACK.
YOU WILL TAKE ME NOW.

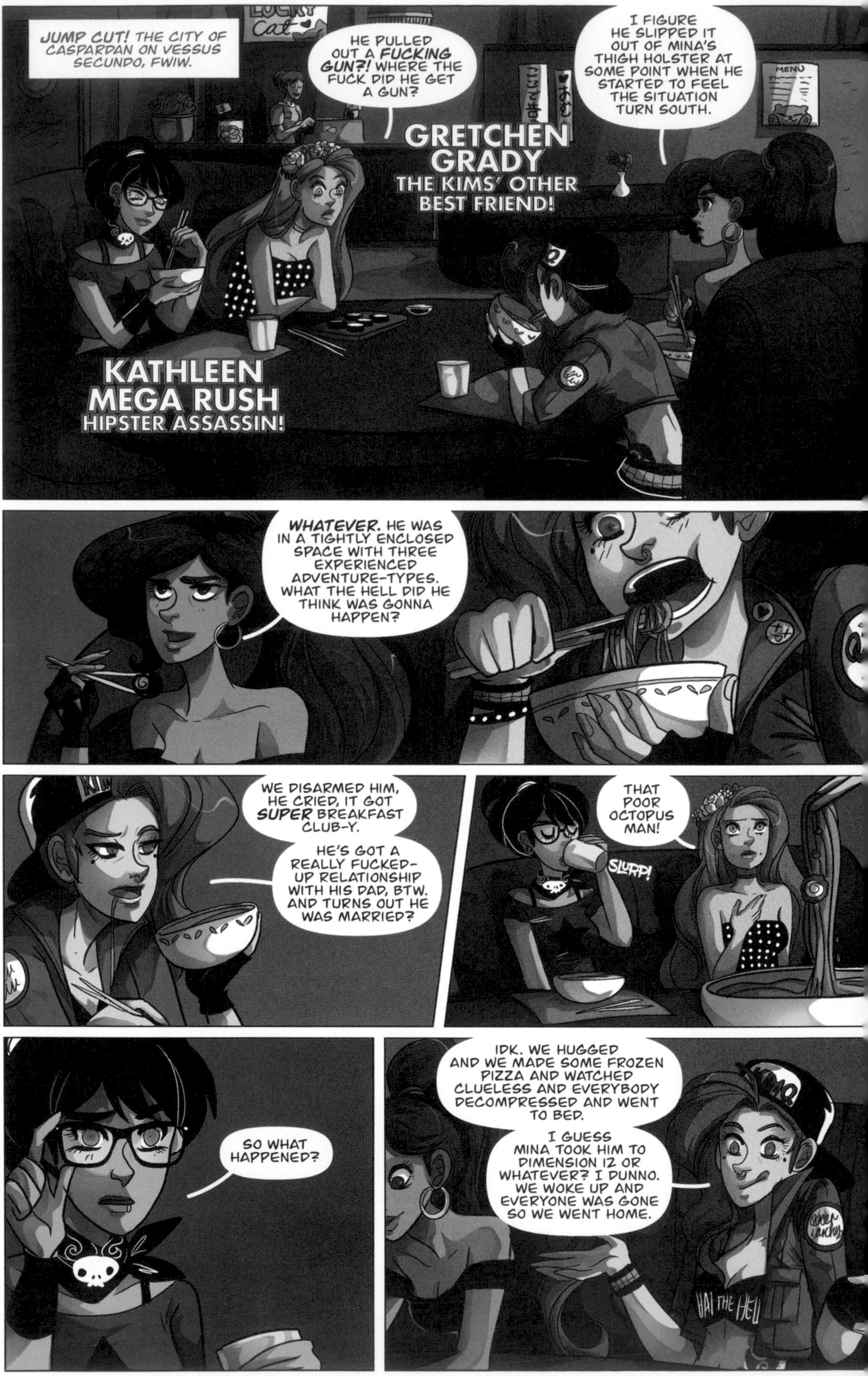

JUMP CUT! THE CITY OF CASPARDAN ON VESSUS SECUNDO, FWIW.
HE PULLED OUT A FUCKING GUN?! WHERE THE FUCK DID HE GET A GUN?
GRETCHEN GRADY
THE KIMS' OTHER BEST FRIEND!
I FIGURE HE SLIPPED IT OUT OF MINA'S THIGH HOLSTER AT SOME POINT WHEN HE STARTED TO FEEL THE SITUATION TURN SOUTH.
KATHLEEN MEGA RUSH
HIPSTER ASSASSIN!
WHATEVER. HE WAS IN A TIGHTLY ENCLOSED SPACE WITH THREE EXPERIENCED ADVENTURE-TYPES. WHAT THE HELL DID HE THINK WAS GONNA HAPPEN?
WE DISARMED HIM, HE CRIED, IT GOT SUPER BREAKFAST CLUB-Y.
HE'S GOT A REALLY FUCKED-UP RELATIONSHIP WITH HIS DAD, BTW. AND TURNS OUT HE WAS MARRIED?
THAT POOR OCTOPUS MAN!
SLURP!
SO WHAT HAPPENED?
IDK. WE HUGGED AND WE MADE SOME FROZEN PIZZA AND WATCHED CLUELESS AND EVERYBODY DECOMPRESSED AND WENT TO BED.
I GUESS MINA TOOK HIM TO DIMENSION 12 OR WHATEVER? I DUNNO. WE WOKE UP AND EVERYONE WAS GONE SO WE WENT HOME.

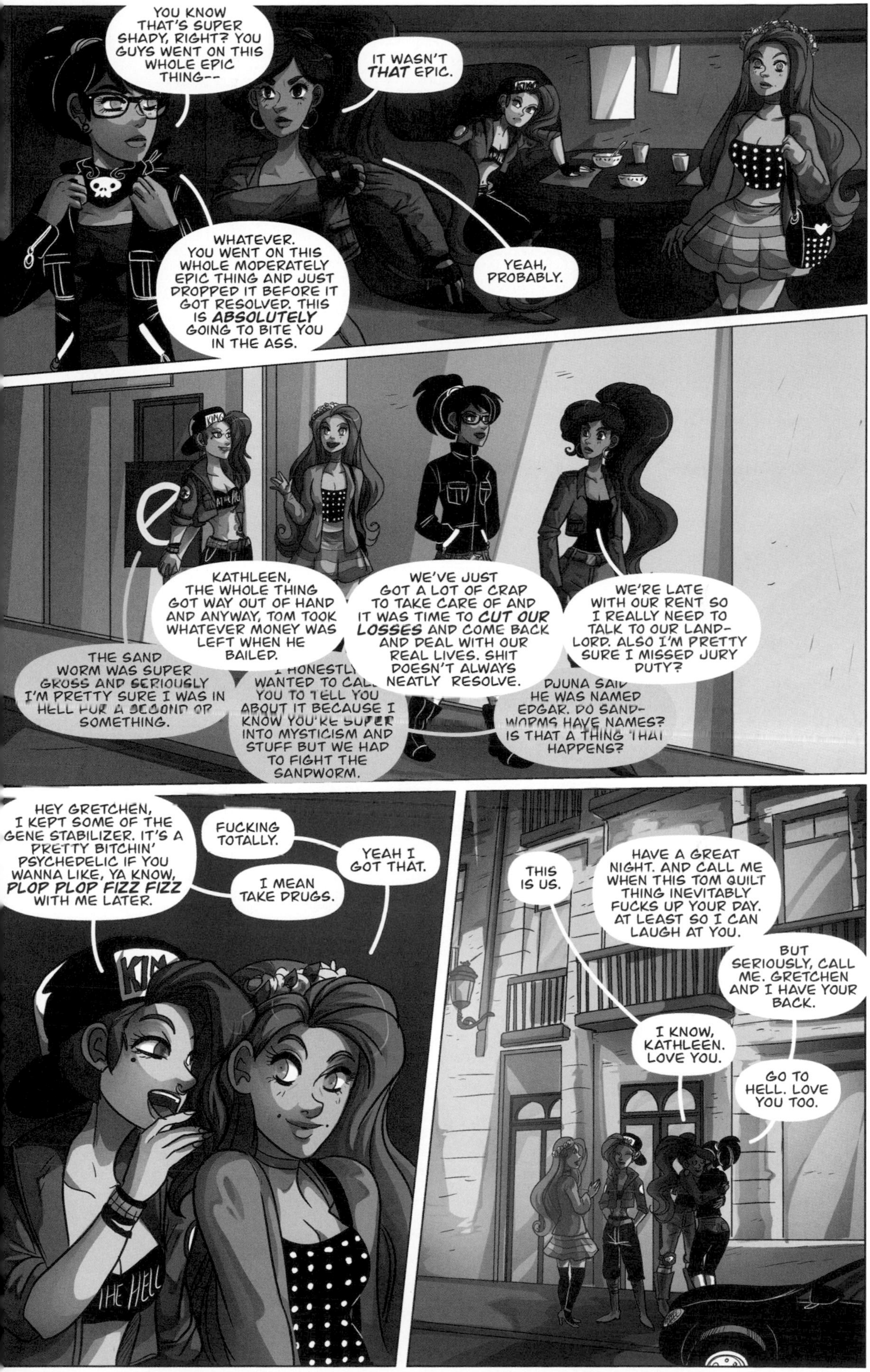
YOU KNOW THAT'S SUPER SHADY, RIGHT? YOU GUYS WENT ON THIS WHOLE EPIC THING--
IT WASN'T **THAT** EPIC.
WHATEVER. YOU WENT ON THIS WHOLE MODERATELY EPIC THING AND JUST DROPPED IT BEFORE IT GOT RESOLVED. THIS IS **ABSOLUTELY** GOING TO BITE YOU IN THE ASS.
YEAH, PROBABLY.
KATHLEEN, THE WHOLE THING GOT WAY OUT OF HAND AND ANYWAY, TOM TOOK WHATEVER MONEY WAS LEFT WHEN HE BAILED.
WE'VE JUST GOT A LOT OF CRAP TO TAKE CARE OF AND IT WAS TIME TO ***CUT OUR LOSSES*** AND COME BACK AND DEAL WITH OUR REAL LIVES. SHIT DOESN'T ALWAYS NEATLY RESOLVE.
WE'RE LATE WITH OUR RENT SO I REALLY NEED TO TALK TO OUR LAND-LORD. ALSO I'M PRETTY SURE I MISSED JURY DUTY?
THE SAND WORM WAS SUPER GROSS AND SERIOUSLY I'M PRETTY SURE I WAS IN HELL FOR A SECOND OR SOMETHING.
I HONESTLY WANTED TO CALL YOU TO TELL YOU ABOUT IT BECAUSE I KNOW YOU'RE SUPER INTO MYSTICISM AND STUFF BUT WE HAD TO FIGHT THE SANDWORM.
DJUNA SAID HE WAS NAMED EDGAR. DO SAND-WORMS HAVE NAMES? IS THAT A THING THAT HAPPENS?
HEY GRETCHEN, I KEPT SOME OF THE GENE STABILIZER. IT'S A PRETTY BITCHIN' PSYCHEDELIC IF YOU WANNA LIKE, YA KNOW, ***PLOP PLOP FIZZ FIZZ*** WITH ME LATER.
FUCKING TOTALLY.
YEAH I GOT THAT.
I MEAN TAKE DRUGS.
THIS IS US.
HAVE A GREAT NIGHT. AND CALL ME WHEN THIS TOM QUILT THING INEVITABLY FUCKS UP YOUR DAY. AT LEAST SO I CAN LAUGH AT YOU.
BUT SERIOUSLY, CALL ME. GRETCHEN AND I HAVE YOUR BACK.
I KNOW, KATHLEEN. LOVE YOU.
GO TO HELL. LOVE YOU TOO.

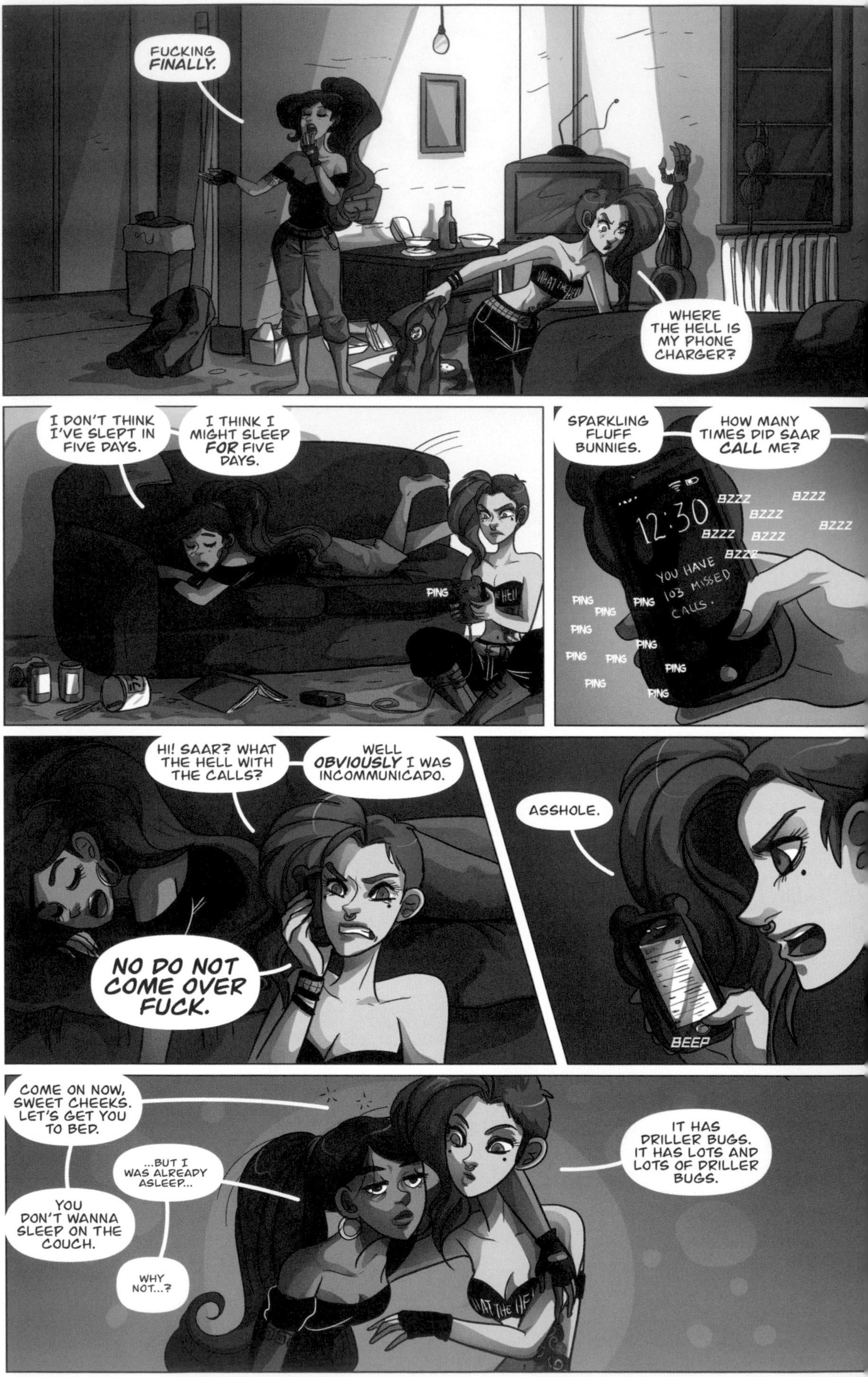
FUCKING FINALLY.
WHERE THE HELL IS MY PHONE CHARGER?
I DON'T THINK I'VE SLEPT IN FIVE DAYS.
I THINK I MIGHT SLEEP FOR FIVE DAYS.
PING
SPARKLING FLUFF BUNNIES.
HOW MANY TIMES DID SAAR CALL ME?
12:30
YOU HAVE 103 MISSED CALLS.
BZZZ BZZZ BZZZ BZZZ BZZZ BZZZ BZZZ
PING PING PING PING PING PING PING PING PING PING
HI! SAAR? WHAT THE HELL WITH THE CALLS?
WELL OBVIOUSLY I WAS INCOMMUNICADO.
NO DO NOT COME OVER FUCK.
ASSHOLE.
BEEP
COME ON NOW, SWEET CHEEKS. LET'S GET YOU TO BED.
...BUT I WAS ALREADY ASLEEP...
YOU DON'T WANNA SLEEP ON THE COUCH.
WHY NOT...?
IT HAS DRILLER BUGS. IT HAS LOTS AND LOTS OF DRILLER BUGS.

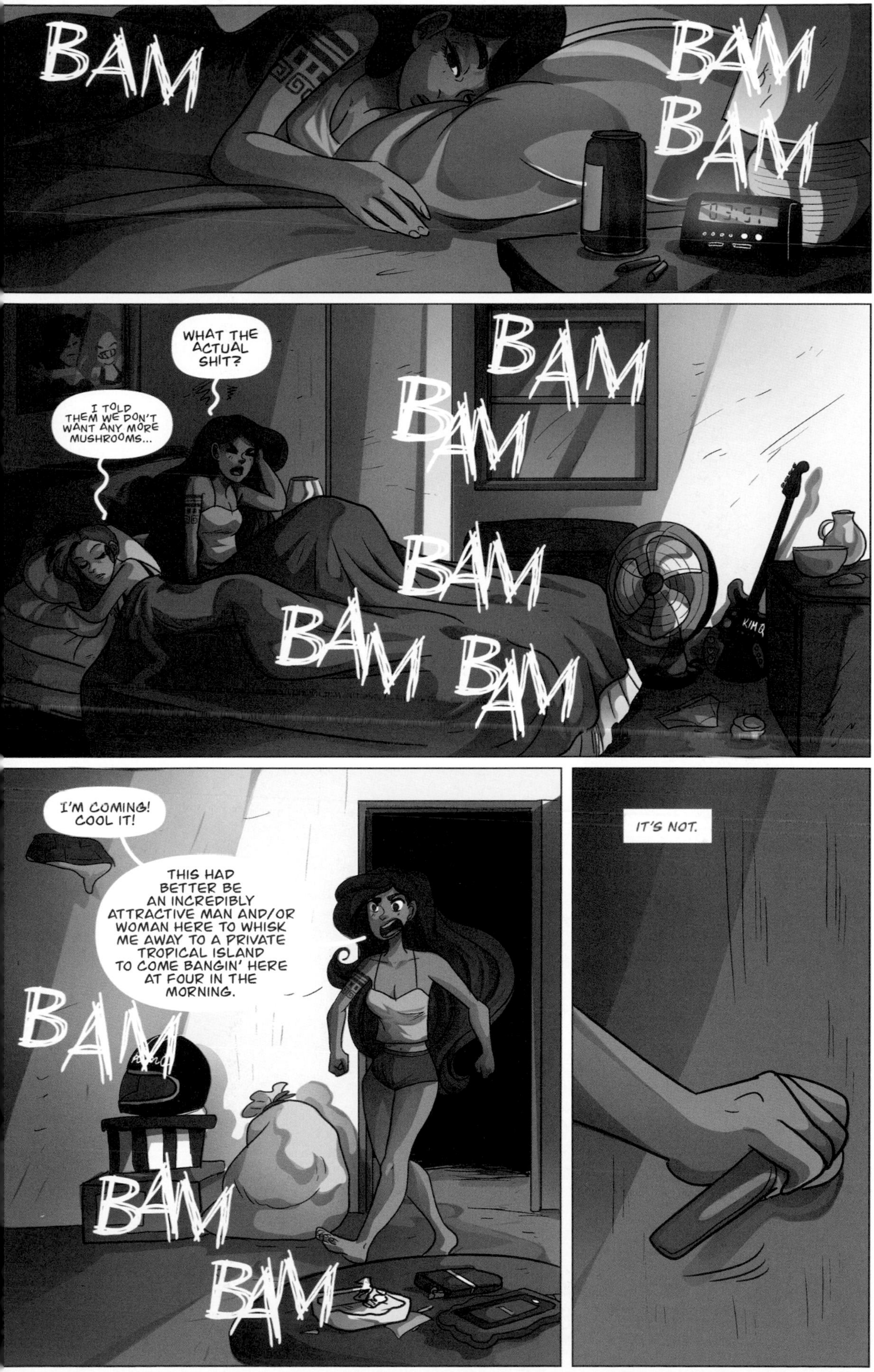
BAM
BAM
BAM
WHAT THE ACTUAL SHIT?
I TOLD THEM WE DON'T WANT ANY MORE MUSHROOMS...
BAM
BAM
BAM
BAM
BAM
KIMQ
I'M COMING! COOL IT!
THIS HAD BETTER BE AN INCREDIBLY ATTRACTIVE MAN AND/OR WOMAN HERE TO WHISK ME AWAY TO A PRIVATE TROPICAL ISLAND TO COME BANGIN' HERE AT FOUR IN THE MORNING.
BAM
BAM
BAM
IT'S NOT.

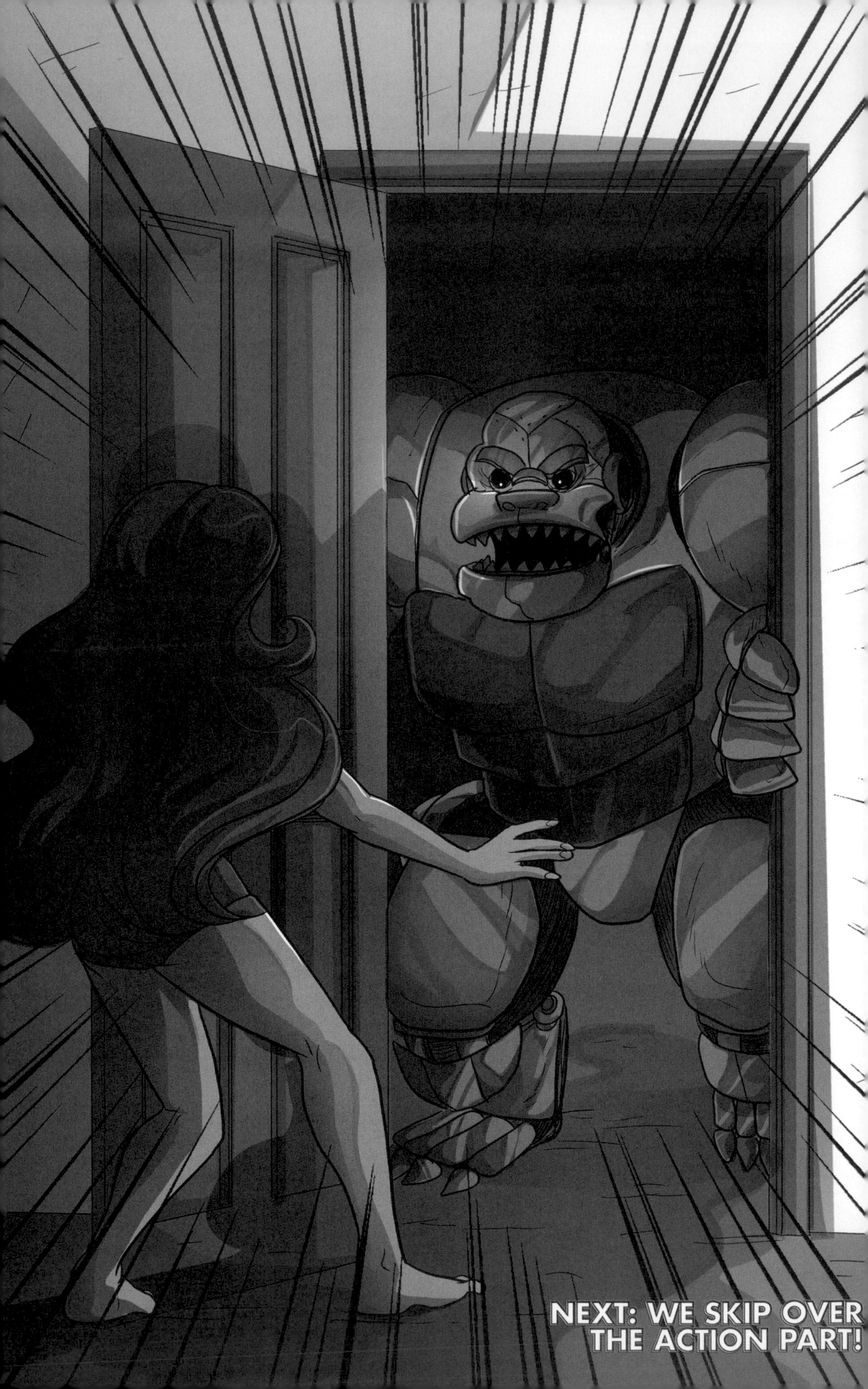
NEXT: WE SKIP OVER THE ACTION PART!

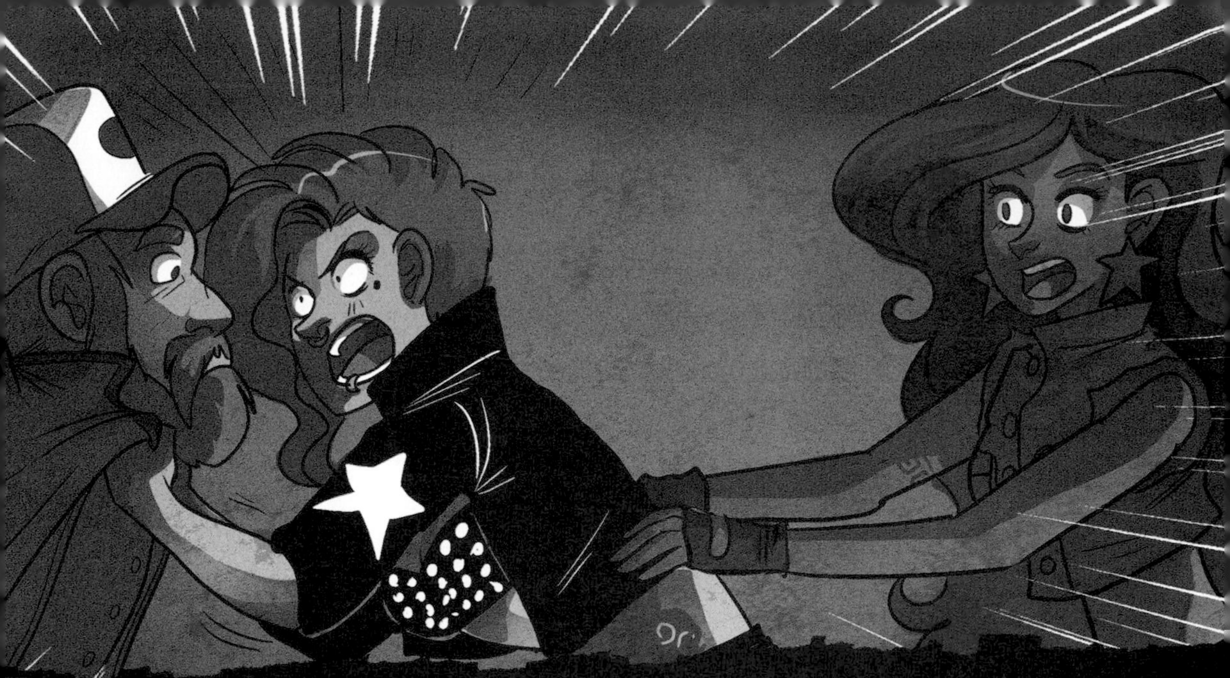

4

"THE SHITTY DAY FILE"

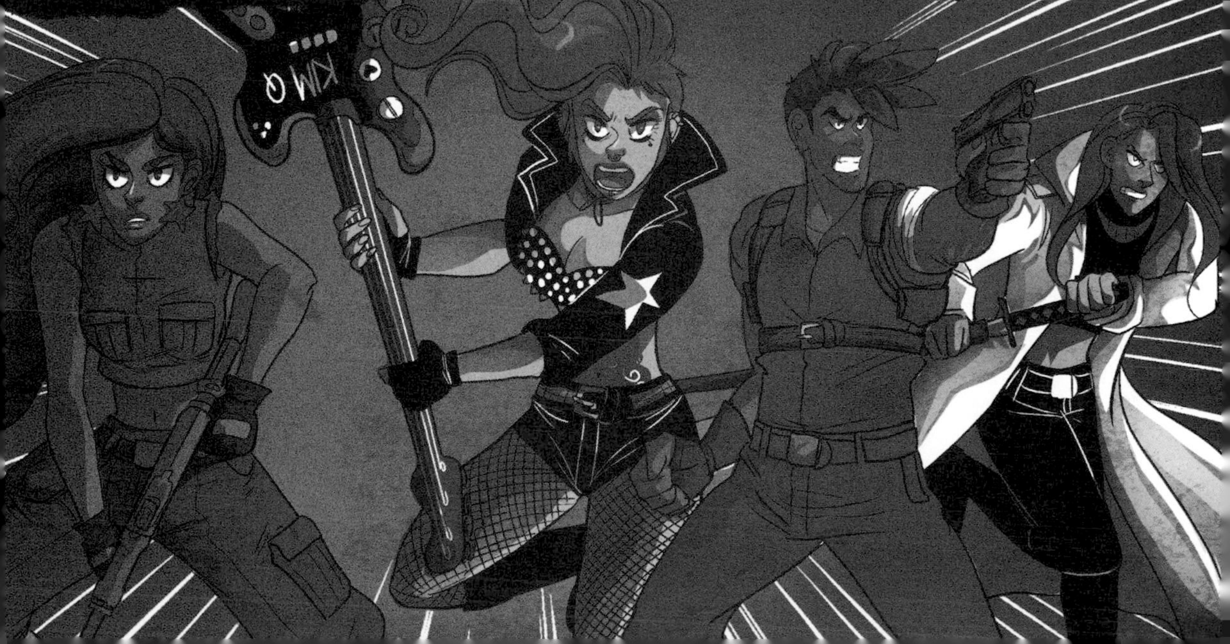
KIM Q

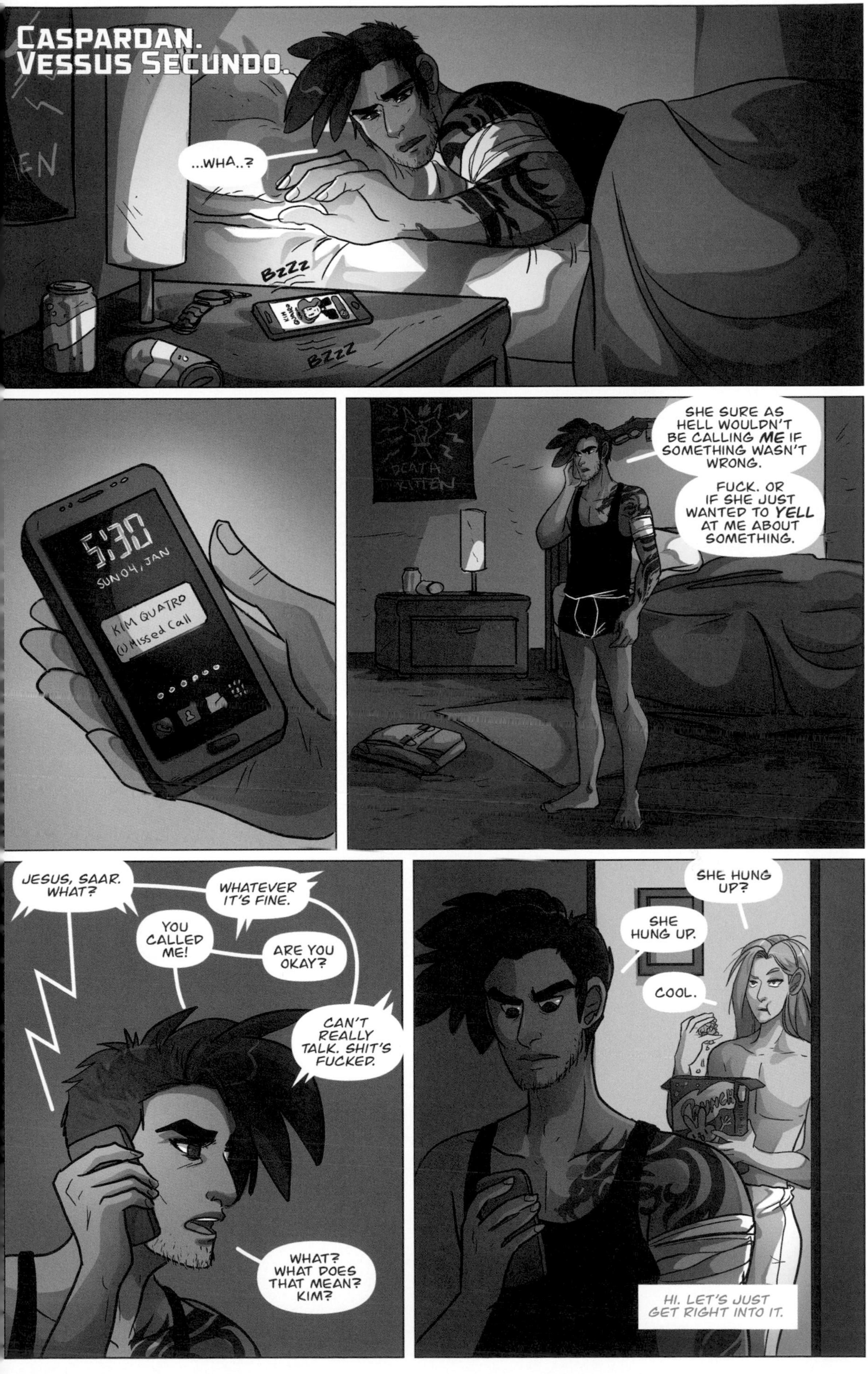
CASPARDAN.
VESSUS SECUNDO.
...WHA..?
BZZZ
BZZZ
5:30
SUN 04, JAN
KIM QUATRO
(1) Missed Call
SHE SURE AS HELL WOULDN'T BE CALLING ME IF SOMETHING WASN'T WRONG.
FUCK. OR IF SHE JUST WANTED TO YELL AT ME ABOUT SOMETHING.
JESUS, SAAR. WHAT?
WHATEVER IT'S FINE.
YOU CALLED ME!
ARE YOU OKAY?
CAN'T REALLY TALK. SHIT'S FUCKED.
WHAT? WHAT DOES THAT MEAN? KIM?
SHE HUNG UP?
SHE HUNG UP.
COOL.
HI. LET'S JUST GET RIGHT INTO IT.

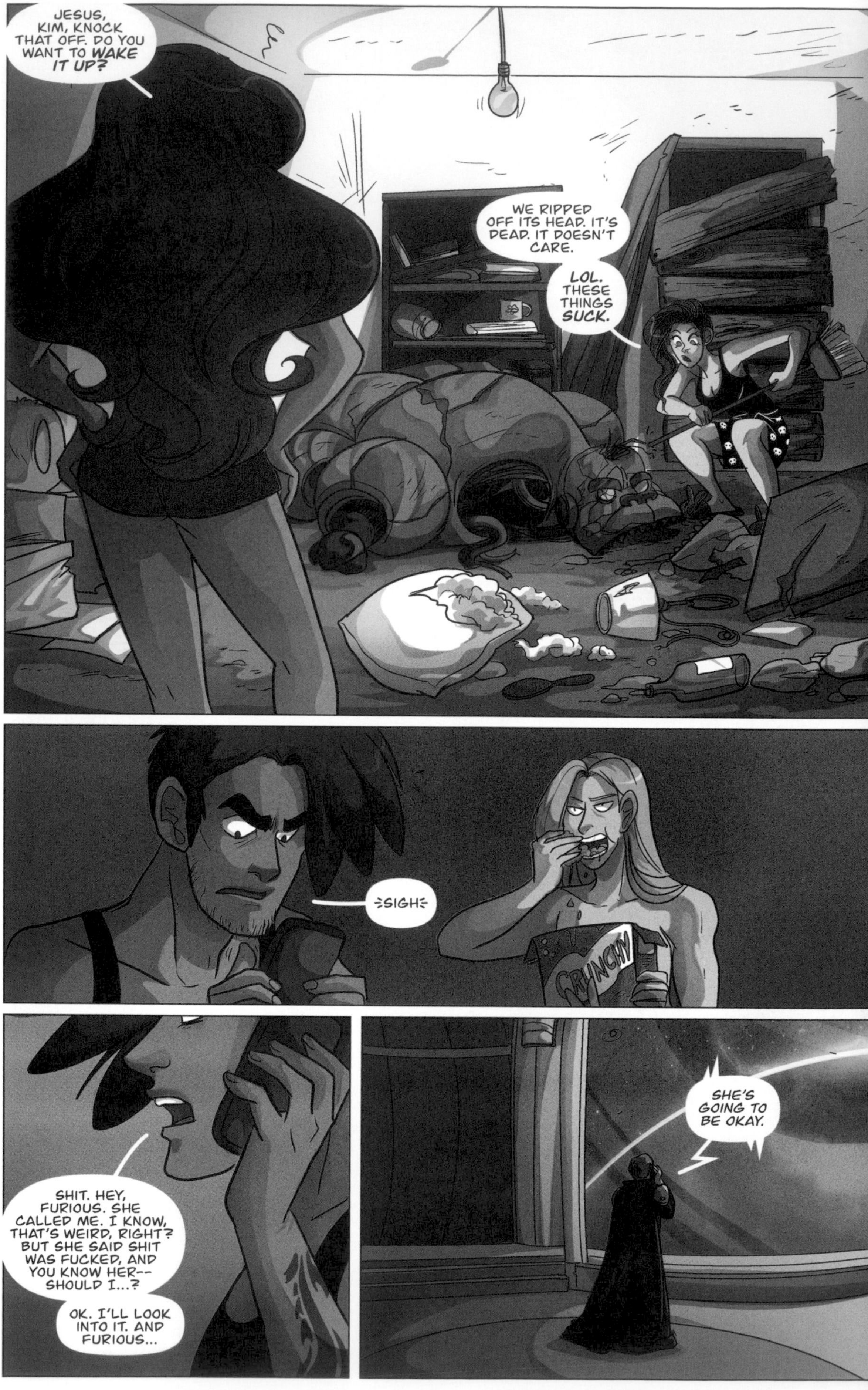
JESUS, KIM, KNOCK THAT OFF. DO YOU WANT TO WAKE IT UP?
WE RIPPED OFF ITS HEAD. IT'S DEAD. IT DOESN'T CARE.
LOL. THESE THINGS SUCK.
SIGH
CRUNCHY
SHIT. HEY, FURIOUS. SHE CALLED ME. I KNOW, THAT'S WEIRD, RIGHT? BUT SHE SAID SHIT WAS FUCKED, AND YOU KNOW HER-- SHOULD I...?
OK. I'LL LOOK INTO IT. AND FURIOUS...
SHE'S GOING TO BE OKAY.

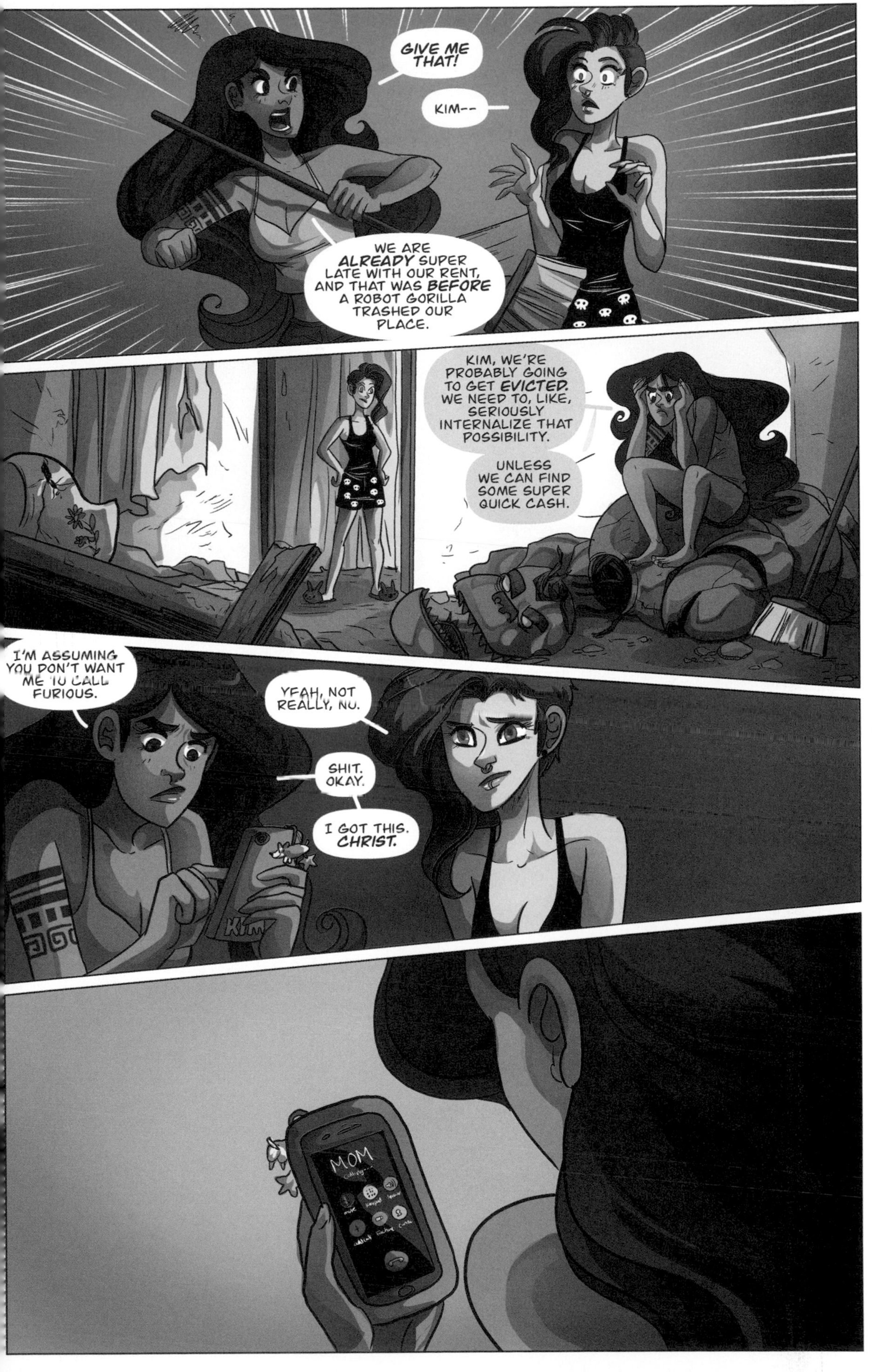
GIVE ME THAT!
KIM--
WE ARE **ALREADY** SUPER LATE WITH OUR RENT, AND THAT WAS **BEFORE** A ROBOT GORILLA TRASHED OUR PLACE.
KIM, WE'RE PROBABLY GOING TO GET **EVICTED**. WE NEED TO, LIKE, SERIOUSLY INTERNALIZE THAT POSSIBILITY.
UNLESS WE CAN FIND SOME SUPER QUICK CASH.
I'M ASSUMING YOU DON'T WANT ME TO CALL FURIOUS.
YEAH, NOT REALLY, NO.
SHIT. OKAY.
I GOT THIS. **CHRIST.**
MOM

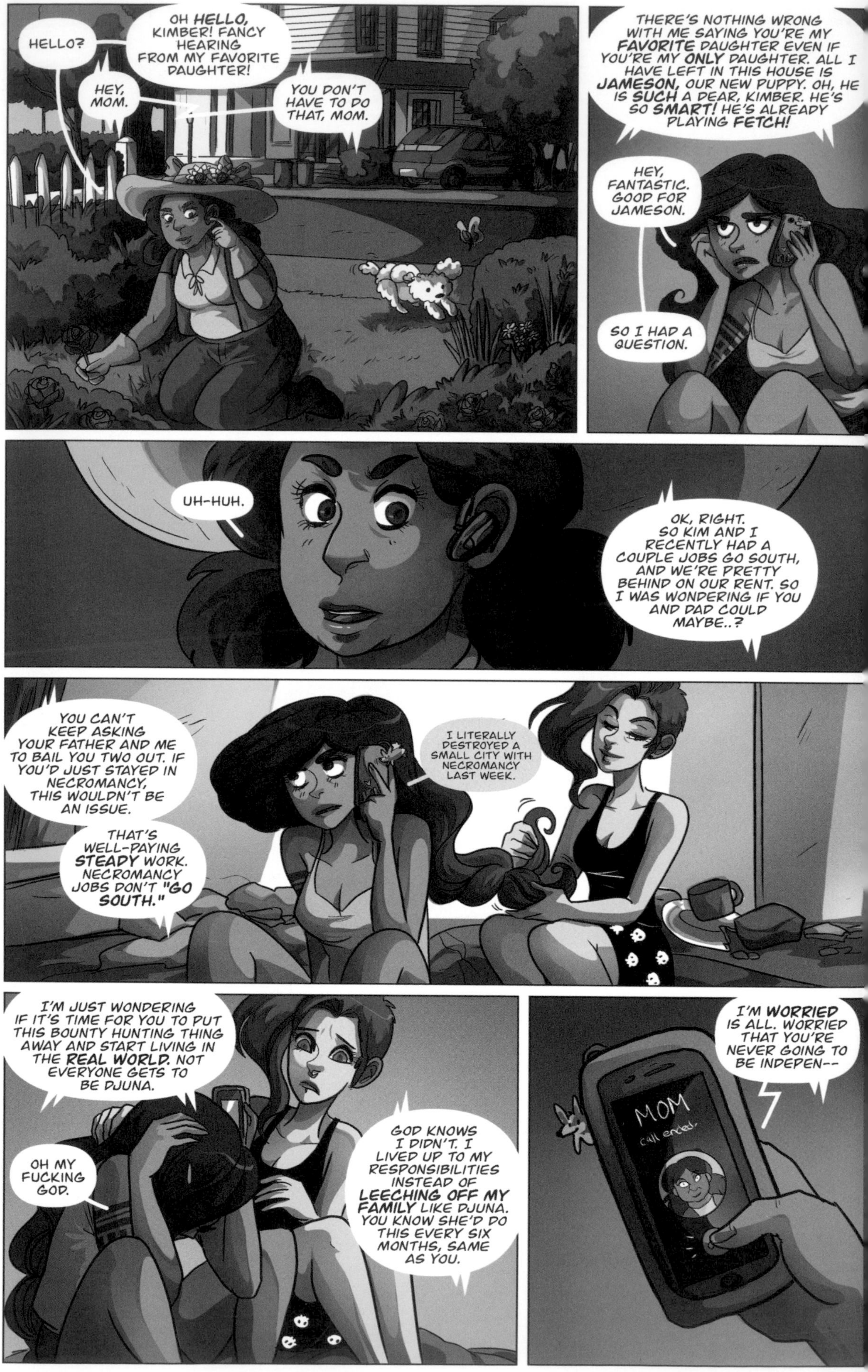
HELLO?
OH HELLO, KIMBER! FANCY HEARING FROM MY FAVORITE DAUGHTER!
HEY, MOM.
YOU DON'T HAVE TO DO THAT, MOM.
THERE'S NOTHING WRONG WITH ME SAYING YOU'RE MY FAVORITE DAUGHTER EVEN IF YOU'RE MY ONLY DAUGHTER. ALL I HAVE LEFT IN THIS HOUSE IS JAMESON, OUR NEW PUPPY. OH, HE IS SUCH A DEAR, KIMBER. HE'S SO SMART! HE'S ALREADY PLAYING FETCH!
HEY, FANTASTIC. GOOD FOR JAMESON.
SO I HAD A QUESTION.
UH-HUH.
OK, RIGHT. SO KIM AND I RECENTLY HAD A COUPLE JOBS GO SOUTH, AND WE'RE PRETTY BEHIND ON OUR RENT. SO I WAS WONDERING IF YOU AND DAD COULD MAYBE..?
YOU CAN'T KEEP ASKING YOUR FATHER AND ME TO BAIL YOU TWO OUT. IF YOU'D JUST STAYED IN NECROMANCY, THIS WOULDN'T BE AN ISSUE.
THAT'S WELL-PAYING STEADY WORK. NECROMANCY JOBS DON'T "GO SOUTH."
I LITERALLY DESTROYED A SMALL CITY WITH NECROMANCY LAST WEEK.
I'M JUST WONDERING IF IT'S TIME FOR YOU TO PUT THIS BOUNTY HUNTING THING AWAY AND START LIVING IN THE REAL WORLD. NOT EVERYONE GETS TO BE DJUNA.
OH MY FUCKING GOD.
GOD KNOWS I DIDN'T. I LIVED UP TO MY RESPONSIBILITIES INSTEAD OF LEECHING OFF MY FAMILY LIKE DJUNA. YOU KNOW SHE'D DO THIS EVERY SIX MONTHS, SAME AS YOU.
I'M WORRIED IS ALL. WORRIED THAT YOU'RE NEVER GOING TO BE INDEPEN--
MOM
call ended.

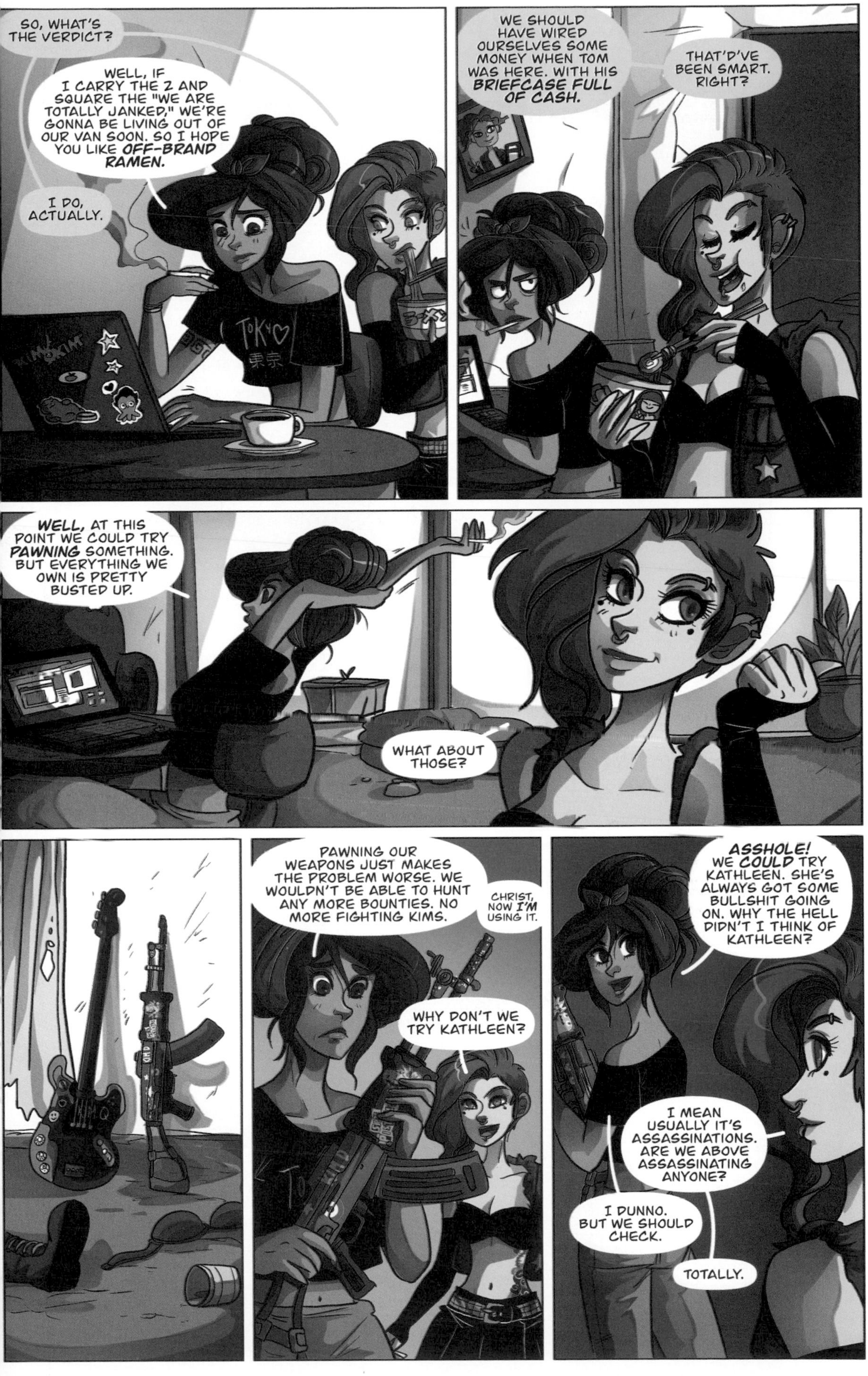
SO, WHAT'S THE VERDICT?
WELL, IF I CARRY THE 2 AND SQUARE THE "WE ARE TOTALLY JANKED," WE'RE GONNA BE LIVING OUT OF OUR VAN SOON. SO I HOPE YOU LIKE OFF-BRAND RAMEN.
I DO, ACTUALLY.
WE SHOULD HAVE WIRED OURSELVES SOME MONEY WHEN TOM WAS HERE. WITH HIS BRIEFCASE FULL OF CASH.
THAT'D'VE BEEN SMART. RIGHT?
WELL, AT THIS POINT WE COULD TRY PAWNING SOMETHING. BUT EVERYTHING WE OWN IS PRETTY BUSTED UP.
WHAT ABOUT THOSE?
PAWNING OUR WEAPONS JUST MAKES THE PROBLEM WORSE. WE WOULDN'T BE ABLE TO HUNT ANY MORE BOUNTIES. NO MORE FIGHTING KIMS.
CHRIST, NOW I'M USING IT.
WHY DON'T WE TRY KATHLEEN?
ASSHOLE! WE COULD TRY KATHLEEN. SHE'S ALWAYS GOT SOME BULLSHIT GOING ON. WHY THE HELL DIDN'T I THINK OF KATHLEEN?
I MEAN USUALLY IT'S ASSASSINATIONS. ARE WE ABOVE ASSASSINATING ANYONE?
I DUNNO. BUT WE SHOULD CHECK.
TOTALLY.

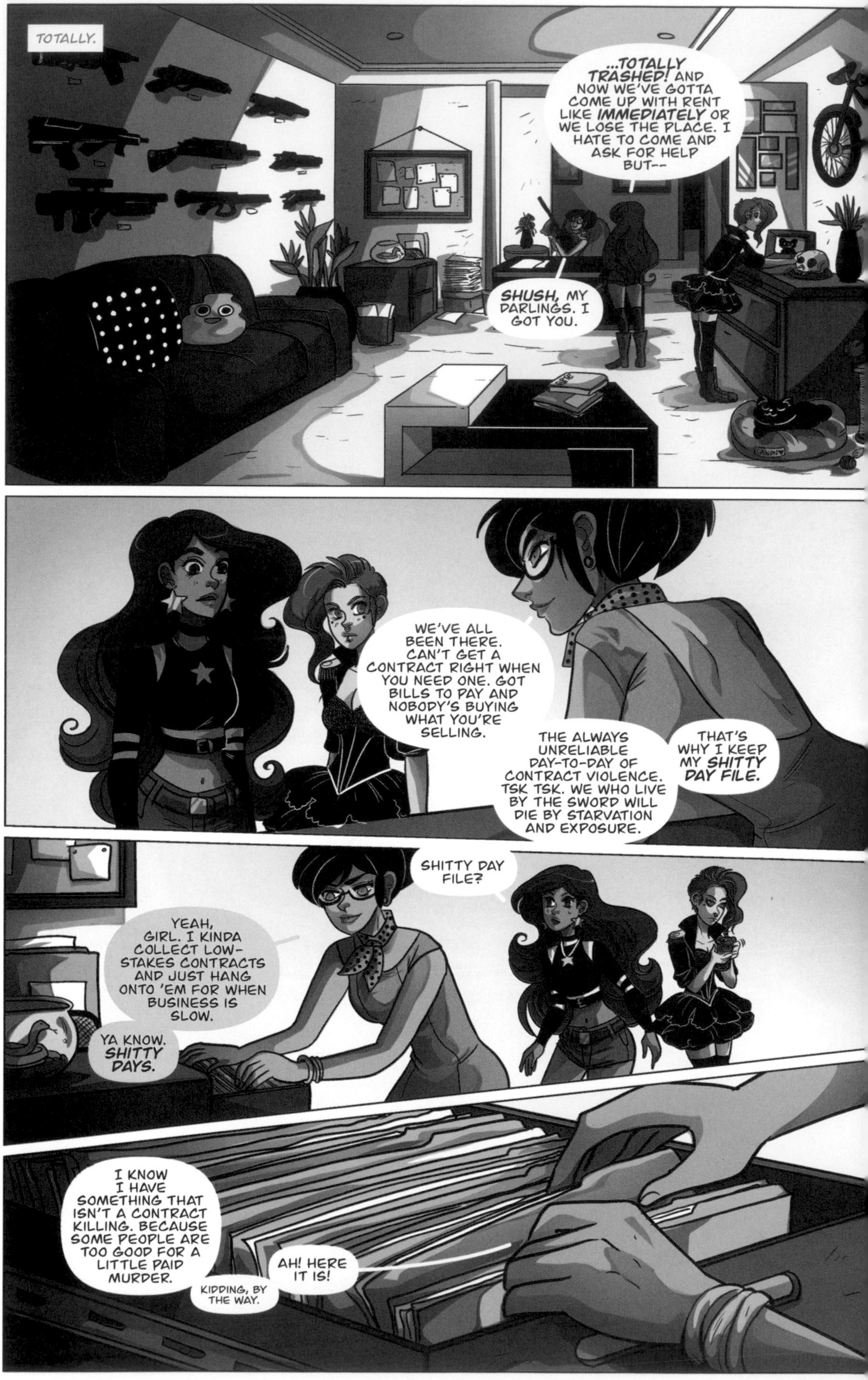
TOTALLY.
...TOTALLY TRASHED! AND NOW WE'VE GOTTA COME UP WITH RENT LIKE IMMEDIATELY OR WE LOSE THE PLACE. I HATE TO COME AND ASK FOR HELP BUT--
SHUSH, MY DARLINGS. I GOT YOU.
WE'VE ALL BEEN THERE. CAN'T GET A CONTRACT RIGHT WHEN YOU NEED ONE. GOT BILLS TO PAY AND NOBODY'S BUYING WHAT YOU'RE SELLING.
THE ALWAYS UNRELIABLE DAY-TO-DAY OF CONTRACT VIOLENCE. TSK TSK. WE WHO LIVE BY THE SWORD WILL DIE BY STARVATION AND EXPOSURE.
THAT'S WHY I KEEP MY SHITTY DAY FILE.
SHITTY DAY FILE?
YEAH, GIRL. I KINDA COLLECT LOW-STAKES CONTRACTS AND JUST HANG ONTO 'EM FOR WHEN BUSINESS IS SLOW.
YA KNOW. SHITTY DAYS.
I KNOW I HAVE SOMETHING THAT ISN'T A CONTRACT KILLING. BECAUSE SOME PEOPLE ARE TOO GOOD FOR A LITTLE PAID MURDER.
KIDDING, BY THE WAY.
AH! HERE IT IS!

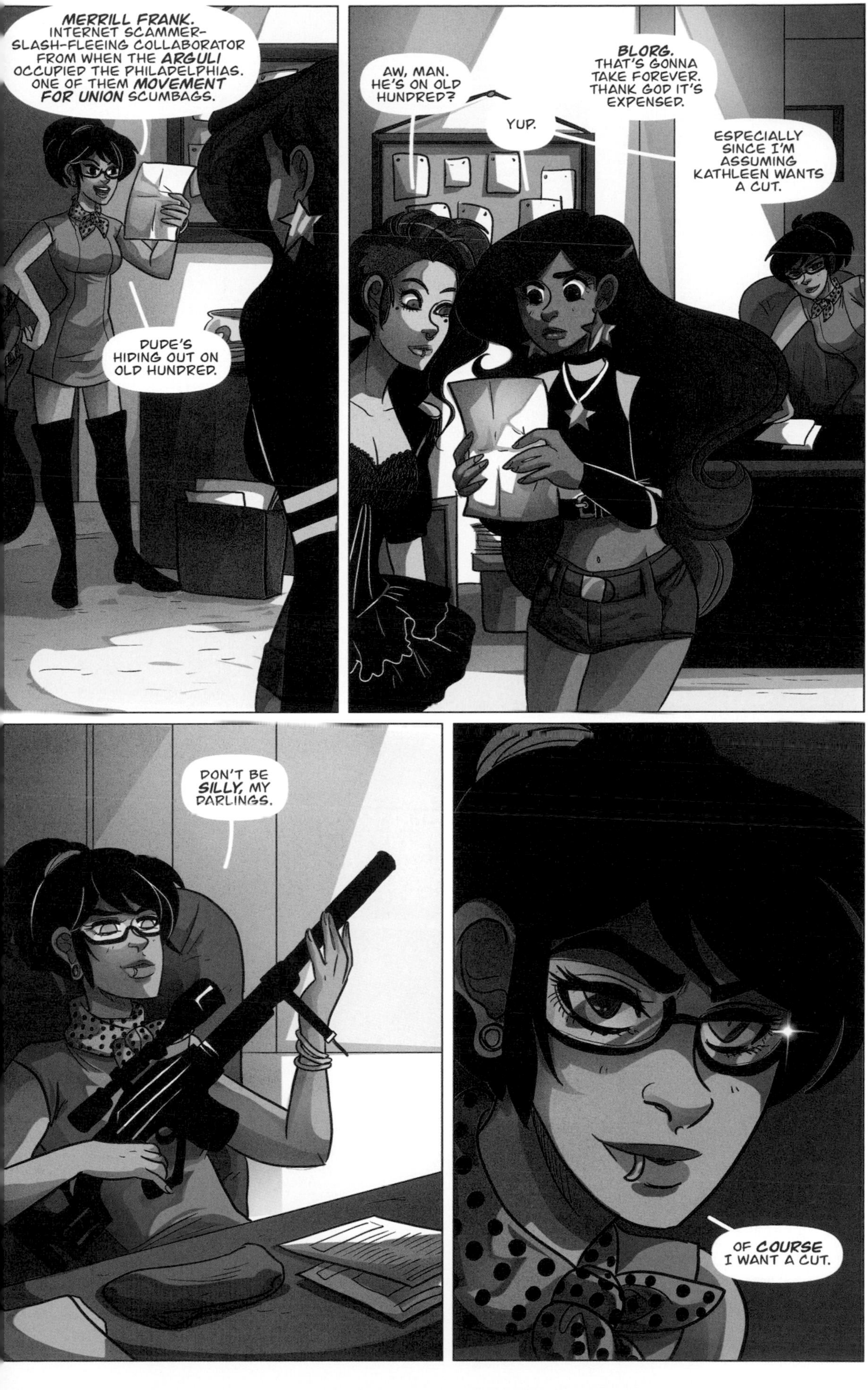
MERRILL FRANK. INTERNET SCAMMER-SLASH-FLEEING COLLABORATOR FROM WHEN THE ARGULI OCCUPIED THE PHILADELPHIAS. ONE OF THEM MOVEMENT FOR UNION SCUMBAGS.
DUDE'S HIDING OUT ON OLD HUNDRED.
AW, MAN. HE'S ON OLD HUNDRED?
YUP.
BLORG. THAT'S GONNA TAKE FOREVER. THANK GOD IT'S EXPENSED.
ESPECIALLY SINCE I'M ASSUMING KATHLEEN WANTS A CUT.
DON'T BE SILLY, MY DARLINGS.
OF COURSE I WANT A CUT.

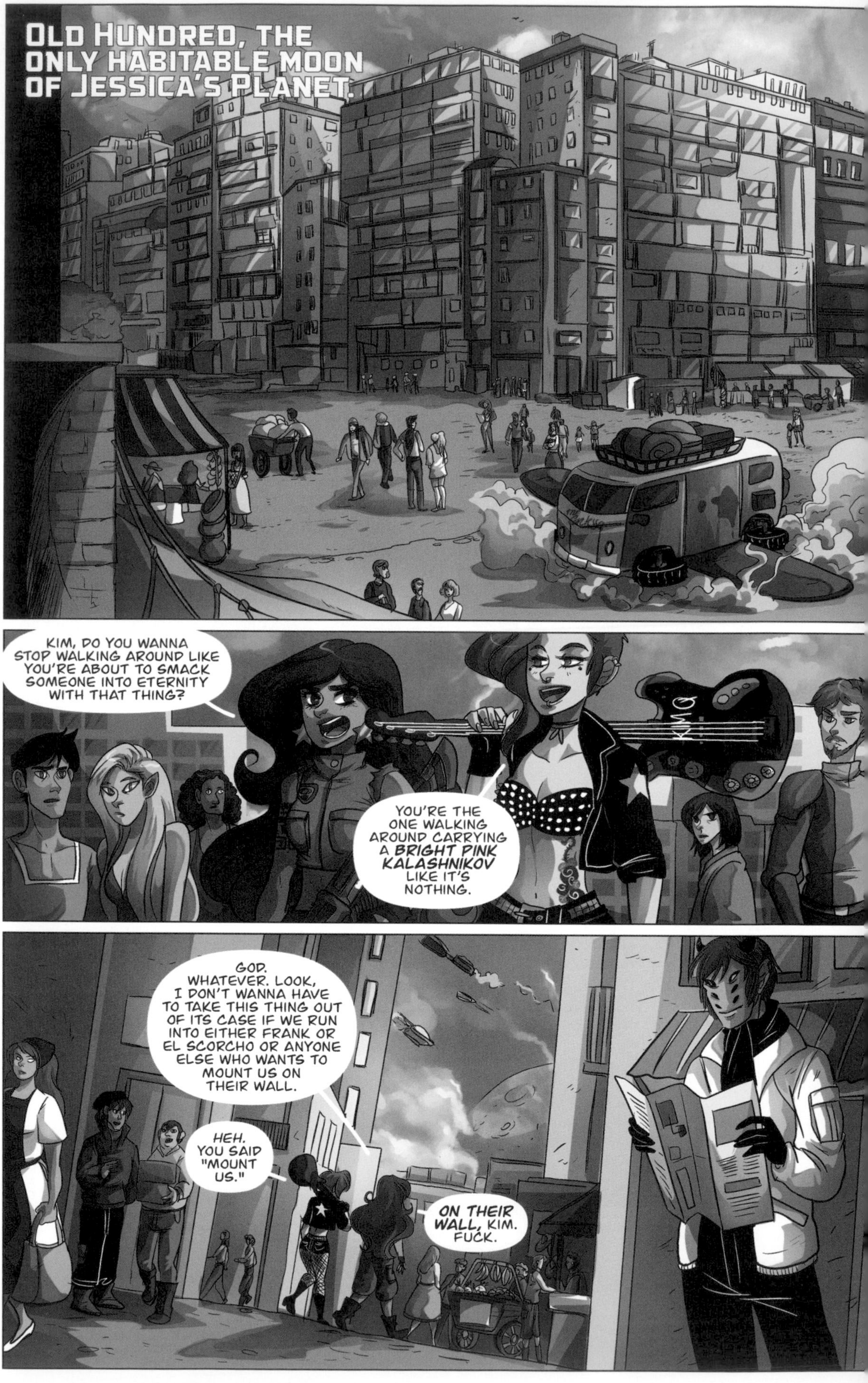
OLD HUNDRED, THE ONLY HABITABLE MOON OF JESSICA'S PLANET.
KIM, DO YOU WANNA STOP WALKING AROUND LIKE YOU'RE ABOUT TO SMACK SOMEONE INTO ETERNITY WITH THAT THING?
YOU'RE THE ONE WALKING AROUND CARRYING A **BRIGHT PINK KALASHNIKOV** LIKE IT'S NOTHING.
KIM Q
GOD. WHATEVER. LOOK, I DON'T WANNA HAVE TO TAKE THIS THING OUT OF ITS CASE IF WE RUN INTO EITHER FRANK OR EL SCORCHO OR ANYONE ELSE WHO WANTS TO MOUNT US ON THEIR WALL.
HEH. YOU SAID "MOUNT US."
ON THEIR WALL, KIM. FUCK.

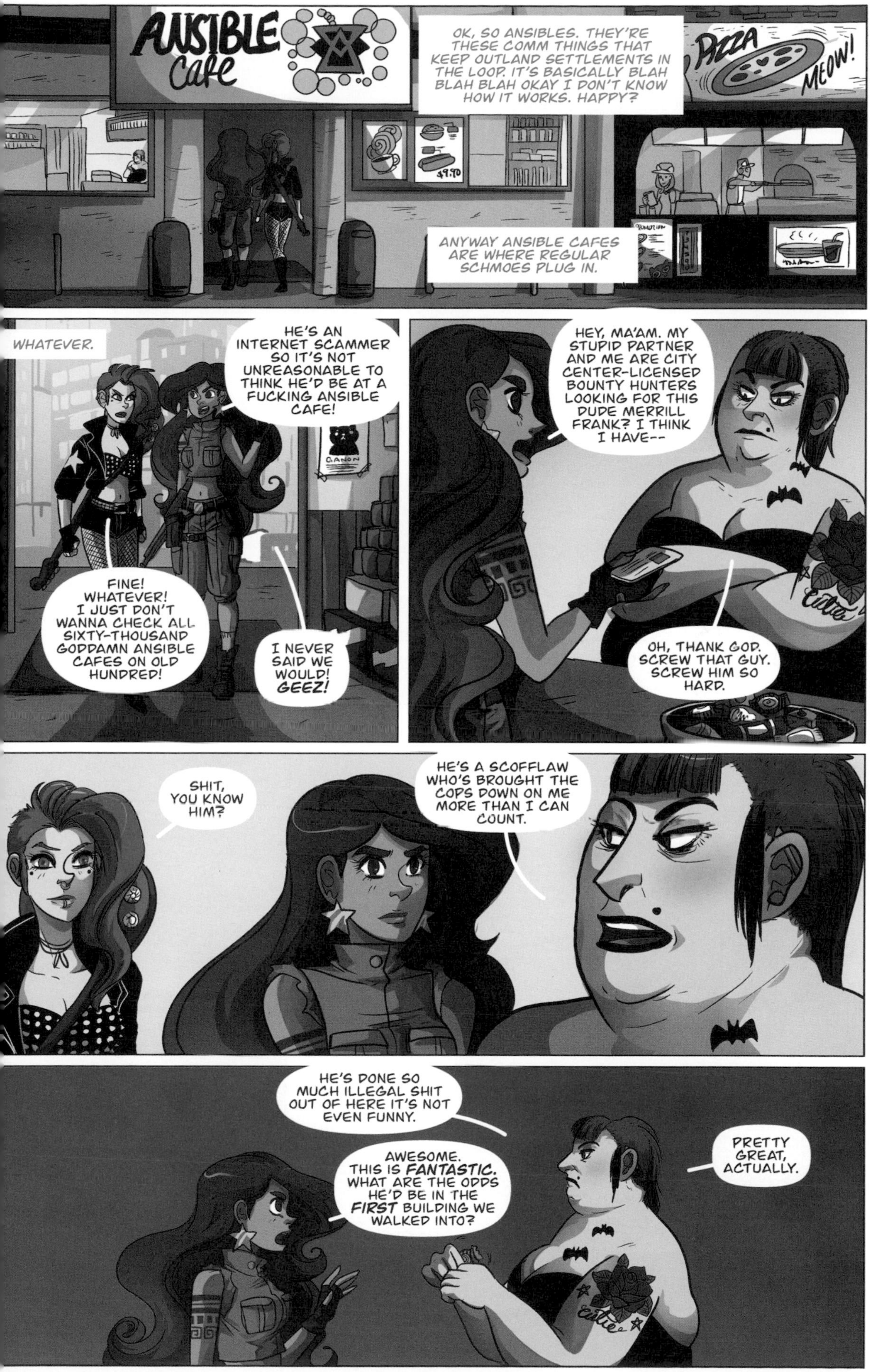
ANSIBLE Cafe
OK, SO ANSIBLES. THEY'RE THESE COMM THINGS THAT KEEP OUTLAND SETTLEMENTS IN THE LOOP. IT'S BASICALLY BLAH BLAH BLAH OKAY I DON'T KNOW HOW IT WORKS. HAPPY?
PIZZA
MEOW!
ANYWAY ANSIBLE CAFES ARE WHERE REGULAR SCHMOES PLUG IN.
WHATEVER.
HE'S AN INTERNET SCAMMER SO IT'S NOT UNREASONABLE TO THINK HE'D BE AT A FUCKING ANSIBLE CAFE!
FINE! WHATEVER! I JUST DON'T WANNA CHECK ALL SIXTY-THOUSAND GODDAMN ANSIBLE CAFES ON OLD HUNDRED!
I NEVER SAID WE WOULD! GEEZ!
HEY, MA'AM. MY STUPID PARTNER AND ME ARE CITY CENTER-LICENSED BOUNTY HUNTERS LOOKING FOR THIS DUDE MERRILL FRANK? I THINK I HAVE--
OH, THANK GOD. SCREW THAT GUY. SCREW HIM SO HARD.
SHIT, YOU KNOW HIM?
HE'S A SCOFFLAW WHO'S BROUGHT THE COPS DOWN ON ME MORE THAN I CAN COUNT.
HE'S DONE SO MUCH ILLEGAL SHIT OUT OF HERE IT'S NOT EVEN FUNNY.
AWESOME. THIS IS FANTASTIC. WHAT ARE THE ODDS HE'D BE IN THE FIRST BUILDING WE WALKED INTO?
PRETTY GREAT, ACTUALLY.

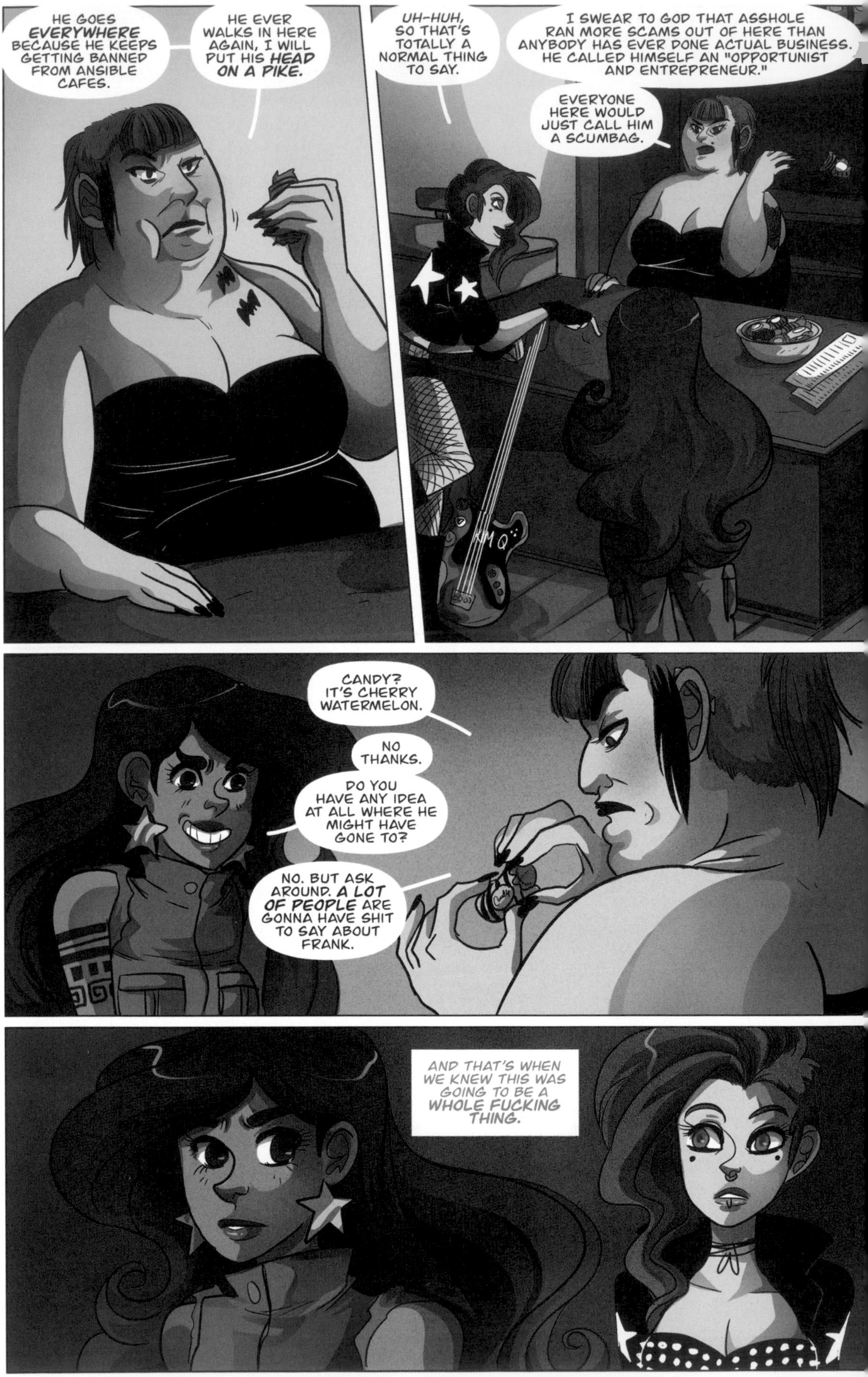
HE GOES EVERYWHERE BECAUSE HE KEEPS GETTING BANNED FROM ANSIBLE CAFES.
HE EVER WALKS IN HERE AGAIN, I WILL PUT HIS HEAD ON A PIKE.
UH-HUH, SO THAT'S TOTALLY A NORMAL THING TO SAY.
I SWEAR TO GOD THAT ASSHOLE RAN MORE SCAMS OUT OF HERE THAN ANYBODY HAS EVER DONE ACTUAL BUSINESS. HE CALLED HIMSELF AN "OPPORTUNIST AND ENTREPRENEUR."
EVERYONE HERE WOULD JUST CALL HIM A SCUMBAG.
CANDY? IT'S CHERRY WATERMELON.
NO THANKS.
DO YOU HAVE ANY IDEA AT ALL WHERE HE MIGHT HAVE GONE TO?
NO. BUT ASK AROUND. A LOT OF PEOPLE ARE GONNA HAVE SHIT TO SAY ABOUT FRANK.
AND THAT'S WHEN WE KNEW THIS WAS GOING TO BE A WHOLE FUCKING THING.

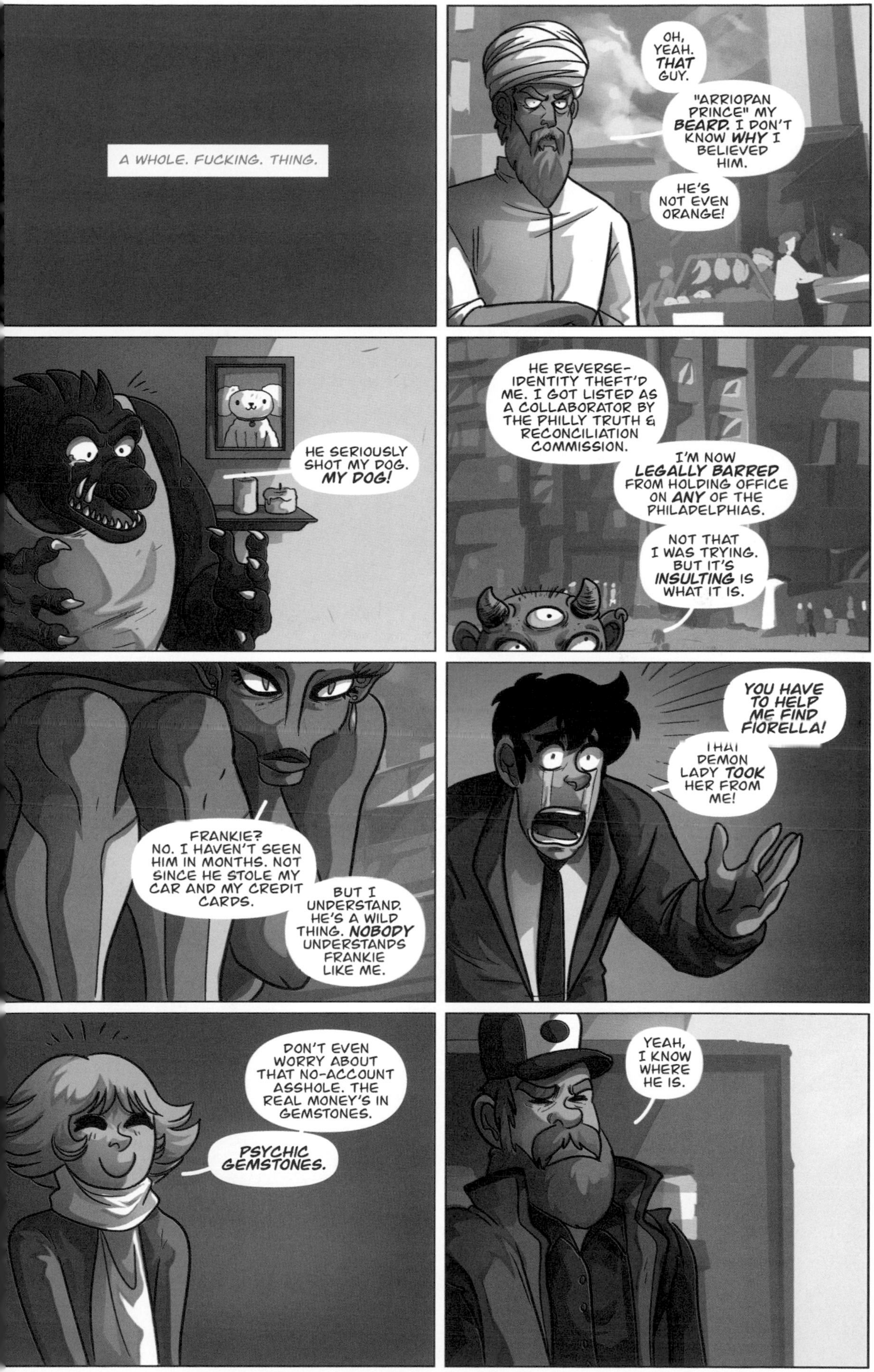
A WHOLE. FUCKING. THING.
OH, YEAH. THAT GUY.
"ARRIOPAN PRINCE" MY BEARD. I DON'T KNOW WHY I BELIEVED HIM.
HE'S NOT EVEN ORANGE!
HE SERIOUSLY SHOT MY DOG. MY DOG!
HE REVERSE-IDENTITY THEFT'D ME. I GOT LISTED AS A COLLABORATOR BY THE PHILLY TRUTH & RECONCILIATION COMMISSION.
I'M NOW LEGALLY BARRED FROM HOLDING OFFICE ON ANY OF THE PHILADELPHIAS.
NOT THAT I WAS TRYING. BUT IT'S INSULTING IS WHAT IT IS.
FRANKIE? NO. I HAVEN'T SEEN HIM IN MONTHS. NOT SINCE HE STOLE MY CAR AND MY CREDIT CARDS.
BUT I UNDERSTAND. HE'S A WILD THING. NOBODY UNDERSTANDS FRANKIE LIKE ME.
YOU HAVE TO HELP ME FIND FIORELLA!
THAT DEMON LADY TOOK HER FROM ME!
DON'T EVEN WORRY ABOUT THAT NO-ACCOUNT ASSHOLE. THE REAL MONEY'S IN GEMSTONES.
PSYCHIC GEMSTONES.
YEAH, I KNOW WHERE HE IS.

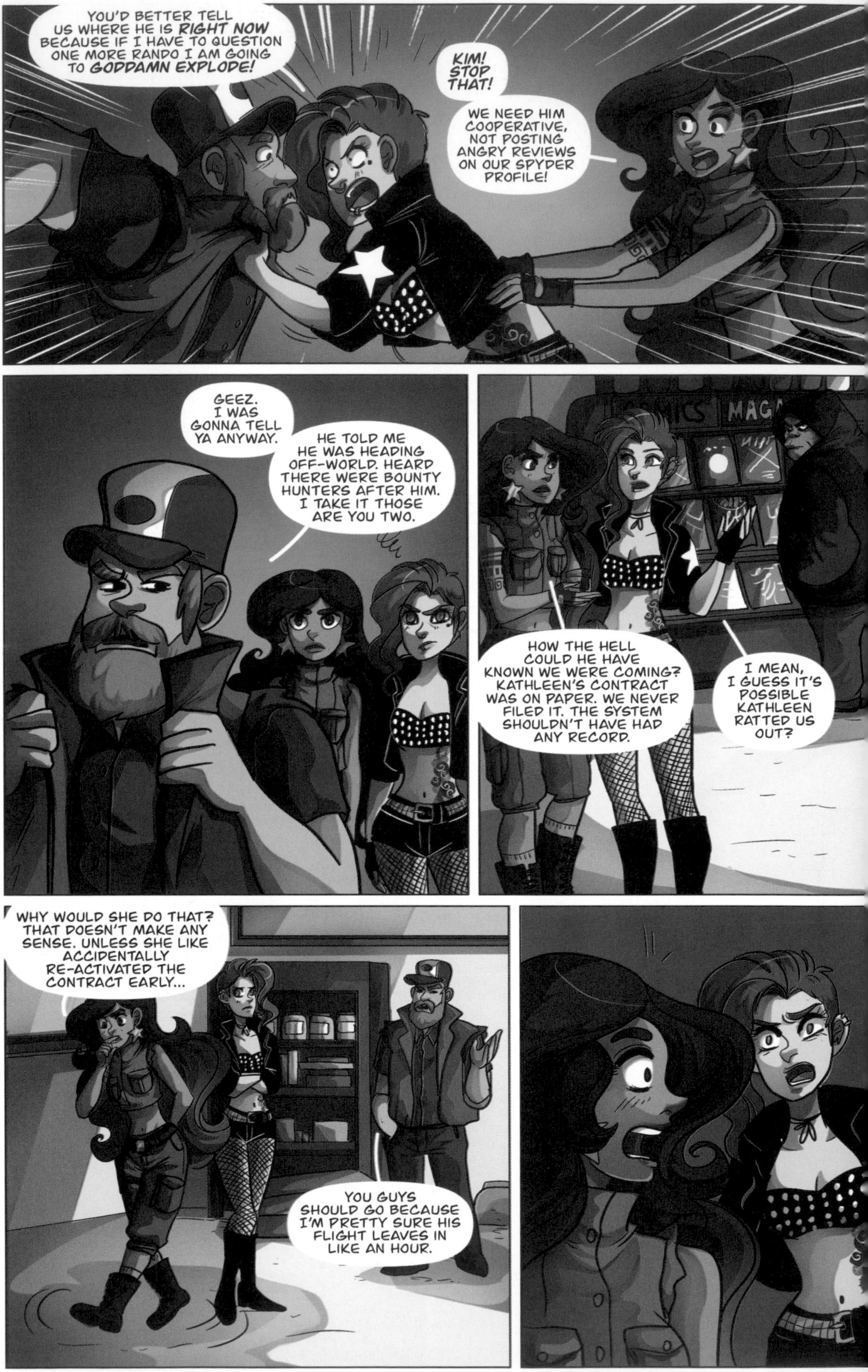

YOU'D BETTER TELL US WHERE HE IS RIGHT NOW BECAUSE IF I HAVE TO QUESTION ONE MORE RANDO I AM GOING TO GODDAMN EXPLODE!
KIM! STOP THAT!
WE NEED HIM COOPERATIVE, NOT POSTING ANGRY REVIEWS ON OUR SPYDER PROFILE!
GEEZ. I WAS GONNA TELL YA ANYWAY.
HE TOLD ME HE WAS HEADING OFF-WORLD. HEARD THERE WERE BOUNTY HUNTERS AFTER HIM. I TAKE IT THOSE ARE YOU TWO.
HOW THE HELL COULD HE HAVE KNOWN WE WERE COMING? KATHLEEN'S CONTRACT WAS ON PAPER. WE NEVER FILED IT. THE SYSTEM SHOULDN'T HAVE HAD ANY RECORD.
I MEAN, I GUESS IT'S POSSIBLE KATHLEEN RATTED US OUT?
WHY WOULD SHE DO THAT? THAT DOESN'T MAKE ANY SENSE. UNLESS SHE LIKE ACCIDENTALLY RE-ACTIVATED THE CONTRACT EARLY...
YOU GUYS SHOULD GO BECAUSE I'M PRETTY SURE HIS FLIGHT LEAVES IN LIKE AN HOUR.

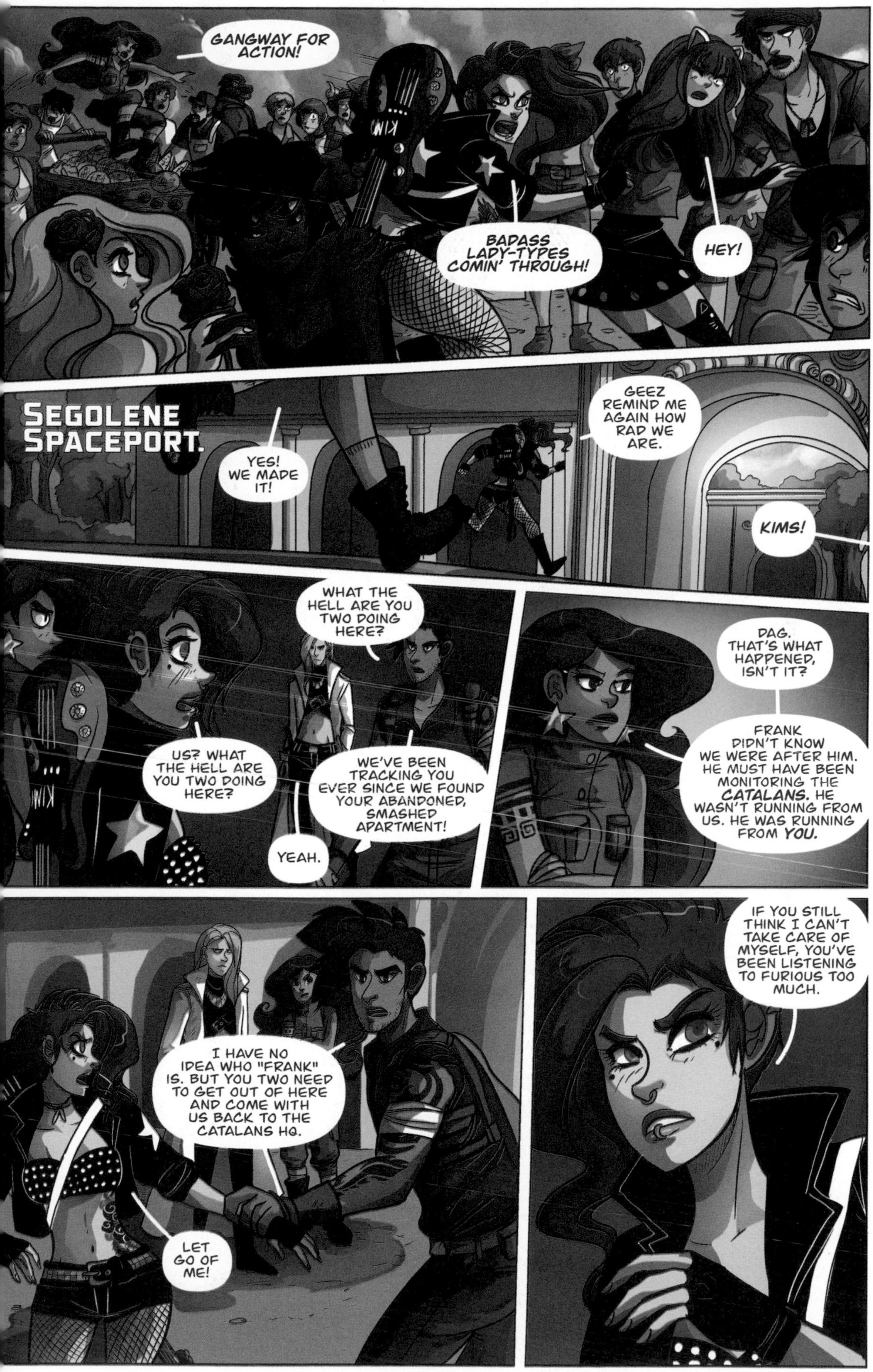
GANGWAY FOR ACTION!
BADASS LADY-TYPES COMIN' THROUGH!
HEY!
SEGOLENE SPACEPORT.
YES! WE MADE IT!
GEEZ REMIND ME AGAIN HOW RAD WE ARE.
KIMS!
WHAT THE HELL ARE YOU TWO DOING HERE?
US? WHAT THE HELL ARE YOU TWO DOING HERE?
WE'VE BEEN TRACKING YOU EVER SINCE WE FOUND YOUR ABANDONED, SMASHED APARTMENT!
YEAH.
DAG. THAT'S WHAT HAPPENED, ISN'T IT?
FRANK DIDN'T KNOW WE WERE AFTER HIM. HE MUST HAVE BEEN MONITORING THE CATALANS. HE WASN'T RUNNING FROM US. HE WAS RUNNING FROM YOU.
I HAVE NO IDEA WHO "FRANK" IS. BUT YOU TWO NEED TO GET OUT OF HERE AND COME WITH US BACK TO THE CATALANS HQ.
LET GO OF ME!
IF YOU STILL THINK I CAN'T TAKE CARE OF MYSELF, YOU'VE BEEN LISTENING TO FURIOUS TOO MUCH.

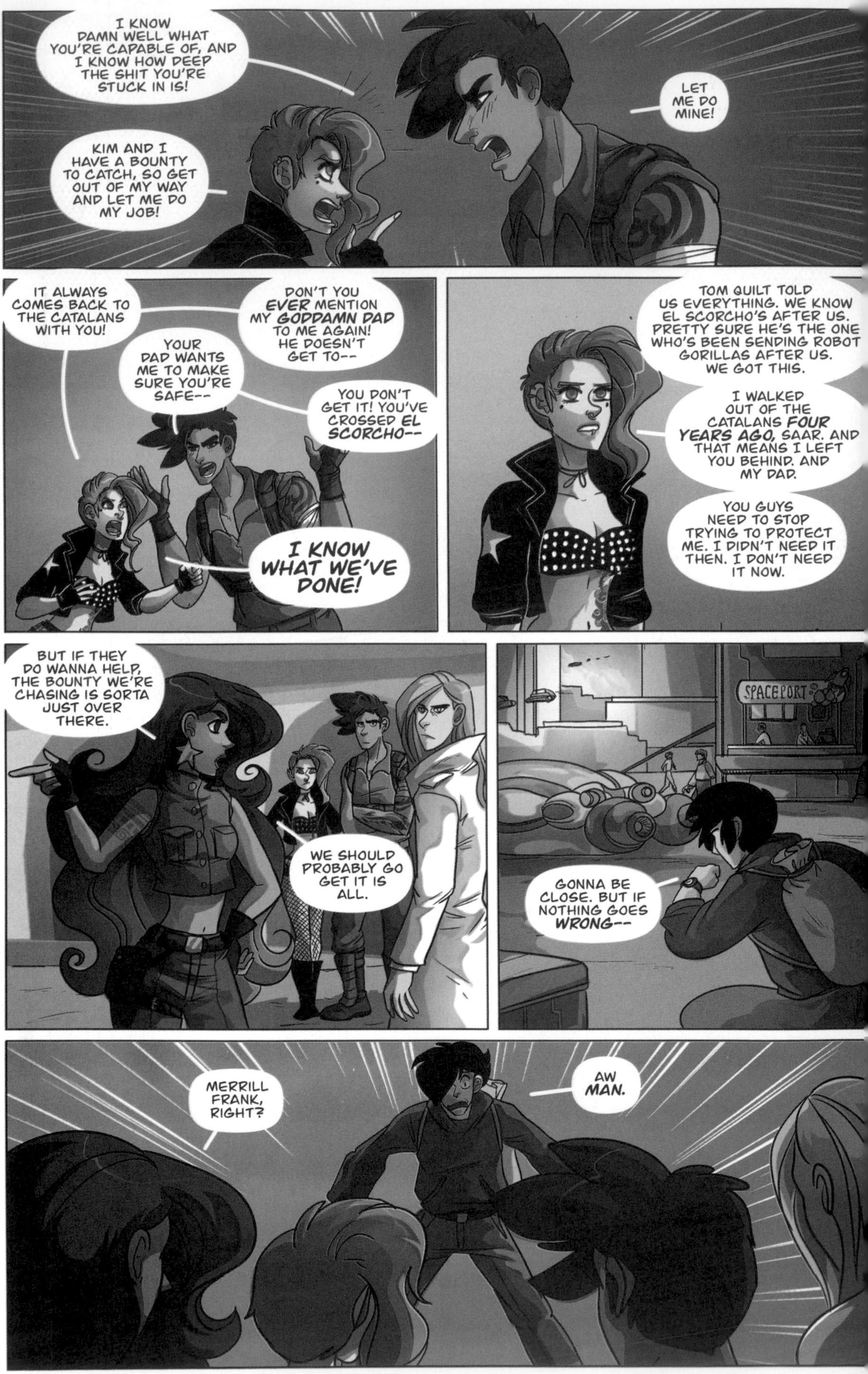
I KNOW DAMN WELL WHAT YOU'RE CAPABLE OF, AND I KNOW HOW DEEP THE SHIT YOU'RE STUCK IN IS!
LET ME DO MINE!
KIM AND I HAVE A BOUNTY TO CATCH, SO GET OUT OF MY WAY AND LET ME DO MY JOB!
IT ALWAYS COMES BACK TO THE CATALANS WITH YOU!
DON'T YOU EVER MENTION MY GODDAMN DAD TO ME AGAIN! HE DOESN'T GET TO--
YOUR DAD WANTS ME TO MAKE SURE YOU'RE SAFE--
YOU DON'T GET IT! YOU'VE CROSSED EL SCORCHO--
I KNOW WHAT WE'VE DONE!
TOM QUILT TOLD US EVERYTHING. WE KNOW EL SCORCHO'S AFTER US. PRETTY SURE HE'S THE ONE WHO'S BEEN SENDING ROBOT GORILLAS AFTER US. WE GOT THIS.
I WALKED OUT OF THE CATALANS FOUR YEARS AGO, SAAR. AND THAT MEANS I LEFT YOU BEHIND. AND MY DAD.
YOU GUYS NEED TO STOP TRYING TO PROTECT ME. I DIDN'T NEED IT THEN. I DON'T NEED IT NOW.
BUT IF THEY DO WANNA HELP, THE BOUNTY WE'RE CHASING IS SORTA JUST OVER THERE.
WE SHOULD PROBABLY GO GET IT IS ALL.
SPACEPORT
GONNA BE CLOSE. BUT IF NOTHING GOES WRONG--
MERRILL FRANK, RIGHT?
AW MAN.

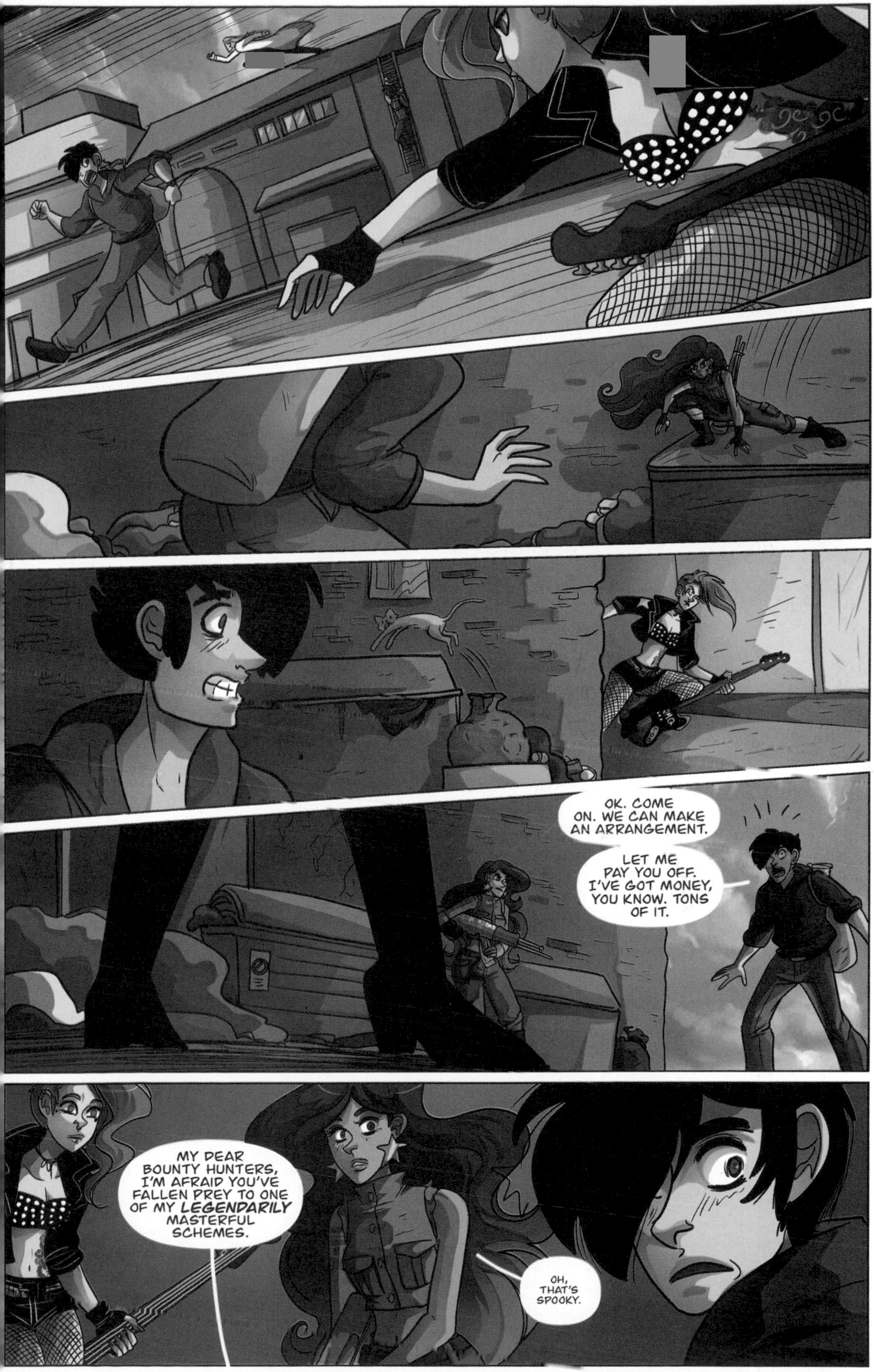

OK. COME ON. WE CAN MAKE AN ARRANGEMENT.
LET ME PAY YOU OFF. I'VE GOT MONEY, YOU KNOW. TONS OF IT.
MY DEAR BOUNTY HUNTERS, I'M AFRAID YOU'VE FALLEN PREY TO ONE OF MY ***LEGENDARILY*** MASTERFUL SCHEMES.
OH, THAT'S SPOOKY.

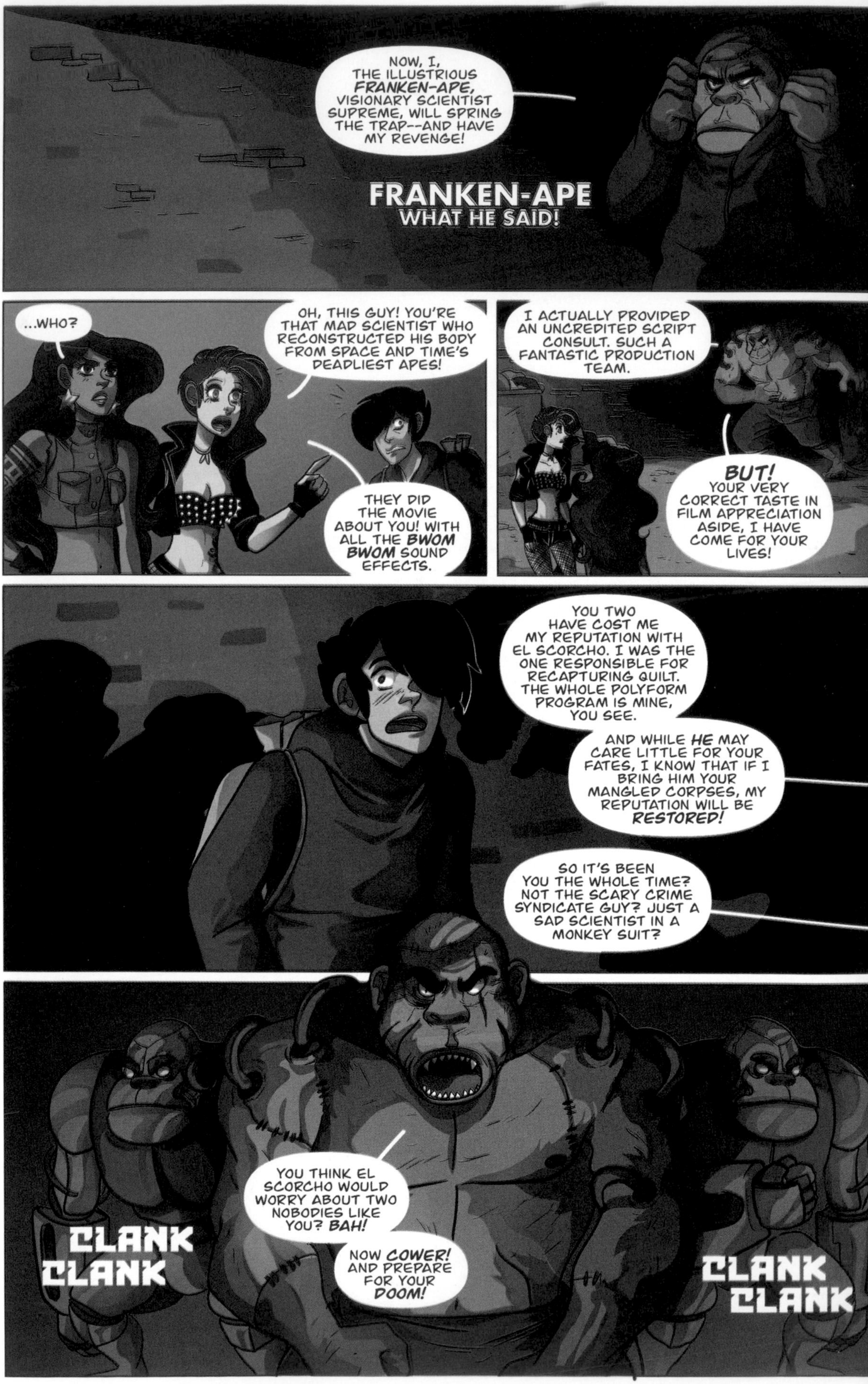
NOW, I, THE ILLUSTRIOUS FRANKEN-APE, VISIONARY SCIENTIST SUPREME, WILL SPRING THE TRAP--AND HAVE MY REVENGE!
FRANKEN-APE
WHAT HE SAID!
...WHO?
OH, THIS GUY! YOU'RE THAT MAD SCIENTIST WHO RECONSTRUCTED HIS BODY FROM SPACE AND TIME'S DEADLIEST APES!
THEY DID THE MOVIE ABOUT YOU! WITH ALL THE BWOM BWOM SOUND EFFECTS.
I ACTUALLY PROVIDED AN UNCREDITED SCRIPT CONSULT. SUCH A FANTASTIC PRODUCTION TEAM.
BUT! YOUR VERY CORRECT TASTE IN FILM APPRECIATION ASIDE, I HAVE COME FOR YOUR LIVES!
YOU TWO HAVE COST ME MY REPUTATION WITH EL SCORCHO. I WAS THE ONE RESPONSIBLE FOR RECAPTURING QUILT. THE WHOLE POLYFORM PROGRAM IS MINE, YOU SEE.
AND WHILE HE MAY CARE LITTLE FOR YOUR FATES, I KNOW THAT IF I BRING HIM YOUR MANGLED CORPSES, MY REPUTATION WILL BE RESTORED!
SO IT'S BEEN YOU THE WHOLE TIME? NOT THE SCARY CRIME SYNDICATE GUY? JUST A SAD SCIENTIST IN A MONKEY SUIT?
YOU THINK EL SCORCHO WOULD WORRY ABOUT TWO NOBODIES LIKE YOU? BAH!
NOW COWER! AND PREPARE FOR YOUR DOOM!
CLANK CLANK
CLANK CLANK

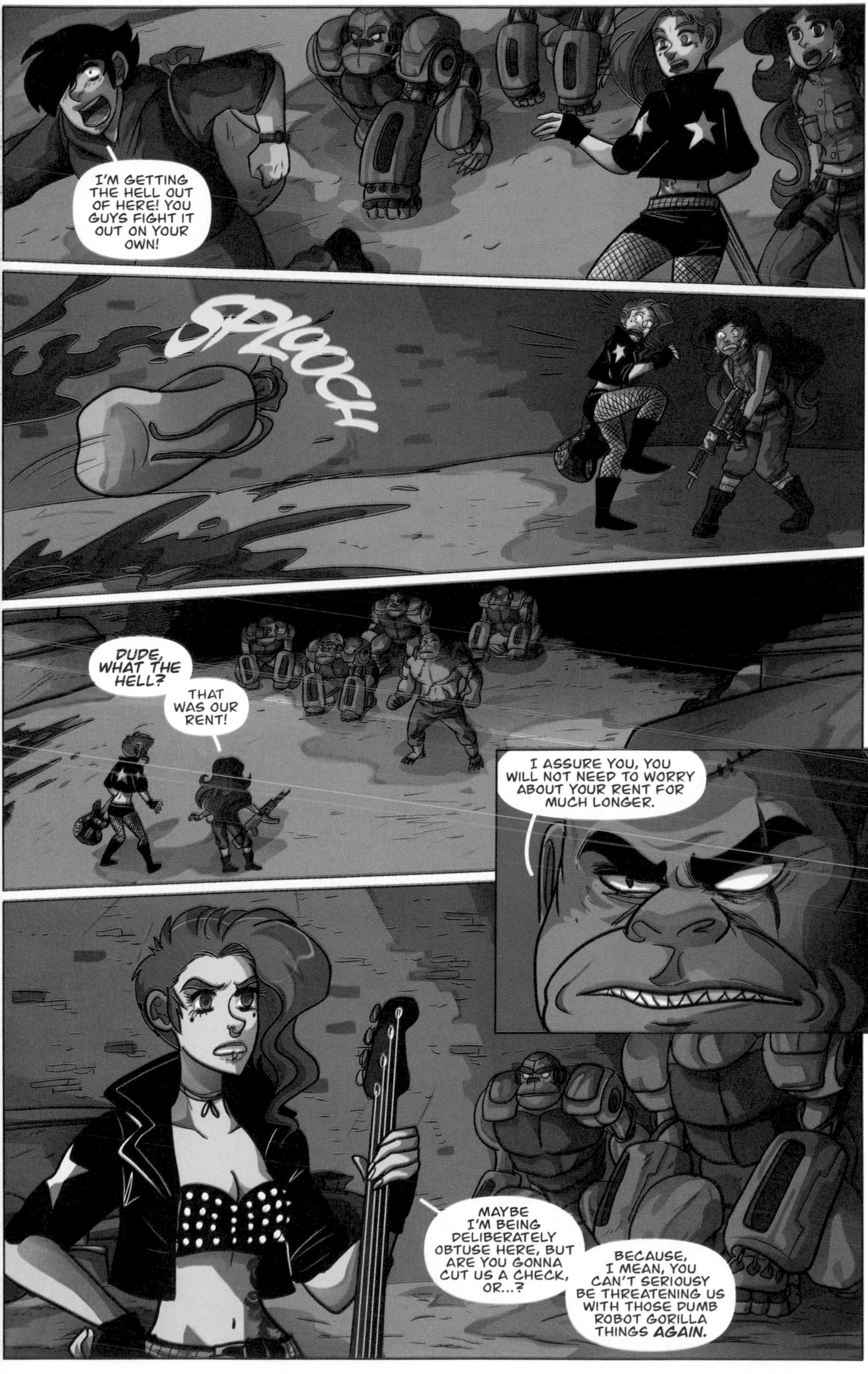
I'M GETTING THE HELL OUT OF HERE! YOU GUYS FIGHT IT OUT ON YOUR OWN!
SPLOOCH
DUDE, WHAT THE HELL?
THAT WAS OUR RENT!
I ASSURE YOU, YOU WILL NOT NEED TO WORRY ABOUT YOUR RENT FOR MUCH LONGER.
MAYBE I'M BEING DELIBERATELY OBTUSE HERE, BUT ARE YOU GONNA CUT US A CHECK, OR...?
BECAUSE, I MEAN, YOU CAN'T SERIOUSY BE THREATENING US WITH THOSE DUMB ROBOT GORILLA THINGS AGAIN.

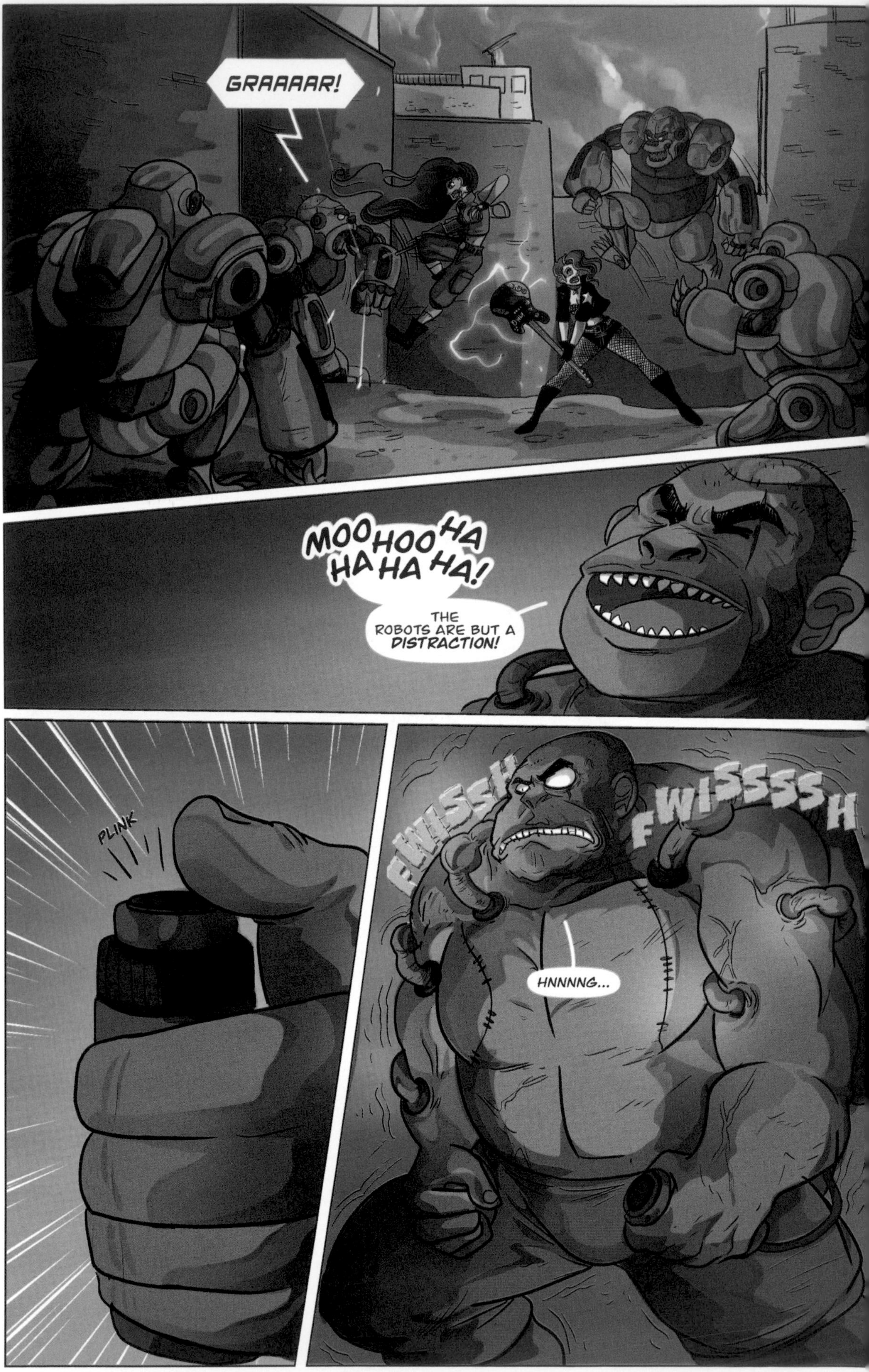
GRAAAAR!
MOO HOO HA HA HA HA!
THE ROBOTS ARE BUT A DISTRACTION!
PLINK
FWISSSH
FWISSSSSH
HNNNNG...

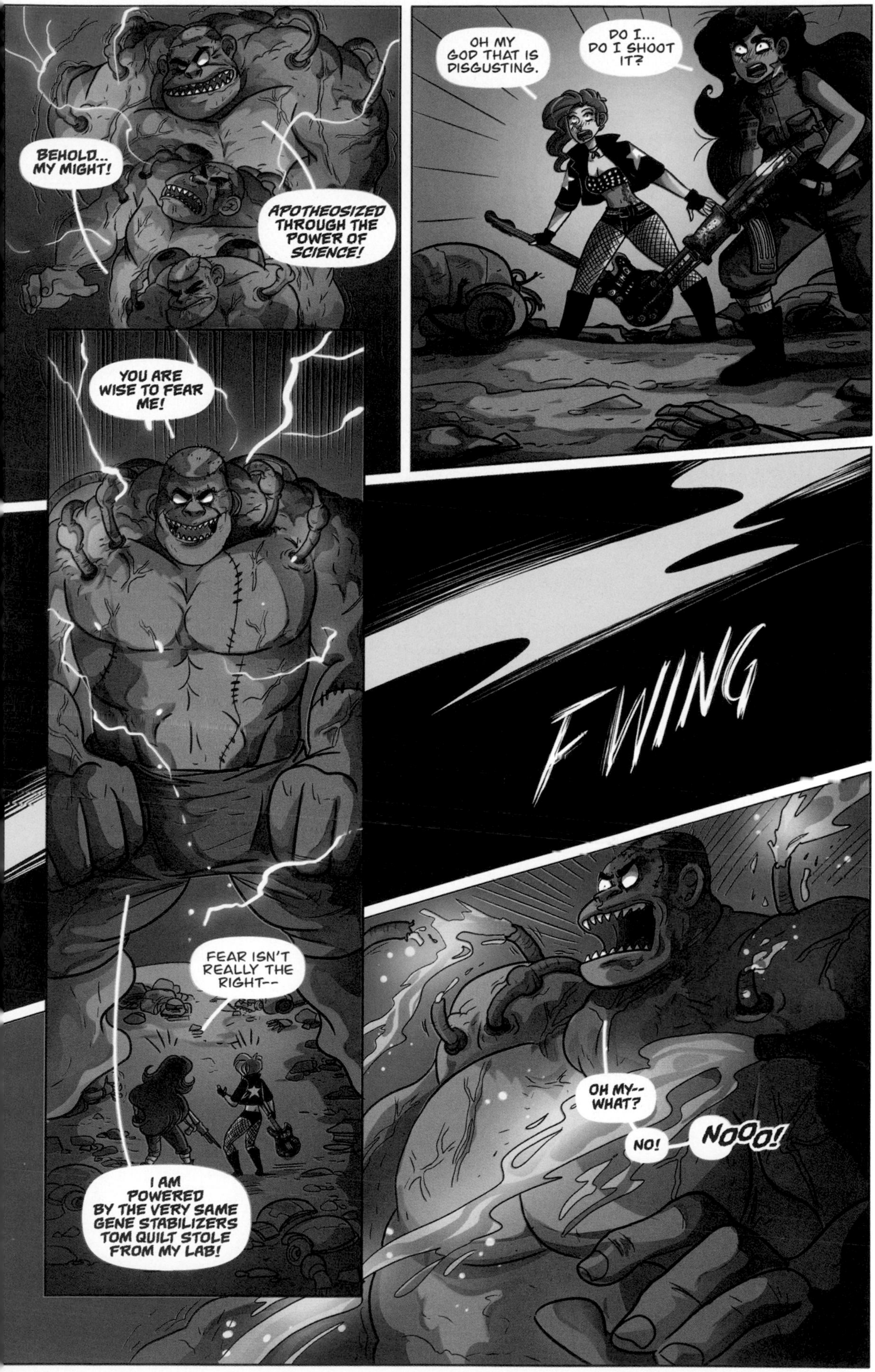
BEHOLD... MY MIGHT!
APOTHEOSIZED THROUGH THE POWER OF SCIENCE!
OH MY GOD THAT IS DISGUSTING.
DO I... DO I SHOOT IT?
YOU ARE WISE TO FEAR ME!
FEAR ISN'T REALLY THE RIGHT--
I AM POWERED BY THE VERY SAME GENE STABILIZERS TOM QUILT STOLE FROM MY LAB!
FWING
OH MY-- WHAT?
NO!
NOOO!

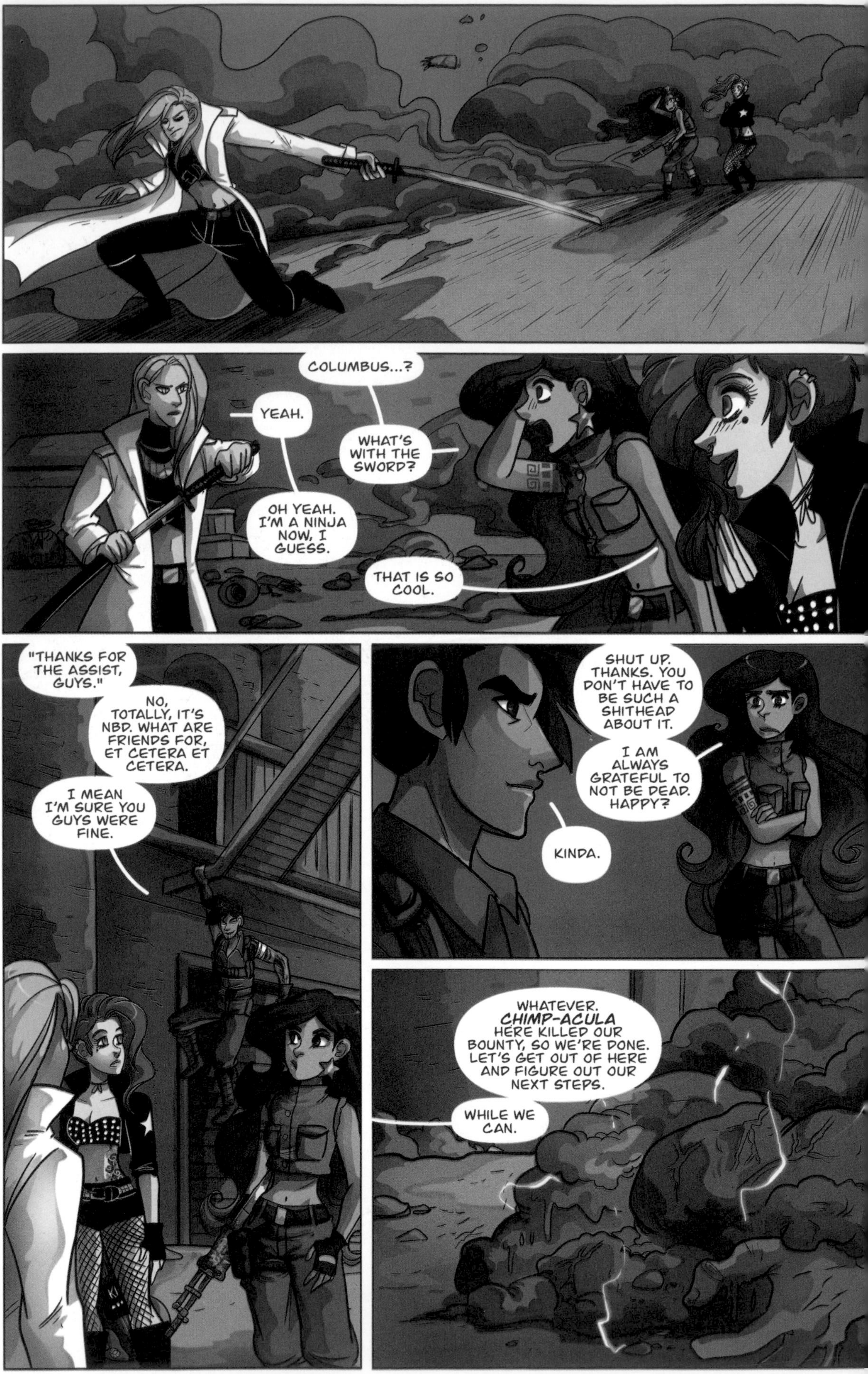
COLUMBUS...?
YEAH.
WHAT'S WITH THE SWORD?
OH YEAH. I'M A NINJA NOW, I GUESS.
THAT IS SO COOL.
"THANKS FOR THE ASSIST, GUYS."
NO, TOTALLY, IT'S NBD. WHAT ARE FRIENDS FOR, ET CETERA ET CETERA.
I MEAN I'M SURE YOU GUYS WERE FINE.
SHUT UP. THANKS. YOU DON'T HAVE TO BE SUCH A SHITHEAD ABOUT IT.
I AM ALWAYS GRATEFUL TO NOT BE DEAD. HAPPY?
KINDA.
WHATEVER. CHIMP-ACULA HERE KILLED OUR BOUNTY, SO WE'RE DONE. LET'S GET OUT OF HERE AND FIGURE OUT OUR NEXT STEPS.
WHILE WE CAN.

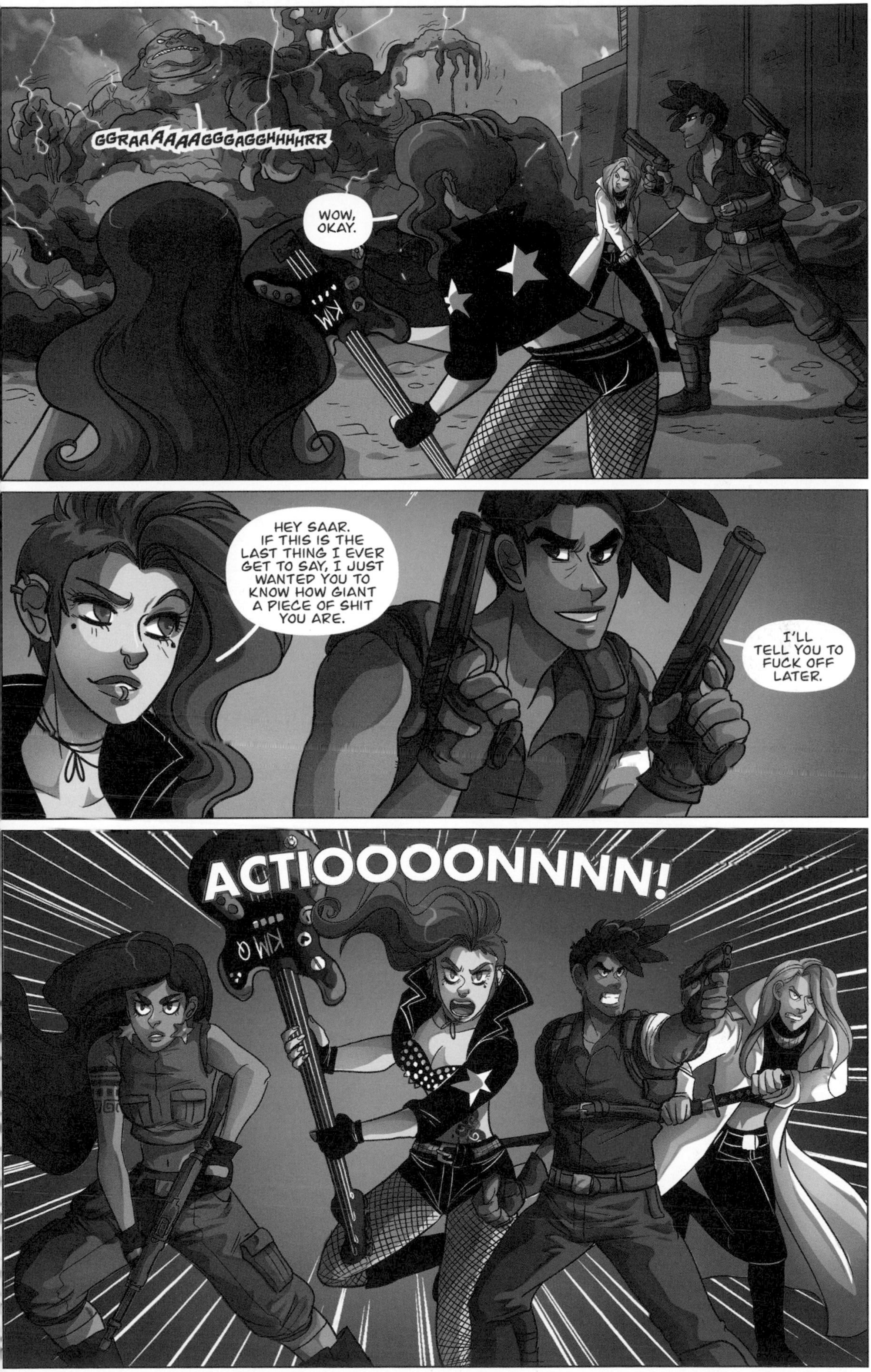
GGRAAAAAAGGGAGGHHHHRR
WOW, OKAY.
HEY SAAR. IF THIS IS THE LAST THING I EVER GET TO SAY, I JUST WANTED YOU TO KNOW HOW GIANT A PIECE OF SHIT YOU ARE.
I'LL TELL YOU TO FUCK OFF LATER.
ACTIOOOONNNNN!

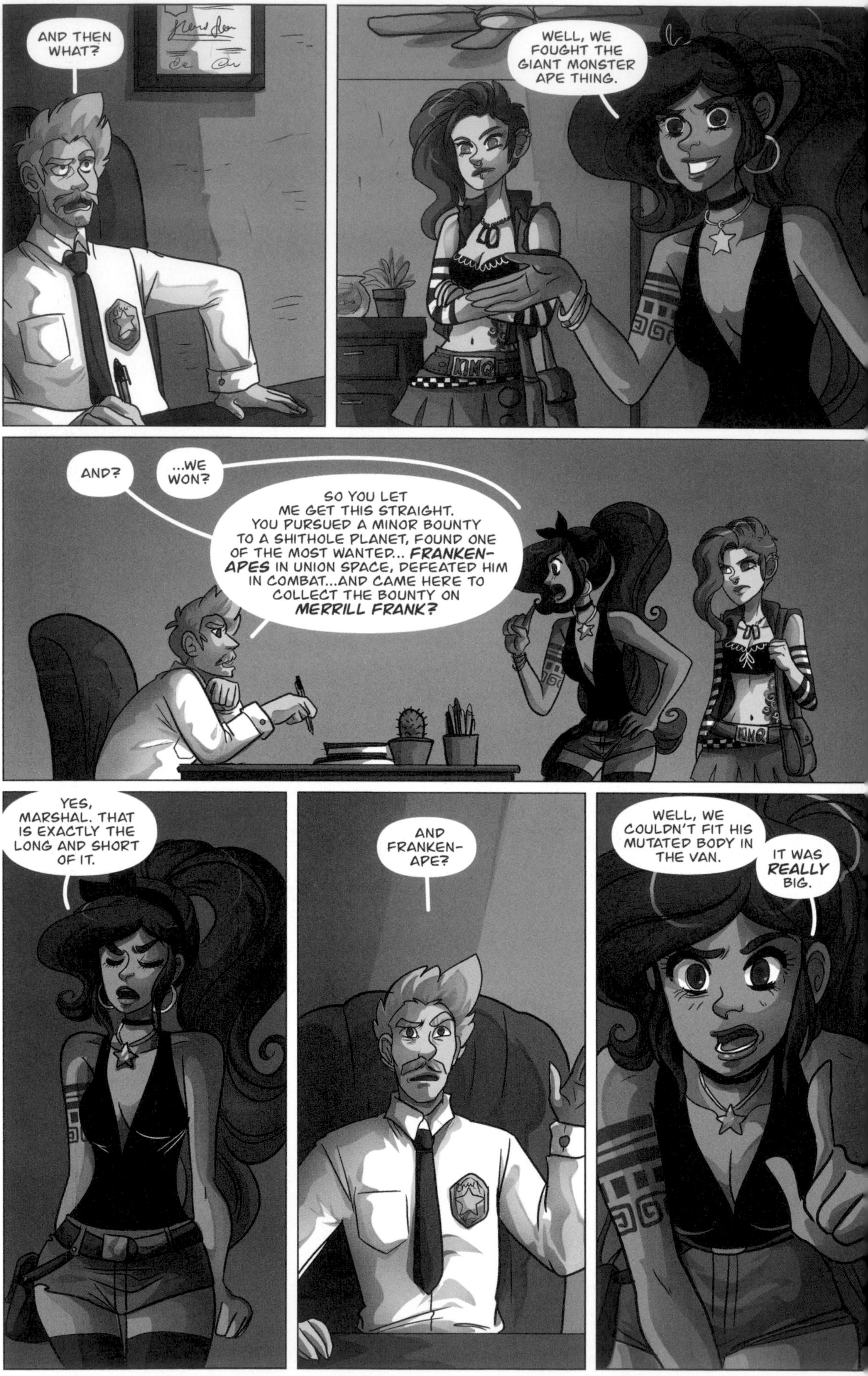
AND THEN WHAT?
WELL, WE FOUGHT THE GIANT MONSTER APE THING.
AND?
...WE WON?
SO YOU LET ME GET THIS STRAIGHT. YOU PURSUED A MINOR BOUNTY TO A SHITHOLE PLANET, FOUND ONE OF THE MOST WANTED... FRANKEN-APES IN UNION SPACE, DEFEATED HIM IN COMBAT...AND CAME HERE TO COLLECT THE BOUNTY ON MERRILL FRANK?
YES, MARSHAL. THAT IS EXACTLY THE LONG AND SHORT OF IT.
AND FRANKEN-APE?
WELL, WE COULDN'T FIT HIS MUTATED BODY IN THE VAN.
IT WAS REALLY BIG.

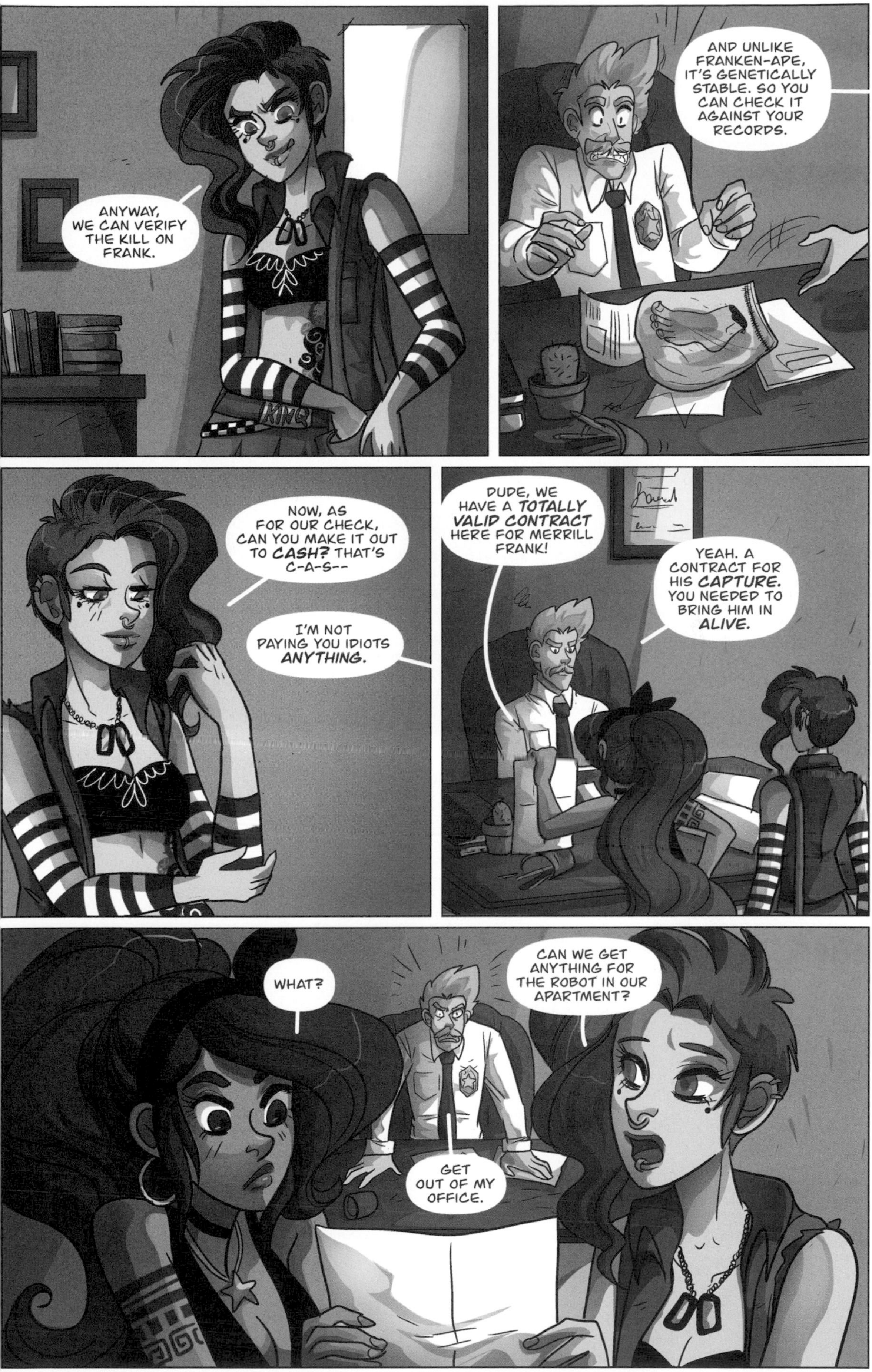
ANYWAY, WE CAN VERIFY THE KILL ON FRANK.
AND UNLIKE FRANKEN-APE, IT'S GENETICALLY STABLE. SO YOU CAN CHECK IT AGAINST YOUR RECORDS.
NOW, AS FOR OUR CHECK, CAN YOU MAKE IT OUT TO CASH? THAT'S C-A-S--
I'M NOT PAYING YOU IDIOTS ANYTHING.
DUDE, WE HAVE A TOTALLY VALID CONTRACT HERE FOR MERRILL FRANK!
YEAH. A CONTRACT FOR HIS CAPTURE. YOU NEEDED TO BRING HIM IN ALIVE.
WHAT?
CAN WE GET ANYTHING FOR THE ROBOT IN OUR APARTMENT?
GET OUT OF MY OFFICE.

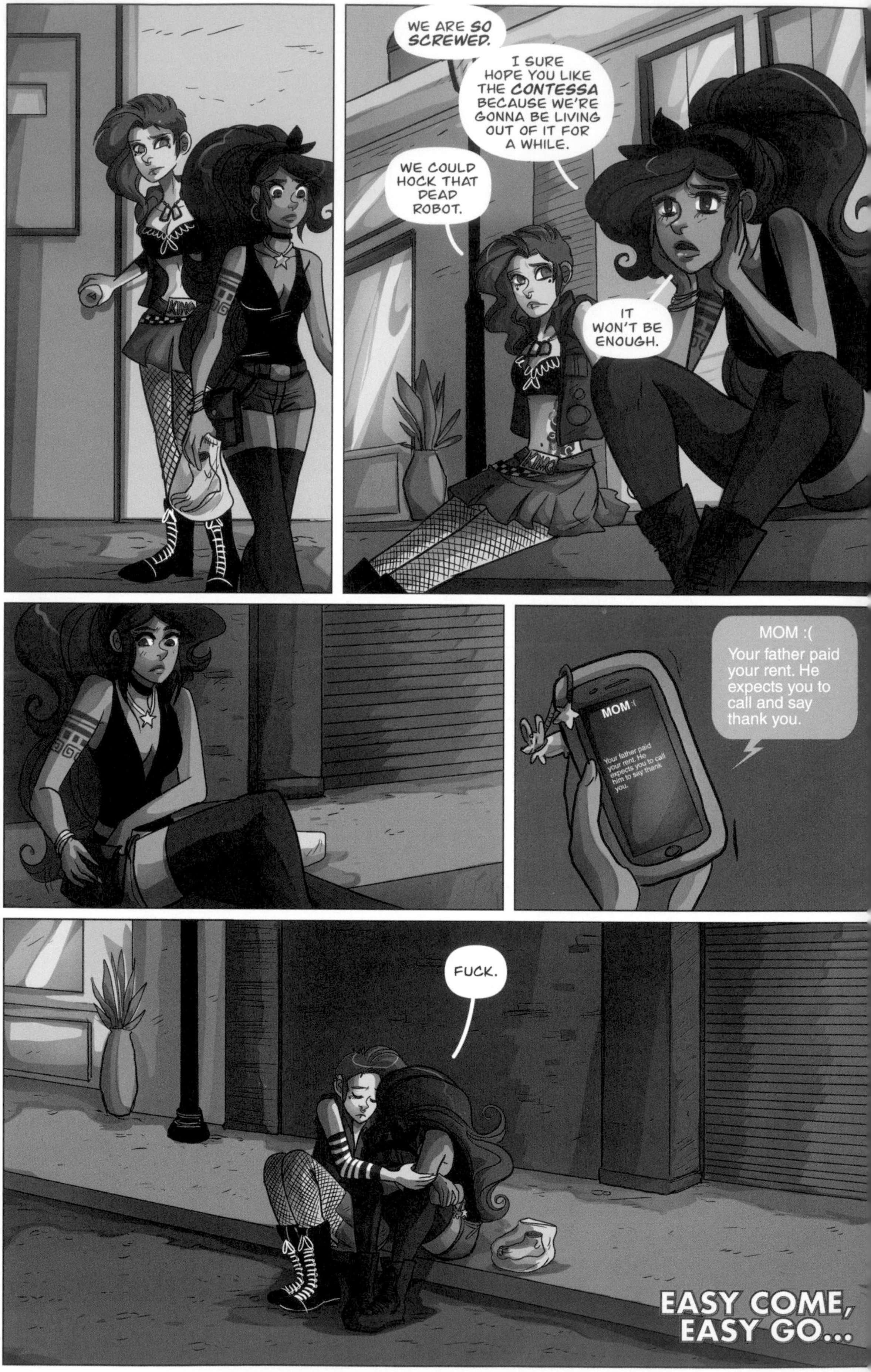
WE ARE SO SCREWED.
I SURE HOPE YOU LIKE THE CONTESSA BECAUSE WE'RE GONNA BE LIVING OUT OF IT FOR A WHILE.
WE COULD HOCK THAT DEAD ROBOT.
IT WON'T BE ENOUGH.
MOM :(
Your father paid your rent. He expects you to call and say thank you.
FUCK.
EASY COME, EASY GO...

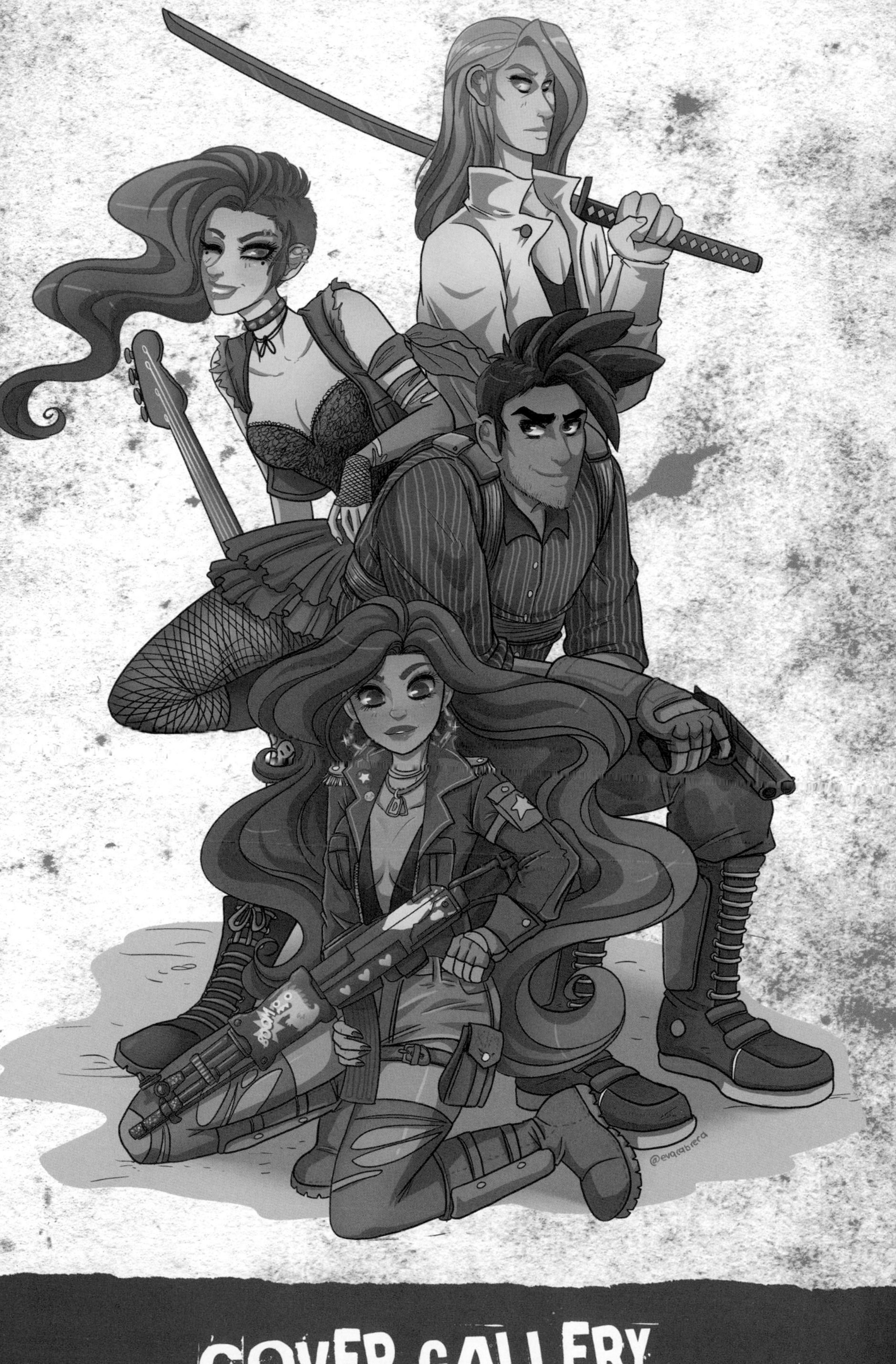
@evacabrera

COVER GALLERY

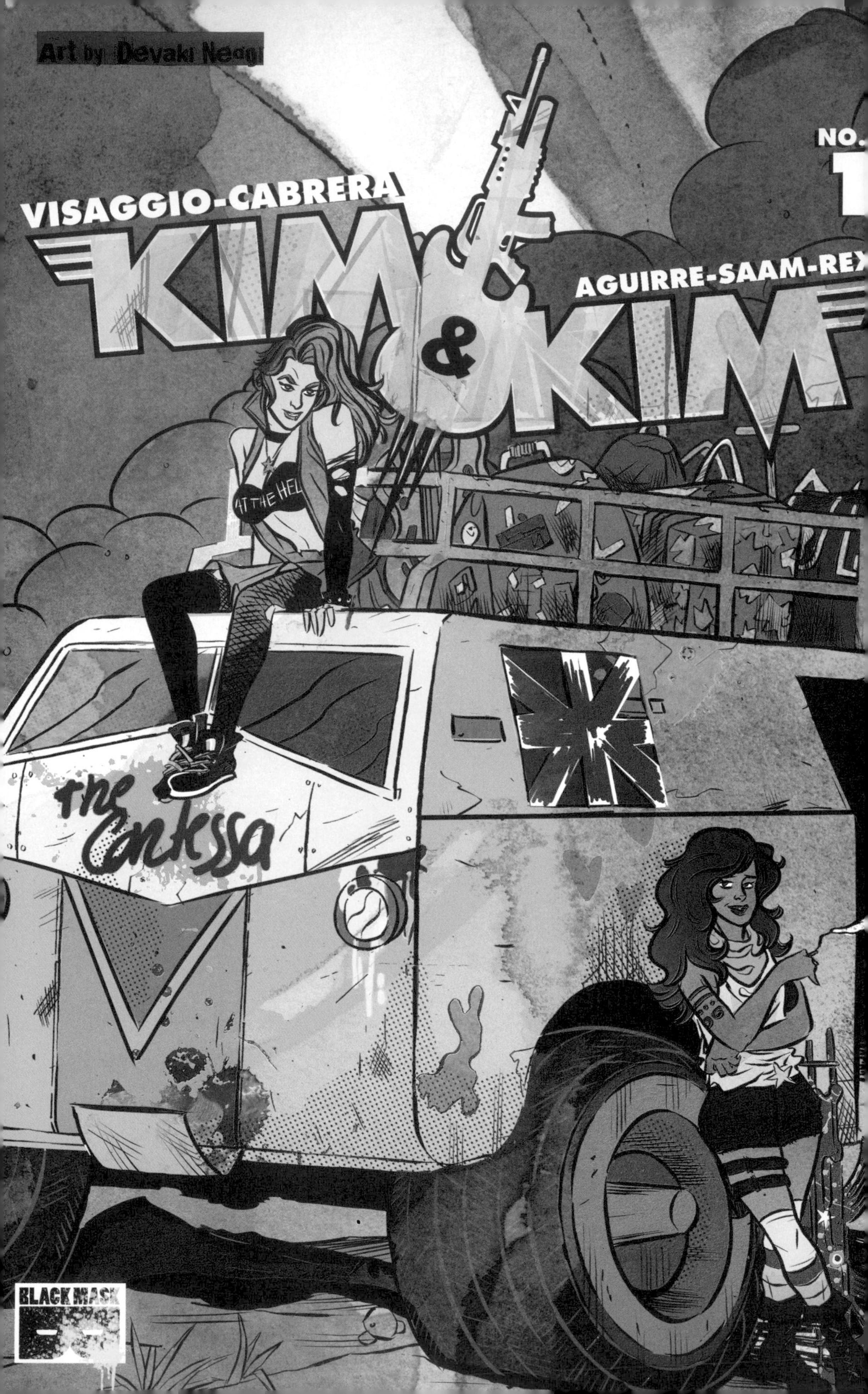
Art by Devaki Neogi
VISAGGIO-CABRERA
KIM & KIM
AGUIRRE-SAAM-REX
NO. 1
AT THE HELL
the Enkssa
BLACK MASK

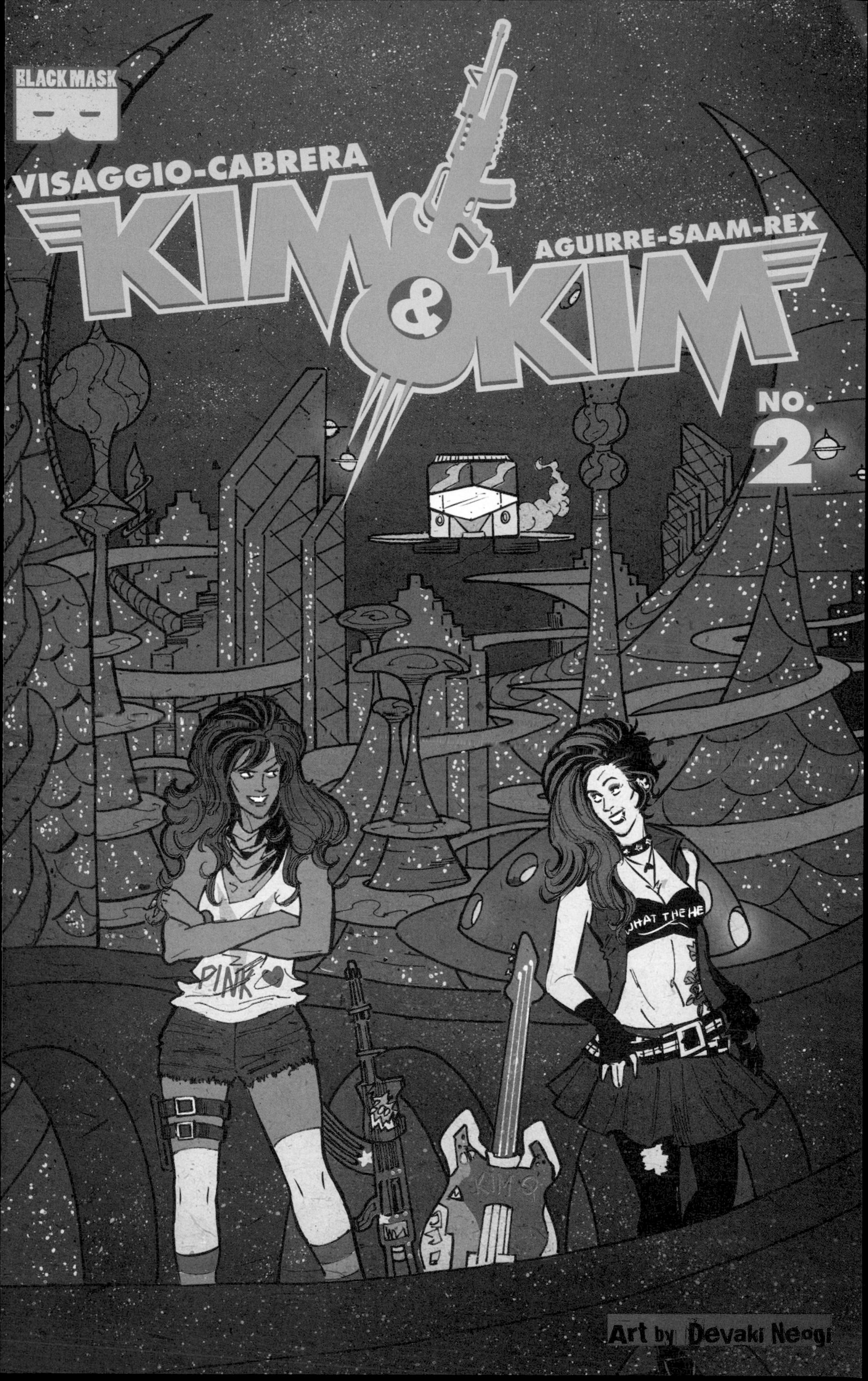
BLACK MASK
VISAGGIO-CABRERA
KIM & KIM
AGUIRRE-SAAM-REX
NO. 2
PINK
WHAT THE HE
Art by Devaki Neogi

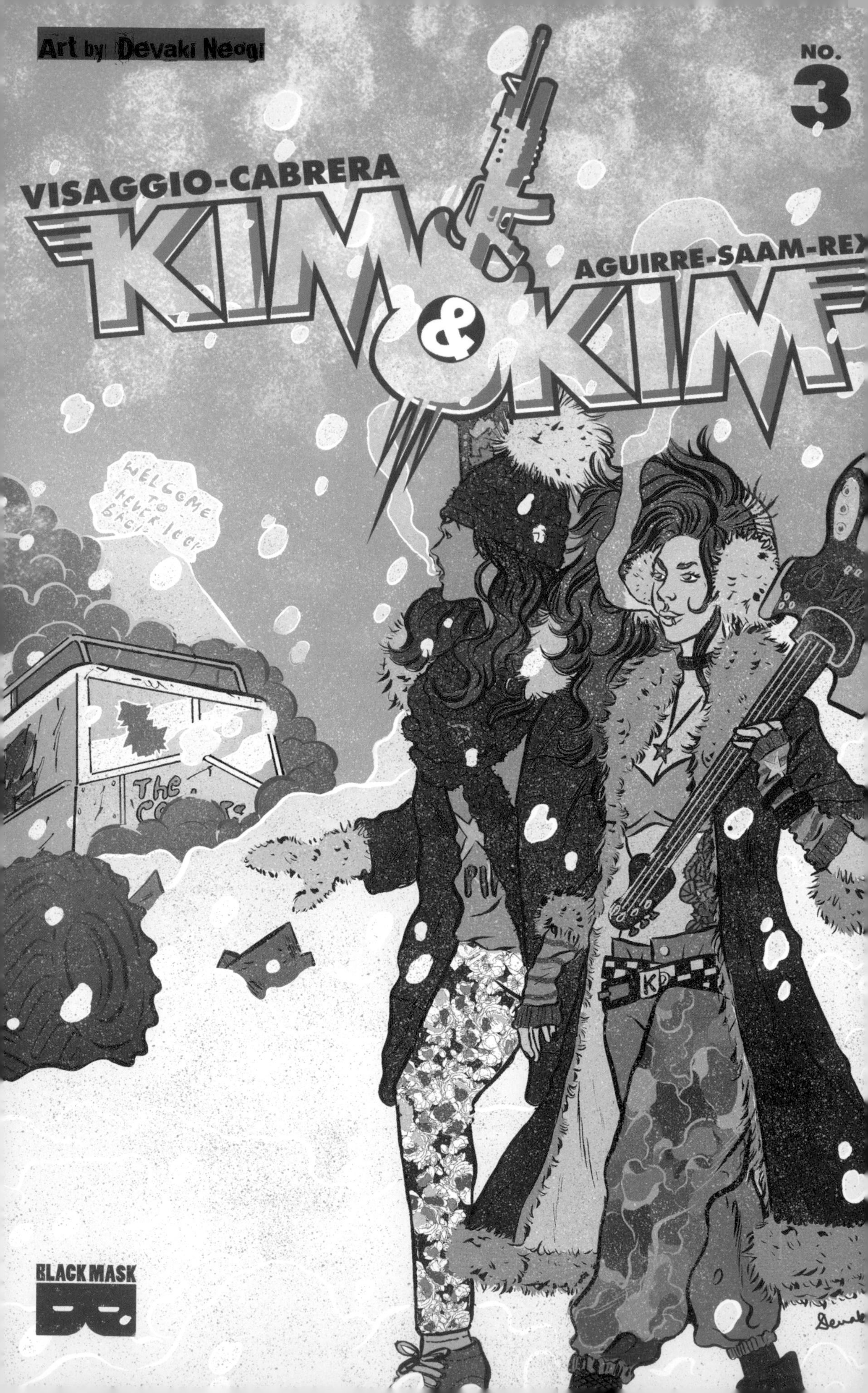

Art by Devaki Neogi
NO. 3
VISAGGIO-CABRERA
KIM & KIM
AGUIRRE-SAAM-REX
WELCOME TO NEVER LOOK BACK
BLACK MASK

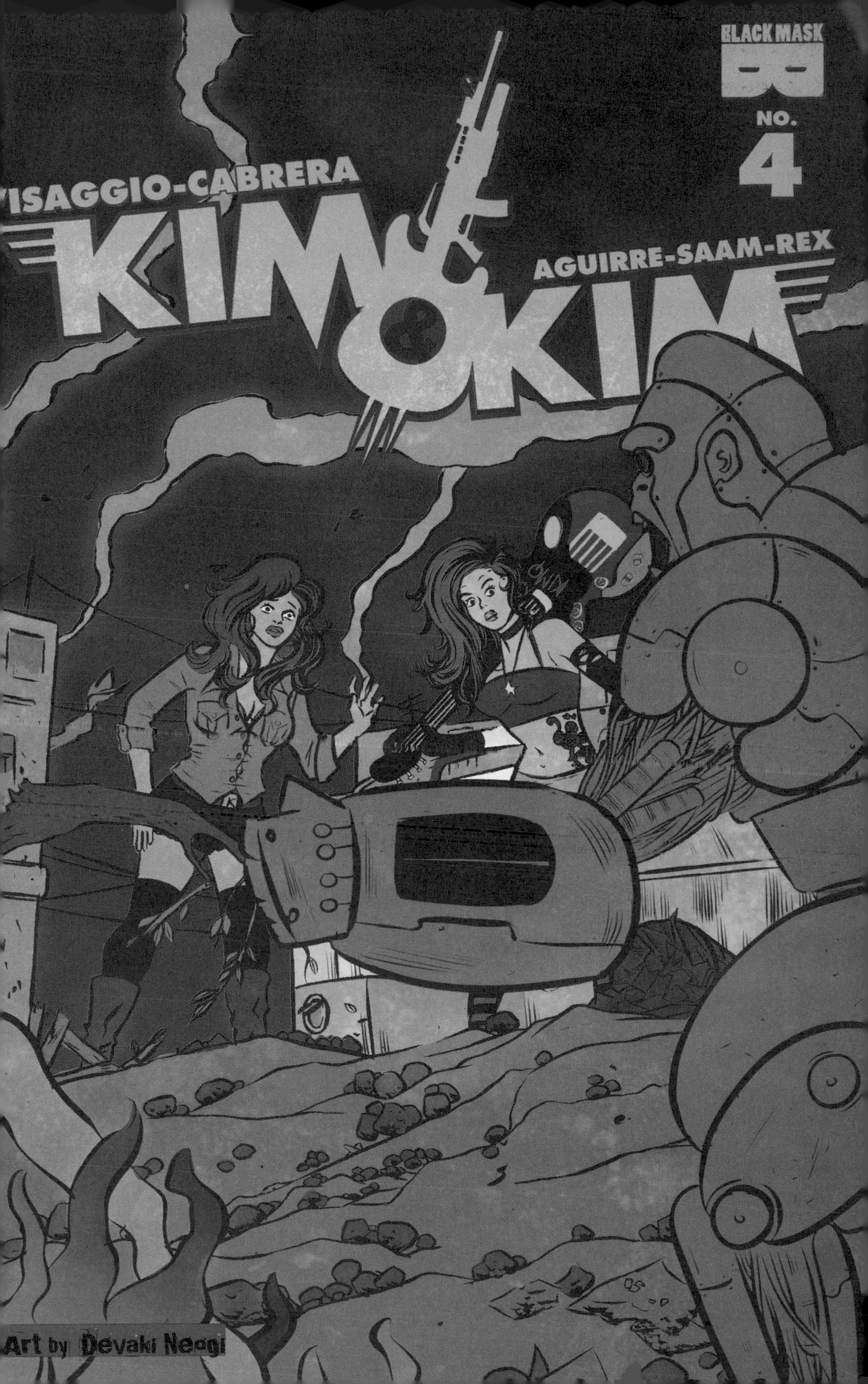
BLACK MASK
NO.
4
ISAGGIO-CABRERA
KIM & KIM
AGUIRRE-SAAM-REX
Art by Devaki Neogi

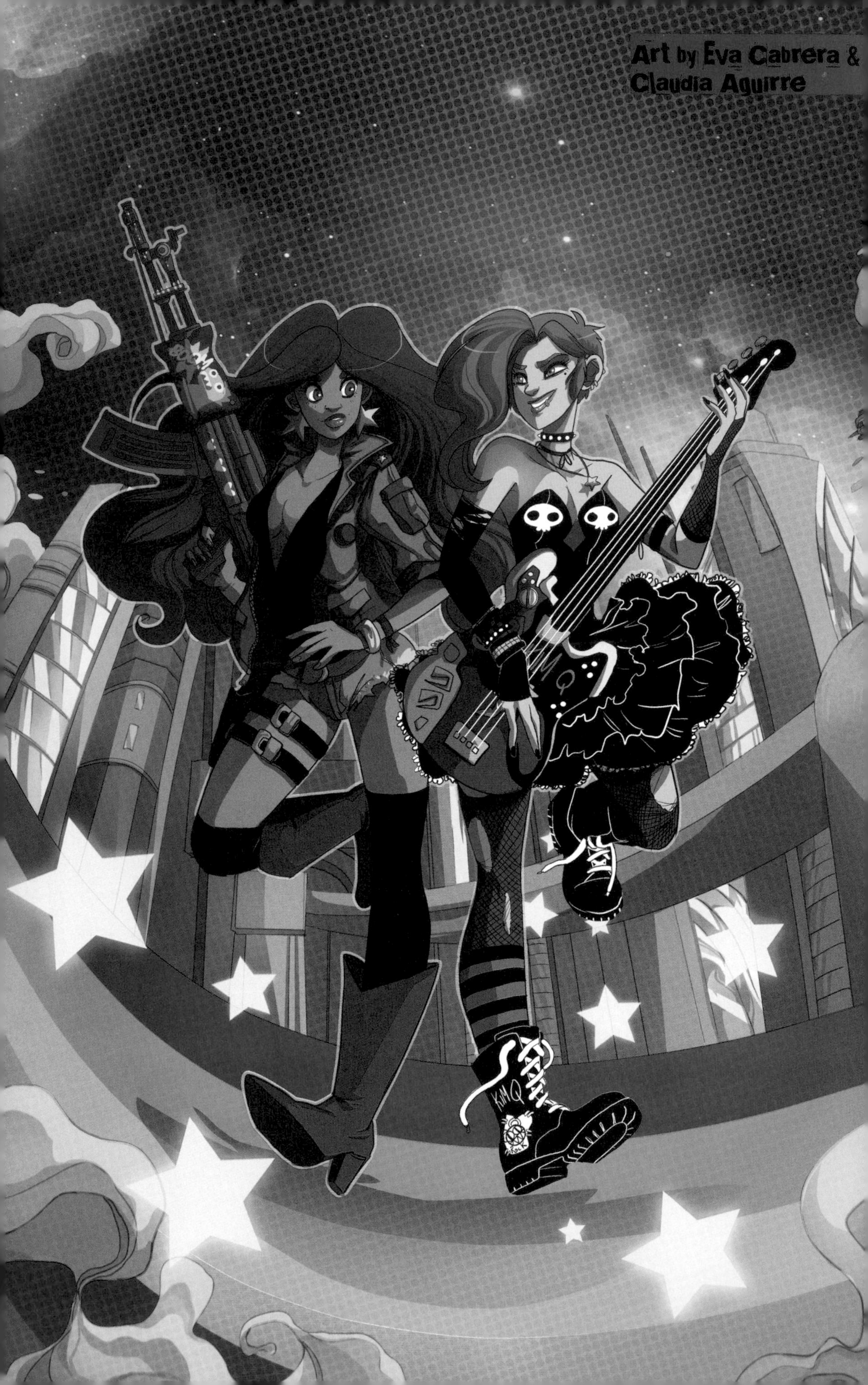
Art by Eva Cabrera &
Claudia Aguirre

Art by Becca Farrow

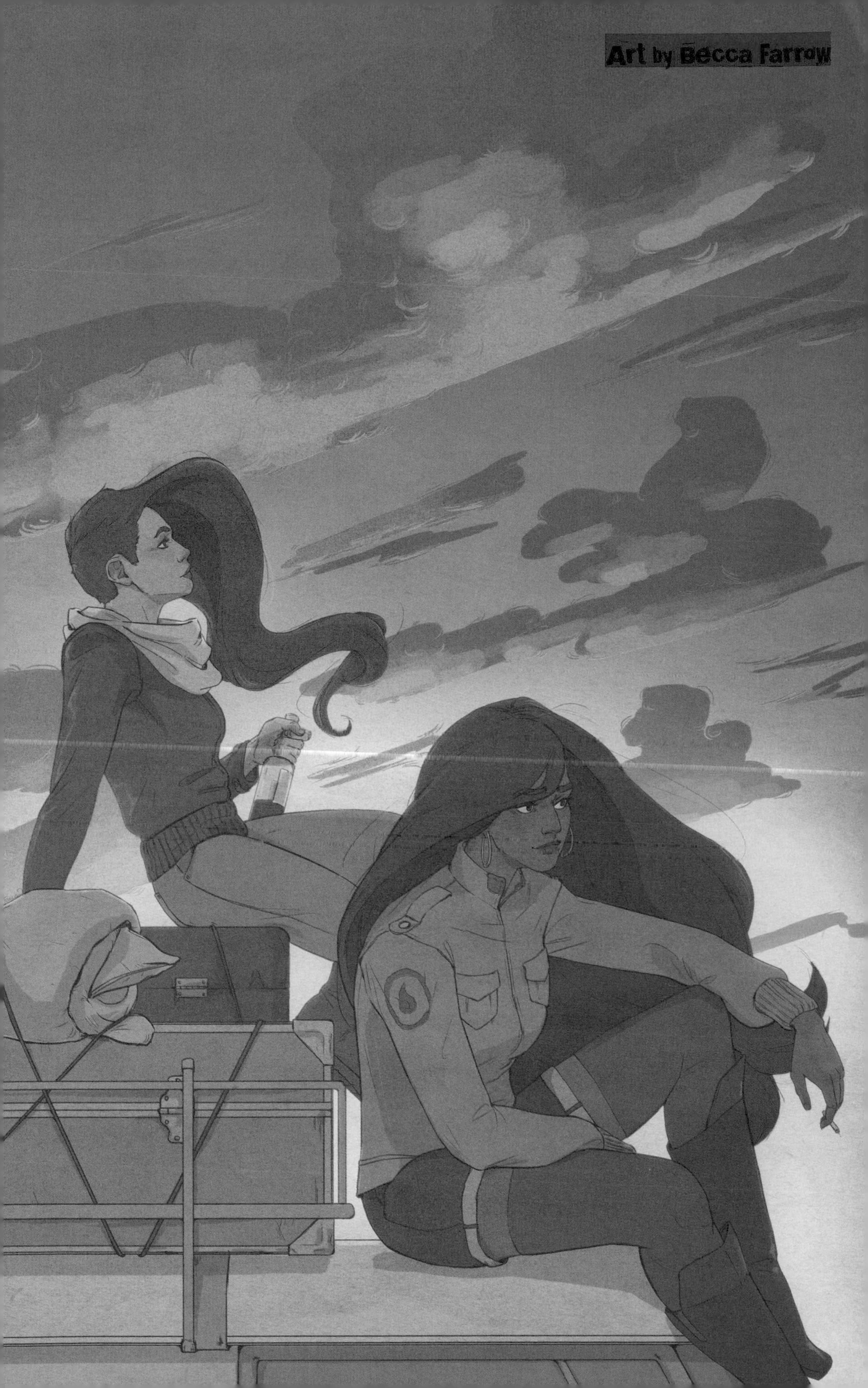

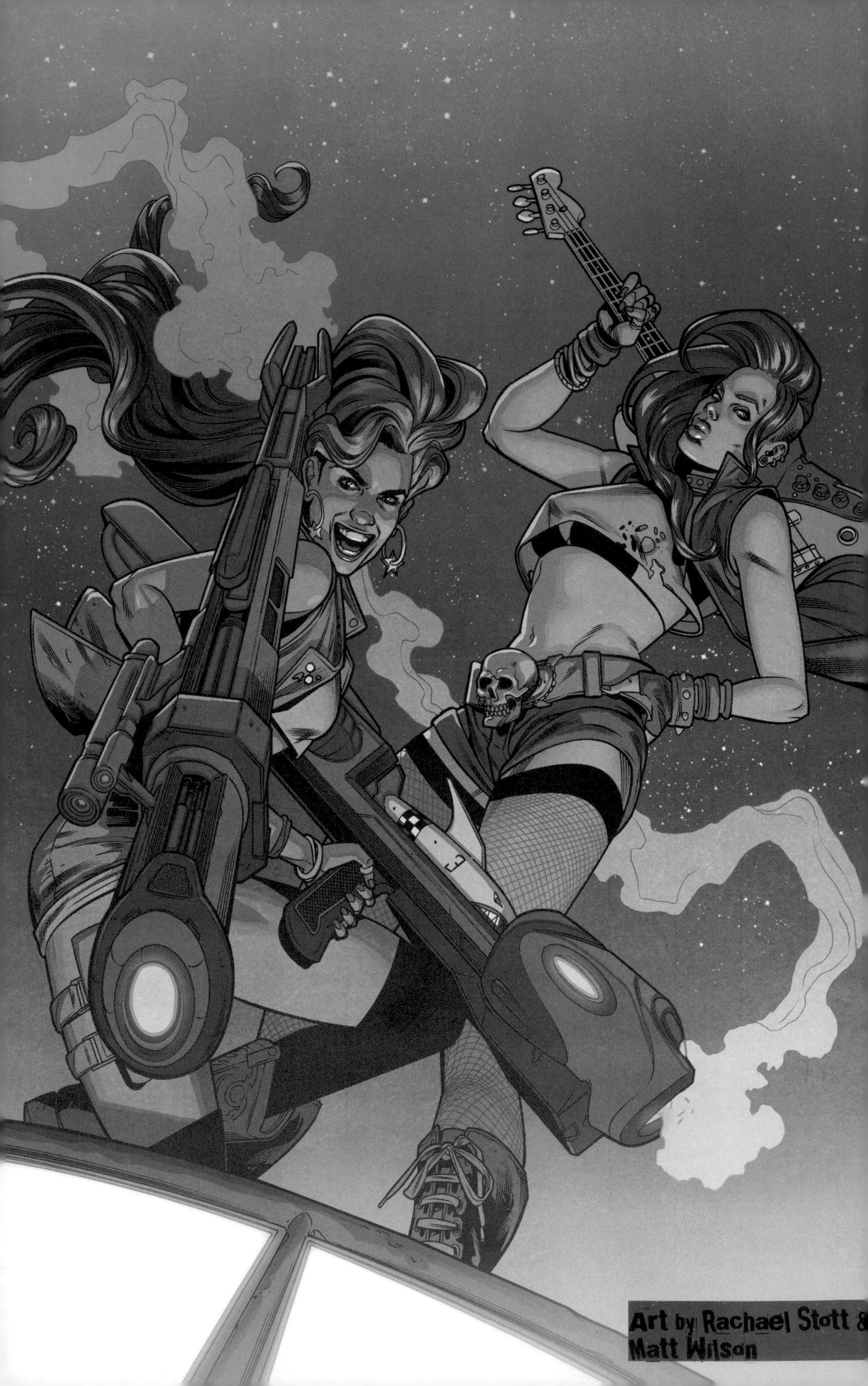

Art by Rachael Stott & Matt Wilson

Retailer Variant Covers by Amancay Nahuelpan

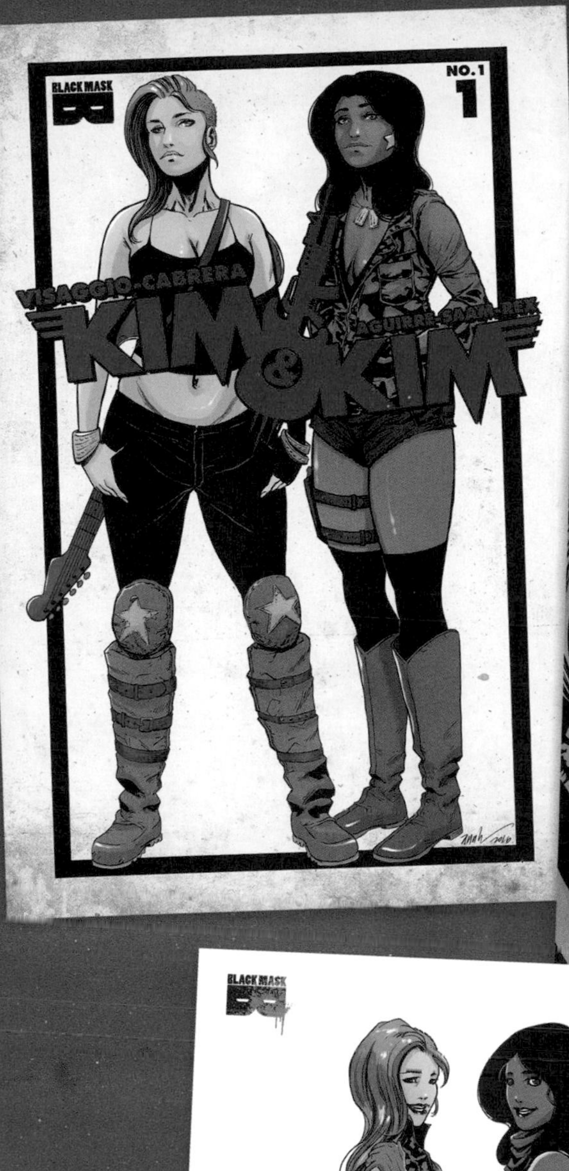
BLACK MASK
NO. 1
1
VISAGGIO-CABRERA
KIM & KIM
AGUIRRE-SAAM-REX

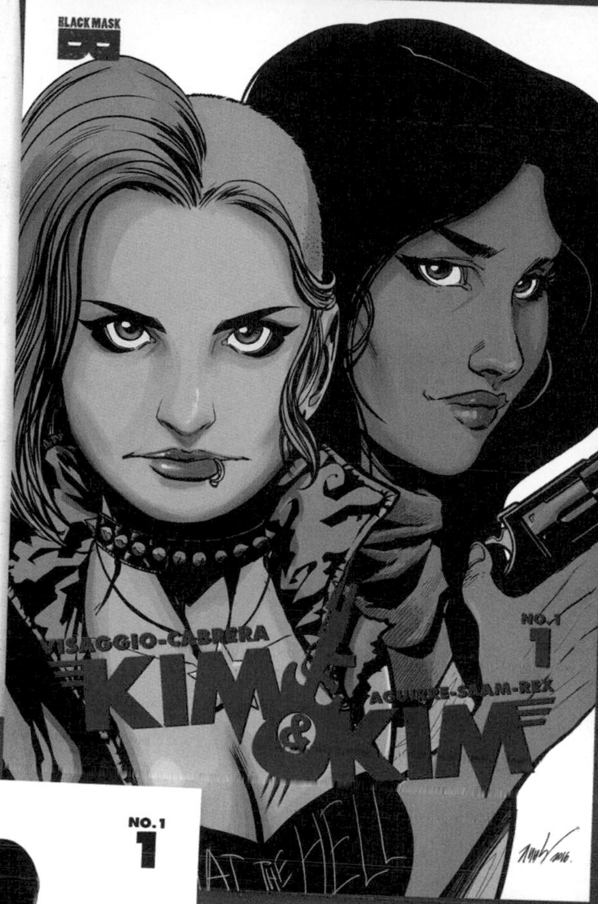
BLACK MASK
NO. 1
1
VISAGGIO-CABRERA
KIM & KIM
AGUIRRE-SAAM-REX

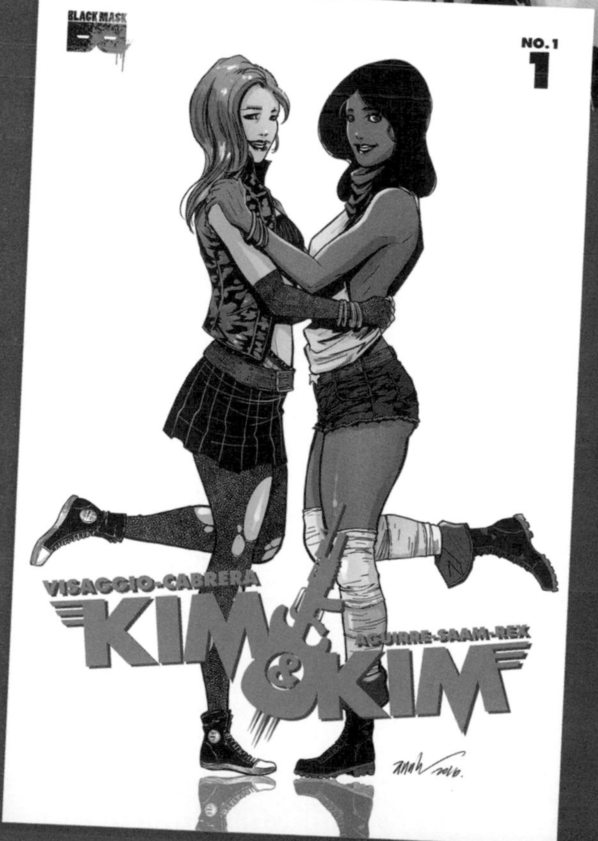
BLACK MASK
NO. 1
1
VISAGGIO-CABRERA
KIM & KIM
AGUIRRE-SAAM-REX

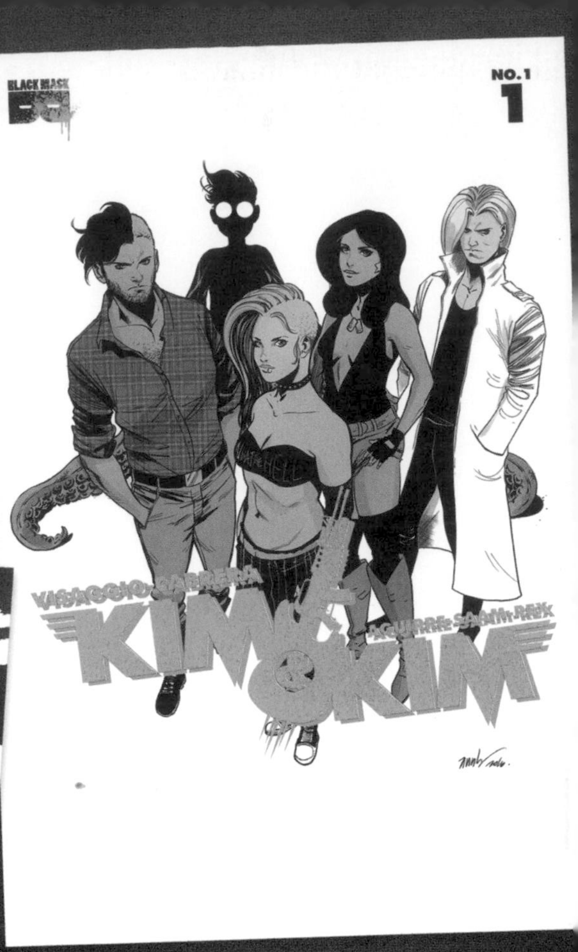
BLACK MASK
NO. 1
1
VISAGGIO-CABRERA
KIM & KIM
AGUIRRE-SAAM-REX

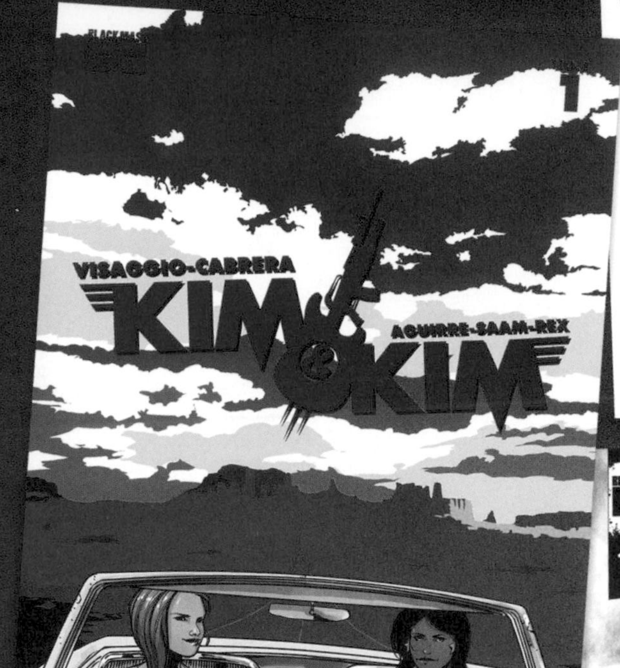
1
VISAGGIO-CABRERA
KIM & KIM
AGUIRRE-SAAM-REX

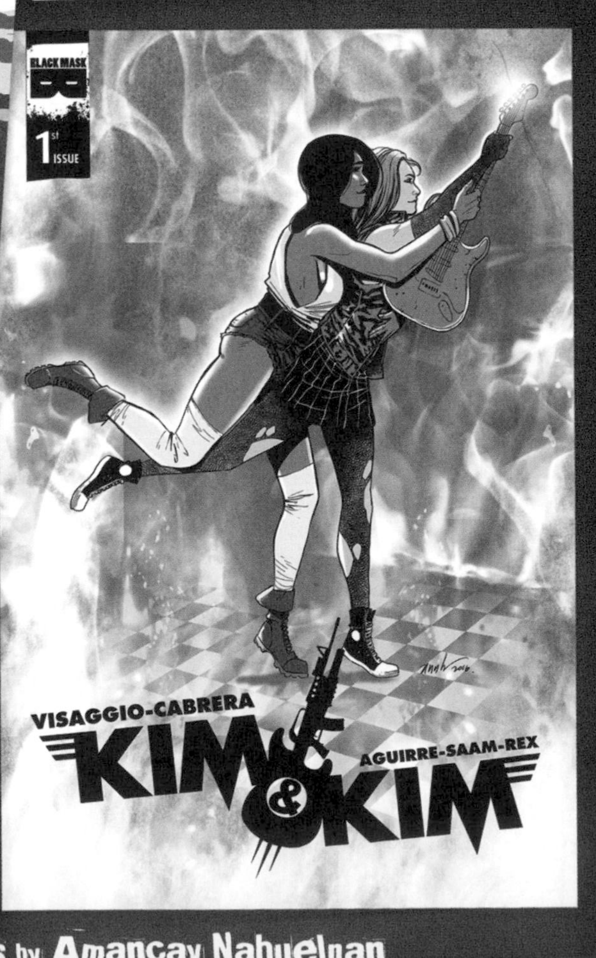
BLACK MASK
1st ISSUE
VISAGGIO-CABRERA
KIM & KIM
AGUIRRE-SAAM-REX

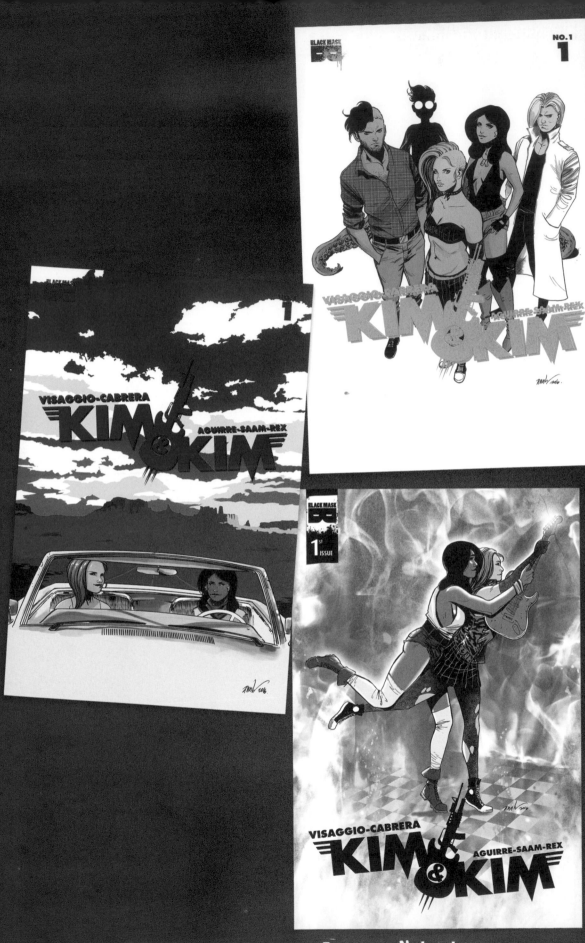

Retailer Variant Covers by Amancay Nahuelpan

Retailer Variant Covers by Amancay Nahuelpan

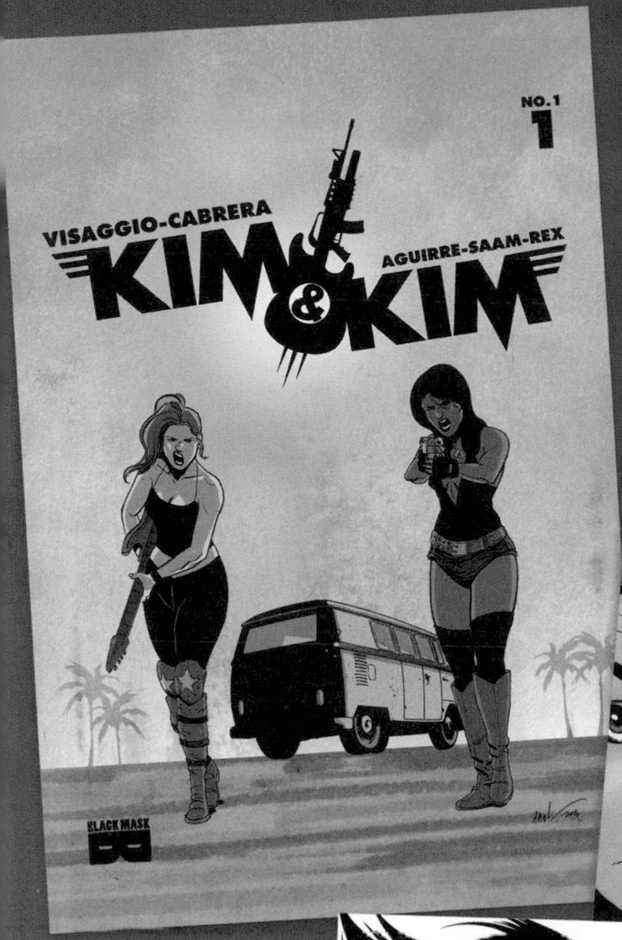
NO. 1
1
VISAGGIO-CABRERA
KIM & KIM
AGUIRRE-SAAM-REX
BLACK MASK

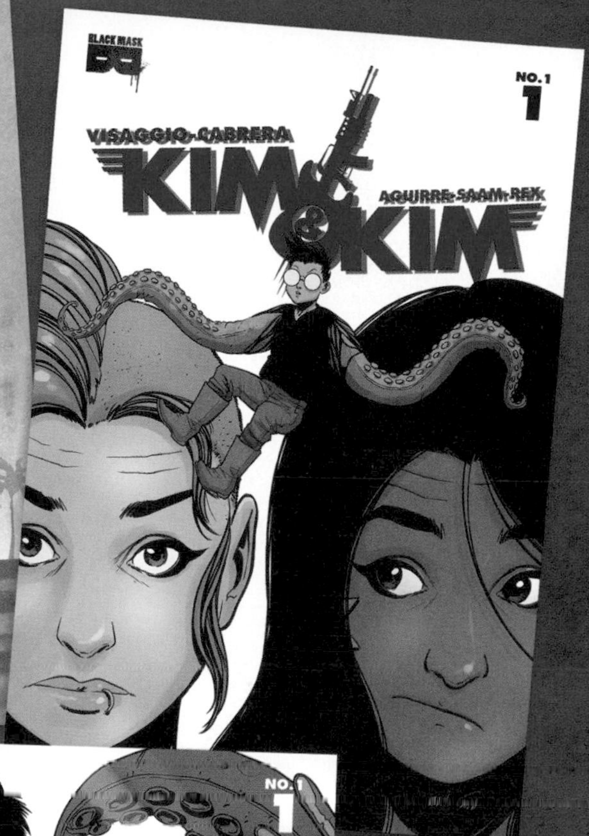
BLACK MASK
NO. 1
1
VISAGGIO-CABRERA
KIM & KIM
AGUIRRE-SAAM-REX

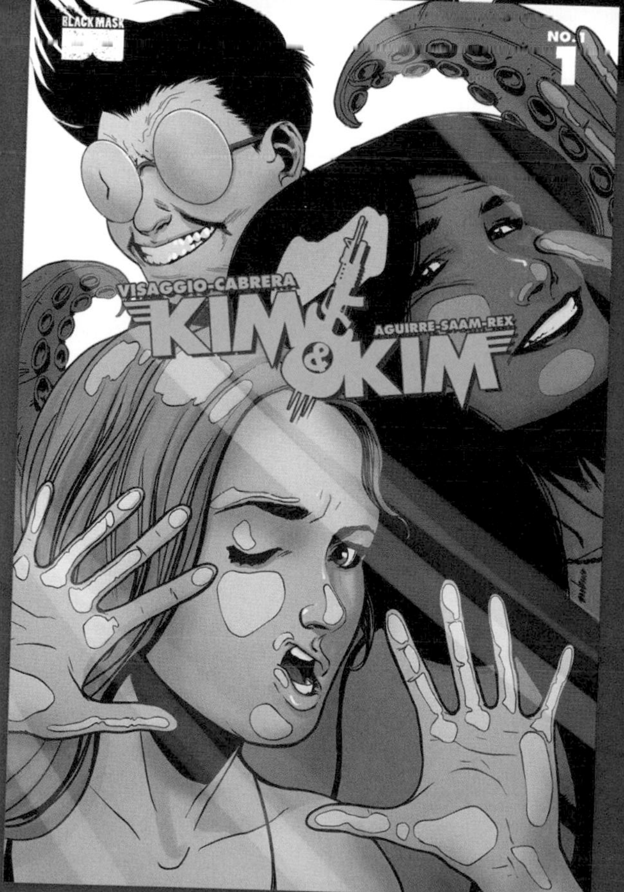
BLACK MASK
NO. 1
1
VISAGGIO-CABRERA
KIM & KIM
AGUIRRE-SAAM-REX

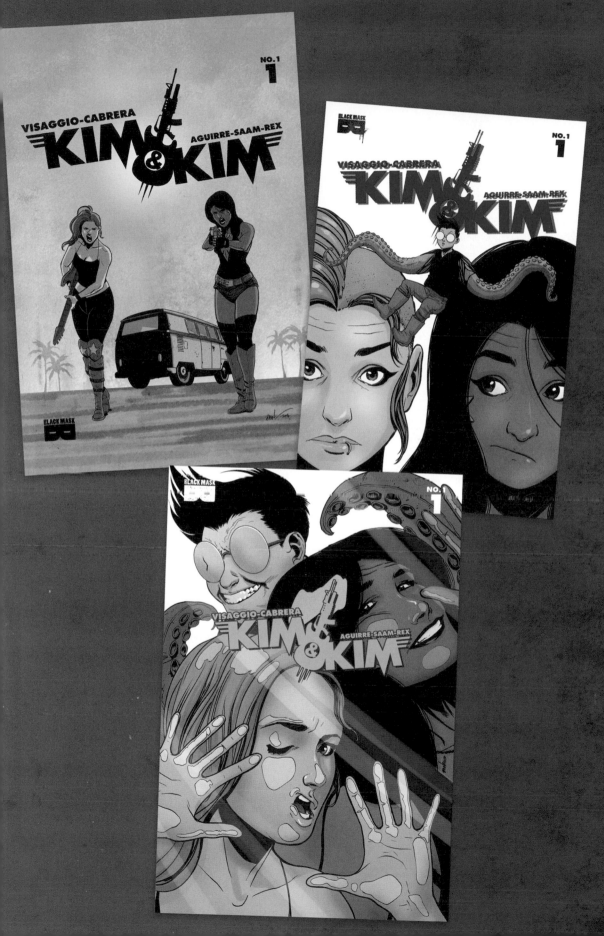